Praise for Jane Lark

*'Jane Lark has an incredible talent to draw the reader in
from the first page onwards'*
Cosmochicklitan

'Jane Lark writes soulful romance'
Big Little Sister Blog

'Every single book in this series is wonderful'
Literati Literature Lovers

*'The book swings from truly swoon-worthy, tense and heart
wrenching, highly erotic and everything else in between'*
BestChickLit.com

*'Beautifully descriptive, emotional and can I say, just plain
delicious reading?'*
Devastating Reads BlogSpot

*'Any description that I give you would not only spoil the
story but could not give this book a tenth of the justice that it
deserves. Wonderful!'*
Candy Coated Book Blog

About the Author

I love writing authentic, passionate and emotional love stories. I began my first novel, a historical, when I was sixteen, but life derailed me a bit when I started suffering with Ankylosing Spondylitis, so I didn't complete a novel until after I was thirty when I put it on my to do before I'm forty list. Now I love getting caught up in the lives and traumas of my characters, and I'm so thrilled to be giving my characters life in others' imaginations, especially when readers tell me they've read the characters just as I've tried to portray them.

The Secret Love of a Gentleman

JANE LARK

Harper*Impulse* an imprint of
HarperCollins*Publishers* Ltd
1 London Bridge Street
London SE1 9GF

www.harpercollins.co.uk

A Paperback Original 2015

First published in Great Britain in ebook format by Harper*Impulse* 2015

A catalogue record for this book is
available from the British Library

ISBN: 9780008135379

Automatically produced by Atomik ePublisher from Easypress

Chapter 1

Life is cruel.

A piercing pain struck Caroline's jaw as the sharp edge of Albert's signet ring cut her skin. Her head snapped back and her gaze left the blue of her husband's eyes. He was a villain, this man she loved.

Her hand lifted to protect her face from another blow while she grasped the back of a chair to stop herself from falling. "Please. No. I did nothing wrong."

"Nothing…" He growled at her through teeth gritted in bitter anger.

His hand lifted again.

She covered her face with both hands, to avoid the next strike. It hit her across the side of her head, a hard slap. Tears flooded her eyes as she fell.

"What have I done?" Caro cried, her hands gripping her head and her body curling on the wooden floor into a position that sought to protect, and yet it was childlike. She longed for comfort, for kindness

"Lived, while my son died!" The accusation rang about her bedchamber. A curse. She was cursed. She could not carry a child, could not give him the heir he needed. He leaned over her, every muscle in his body taut with accusation.

She loved him, regardless.

He hated her.

"Your doctor spoke to me today. He believes you may never bear a child. He believes your womb is damaged."

Caro swallowed back the tears catching in her throat. She knew. She had been told. Yet did it justify such brutality and bitter hatred? *He hates me, and I have always loved him…*

There was nothing to say in her defence. She had lost another child, his child, and she might never be able to carry an infant full-term. Tears flooded her eyes. How many times? How many children? How long could she endure this?

"I need a son! Give me a son, Caro! That is all I ask. You are capable of conceiving, you must be capable of giving birth!"

She lifted a hand so she could look at him. His gaze softened.

His eyes were like azure stones, an entrancing blue. Even in his vicious moods, when he was cold and callous, she still saw the man she'd married, the man who'd given her months of happiness and hope.

But each time he behaved like this, a little more of her hope died.

He turned away and walked across the room.

How could she love and hate the same man? How could she love a man who terrified her?

She struggled to her feet. "I am trying to give you a son." Yet she no longer believed she could. She had lost five children.

He stopped and turned, his eyes expressing pain, pity and disappointment.

Long ago, once upon a time, Caro had believed him in love and her marriage a happy-ever-after, like a fairytale. There had been gifts and balls, and their gazes holding across rooms, and gentle touches on her waist and her back as they walked together, which said, silently, *I love you*. But it was damned—doomed.

"Trying is not enough. I need a son. You will do your duty." He turned again and walked away.

She stared at the door when it shut behind him.

Before their marriage, and after it, throughout the first year, Albert had seemed love-struck. He'd begged the Marquis of Framlington for her hand, and the marriage had been arranged swiftly so he could be rid of his wife's illegitimate daughter.

Albert had been attentive, walking and standing close to her wherever they went, and devouring her body at night, but it had not been love, it had been obsession, and when she'd become pregnant and sickly, his interest had waned. He'd found a mistress and ceased to come to her bed. It had broken her heart. Especially when he continued to touch her and look at her as though love hung between them in the day and at balls. Then she'd lost the child.

That was when the beatings and the hatred had begun. He would not forgive her for the loss of their first child and now when she was with child he was so used to beating her he would not even think of her condition.

Yet the old Albert still shone through: the handsome, powerful man who'd entranced her in the beginning. Every night she had an unbearable reminder of how things should be between them, of how they had been. Even when he was angry with her, when he came to her bed he still joined with her as though he cared. That sense of being loved was still there—when in her childhood she had known so little love. She'd clung to the moments of intimacy and affection for years.

She cared for him.

"Ma'am, may I help you retire."

Caro had forgotten the maid was even in the room. "Yes, and please bring some fresh water." To wash the blood from her cheek and her lip. Albert would expect her to look well when he came to her later.

~

Sunset had passed long ago when Albert returned to the house, and Caro's bedchamber was entirely dark when he entered. He'd

3

not brought a candle.

His footsteps quietly crossed the room, then the sheets beside her lifted. The mattress dipped when he lay down.

"Caro," he whispered as his hand reached for her waist and pulled her to him. The scent of brandy carried on his breath. His lips pressed onto hers and his hand slid to her breast, gentle now.

His kiss eased away all the pain from the blows. The thoughtfulness he showed her at night wrapped about her soul and held her heart as his prisoner. The Albert she'd fallen in love with was here.

This was how it was with him—cruel, heartless, beautiful love. He would beat her and then he would devour her tenderly.

His fingers rubbed and gripped her breast through the cloth of her nightgown for a while, then he unbuttoned it.

He was passionate in all respects, in anger, in admiration, and in bed. Yet where his heart ought to be, there was a lump of stone.

His fingers slipped inside her open nightgown and skimmed over her skin, searching out her nipple. He teased it to a peak.

She yearned for more than this, she yearned for love. Her palm rested on his shoulder then slid down across his warm, naked chest. Soft skin covered the firm muscle beneath.

His hand began drawing up the hem of her nightgown and his lips left her mouth to kiss the bruise beside it, then kiss across the bruises on her neck, where his fingers had gripped earlier.

He did this every day, ripped her apart and then put her back together at night, and she did not even think it deliberate or mean, he was simply cold-blooded. She truly believed he had no idea how his behaviour hurt her.

When the hem of her nightgown reached her waist, his fingers touched her between her legs, gently caressing and calling to her body.

The magnetism in his character, his presence, his touch, pulled her to do things for him, to wish to be near him, to love him.

When he entered her she was damp between her legs and hot, and his intrusion was hard and fast, yet not painful. This was always how he loved her, with a force and strength that sent her reeling.

The little death swept over her in moments, and in a few more moments he spilled his seed inside her. Another minute's tick of the mechanism of the clock on the mantle above the hearth and he was withdrawing, disengaging, mentally and physically denying her again.

The pain of her bruises flooded her senses, while the pain of his lack of care filled her soul.

He kissed her cheek. "Thank you. God willing there will be a child soon." Then he got up and returned to his rooms. His departure ripped another little hole in her heart.

When Caro rose in the morning she had her maid carefully powder her face and neck, and she chose a gown with long sleeves. They hid the bruises, but not the swelling about her lip. She tried to hide that with rouge. It was not the worst it had been.

Her stomach trembled, along with her hands, as she walked down to break her fast with Albert before he left. The marble-lined hallway was cold.

A footman bowed his head when she reached the door of the morning room. He held the door open for her.

Her stomach tumbled over. Every servant in the house must know how she was treated.

Albert looked up. He'd been reading the paper while eating scrambled eggs, his fork lowered to the plate.

She longed to see that old look of want and reverence that used to hover in his brown eyes, but instead he stared at her as though she was an oddity in a village fair.

A sharp and violent sensation raced through her blood, reaching into her limbs—terror. She hoped it did not show on her face. Had she done anything wrong today? He did not only beat her for her lack of ability to breed; everything that went wrong in the house was her fault, a fork out of place, a glass broken, something he did not like on a menu. The servants were her responsibility and therefore their errors were hers.

"Caro." He stood up and gave her a shallow bow. "Good morning." Then he sat again.

She took her seat at the far end of the table, her fingers shaking when she accepted her food.

Albert was a dozen years older than her. His maturity and strength of character had seemed a blessing to her younger self when they'd met, when he'd been adoring and attentive. She'd felt sheltered by him then.

Now, this was their day; they would take breakfast together and then he would leave, and perhaps return to dine with her, or to accompany her to a ball, or ask her to entertain his political friends. Then at night he would lay with her, at whatever hour he returned home from his mistress, or mistresses.

"I shan't be home for dinner." Albert set his napkin down and rose.

Caro looked up. There was no emotion in his blue eyes.

She had tried. She had tried to be a good wife. She loved him. She had tried to give him children. She could not. She had failed.

The blood from her torn heart dried at little more, just as the blood had dried on the cut his ring had ripped in the flesh of her face last night.

How much longer could she live like this? If she lost another child…

In the last six weeks he'd beaten her a dozen times.

After the loss of the last child he'd left her in bed a day later, unable to move, her face grotesquely swollen.

If she lost another child would he kill her?

Would anyone care?

Her brother would care. Drew. He would. Like her, he'd been a cuckoo in the Marquis of Framlington's nest, and their parents' rejection had forged a bond, which had held. She'd clung to Drew for security as a child, for the love and attention their parents never gave. Drew was the only person who had returned her love.

Her closeness to her brother was the only thing in her life that had lasted.

She finished the last mouthful on her plate to make it appear to the servants that all was well, then rose and left the room, passing through the cold, austere marble hallway.

Drew had begged her to leave Albert. He had offered to keep her. He'd recently married a woman with money and he'd said he would buy Caro a property somewhere in the country where she would be safe. But how could she run from someone with the power of the seventh Marquis of Kilbride, and how could she leave when she still loved him, and yet… *How do I stay?*

The blood about her heart congealed and the bruises in her soul ached.

If she stayed there would be more beatings and more children lost.

Drew had promised her security.

Her fingers slid along the stone banister as she climbed the stairs to her rooms.

If she stayed nothing would change. Nothing would become better, it could only be worse. The doctor had said she would never have a child and she would always have to look into the eyes she loved, which had once held a look of adulation and were now hollow windows, which merely acknowledged her existence.

She would run. She had to leave Albert. Yet if she did, she would leave herself here, her soul and her heart. They might be wounded but they were not dead, and they still loved Albert with a loyalty that she did not think would end. She had been so starved of love, to have known what she had with Albert, even for a year, would stay with her forever.

But there was no other choice than to leave. This was a poisoned marriage. He would kill her in the end.

Chapter 2

Caro descended from the coat-of-arms embossed carriage her husband provided for her use, gripping the hand of a footman.

Her foot touched the pavement of Tavistock Street, the address of her modiste, and her heart raced, its rhythm running through her veins. The air petrified in her lungs, yet she refused to let her hold tighten about the footman's hand or tremble. He must not sense her fear. Her husband may not love her, but he had her watched, like a hawk. Her family had a reputation for setting up intrigues, her own birth was evidence of it, and her eldest sister was as bad as their mother. The Marquis of Kilbride did not wish to be cuckolded. He might play away from the marriage bed, yet she must stay loyal, and to ensure her loyalty he surrounded her with his staff.

The street was busy, a throng of people flowed past, even though it was still relatively early. She hoped the crowded pavement would help her.

The footman bowed low over her hand, then let it go and turned to force her a path through the people.

The broad bow window of the shop displayed fabrics and fashions. The footman opened the door and held it open as the bell above jangled.

She walked in. He followed.

How long would it be before he guessed something was amiss once she'd gone?

Half a dozen customers touched fabrics and accessories, which had been put out on the counters for them to consider.

Caro's eyes scanned the occupants through the fine net of the veil she'd worn to cover the bruising on her face, and her identity. Her heart hammered against her ribs. She knew no one, and she hoped no one, bar the modiste, would know her. She did not want to be stopped by anyone.

She held her heavy reticule carefully as she crossed the room, so it appeared light, hiding the weight of the jewellery within it. She'd taken nothing that belonged to Albert, only what he had given to her as gifts in their first year—the year she'd believed he'd loved her.

It was what she hoped to live on. She did not wish to be entirely dependent on Drew nor to become a burden. She would live quietly and spend little.

"May I see some fabrics for a new ballgown?" Caro pointed out some bolts. The modiste's assistant took them down and lifted a pattern book out from beneath the counter.

Caro touched each fabric as the assistant unravelled lengths. This would be the last time she would have the chance to look at such fine things. She picked a very delicate pale pink, then thumbed through the fashion book. Her heart racing, she stopped suddenly and left it on an open page as she leant across the counter to ask the assistant discreetly, "May I use your convenience, please?" Her voice had trembled. She coughed as if clearing her throat.

When Albert's footman attempted to follow them through a door at the back of the shop, the assistant shooed him away.

Caro was led through a workroom and then out to a cold, short corridor. The closet was at the end of that. Caro had used it before, and she knew how it was situated, next to the rear entrance into the yard behind the shop.

"I will find my own way back," she said to the girl when she went into the closet. Caro shut the door for a moment. But she did not make use of the chamber pot, which had been left in the room. Her fingers gripped at her waist while she listened to the assistant walk away. Caro came out and turned to the door, her heart thumping against her ribs. She opened it and shut it quietly.

Drew was there.

"Caro," he whispered as he took her hand. "Come." He led her out of the shop yard. "Did they query your exit?"

"No, I asked the modiste if I might use her closet, but there is a footman waiting for me in the shop."

"Then we had best hurry."

His grip on her hand pulled her into a run along the narrow cobbled alley at the back of the row of shops.

"There is a hired carriage at the end of the alley. I ordered it in a false name. We will change carriages once we are out of London and go the opposite way, and then change again. No one will be able to trace you. Where was Kilbride when you left?"

"I waited until he'd left for the House of Lords. He will be there hours before he knows I am gone. He cannot abide being interrupted while he is in the House."

When they reached the end of the alley, the door of the waiting carriage was ajar. Drew pulled it wider and handed her up, then climbed in behind her.

"Go!" He called up to the driver, before shutting the door. He pulled down the blinds to hide them from view.

Caro's hands shook as she opened her reticule. "I have brought something to help. I cannot allow you to support me entirely, Drew." Gold and jewels glinted in the low light of the carriage as she opened the handkerchief she'd hidden them in. "They are all gifts he has given me, they were mine to take, earbobs, hair slides, bracelets and necklaces."

Drew smiled awkwardly.

He'd expected nothing and yet he was not a wealthy man. He needed the dowry he'd received from his wife to find his own happiness, not hers.

He said nothing, turning away to lift the edge of the blind and peer around it as they passed the front of the shop, and Albert's carriage.

Drew looked back at her. "They do not appear to have noticed your absence yet."

When they did discover her gone there would be bedlam. They would fear Albert's response. She would always be terrified of her husband's influence.

What if he found her?

Drew's hand held hers, offering comfort and reassurance.

She was grateful and yet his own marriage was falling apart, his wife had left him.

They were both flawed.

They'd been scarred as children by their mother's betrayal and their stepfather's hatred. But on top of that Drew had the curse of male pride. He would not plead his case and try to persuade Mary to have him back.

~

"We will leave the carriage here and walk," Drew stated when it jolted to a halt. It was the last stage of their journey.

He opened the door and took her hand. She climbed out, her eyes wide and heartbeat racing. He kept a hold of her, leading her out of the inn's courtyard.

They turned a corner and walked down another street. Then past a shallow ford across a river and a large, ornate building.

Drew continued walking until they reached a row of terraced, whitewashed, thatched cottages. Most had gardens filled with vegetable plants, but the one in the middle was full of flowers in bloom. When they reached it Drew opened the gate in the stone wall that ran along the edge of the road.

They walked up the path.

The cottage door was small, but it was the entrance to her new life. In that context it was a giant step.

Drew knocked and the door opened. A thin, middle-aged woman, dressed in unrelenting black, stood there. Drew hurried Caro in and shut the door. It was dark inside and the ceilings were low. It felt a little like a prison cell—gloomy, cold and desolate.

She had come from affluence to this, tumbling down the stations of society, simply because she could not bear a child.

Drew stayed with her for a while, as the housekeeper who had opened the door showed her about the small four-roomed cottage, and then he drank tea with Caro. But he could not stay forever.

"Caro, you know I cannot return for a while. Kilbride will have people watching me for weeks. We both know it. Do not write either. It is not worth taking the risk. I will come as soon as I can, but in the meantime, simply live quietly here."

She nodded as he stood. She rose too. Then she lifted to her toes and hugged him, crying, clinging to him. The one person in her life who had proved themselves constant—who loved her truly.

"You must be brave, Caro, stay calm and stay strong and sit it out here. He will not find you, I promise."

She nodded again, but Albert would never cease looking. She knew him better than Drew. Albert would take her flight as an insult. He'd wish for revenge. He would continue to live his life without her and yet ensure she never felt able to live hers without fear.

Chapter 3

The knocker struck on the cottage door with four firm raps.

Caro rose from her chair, fear clasping in her chest as she walked into the hall.

This was her haven—no one knocked on the door.

Beth, the housekeeper, had come out from the kitchen. She wiped her hands on the skirt of her white apron.

Caro had lived here alone for days, a prisoner in her new home, communicating with no one except Beth and no one else ought to be here. Drew had said he would not come.

Caro could not look from the window without giving herself away. Instead she stared at the door, willing her eyes to see through wood.

No word had come from town and she had not asked Beth to purchase a paper for fear that local people would wonder why a woman of the class she was now supposed to be would wish to read. She was living humbly, trying not to rouse suspicion.

"Madam, should I open the door?" Beth whispered as Caro merely stood there, her heart pulsing hard.

Foolishly she longed for Albert, for someone to turn to and say, *what should I do?* She missed none of her finery but she missed her husband. She missed the man who had felt like her protector once, the man who had come to her at night and touched her as though he loved her. A part of her foolish heart longed to be found, but not by the man who beat her.

"Ask who it is." Caro whispered.

"Who is there?" Beth called as she looked towards the door.

"It is Lady Framlington. Your brother sent me, he could not come himself." Mary's soft voice penetrated the wood and pierced Caro's heart. Drew's wife should not be here if all was well.

Caro looked at Beth. "Something is wrong. Why would my brother not come himself? They are estranged…" Of course, it was foolish asking her housekeeper. How was Beth to know? But the anxiety skittering through Caro's nerves stopped her from thinking clearly.

"Ma'am, I cannot say—"

Panic gripped and solidified in Caro's stomach, and froze her limbs as though ice crept across her skin. She imagined Drew beaten or dead. "Should I trust her, do you think?"

"Ma'am." *The decision must be yours*, Caro heard the words Beth did not utter.

Drew's wife was from a good family, a family renowned for its loyalty and high morals. Surely Mary had not come to entrap her.

"Let her in," Caro ordered in a broken whisper.

"Very well, my lady?" Beth's hands reached behind her back to untie her apron as she turned away and went to hang it up in the kitchen.

When Beth returned, her black dress still dusty with flour, she freed the bolts that held the door.

When the door opened, a silhouette of the young woman standing outside was framed by the daylight.

Beth bobbed a curtsy. Mary looked at Caro, her gaze assessing the brown shawl Caro had wrapped around her shoulders to shelter from the chilly draughts in the cottage.

Embarrassment lay over Caro and her skin heated, probably colouring. Where was Drew?

Her fingers gripped her shawl tighter to hide the tremble in her hands.

"May I come in? My brother is with me."

The Duke of Pembroke…

The thought of a man, a stranger, within any distance of her sent terror racing through Caro. She'd become used to this little four-roomed prison cell—used to there being no risk. He had once been her elder sister's lover, and rumour had cast him as rakish and rebellious when he'd followed the route of the grand tour at the same time as Drew, but now the imposing duke was married, and all gossip and talk of him had died in town. He'd absorbed the morals of his family, people said, and Caro had heard his marriage discussed as a love match.

Her gaze reached past Mary as the housekeeper stepped aside, and her heart hit against her ribs like the beat of hooves on hard ground in a canter.

"I have this from Andrew, so you know that what I say is true." Caro looked at the letter Mary held out. Then looked at her sister-in-law.

Mary was dressed in the fashion of the capital. In the finery Caro had been accustomed to, until she'd fallen out of favour and been forced to run. She was no longer a Marchioness. She no longer had a right to such things.

The letter trembled when Caro took it and unfolded it.

Drew's familiar bold, assertive letters stretched across the page. She spotted words. *Kilbride. He has accused us. I have to go to London to face the charge.* She stopped and read it in full, her heart pounding harder.

When Caro looked up, Mary had turned to beckon her brother forward.

"He has accused Drew of being my lover. Incest is a crime. I never thought… Oh God." A dark cloud crowded Caro, and a heavy sensation pulled her down. She'd never imagined this.

"This way Ma'am." Beth directed them to the parlour.

"Here" Mary held Caro's arm as the Duke of Pembroke removed

his hat to pass beneath the lintel.

His presence robbed the dark cottage of even more light.

Caro's heart kicked against her ribs, like Albert's boot had often done and she shivered.

She'd grown too used to her own company, to the safety of her solitude. She wished to run, and yet Drew had been imprisoned. He'd asked her to go with these people.

The letter trembled in Caro's cold hand.

"You must sit," Mary said.

They'd been accused of incest…

Caro sat in an armchair and looked up. Drew's letter crumpled in her fingers. Nausea twisted through her stomach. "Drew will regret helping me."

"He does not. The last thing he said to me was that he could not regret it."

The Duke, who could not stand straight beneath the low ceiling, took the other chair in the room. Now he was not looming over her, Caro remembered her manners. "Your Grace." She moved to rise, but Mary pressed a hand on her shoulder to keep her seated.

"Forgive me, I would stand myself but it is a little awkward," the Duke said "and I would rather you felt able to be informal in my presence. Besides, it is far easier to converse with us both seated."

Caro's fingers clung to Drew's letter in her lap. She did not understand this. Drew had eloped with Mary and had made an enemy of the Duke. Why would he be here? Why was Mary here? She had been estranged from Drew… She'd left him…

"I have promised to protect you," The Duke continued, as Caro looked her bewilderment, she could take none of this in. "You will be safer at Pembroke Place. No one can get within miles of the house without being seen, and my wife, Katherine, and Mary and I will be there to keep you company. Of course the house and grounds will be at your disposal. You may mix with the family or avoid us entirely if you wish. But there is a music room and a library to entertain you. It need not be confinement as this must feel, and you need not live in fear, Lady Kilbride?"

"Why would you help me?" Caro looked from the Duke to her sister-in-law.

"Because you are my sister now." Mary dropped to her haunches and gripped one of Caro's hands.

"You are together again?"

"Yes."

"How?"

"I thought he had been disloyal and betrayed me. He was seen with another woman in a draper's and I was told and I heard him saying he was setting up a woman in a house. I thought he'd taken a mistress. I was mistaken. The woman he was taking care of was you. He has forgiven me my misjudgement."

Oh, Caro was glad for Drew. "He deserves to be happy. I knew you would make him so, you are good." Yet he would not be happy because of Caro, he was in a true prison, locked away for helping her.

"And Drew is a good man."

"Yes." Caro's vision clouded with tears. He was not known for his goodness, but he had always shown it to her. His love had been precious to her as a child, when he'd protected her from the cruel taunting of their siblings and tried to shelter her from their lack of parental love. He'd been her safe harbour when her marriage had turned sour. He deserved happiness. "I owe him much."

"The two of you are not alone anymore. Will you come with us?" the Duke asked, his baritone cutting the stillness in the room and making her jump.

When Caro looked at him a tingle like hackles lifting on her spine rippled across her skin, cat-like. His authority and arrogant stance reminded her of Albert. "I will come." *Because Drew asked it of me.*

"Then we should go directly." Mary stood. "John can send a cart back for your possessions."

A new sensation, a sense of drowning, overwhelmed Caro,

stealing her breath, as though the water about her was icy.

To be outdoors again.

To be amongst people again.

She took a deep breath, fighting against panic. Yet Drew would not have asked her to do this if he did not think it right. "I have barely anything… Lady Framlington, I left everything in town."

"You must call me Mary. You are my sister."

Yes, and that is what Caro must think. This was not accepting charity from strangers, and this was for Drew.

Chapter 4

"The magistrate wishes to speak with you, Lady Kilbride."

Was she to be charged now too? Caro's fingers clasped together at her waist as the nervous discomfort that had claimed a hold over her ever since she'd left her cottage roared through her. Her heart pounded so loud in her ears it was deafening.

The Duke of Arundel, Mary's uncle, stood before her, in her private sitting room. He'd come to speak with her, in Mary's company, while downstairs the magistrate who had the say over Drew's situation waited in the formal drawing room.

"If you wish to help your brother then you must speak. He has told us of the Marquis of Kilbride's violence and sworn that is the only reason you accepted his protection, yet unless you confirm it I fear Kilbride's word will be taken over Drew's."

Then she must speak. She would not see her brother hang because of her.

But to speak of such private things… Shame touched her skin with warmth. She had lived with the Duke of Pembroke for only two days and yet she had seen love as it ought to be returned here. He loved his wife and Mary loved Drew—Caro still loved Albert too, the Albert of her fairytales, the Albert who for a little while had seemed so similar to the Duke of Pembroke and how the Duke was towards his wife, Kate. Yet Albert had never looked at Caro quite as the Duke looked at Kate. Caro knew what she'd lacked. She had been right to run, but her heart still remembered all the emotions of her first year with Albert, and it clung to the only time she'd known such tenderness and admiration in her life, even if it had been a shallow image of it. It also clung to the moments Albert's touch had been gentle and tender in her bed. Those had been the most precious moments of her life…

And the times he had hit her the worst. It had been betrayal.

"Do you wish me with you?" Mary asked.

"No. Thank you." She could not bear to tell the truth of her humiliation before Mary, she wished no one to know. Yet she must speak to save Drew. "If I speak, will the details remain private?"

"I shall ask for the records to be handled discretely."

Caro took a breath trying to calm her heart and the terror in her blood. "You may take me to him. I will speak."

The magistrate rose as she entered the room. He was a large, tall man. His gaze studied her as she walked across the room. He knew things about her and she could see in his eyes that he assumed other things. But she doubted Drew had spoken of the children; she hoped he had not. Yet it was the reason she was here. If there had been living children perhaps Albert would have adored her still.

"Please sit." The magistrate lifted a hand.

She did so, as he sat too. Lord Wiltshire sat beside him.

"Please tell me about your relationship with your brother, Lady Kilbride?"

She took a breath, then began from when they were children, because the isolation and ill-treatment they had suffered then was what had truly brought them together and held them fast.

"And since your marriage?"

"We have not been so close. My husband did not wish me to go out alone, but Drew and I have managed to speak." She'd spoken to Drew mostly about the beatings since her marriage.

"To speak…"

She took a breath. She did not care for the inflection in the magistrate's tone. If she was to save Drew she must tell him what she spoke to Drew about. Tears welled in her eyes and her fingers shook as nausea spun in her stomach.

"Here." Lord Wiltshire passed her his handkerchief.

"I spoke to him mostly when my husband beat me. Drew would give me comfort."

"Comfort…"

She had looked at her hands, but now she looked up and glared at the magistrate, her heart racing wildly. "Not the physical kind. I sought words of comfort. He was someone to speak with when I had no one else. As I said, neither my mother nor my sister will speak with me."

"And so you turned to a brother."

"Yes. Because my brother is a good man." She stared at the magistrate, denying the accusations in his eyes, as fear danced through her nerves, running up her spine.

"It has never gone further? Never become something beyond what it ought to be? You have been accused of incest by your husband."

"My husband is a liar. He does not like to lose. There has never been anything inappropriate between myself and my brother. My husband is merely angry because I have left him and my brother has enabled it." *And she had once thought that man cared for her…* She was a fool. Her heart had been deceived. Yet it could not forget the web of emotions his shallow devotion had cast. It wished to believe his devotion continued to lie beneath all else, and guilt had hung over her since she'd fled because, despite everything, her heart told her she'd been disloyal and had disgraced herself—and him.

"And you have left your husband because?"

"I cannot breathe," she said to Lord Wiltshire as the vice of terror tightened about her chest.

He rose and turned, going to a table across the room, then returned with a glass of amber liquor. "Here."

She swallowed a mouthful. It burned the back of her throat, but it relaxed the muscles in her chest. "Because he beat me, violently, sometimes daily. If I had stayed with him he would have killed me. Is it a crime to wish to be alive?" Her words echoed through her head. Was it a crime? She felt as though it was, and now she served her sentence. She had spoken the words to her foolish heart as well as to these men.

"It is no crime. But nor is it crime for your husband to reprimand you, yet neither point is the cause of my investigation. Did anyone witness the Marquis strike you? I am not entirely insensitive to the fact that such a thing would justify and explain your brother protecting you."

Nor is it a crime for your husband to reprimand you… So the men agreed to her guilt—that she ought to be blamed and chastised for her inability to breed. Hearts should not be involved in marriage—love like that which Drew had found was abnormal. Most couples in society lived without love.

Yet what the magistrate said meant there was hope for Drew, if there was a witness who would dare to stand against Albert.

Caro drank the last of the brandy, then passed the empty glass to Lord Wiltshire. Her fingers curled tighter about the handkerchief in her hand. "My lady's maid would be able to give you an account of the events which she witnessed, but I cannot say where she will be, she will have been dismissed, and if you find her you will need to promise that her name will not be released." She looked at the Duke. "She will need to be protected if she is willing to speak." Albert's temper may turn against her as it had turned against Drew.

But all would be laid bare if they spoke to her maid. Betsy would tell them the words Albert spoke when he'd beaten Caro and then they would know she was incapable of providing him with a child.

Heat burned in Caro's cheeks and tears made the Duke shimmer. She looked at the floor, shame lancing through her breast as the tears ran on to her cheeks.

"Thank you, Ma'am. We are finished." The magistrate and the

Duke of Arundel stood.

Caro wiped the tears from her cheeks.

The Duke walked past her and then opened the door to let the magistrate leave.

"I believe Lady Kilbride would appreciate your company, Mary. John, may I stay with you and dine here before I return to town?"

Caro rose and turned as Mary came into the room. She clasped Caro's hands. "I am sorry you had to endure this."

Mary was kind and generous in nature. She loved Drew deeply and she never hid those feelings. Caro could see now how Mary had drawn out the best qualities in Drew.

"Better that than for Drew to suffer because of me." Caro would never forgive herself if her failure destroyed Mary's and Drew's chance of happiness.

Tears sparkled in Mary's eyes, then fresh tears spilled from Caro's. She leant to embrace Mary as Mary embraced her, both offering comfort. Caro broke the embrace, heat burning in her cheeks. "I am sorry."

Mary wiped away her tears with the sleeve of her dress. "You have no cause to be sorry."

"I do. This is my fault."

"It is not… It is no one's fault, and we are going to remain calm. That is what is best for Andrew, and we are going to feel confident and trust Richard to return him to us."

"The magistrate did not believe me, not wholly. He is going to speak with one of my lady's maids to ask her to confirm what I have said. The whole thing is mortifying… and then I think of Drew in a cell, alone. When he has done nothing to deserve it."

Mary gripped Caro's hand. "I know. I know you are both innocent. I know you have both been through so much. But that is over now. We will have faith."

Caro gave her a tentative smile. "Thank you. Thank you for your concern. But most of all, thank you for loving Drew. He needed a woman like you—"

"And I need him—" Mary smiled, but a tear escaped.

Caro wiped it away with the handkerchief she held. "I am glad for you both."

A light knock struck the door, which had been left ajar. "Come!" Mary called.

"Sorry to interrupt." It was the Duchess of Pembroke, Mary's sister-in-law. "It is just, I wished to let you know we are serving dinner. Your uncle is staying with us to dine, Mary, and he sent me to fetch you to ensure you came to the table. "Will you dine with us, Lady Kilbride?" The Duchess looked at Caro and Mary, as they looked at her.

The Duchess had requested Caro's attendance at the table daily and yet Caro had kept to the rooms she'd been allotted. She felt safe there. Among people, the sense of shame and discomfort was overwhelming.

Caro shook her head.

"I will leave you, then. Come when you are ready, Mary."

"I'm sorry," Caro whispered. "I feel as though they must think I am rude and disrespectful of their hospitality, but I… I cannot tell you how I feel. I… Do you think the Duchess would send my dinner to my room?" How could she explain her feelings to Mary? She was beginning to feel as if she were mad.

"Of course she will. You must not feel pressed."

"Thank you, Mary. I will retire, then."

"Yes. But send a maid to fetch me if you need me."

Caro nodded.

They left the room together, but when Mary turned towards the dining room, Caro turned to climb the stairs.

~

Caro waited in the drawing room of the Pembrokes' giant Palladian mansion, seated in a corner, beside Mary's mother, her fingers clasped in her lap, struggling to control her breathing and the pounding of her heart.

But Drew was here. Free. She had been told by the Duchess an hour ago that he'd arrived. They'd all hoped today. She'd heard them talking even from upstairs.

The house was full of people. All of Mary's extended family had come from town to celebrate on Drew's behalf, and they were all in the room. Caro felt crowded as she waited, smothered by them. Her nerves screamed.

Mary's mother had said he was with Mary still. Yet he must come down soon. Caro had been waiting nearly half an hour.

When Mary came into the room she was alone. She walked across it and whispered something in her father's ear, then they left together.

Caro's gaze hung on the door while Mary's mother talked of her younger children. Caro was not listening.

The noise of conversation was intense, deafening. A shiver ran up her spine. It was more than simple fear, though. There was annoyance and anger inside her too. She wished to scream as much as run.

She was falling to pieces. At any moment the panic inside would explode and she would shatter like glass.

But Drew was free…

Maybe she ought to retire to her rooms. He would come up to her.

She was about to stand and declare her apology when he came into the room, his hand holding Mary's.

The room broke into applause and he smiled self-consciously. She had never seen him look humble as he did in that moment, and yet there was pride in his eyes when he looked at Mary. He had won himself a place in this family. He had achieved what Caro never would—a good marriage. He deserved this. She did not begrudge him it and nor would she spoil this moment for him. She would not run.

While the men moved to speak with him, Caro tried to make

conversation with Mary's mother, but all the time her awareness was on the proximity of her brother. She looked up. Drew spoke with Mary's younger brother, Robert, a tall, slender youth. Mary lifted a hand and pointed Caro out, and then Drew looked and a moment later he turned towards her. But his progress towards her was hindered by well-wishers.

The sight of him filled Caro with a mix of emotions, relief and happiness, he was her home, the only place she felt safe, but there was sadness too, to know that she was dependent on him.

When Drew reached her he sank down onto his haunches and took her hands in his, looking concerned. "How are you, Caro?"

Caro hugged him and broke into sobs, the pent-up fear and pain spilling out of her. He held her in return.

"I am glad you are safe. I am sorry. This was my fault," she whispered in his ear.

"No," he whispered back, speaking into her ear too. "It was not. It was Kilbride's, but it is done with, and all will be well now, I promise."

"I feared for you, but it seems now you have all you deserve."

"I was afraid for me too," he jested. "This feels strange, doesn't it? I shall not lie. I am ready to run as much as you are, I should think… But these people are not like ours, Caro—"

"I know."

"The Duke of Arundel, Lord Wiltshire, Mary's uncle, told me Kilbride is going to sue for divorce. You will be free soon, too, and then you may begin a new life."

Fresh tears gathered in her eyes. Albert wished to be rid of her entirely, and then he would find a wife who would bear him children. The pain of that cut at her heart. Drew pulled away and gripped her hands gently.

He would never understand if she told him she loved Albert still.

Mary touched Drew's shoulder and Caro looked up to see her holding out a gentleman's handkerchief. Lord Marlow's, Mary's father's.

"Thank you." Caro forced a smile, then looked away as she dabbed at her tears.

"All will be well, now," Drew said, his hand patting her arm. Then he stood and looked at Lord Marlow. "I thought you were hungry. Are we not going to eat?"

Lord Marlow turned and in a moment the dinner gong sounded.

Caro's heart pounded, but Drew gave Mary an apologetic smile and raised his arm to Caro.

She stood and lay her fingers on his sleeve. Drew was her security—and now her only hold on sanity. She could not have walked into the room to dine without him.

"I shall buy you some new clothes," he said quietly as they walked ahead of Mary and her father. "Living among the Pembrokes is not the same as living in a cottage."

"I cannot bear this, Drew, is there nowhere else—"

"I have a home. I am buying a property bordering Pembroke's. You will have a home there too, Caro."

Tears blurred her vision again. She was grateful, and yet she did not wish to be a burden and beholden to him for the rest of her days, a poor, shamed, dependent relation.

She would be a blight on his happy home.

Chapter 5

Three years later

Rob leaned on a windowsill in the first-floor drawing room, looking out onto the gardens below. His gaze caught a sudden movement across the lawn. It could have been the shadow of a cloud sweeping across the sky, if the movement was dark and not light. But it had been something pale blue.

It could have been a ghost if it was night and not midday. But it was not a spectre. He would lay strong odds it was the tail end of Caroline Framlington's skirt disappearing behind the hedge. Perhaps a ghost of sorts, then.

Rob leant more firmly onto the windowsill.

Her fingers had held the rim of her bonnet, hiding her face as she'd hurried away, head down, scurrying from the house.

He assumed she'd left the house because he'd arrived. He had not even come within ten feet of her. It did not bode well.

"Do not take it personally." His brother-in-law said jovially, in a low tone, resting a palm on Rob's shoulder. "Caro does not appreciate company."

Rob turned to look at Drew "And male company particularly… Yes, I know. Are you sure it is a good idea for me to stay here if it will disturb her?"

"Life must go on, Robbie, she cannot orchestrate what we do. Caro will keep to her rooms as she does most of the time. I wish she would be braver, but I do not have the heart to force her into facing her fears, and yet nor will I pander to them. She'll cope because she has to. We have servants, after all, and men among them. It is not only Mary and I who live here. It is just because your presence is unfamiliar and so she feels threatened."

"I could stay at John's."

"Rattling about your brother's monstrosity of a mansion on your own. No, Robbie. Mary invited you for the summer because she wants to spend time with you. You and I can go out shooting and fishing, and riding."

"I can ride over daily from John's and do that. His property is only a few miles from yours."

"And kick around the house alone all night, bored. Do not be foolish. You will stay, and Caro will adjust. It is only going to be for the summer. Caro will survive."

"Or hide."

"Well more likely that. But either way, it will do her no harm."

"Uncle Bobbie!" George, Drew's son, charged across the room and barrelled into Rob's leg. The boy was barely two, and a little tyke, but adorable despite it. He still refused to sound his "r"s and thus Rob, known to his family as Robbie, had become Uncle Bobbie to the boy.

Rob bent and caught the child by his chubby arms, lifted him and tossed him in the air once, then caught him and turned him upside down. George laughed in his childish giggle.

His nephew was another good reason to stay, as was his infant niece, whom his sister currently cradled on her arm while speaking with their mother.

Rob loved the children. There was something very endearing about being hero-worshipped by George, something his younger brothers rarely did.

Mary was the sibling he was fondest of. She was the closest to him in age and temperament, and her notorious husband had always treated Rob like a grown man, even when Rob had been scarcely that. Rob had been eighteen when Drew and Mary had eloped.

"And I have been looking forward to your company, as has this rapscallion."

"Uncle Bobbie, I want to fly!" George cried.

Rob carefully let him descend to the floor, head first.

The boy rolled onto his back, then rose and turned to his papa to be caught up again, in a firm hold. "Your uncle Robbie is not going to swing you about all day, George."

"Boats!" The boy yelled.

Rob ruffled the child's hair. "Yes, I will play boats and kites, and ball, George. We'll do lots of things."

"Aun'ie Ca'o too."

"Perhaps." Drew avoided the true answer.

"We ought to be getting back to John's, if you are ready, Robbie?" Rob looked at his mother as she stood up.

Mary stood too, with the baby sleeping in her arms. "We shall see you at John's tomorrow. I believe we have even persuaded Caro to come, because the children are. But I doubt she will speak to anyone but them."

"I do feel sorry for her. I wish there was more I could do." Their mother smiled at Mary, then Drew. "But I have no idea how to help her, she always looks so uncomfortable the moment I begin any more personal conversation."

"She is not so unhappy, Mama. She adores the children. She would be more distressed to think you pitied her."

Unease swung over Rob, like a cloak settling on his shoulders, as Drew continued reassuring Rob's mother.

Rob was still unsure about staying, but he did not really wish to remain at John's. He turned to look from the window again.

His eldest brother's, his step-brother's, property was vast. So vast it currently housed every branch of the family. But after the garden party the family would splinter again and each aunt, uncle and cousin would return to their own homes, and John and his wife, Kate, were retiring to a smaller estate for the summer.

Rob could change his mind and go home with his parents or stay with any of his uncles and aunts, but he would still be one of a dozen wherever he went with them. He wanted to spend some time just as himself.

He'd finished at Oxford at the beginning of the summer. He wished for independence. If he went home he would be lost among his siblings, and with his aunts and uncles, lost among his cousins, and being lost among his cousins was worse because most of the men his age were titled. He was not. Rob was the odd one out in his extended family, the only firstborn son without a title or a huge inheritance awaiting him.

Here with Mary and Drew that did not matter. Rob could be himself, independent, respected, and hero-worshipped by his nephew, and it was close enough to town that he could also begin to plan for his future. He could hunt for lodgings in London and move into them in the autumn. All he needed to do then was choose a living. In his mind he had a grand idealistic plan, yet in practice he was unsure how this great feat of his might be managed.

Not that he needed an occupation, he had an income provided by his ducal brother. He'd come of age, he was one and twenty, and on the day of his coming of age he'd received his first quarter's allowance—but the idea of living off John jarred brutally.

John had everything. He was rich, titled and successful in both the management of his estates and in the House of Lords. He'd lived abroad for several years and explored archaeology in Egypt, returning with his finds as trophies. He drew like a master, sung with the voice of a professional and played the pianoforte equally well.

What do I have, what can I do? Rob wished to make something of himself. To make some mark on the world. To do something worthwhile with his life, but he wished to achieve it through his own efforts. His cousins and brother might mock him as a philanthropist but he did not think it a bad thing to wish to make a difference. He refused to sit back and live on the largesse of his brother. He wished to do something meaningful and inspiring. Something more than being dependent and idle.

He was the grandson of an earl and a duke, but not within the line of inheritance for either, and his father's estate was small, too small for his father to require assistance. Rob could paint with moderate skill, sing with pleasing countenance, ride as well as any man, and shoot well, but he could not join a regiment, he was still an heir. He was good at many things, but a master of nothing, so numerous occupations were beyond his reach, while his step-brother had set a bar above him that was so high it could never be achieved.

But he still had his plan that would, he hoped, give him the sense of pride in himself that he craved, some separation from reliance on his family and bring benefit to thousands.

He longed for a position in government. That was his great plan—to carve out his place in the political world and create a niche for himself.

Yet to be elected he needed money for a campaign, and he did not wish to involve his father, or John, or anyone else in his family because they would simply offer him one of their pocket seats, which they owned through bribery. The whole idea of that rankled. It would feel immoral, and then again Rob would have achieved nothing on his own. There would be no pride in it. If he were to respect himself, when he spoke out for the poor, he could not do it when everything that had got him to that point had come from the wealthy.

He'd rather give the money he received from John to the poor and bypass himself, if that was the way he had to earn a place in parliament. *Perhaps I am a philanthropist.* But he hadn't a clue where to begin without using John's money. The only detail in the conception of his plan to date was that he did not wish it to become John-shaped.

This summer, therefore, was his time to think things through and develop his method to win himself a place in the governance of the country which had been earned and not inherited.

"Robbie." His mother touched his elbow.

His thoughts had been a mile away.

Looking at her, he smiled. He'd driven her over here to see Mary. His father was with John, looking over John's estates.

"We ought to go, and leave Mary to settle Iris and George down for a nap."

He agreed. He kissed his sister's cheek, before bending to kiss his niece's forehead as his finger brushed over the wispy hair on her soft head.

He would stay here. With Mary and Drew, where he did not feel such a lesser mortal, or so lacking in achievements and ability.

Drew slapped Rob on the shoulder. "We shall see you tomorrow, and we shall have a merry time over the summer."

~

Caro looked out of the open French door at those gathered on the terrace and the lawn beyond it. It had been over three years since she'd first visited the Duke of Pembroke's. She had felt then as she felt now, overwhelmed, afraid, and yet angry. Nervous sensations tingled across her skin, as her heart raced.

There were dozens of people here, adults and children, all laughing, smiling and talking.

Drew was among them playing cricket as Mary sat on a blanket beneath a canopy watching him, with Iris in her arms.

Many of the women held young children.

Caro was the only parasite—unmarried and childless, sucking the blood from this family, hiding among them, dependent and clinging to her brother. She hated her reliance on Drew, it pressed into her side, a steel-hard pain. Sometimes she felt as though

Albert's hands were still about her neck, cutting off her breath and that she had not taken a breath since she'd left him three years before.

Yet this family accepted her, all of them. She could not blame her misery on them. They were simply a constant reminder of what she had failed to possess, she had not succeeded in winning the love of her husband, or to bear his child. Guilt, shame and longing hung about her and whispered in her ears as constant companions.

Caro sipped from the glass of lemonade she held. If the family had gathered at Drew's house she would have retired to her rooms and found a book or embroidery to absorb her thoughts. But today she had been foolish enough to agree to travel with them. Yet Mary had asked specifically and refusing would have seemed too rude.

"Throw!" The Duke of Pembroke yelled from his position behind the wicket, holding up his open hands. The ball was thrown to him and his uncle was caught out.

Some of the women and children cheered and others booed, depending on who their allegiance lay with.

The Duke slapped his uncle's shoulder and his uncle laughed.

The Pembrokes were a happy, harmonious clan, and Drew was now one of them. He'd thrown the ball to John.

The crack of hard leather hitting willow echoed across the open space above the sound of conversation. Mary's brother Robbie held the bat and ran.

He was to stay at Drew's for the summer.

Caro watched him run from one wicket to the other. He was tall but lithe. He touched the bat to the ground, then ran back.

Discomfort rippled through her nerves.

"Papa! Uncle Bobbie!"

Caro's gaze turned to Drew's son. He'd escaped the women and was running on his little legs to join the game.

Before he'd run more than a dozen steps, Mary's father caught him up and tossed the child, squealing, into the air.

Drew's children were the only part of Caro's life that brought her happiness. She spent hours with her nephew and niece.

Applause echoed over the lawn as Robbie ran his fourth length and beat the ball back to the wicket. He turned and braced himself to hit again, his dark-brown hair falling forward over his brow.

He was different from most of the Pembrokes, and from most of Mary's family. He looked like his father, not his mother. He did not have the Pembrokes' dark hair or their pale-blue eyes.

Drew had told her Robbie had seen her leave the house yesterday. Drew had said she'd made Robbie concerned about staying. Then Drew had waited as if he hoped she would say she did not mind Robbie coming.

She had not answered. She did not wish to discuss her silent madness with her brother. Guilt and shame had eaten away at her in the last three years and she was not a whole woman; she could not simply snuff out her feelings like the flame of a candle. She did not understand it herself, so how could she discuss it anyway. He'd encouraged her to speak with doctors in the early years, and yet the only one she had told had offered her laudanum to calm her nerves—nothing else.

She did not wish to feel ill as well as mad.

Perhaps Drew ought to have her admitted to an asylum and be done with it. She felt as though she was trapped within a prison anyway—a glass gaol of her own making.

A raucous cheer rang across the lawn outside as Robbie's wicket was smashed by the bowling technique of one of his cousins. Once the cheering was over the men began to walk back up the hill towards the house.

Her heartbeat pounded violently in her chest.

Drew spotted her. Of course, he knew where to look. He knew she would not be outside among Mary's family. He lifted his hand, peeling away from the others, who walked towards the women.

Her brother was a man to match the Pembrokes, he was tall, athletic and handsome; brown-haired and hazel-eyed. He'd carried

35

his own insecurity before he'd married Mary, but not now. Mary and her family had healed him—made him a complete man. He was at peace with himself, confident and in love with Mary. He deserved more than to have a sister who clung like a shackle about his neck.

"Caro!" he called as he drew nearer. "Come and sit with Mary and me!"

"I am happy here!" she called back.

"Are you?" he responded with a smile. "You need not exclude yourself, though! Come!" He held out his hand as he walked closer.

Unfortunately, he was also stubborn.

Her lips trembled when she tried to smile.

Then he was there, taking her hand, whether she willed it or not. He pulled her outside. "Kate will take it as an insult if you do not join us."

"She will not. The Duchess will not notice." Yet Caro gave in to his urging rather than cause a scene.

His hold on her hand was loose as he pulled her on.

The only people she felt comfortable touching her were Drew and the children… and yet she craved touch. She felt starved of it at times. It was another anomaly of her madness.

He flashed a smile across his shoulder. "She notices. They all do. But admittedly no one thinks ill of you, and yet you still hide."

She said nothing to that.

The family groups were gathered about the refreshment tables. Some of the children ran between people's legs, playing a game of chase, until one of the Duke's uncles called a stop to the game. "Enough, children, you shall knock one of us over!" Caro flinched at the tone of his voice. It rattled through her nerves.

"Come on." Drew's hold tightened on her hand as he felt her hesitation.

Caro focused on Mary, her heart racing with the pace of a galloping horse. Her panic was irrational, there was no threat and yet every one of her senses tingled with a need to run. Fear hemmed her in and tightened in a heavy grip about her chest, making it difficult to breathe.

Flashes of memory stirred, images sparking through her thoughts like flashes of lightning—there and then not.

"Look what I found," Drew said to Mary.

Caro fought the growing pain in her chest when Drew let go of her hand and tried not to gasp for breath as her heart pounded out a wild rhythm.

Mary smiled and patted a vacant space beside her on the blanket. Caro sat down.

"Caro was in the house. I thought I'd bring her out here so that she could converse with you at least."

Caro's gaze fell to Iris—her niece was asleep in Mary's arms. Instantly the panic eased, replaced by love and longing.

"Would you like to take her," Mary offered.

Mary was a few years younger than Drew, but she was so good for him, and good to Caro.

"Thank you." When Caro took Iris from Mary, the child stirred, her little hands opening as her eyes did.

Drew's fingers brushed his daughter's cheek. Iris looked up at her papa.

"Poppet," he whispered.

Iris gurgled in recognition.

"Aun'ie Ca'o!" George barrelled into her side, tumbling onto the blanket with a roll. She clasped one arm about George while the other held Iris, and the world was at peace again.

"I hit a ball with Uncle Bobbie." George announced.

"I held the bat with him." The words came from above them.

Mary looked upward. Caro did not. Robbie's voice grated on her nerves.

"I hit it far," George declared slipping from beneath Caro's arm to hug his mother instead.

"Clever boy," Mary praised her son. "Perhaps Uncle Robbie will teach you how to hold the bat yourself in the summer."

"And I missed this marvellous feat," Drew said. "You will have to do it again after luncheon so I may see you."

Robbie stepped closer.

Tremors ran across Caro's skin and unravelled into her veins. She wished Robbie to move away.

He dropped down to sit on the end of the blanket, near Mary's feet.

Panic claimed Caro in full force, her chest becoming so tight she could not pull the air into her lungs.

The baby made an impatient sound in Caro's arms.

"Sorry, she's fractious, she is hungry, I ought to take her in and feed her." Mary gave her son another squeeze, then let him go and stood up. "Come along, little one." She reached down so Caro could pass Iris back.

Robbie's gaze rested on Caro as she held Iris up.

When Mary walked away, Drew sat down beside Caro and leant back on his hands, stretching out his legs. "You know your mother is taking your absconding personally," he spoke to Robbie.

Caro's limbs filled up with the weight of lead and she adjusted her sitting position, bending up her knees within the skirt of her dress and hugging them, as George crawled towards Robbie.

Robbie laughed and his hand ruffled George's hair. "She is not ready for me to leave the nest. She thinks we are all growing up too fast."

"I suppose that is my fault, for snatching Mary from it."

"She does not hold that against you. You have given her more grandchildren in return. It is an exchange. I am just a loss."

"Shall I tell her to stop henpecking and let you fledge?"

Drew was joking. He was close to Mary's and Robbie's parents. They were his parents too—because theirs had never fulfilled that role.

"Papa spoke to her. He supports me. He knows I cannot live on his estate, there is nothing for me to do there."

When Caro had first come to the Duke's home Robbie had

been eighteen. He'd smiled and laughed frequently, but as a man he seemed more serious than the others. Most of his cousins had no interest in the children, his peers within the family always kept to their own group, but Robbie never stood with them. Yet his younger brother, Harry, did. Drew at his age had been wild, playing with danger, fighting everyone and everything.

"Of course you cannot, if you wish to sow a few wild oats?" Drew added.

"Not my style," Robbie answered.

Drew's face split into a broad smile, "So your brother told me."

"Harry?"

"Harry…" They laughed again. Caro did not know the joke.

"Well, you may tell Harry to mind his own business, not mine," Rob said, with a smile.

"But younger brothers are born to be a thorn in the side. Mary and I are working on one for George solely for that purpose"

"I have never been a thorn in John's. He'd win whatever argument I started with a simple glance."

"True, your older brother does have a way of making a man feel as small as a mouse. I ignore it."

"I do not risk it. I never give him cause to deploy that look on me."

Another laugh was shared between them as George scrambled back across the blanket to Drew, then began using his father as a climbing frame. He clambered up Drew's back and then tumbled over Drew's shoulder. George's legs flew out towards Robbie.

Robbie reached to catch him and slow his fall.

Caro instinctively leant back.

Robbie and Drew looked at her, but Robbie did not move back, instead he shifted forward on to his knees, leaned over and tickled George's tummy, making him giggle.

It left Caro sitting two feet away from him.

When Robbie stopped tickling, George crawled to her, to escape his uncle, still giggling.

The attention of both men followed George. Heat burned in Caro's cheeks as the rhythm of her heartbeat rose. She pulled George onto her lap and hugged him, perhaps a little too tightly, but it helped relieve her discomfort.

"I am sorry I missed you yesterday, Caroline."

Robbie was being polite, nothing else, but yet again her senses revolted. He knew she'd avoided him on purpose.

"Caro," Drew prompted, when she did not answer, as though she was a child to be corrected.

Her gaze lifted to Robbie's eyes. They were blue, but a much darker blue than Mary's.

Caro had never spoken to him before, never been this close to him. He did not have the imposing presence of his elder ducal brother, his body was relaxed and his appearance therefore more approachable as he smiled at her. But he was still a man, even though he was young and behaved with good manners, and she was still uncomfortable with him so near.

He leaned sideways, resting his weight onto one hand. His shirtsleeves were rolled up and she could see his forearm covered in a dusting of dark hair.

George broke free from her embrace. "Papa, I need the pot," he declared with extreme urgency. He always waited until the last moment.

"I'll take him." Caroline moved to rise, but Drew pressed a hand on her shoulder as he did.

"You stay here, I'll take him." He rose.

She knew what Drew was doing—he was forcing her to endure Robbie's company. He'd expressed his view over her "flighty nature" dozens of times and he was never cruel about it, but he'd insisted often that she should try harder to overcome it. He was stubborn.

"I will do my best not to discompose you when I stay at Drew's."

Caro's gaze spun back to Robbie. Every one of her senses screamed.

Robbie had a physical energy about him, an aura that said he

40

was an active man and he was athletic in build.

"I… I…" Her gaze turned to where his elder female cousins sat a little way away. They had their husbands beside them.

She had never felt more desolate.

The tears which threatened caught in her throat as she clutched her knees, holding them close, clinging to herself as if she were driftwood on a swirling sea.

A family group the other side of them laughed. Caro unfurled and rose instantly. She could not do this. She turned and began walking, uncertain where she was going, but knowing she could not stay there.

"Caroline." Her name was spoken quietly. Robbie had followed. She glanced back, her gaze apologising. It was not his fault. He'd done nothing wrong.

But then she turned away and fled, striding across the lawn in the direction that Drew had taken.

She had truly cast herself a gaol cell.

~

Rob was torn. *Should I chase after her?* He'd said nothing wrong and yet guilt gripped in his chest. Caroline had braved his company and he'd scared her off.

He cursed himself as he watched her ascend the shallow flight of stairs leading to the stone terrace and then disappear into the house, a phantom again.

He'd have to apologise this evening.

When they ate dinner he watched Caroline often, glancing at her across the table. Kate had pandered to Caroline's insecurities, she'd been seated between his mother and Mary, disobeying the male, then female, structure of the entire group. But between the women who she knew and perhaps felt a little more comfortable with, Caroline had animation. Deep in conversation, she smiled at Mary on occasions and her hand gestured as she spoke.

41

She was beautiful, but not in the striking way of his family. Caroline's beauty was almost indefinable—there was no particular notable element—but the elements put together…

Her hair was blonde, a golden yellow, her skin clear but not remarkably pale, and her eyes hazel. Her nose was slender and long, and her lips generous, but when they parted in a rare smile, it lit up her face, awakening her overall beauty. He was fascinated. He hardly spoke to his aunt Jane and his cousin Eleanor, who flanked him at the table.

Watching Caroline was like watching a wild creature. She required patience. To observe her in reality you must sit in silence because if you moved she would know you were watching and be scared away.

Her gaze caught on his, only for an instant. Then she looked at his mother. But in that instant something hard struck him in the chest.

The candlelight from the candelabra on the table made her skin glow, and the different shades in her eyes became darker as the light flickered.

When the women rose and left the table, Rob spoke with his uncle James. They walked into the drawing room together later, once they had finished their port, and as they did, Rob's gaze searched for Caroline.

She was sitting in the corner, beside Kate.

Every time he'd seen Caroline here over the years she'd hidden in corners.

"Robbie." Rob turned at his ducal brother's greeting. "I imagine you have been longing for this summer, to have your freedom and stretch your wings. I know I was excited at your age."

"You did not just stretch your wings, you flew off." John had been the ideal Rob aspired to when he was younger—but John was so damned perfect Rob would never match him. John irked him now. They were not particularly close. In Rob's formative years John had been away at school and then abroad for years.

When John had returned to take up the role of duke, he'd been a grown man and Rob still a boy.

"Yes, well, this country held no appeal when grandfather was alive, and I had a contrary nature. Leaving was the only way I could influence my life. You could do the same if you wished—go abroad. Your allowance is yours to do with as you will."

Rob held his brother's gaze as the words kicked him in the gut. Living on John's generosity was not the life he chose. "I've no idea what I wish to do." That was not true, but he would not share it with John because he knew one thing clearly, *I do not wish to mimic you.*

"Except escape Mama's nest."

"Well, yes, that, obviously." Rob's gaze swung away and reached across the room, only to find Caroline watching him. His heart thumped in his chest as he met her look. She turned away, and his gaze turned back to John.

"Will you run riot in town, then?"

"That's Harry's style. You know it is not mine." Harry was the hell-raiser. Rob had never been that.

John gripped Rob's shoulder. "Well, whatever you do, do not become a stranger."

Rob nodded. John turned away. Rob looked back at Caroline. She was alone.

She was looking at her hands, which rested in her lap, trying to hide amidst a crowd. A phantom.

He walked over to her. "Caroline." The muscle of her upper body jerked, her gaze flying to his for an instant. She hadn't noticed him approaching. She looked down again.

Her hair was curled and coifed, with a few wisps trailing the length of her slender neck and kissing her cheeks. Those curls danced with her movement.

She was a slender woman, neither short nor tall, but fragile in appearance, and yet she had a generous bosom.

Rather than tower over her, he dropped into the seat beside hers.

She leant back a little.

"I am sorry for upsetting you this afternoon, but there was no need to run."

Once more her gaze flew to him, before falling away.

"Look at me." Rob urged quietly, sitting forward in his chair and leaning towards her. No one ever challenged her, *no one*. Everyone protected her.

The memory of his younger sister, Jemima's, aversion to spiders came to mind. He'd caught one and kept it in a glass so that she could look at it, and eventually he'd persuaded her to touch it, now she could let one run across her hand. Fears ought to be faced.

Her gaze lifted to his, and her eyes shone from behind blonde eyelashes; her eye colour in candlelight was a dark amber. Her eyebrows arched as her fingers clasped more firmly in her lap.

"I am staying with Drew and Mary for the summer..." He searched for words.

"I know, Mr Marlow."

Her gaze left his and looked for someone to rescue her, probably Drew.

"Rob, Caroline, not Mr Marlow. Look at me," he said again. If she would look at him, then maybe he could begin to help break her fear.

She did, but her gaze raged at him, bidding him to leave her alone.

"Why do you not feel comfortable?"

She looked away. She was about to rise and run again. Instinctively he reached out and caught hold of her wrist. "Caroline..." But immediately he realised what he'd done. No one touched her except Drew, Mary and the children. Everyone knew Caroline could not abide to be touched.

It was as though a lightning bolt struck between them her reaction was so violent and sudden. Her gaze accused him of committing murder as his fingers opened. Her arm slipped from his hold when she rose from her chair and fled again, crossing the room to the safety of Mary.

Rob watched her flight and felt a heel. He should not have pushed her.

He looked at his sister and awaited a glance of condemnation. None came. Caroline did not tell Mary, and no one in the room had noticed that he'd approached Caroline.

He rested his elbow on the arm of the chair and his chin on his fist, still watching Caroline.

"You're miles away, where are you?" Rob's uncle Robert, the Earl of Barrington, occupied the chair Caroline had vacated.

As Rob leant back, his ankle lifted to rest on his opposite knee and he smiled. Uncle Robert was his favourite uncle, his father's brother. Rob had been named for him.

"I did not think you were coming. I thought you were going home to Yorkshire."

"Jane wished to spend some time with everyone before we left. I gave in to her coercion."

Aunt Jane was sitting at the pianoforte, in the company of his cousin Margaret, sorting through music.

Rob had been close to them from a young age. Their eldest son, Henry, was of an age with Harry, so Rob and Harry had stayed with them frequently as children.

Henry was more like Harry, though. They were both currently standing to one side of the room drinking and laughing with the others of their age group.

Rob looked back at his uncle. Robert had undertaken a grand tour, as John had. "Did you enjoy the continent when you were there?"

Robert smiled, then looked at his wife. "Jane grew up on a manor bordering my father's land. We were close as children. I was in love with her, but she married someone else, an arranged marriage. She broke my heart. I left England because I was miserable. My time abroad was equally miserable."

Rob shifted to sit upright, his leg falling from his knee. He'd known Jane grew up with his uncle and his father, but he had not known his uncle had loved her then. His father often likened Harry to their uncle Robert, but in that context there was nothing similar. "I thought you'd gone abroad for fun, like John."

"No, I was sent there in disgrace by your grandfather. I'd dropped out of university and become an embarrassment."

"I did not know. I'm sorry."

"Why should you have known? What of you? Have you decided what you will do?"

"No, beyond finding rooms in London during the summer." He'd told none of his family about his great plan. He knew if he spoke of it they would grasp upon the idea, and in the name of helpfulness take it over and manipulate it all so that the achievement would not be his. If he wished to take up a place in the House of Commons and speak for the working class he needed to first earn the people's trust and win a true vote, not one contrived by his family.

"You know you would be welcome with us, if you wished to come. The tenants are due to leave the estate, which used to belong to Jane's father. I'd be happy for you to take it over and cut your teeth managing that."

Rob's father had done that, he'd managed all of the Barrington Estate, while Robert had been abroad and, like John, Rob's father set the bar high for any comparison. No, Rob wished to take his life in a direction that no one in his family had gone. Following in his father's footsteps and relying on his uncle held no greater pleasure than living off his brother's generosity.

"It is only an offer, Robbie…"

Rob's gaze travelled to where Caroline stood. She had been looking at him; she looked away.

A spasm seized his stomach. It was odd to have her look at him.

"If you change your mind write and let me know. I'll probably not re-let it for a few months; there is some work to be done on the house."

Rob looked at his uncle. "Henry may want it in a couple of years?"

"Henry will have plenty to occupy him on my other estates and Henry is not you. My son is reckless and self-absorbed. He'll not settle to anything that requires sobriety and forethought for years. The only thing he is currently interested in is racing horses. He spends more time with Forth than me."

Lord Forth, who bred horses, was a neighbour of Uncle Robert's and a friend of Rob's father's too.

"Racing is Henry's passion and his weakness," Rob stated.

"What is your weakness?" His uncle lifted an eyebrow.

His whole family believed he had no weaknesses, thanks to Harry's mocking. His brother liked to taunt Rob for being staid. Or boring, as Harry put it. But Harry was so damned wild Rob had always been too busy hauling his brother out of scrapes to get into any of his own. Being the eldest boy he'd been forced into responsibility for his siblings.

Yet his peers in the family had never done the same.

It was true he had no vice, though. But he did not think himself dull.

He'd drunk excessively once, and woken up hating the fact he could not recall what he'd said and done. He'd played cards for money once and lost half his allowance, then considered gambling a fool's game.

Perhaps his weakness was idealism. But in truth, now... "A lack of inspiration." The look he shared with his uncle mocked himself. He had this great plan, but really it was no plan at all, simply fanciful, he did not have a method by which to achieve it.

"Something will come along to give you purpose. Wait and see." His uncle looked away, turning as his eldest daughter, who was fifteen, joined them.

"We are going to dance, will you dance with me, Papa?" She gave Rob a smile. Julie had her mother's unusual green eyes.

"Julie." Rob nodded.

"Robbie," she bobbed a shallow curtsy. It was unnecessary but the girl was already practising for her debut. He smiled more broadly and she smiled brightly.

"I shall be honoured, young lady." Uncle Robert stood.

Rob looked across the room. Caroline was standing beside his sister, looking at him. Before she had chance to look away, he smiled as he had just done at his cousin. Red stained Caroline's cheeks when she did look away.

Rob rose. It would be crass of him not to offer to escort one his female cousins in the dance.

They danced a string of over half a dozen country dances, and he participated in every one with one of his cousins or sisters, but as he did so, he noted Caroline watching him frequently. If he'd been more courageous he would have offered to partner her, but she never danced.

He wondered if she wished to dance, if perhaps she was trapped by her fears and they were just as disturbing for her as they were for those trying desperately not to upset her.

Idealism was certainly his fault, because in his mind's eye he saw her dancing. She'd come to life when she'd spoken with Mary. How much more would she come to life if she danced without fear.

I shall dance with her by the end of the summer. The promise whispered through his soul. He abhorred dares, dares were another thing that was Harry's forte—but if Rob wished to achieve something, when he set his mind to it, he did so with determination. He would see her dance because he firmly believed, from the amount of times she had looked at him this evening, she was not happy to be withheld by her fear. She wished to dance.

If I wish to achieve something, when I set my mind to it, I do so with determination… He'd hold that thought fast through the summer, and find a way to win himself a seat in the House of Commons without the assistance of his family.

Chapter 6

"Aun'ie Ca'o, look." Caro turned her gaze from the window to her nephew, who held out the wooden horse his grandfather had given him the day before. He was playing with his ark full of wooden animals.

"I can see, darling."

His nanny was kneeling on the floor beside him, while Iris lay sleeping in a cradle across the room. There was no need for Caro's presence in the nursery other than that she wished to be here.

"It's nearly three, ma'am. Will you stay here for tea?" the nanny asked, rising from the floor.

Caro turned fully away from the attic window. Robbie had been due to arrive at two. He was an hour late. Drew would expect her to go down for tea once he came, but Caro was a coward to the core. "Yes, I will. I have nothing else to do."

Caro walked over to George, who was galloping his horse across the rug, she bent and caught hold of his waist, then lifted him an inch or two off the floor. He laughed and wriggled. "Aun'ie Ca'o."

"Tyke, you will be a monster when you are grown."

"Papa, says I'll be a 'ogue and I'is a diamon'."

"You'll be a star and outshine everyone, and Iris will be sunlight, too bright for anyone to look at." Caro lifted him up and balanced him on her hip. From outside came the loud sound of an arrival, carriage wheels turning on the gravel and horses' hooves crunching in the stones.

"Uncle Bobbie!" George bellowed, pointing to the window with his horse.

Caroline's heart thumped in her chest.

"Let me see, Aun'ie Ca'o."

She wished to look as much as George did. She crossed the room and leaned to the window. She could still feel the sensation of Robbie's fingers brushing against her skin last night when he'd touched her arm, and then she'd risen and her arm had slipped from his hold. His grip had been gentle. He'd not held her hard.

Robbie's fashionable phaeton stood below and two thorough-bred chestnuts shook out their manes in the traces, while one of her brother's grooms held their heads to stop them bolting.

Robbie jumped down as Drew walked forward. She'd watched Robbie moving last night as he'd danced. His slender, athletic build gave his movement grace. He'd not meant to disconcert her yesterday. She knew it. He was simply being thoughtful, and she had watched him dance with his sisters and his cousins, displaying the same thoughtfulness, while his brother and his male cousins stood to one side of the room talking amongst themselves and laughing frequently.

"Uncle Bobbie!" George cried again, his legs straightening, expressing his desire to get down as he wriggled to be free.

Caro set him down. Immediately he ran to the door and tried to reach the handle.

"Master George!" The nanny reprimanded, but George would never be deterred from the thought of someone new to play with.

"I shall go with him," Caro stated as George managed to turn the handle and run out. "Forget the tea. I doubt we shall be back,"

Caro's heart raced as she followed, but it was not with fear. She felt inexplicably excited. *Why was she excited?*

"George!" she called, as he ran along the hall. He always looked like a little caricature of Drew when he ran. "George!" He did not stop. "George! Wait! Or I will tell your papa you misbehaved and you shall not see Uncle Robbie!" Her heart thumped harder as George neared the top of the narrow stairs leading down from the attic. "George, stop!" She clasped her skirt and held it high as she ran too, terrified he'd fall.

The child was an absolute nightmare when he chose to be, but thank the Lord he stopped and turned back, waiting for her as he grasped a spindle of the banister.

"Good boy, George, darling," she praised breathlessly when she reached him, dropping to her haunches to hug him in relief. "Remember, you are not to run near the stairs, nor near horses or water, they are the three things you must never do."

He nodded, his face twisting in a look of concern over her distress.

"Good boy," she gave him another squeeze as love spilled from her heart into her blood. Drew's children were her life. Without them she would have nothing to hold her together.

When she rose she lifted him to her hip and kissed his cheek, then said near his ear, "Come along, then, let us find your Uncle Robbie."

She carried him down, with one hand sliding along the stair rail.

"May I see Uncle Bobbie's ho'ses?"

"They will be in the stables. You may see them another day."

"Will Papa let me 'ide them?"

"One day, yes, I'm sure he will."

George's short-sentenced conversation continued down the stairs. He so rarely ran out of enthusiasm or energy.

When they reached the first floor, Caro heard loud, masculine voices echoing along the landing. Robbie was already upstairs and he and Drew were heading towards the drawing room. She stopped on the stairs, looking down through the stairwell and saw the servants carrying in Robbie's luggage on the ground floor.

She'd hoped for a moment more of obscurity, but her hopes wilted as George shouted loudly, "Uncle Bobbie!" and then he fought for freedom. She finished her descent and set him down. He charged off in the direction of the voices.

Caro did not follow. Her excitement ebbed as she saw them.

"Uncle Bobbie!"

They looked back.

Foreboding crept over Caro and then the familiar discomfort—panic. Her lungs emptied of breath. Rob was looking at her not George, his gaze briefly skimmed the length of her body, then lifted back to her face. She felt hot as well as uncomfortable. The recollection of his touch now gave her a sense of self-consciousness. Her discomfort with other people had been her companion for too many years.

"Oh!" The cry came from George. He'd caught his toe on a wrinkle in the carpet and he tumbled forward, still gripping his wooden horse.

Caro lifted the hem of her dress and ran as the poor child's head hit the floor with a bump. Thank the Lord it was wood and not stone.

Drew reached him first, but George was now howling, the broken wooden horse still grasped in his hand. It had lost a leg, but it was also covered in the child's blood.

"What has he done?" she asked, stopping before them, breathing hard.

Drew wiped his thumb across his son's swollen lower lip as Robbie held out a handkerchief.

"He bit his lip when he fell. No real harm, Caro," Drew answered.

Caro's fingers pressed against her chest, then reached to brush through George's hair. He was crying still. She sensed Robbie watching her, but she did not care. George was everything to her. "Poppet," she whispered, "did you break your horse?"

"Grandpa will buy you another," Robbie said, his fingers brushing across George's brow. They touched Caro's. She pulled her hand away as she met Robbie's dark gaze.

Her heart raced into a gallop, calling her to flee.

But if Robbie was to be here for the whole summer she must force herself to feel easier with him. "I brought him down because he wished to see you."

George's wails had turned to quieter sobs and sniffs. Robbie held his hands out and George reached for him in return. He set his arms about Robbie's neck as Robbie took him.

Robbie's ease with George moved something within Caro. If she had given Albert a son he would not have held the child, he would have probably looked into the nursery for a few moments each day and no more. It was more evidence that Robbie's actions towards her had been nothing more than kindness. He was simply a good-natured young man.

"Mama," George cried, pressing his face into Robbie's neckcloth, probably getting blood all over it.

"Your mama is asleep," Drew ruffled George's hair. "Iris woke her in the night and she needed to rest. She will be down in a little while."

Robbie's gaze lifted to Drew then passed to Caro, and he smiled. It shone in his eyes, not simply parted his lips. He was as open in nature as his sister.

The rhythm of Caro's heartbeat was painful. Something solid tightened in her chest. He'd smiled at her last night, across the room, and anger and discomfort had taken up their swords and begun a war inside her. That was her irrational madness. But when he'd touched her arm, his fingers had gripped her gently.

"Are you going to join us for tea, Caro? You could act as hostess..." Drew lifted an eyebrow at her. It was a challenge.

Forcing a smile, she looked from Drew to Robbie, fighting the urge to run. Yet, bizarrely, as much as she wished to run, she felt pulled towards Robbie when he smiled again. His smile tried to reassure and pleaded with her to stay.

Her skin burned as she blushed, but she nodded, then turned to lead the way towards the drawing room. A maid was already there, laying out the tea tray. Drew must have ordered it when

Robbie arrived.

Caro breathed slowly, trying not to show how hard it was to draw the air past the panic in her chest.

A plate of almond biscuits stood beside the teapot, and as the men came into the room, George released a deep whimper of longing.

Caro picked up the plate and held it out for George, who was still balanced in Robbie's arms. George took a biscuit and sucked it. Tears stained his cheeks.

Caro's gaze lifted. Robbie had been watching her again.

"Your neckcloth is ruined," she said to him.

Drew was watching her too.

Robbie's hand lifted and he took a biscuit. He had long, slender fingers and beautifully proportioned hands. They looked as gentle as they'd felt.

Albert's hands had been broad and brutal.

A spasm caught in Caro's stomach, as though her womb ached. *It is because he's holding the child.*

Her gaze met Robbie's again as he bit into the biscuit. She looked at Drew and held out the plate.

~

Rob watched Caroline as they ate breakfast the day after his arrival. He'd experienced a strange sense of recognition, *déjà vu*, when she'd offered him the plate of biscuits as George had held his neck.

Something had passed between them, her eyes had said something he did not understand. Yet after serving their tea she'd disappeared into hiding, leaving Drew to take George to see his mother and Rob to unpack.

She had not come down to dinner.

But this morning she'd risked Rob's company again. He'd entered the morning room after her and seated himself opposite her. She'd mumbled good morning as he sat, but she had not looked at him.

Rob was unable not to look at her. The more he watched her, the more he became fascinated.

Mary spoke to Caroline about a book she'd read, probably trying to ease Caroline's discomfort through conversation. Flashes of expressions passed across Caroline's face, but they never fully formed. She hid her thoughts and emotions as she hid herself. Her smile was tempered and frowns fleeting, and he'd not once in all the years he'd known her, heard her laugh.

Her gaze lifted and the morning sunlight spilling through the windows caught her eyes. It turned them from the hazel with a look of amber to a remarkable gold.

He wished he could make her see he was no risk, that at least with him she might be free of fear.

She looked at Drew.

What would she look like if she were to laugh, while her eyes, cast in gold, sparkled? Rob wished to see her laughing.

I will have her laughing and dancing by the end of the summer. He smiled as a sound of humour slipped from his throat. It was his idealism speaking. He wished everything ordered as it should be, and no one should feel as restrained as Caroline did. That was why he saw himself in government, because he cared about the people who desperately needed help.

Yet while he worked out how to win himself an elected seat and change the world for them, the aim of bringing Caro out of her shell would give him a purpose he could fulfil more quickly.

Caroline had looked back at him when he'd made a sound, as had Mary. He did not explain it, but looked at Drew. "Is there any interesting news?"

"Not really," Drew folded the paper and threw it across to Rob. "It's all gossip and insinuation. What are we doing today? Riding out? I could show you all of the estate. You've never ridden the boundary."

"Your son has a prior claim on me. I promised to teach him

how to bat alone, and you will need to help me with that."

Drew smiled. "Then I'll defer to my son. We can ride out tomorrow and I'll take George with us on my saddle. He'll—"

"Not be going," Mary interrupted, "That is too much for him."

"Nonsense, he loves riding up with me, he likes watching everything and he loves the horses." Drew gave Mary a smile that said do not challenge me. "He is my son, he has backbone."

"He is a two-year-old child—"

"Who has a healthy interest in the world."

Rob looked from Drew to Mary. "I did not come here to cause a rift between you, but I'm sure George will cope. He will have the two of us to entertain him, and he will be unhappy if we leave him behind."

Mary glared at Rob and rose from the table. "We will see. I am going to the nursery." She turned, her skirt swaying with the movement, speaking her annoyance without words. Then she walked away.

Drew laughed for an instant, but then he rose. "Mary..."

She did not look back.

Drew's hand touched Rob's shoulder and he leaned down. "Do me a favour, in future do not side with me. You are *her* brother. She'll hold it against me." Laughing again, then, he walked on, while Mary made a disgruntled noise as she left the room.

Drew's lack of respect for her irritation would rile her further and she'd be angry for a while. Poor George would have to wait for his lesson until Drew had finished patching things up.

Rob looked back at Caroline, expecting her to rise immediately and leave. Instead her gaze met his.

"I'm sorry," she breathed in a quiet, blunt voice. "If I have made you feel uncomfortable. I will try to accept your presence here. But it is not easy for me, Mr Marlow, and I wish you would not stare at me as you have been."

"Caroline..."

She rose, leaving her napkin on the table and her meal half-eaten.

But Rob carried on quickly, before she could walk away. "...I will be no threat to you. I am staying here only because I love my sister and I love the children. I have no desire to discompose you. I hope you will come to feel at ease in my company as you do in Mary's."

She nodded, slightly, but then she turned.

"Good day!" he called in her wake, feeling as though he'd taken a step towards dancing with her. It was the first time she'd voluntarily spoken to anyone in his family beyond his mother and Mary, as far as Rob knew.

~

Love. The word echoed in Caro's thoughts like a bell that kept tolling, as she crossed the hall, then climbed the stairs. *Because I love my sister and I love the children.*

Love. The word had seemed odd on Robbie's lips. Yet she heard Drew say it often, and she saw love everywhere in Mary's extended family. But for a young man like Robbie to use the word so freely about his sister and his niece and nephew.

Even in the first year of their marriage, when she'd thought herself loved, Albert had never used that word. But nor had she spoken it to him. It was a word that had never been spoken in her childhood. She had never dared to risk the mention of it to Albert in case it had broken some spell!—the spell had broken anyway.

She walked past the stairs to the nursery. Drew and Mary would be up there, either continuing their disagreement or ending it.

Caro went to her rooms and collected her bonnet, so she might walk outside. The sunshine and the sounds of nature would calm the turmoil inside her.

When she came down she used the servants' stairs to avoid the possibility of another encounter with Robbie.

The servants' hall brought her out into the walled garden. It was full of vegetables waiting to be harvested for the table, and rows of flowers to be cut to fill the vases in the house. The scent of herbs caught on the breeze as her skirt brushed the leaves of the thyme, mint and rosemary.

A flock of sparrows chirped riotously, chasing each other through tall beanstalks, seeking insects.

Caro walked on, smiling at the gardeners, who lifted their caps, as she had smiled at the servants who'd curtsied and bowed within the house.

She felt no unease with them.

But they bore no comparison to the life she'd left—she had no need to feel judged by them.

She walked from the walled garden through the narrow wooden door onto the lawn, which fronted the house and followed the path that would lead her about the hedge into the parterre gardens. New scents greeted her: lavender, roses and the sharp smell of the pelargoniums that grew in pots positioned along the path.

~

Rob watched Caroline from the library window as she walked the path at the edge of the lawn, heading towards the parterre gardens.

He'd not gone up to the nursery for fear he'd be intruding on Mary and Drew. He'd go up later, but that meant he was currently at a loose end.

He freed the latch and opened the French door, then stepped out as Caroline disappeared behind the same tall hedge he'd seen her go behind the other day.

When he walked across the lawn he realised he'd come outside hatless and gloveless, but his stay was informal.

He turned the corner and saw her on the other side of the hedge.

She stood at the edge of a flower border, reaching down and leaning forward, pulling a flower to her nose.

His heart made an odd little stutter. If he could draw as well as

John, it would have been a perfect pose to capture—the serenity of a summer morning.

He walked closer, the grass silencing his footsteps. "Caroline."

She jumped half out of her skin, turning and stumbling.

He was close enough to catch her arm and stop her falling. Her bosom lifted with a sharp breath, and her hazel eyes, in the shadow of her bonnet, burned like soft amber.

"You frightened me." When he let go of her, she stepped away.

"I'm sorry. I did not intend to. I saw you come out, and I had nothing to do…"

She looked into Rob's eyes as though she saw a puzzle that confused her.

It made him unsure what to say. *I wish she would be braver,* Drew had said the other day. *We have male servants, after all.* "Do you think it possible that by the end of the summer we may be friends?"

Her bosom lifted with a breath. "That would b-be nice. But you will have to f-forgive me. I-I am not b-brave. I'm sorry."

She turned away and she would have left him again, but he gripped her arm. It would discompose her and yet, when the woman kept running, how else was he to keep her there long enough to speak?

The muscles in her arm stiffened within his hold. "We may progress at your pace. But I do not see why it is not possible. That is what I hope for."

She nodded.

When he let her go she turned away and walked further into the garden; he presumed to find solitude and security.

She must have endured much in her past. He knew Drew had helped her leave her violent husband, but her husband must have been very violent for her to still be affected by it after so many years.

Pity clasped in his stomach. Perhaps it was that which had caught him in the gut the other day. She might suffer with fear, but he also thought she suffered with wounded pride, because she was embarrassed, by her husband perhaps…

Chapter 7

When Rob walked into the drawing room, in time for the dinner gong, he hoped Caroline would be there.

She was not.

He'd not seen her since they'd spoken in the garden and it would be hard to make a friend of her, to the point that he might make her laugh and dance, if she was never about.

"You are late, Robbie. Did my son exhaust you?" Drew walked forward and grasped Rob's arm, turning him around so they could go to the dining room, leaving Mary to walk behind them for a moment.

Rob glanced back at Mary, wondering what Caroline did in the evening when she did not come down to dinner. "Did Drew tell you, your son is a natural with a bat. He quite surprised me. By the end of the afternoon I had him hitting nearly every ball Drew threw."

"When I am sure they were very carefully thrown to hit his bat." Mary smiled at Drew.

He let go of Rob's arm, turned back and took her hand. "Perhaps."

The two of them walked beside Rob as they continued.

Rob longed to ask Drew more about Caroline. He wished to understand her.

"Caro. I did not think you were coming down."

Rob looked forward when Drew spoke. Caroline stood at the foot of the stairs to the second floor. Her fingers were clasped together at her waist. She had not been there when he'd come from his rooms a moment ago.

She wore a shimmering amber silk dress. It drew out the variety of colours in her hazel eyes, and in her blonde hair too. Nothing about her was one shade. One lock of gold hair fell to her throat and a necklace with a single amber cross pendant lay in the cleft between her breasts.

A moment ago, as he'd made his way to the drawing room, a dozen topics to encourage her into talking had been spinning in his head. There were no words there at all now. He swallowed against the dryness in his mouth. He was thirsty tonight.

"I changed my mind," she answered Drew, only looking at Drew.

"Caroline," Rob stated, as she walked nearer.

She looked at him and dropped a very slight curtsy, then turned to walk beside her brother. There was not room for them to walk four astride, so Rob held back and Mary let go of Drew's hand, then dropped back to walk beside Rob.

How many times had Mary given up her husband for the comfort of his sister? It seemed an odd scenario. Surely Caroline could not enjoy such a life.

When they reached the dining room, Drew pulled out a chair for Caroline. "Caro."

A footman pulled Mary's chair out and Rob walked about the table to sit opposite Caroline, while Mary sat at the other end of the table to Drew. It was not like dining at John's. Drew's manor was small, and their dining table arranged for a small family, not a stately affair.

Once seated, Rob leaned back to allow the footman to pour him a glass of white wine, and across the table, although he kept his gaze lowered, he could see Caroline's slender fingers reaching for a small fork and spoon as she was served muscles in a cream

61

sauce. Her hands shook.

Rob lifted his glass of wine and took a sip as Mary and then Drew were served, and then he leant back as he was too, the glass still in his hand, his eyes turning to the footman.

It was hard to avoid looking at Caroline, especially when he was so pleased she had come downstairs. Yet he did not wish to do anything that might upset her and dissuade her from coming down again.

When the footman finished dishing up the mussels, Rob looked up. He caught Caroline watching him. She looked down at her meal, her cheeks colouring a little.

Friends. He hoped they could achieve it. He thought it would be good for her, and it was a good foundation on which to build the hope of making her laugh and dance with him.

His gaze followed her hand as she freed a mussel from its shell and lifted it to her mouth. Then his gaze ran from her wrist up to the hem of the short sleeve of her gown. She was so very slender, frail and vulnerable in appearance. Yet she'd borne beatings. Had she suffered broken bones? He would probably never know the answer.

He looked at Drew. How much did Drew know?

Drew spoke about where they would go tomorrow and who he would take Rob to meet.

Rob looked at Mary. Did Caro confide in her?

Caro looked up and met his gaze. He swallowed against the dryness in his throat once more, then took a sip of wine to clear it and smiled, trying to make his smile as warm and unthreatening as he could. Her lips lifted at the edges, and they seemed to lift a little more than they'd done yesterday.

He looked at Drew and asked some questions about Drew's tenants, suspecting that Drew was keener on showing off his son than he was on entertaining Rob. But Rob would not fault him for it. George was a sweet bundle of boyish energy whom Drew should be proud of.

When Rob finished his mussels he left his cutlery resting on the rim of the bowl and looked over the table once more. Caroline had finished eating too.

He tried to think of questions he might ask to draw her into the conversation, but his mind remained blank.

She leaned back to let a footman clear her place. Then on the next plate she was served fish terrine, chicken in aspic and sliced venison.

He lifted his glass and took a sip of wine, as she did, and their gazes collided. He smiled. In the candlelight her eyes were more matt than they were in daylight, but there was still a warm glow in the colour about the wide onyx circles at their centre.

She looked at Mary, her skin turning a deep red. "What will you do tomorrow, Mary?"

"We could drive to Maidstone if you'd like, Caro, and visit some of the shops?"

"That would be pleasant."

~

As Caro listened to Mary speak of the things she would buy tomorrow, she took a deep breath and let it out slowly, trying to slow the beat of her heart and loosen the vice tightening about her chest. She was too aware of Robbie, of the way his dark-blue eyes studied her. Yet he was sitting opposite, it was only natural for him to look at her, and she had watched him too. It had been mean to ask him not to stare.

Friends. He had proposed this morning. *Friends!* And she had said *that would be nice.* But she'd never had a friend. Mary, perhaps, was the closest person to such a thing, but Mary was Drew's confidante and Caro had deliberately avoided interfering too deeply in their closeness.

Caro thought of Albert and heard Robbie's words. *Do you think it might be possible that by the end of the summer we will be friends, Caroline?*

Even from the beginning, when Albert may have adored her and admired her, he'd never treated her as an equal. He would never have considered a woman his friend.

She looked at Robbie and he smiled as he leant back to let a footman serve him. His smiles were swift, open and warm. There was no malice or artifice in him. He was a kind man. Thoughtful.

Friends. The idea appealed to her, and terrified her. She could not have seen it as a possibility if he'd asked in the company of his extended family. But here… She could imagine they might achieve it when it was the four of them. He was likeable.

He lifted his wine glass. She could see how gently his fingers gripped the stem, as they'd touched her twice. She could not see his hands about a woman's throat. They were hands designed for creativity, writing, art or music, or honest labour.

He was different from his cousins and his younger brother, not brash and assertive, simply confident. Drew at his age had been an inferno of aggressive, defensive anger, fighting against the world. But Robbie seemed to sit back and watch it.

She tried to imagine Albert at Robbie's age. Albert had been handsome, but not in the way Robbie was. Robbie had a masculine beauty, not simply a handsome face. The women in his family had a beauty that was breathtaking, and in Robbie it was striking, he had elements of his father's angled features, marked with the Pembrokes' large eyes and full lips.

He spoke to her brother, joining in a conversation Drew and Mary were having about George.

Robbie laughed as Drew admitted that he intended to pamper George in everything. It was a deep, low sound.

He glanced at her, as if he knew she'd been watching him, and smiled again, even more warmly.

His dark-blue eyes glittered in the candlelight.

She smiled again too, weakly, then looked at Mary and tried to join the conversation, her heart thumping steadily. She was not wholly comfortable, yet she did not feel the onset of panic.

Chapter 8

The day had indeed been pleasurable, using the word Caroline had applied to her anticipated trip into town. Rob liked Drew's company, and he was actually impressed with the way Drew handled himself among his tenants. He'd earned their respect in the years since he'd taken over this property. People looked up to him because they liked him, not simply because he was the land-owner, and they sought his opinion on subjects that four years ago Rob doubted Drew could have even discussed.

Then, of course, everyone they'd met on their circuit had enthused over George, and the boy had lapped up all the atten-tion with his usual gusto.

But as Mary had predicted, George had become tired. He'd been complaining for the last hour and asking to go home, and now he was stretched sideways across Drew's saddle, one of his arms draped about Drew's hip, where he'd been holding his father before he'd fallen asleep with Drew's forearm as his pillow.

George's other hand was at his mouth, and his thumb hung at the corner of his lips, where he'd been sucking on it.

It meant their return ride was restricted to the pace of a walk as Drew cradled George on one arm and tried not to dislodge him with the rock of the horse.

They were still about twenty minutes away from the house

when Rob heard the sound of a single horse cantering along the dry mud track and the creak of a vehicle. Gripping the pommel of his saddle, Rob turned to look back, steering his animal off the track and out of its path. He recognised the trap, even though it was a distance away. It was the vehicle Drew had bought for Mary to drive when she wished to go out alone. He saw the two women.

Mary wore a wide-brimmed straw bonnet and she was clothed in pink, while Caroline was wearing pale-lemon yellow, with an ivory shawl and parasol. The pair of them made a tableau from a ladies' magazine.

"Mary." Rob stated, looking back at Drew, knowing that Drew would not have been able to look with George sprawled across his thighs. "You're in for it now. She said you'd wear George out."

Drew laughed, but he pulled his horse to a halt as the trap approached.

"Whoa," Mary called to slow her horse. Obviously she'd recognised them from a distance too. She stared at Drew as she slowed the trap to a halt.

Drew looked downward and gave Mary a devil-may-care smile, which dared her to challenge him if she wished to.

"He is exhausted," she said, her gaze shifting to George.

"He is asleep," Drew answered. "Because he had a wonderful time and needed to rest."

Mary clucked her tongue and made a face at Drew. She knew her husband well. There was no point challenging Drew, she would not win the argument.

"He did have a wonderful time," Rob assured her, "Everyone made a fuss over him and he spent his first hour laughing his head off with glee at the opportunity of such a long ride, and he has been given a dozen biscuits."

Mary frowned at him, reprimanding him for siding with Drew.

"Don't turn your wrath on me," Rob stated jokingly, "I am not to blame. But George did enjoy it."

"Will you hand George to me, Drew? At least then we can get

him home sooner, and securely." Caroline stood. Of course she must know Drew best of all.

Drew smiled at her, let go of his reins and lifted George, then leaned over. Caro put down her parasol to receive the sleeping child.

Yellow suited her colouring. It gave her freshness and made her look younger. She sat, as though George was heavier than she'd expected, and settled him across her lap, cradling his head on her arm.

When she'd been married she must have had to organise a huge household, the size of John's probably. The other day Rob had sensed wounded pride within her distress. When she'd left her husband, she'd also left the position of marchioness, with respect and finery to the style that Katherine had, to then become a penniless dependent of her brother. It must have tilted her world upside down.

Another hard, sudden feeling gripped at his gut as Mary pulled away and he watched Caroline. It was pity.

What she'd left behind was another signal of how much she'd suffered. It would have taken a lot to make her choose to leave that life.

But he was certain that Caroline would abhor pity. Perhaps that was a part of her discomfort, that she must be reliant on others, and therefore be in need of pity. Perhaps she was embarrassed by her reliance on Drew as much as by her husband.

The pity in his gut swelled to admiration in his chest as Drew turned his horse off the track and kicked his heels, rising into a canter. Rob followed, racing the trap back to the house.

The first night he'd met Drew, Rob's family had applauded Drew when he'd entered the room, out of respect because he'd helped Caroline escape her marriage. They should have applauded Caroline because she had survived years of cruelty and then had the courage to leave Kilbride.

When they reached the house Rob dismounted and handed the reins of his horse over to a groom, then waited for the trap beside Drew. It was a few yards away.

A groom came to hold the horse's head as the trap pulled up. Drew lifted his hands up to take George from Caroline.

Another groom helped Mary down. Rob stepped forward, offering his hand to Caroline, forgetting entirely that she'd never taken anyone but Drew's hand in all the years he'd known her. But he could not retract the offer, that would look crass, and so his gloved hand hovered in the air a foot away from where she stood in the trap.

Drew's arms were full, the grooms were not near her, she accepted Rob's hand, or rejected it and climbed down unaided; those were her choices.

She looked at him, her eyes gilded gold in the sunlight.

"Caroline." He bowed his head, slightly.

She took a breath, which lifted her bosom. Then her fingers gripped his. They'd been trembling, but her firm hold denied it as she stepped down.

She immediately let go, when her feet touched the ground. But it was another step they'd taken towards friendship.

He turned to see Drew and Mary walking towards the house. They had not even noticed. He glanced at Caroline. "If you like, we could walk about the side of the house across the lawn and go in through the French doors of the morning room, to stretch our legs a little. Drew and Mary will be going up to the nursery anyway. Then we can call for tea."

She looked at him, challenge bright in her eyes, but he guessed the challenge was to herself. "Yes, if you wish." She was being brave today.

He turned and began walking. She fell into stride beside him.

He clasped his hands behind his back, refusing the instinct to offer her his arm.

It was not only Caro who felt awkward; he felt awkward too. He was not overly used to spending time with women outside of his family. Again, women were Harry's forte, not his. There were many years to be lived before the time came for him to think about a wife, and he was not interested in mistresses, or casual liaisons. He was happy as he was. And unlike his peers in the family he believed in morality.

Rob had seen how the whores his brother and his cousins favoured lived. He pitied them. He had no desire to lie with them, and if he held a seat in the House of Commons then he would be speaking out for the safety of those women. His brother and cousins used the brothels, but there were many women on the streets who were only there because they needed food. It was not right.

But if Caroline were to be a friend, he supposed he ought to treat her as he would his friends—he would not offer his arm to a male friend.

A humorous sound escaped his throat.

She glanced at him, but said nothing as they walked on, side by side, in steady strides, she gripping the handle of her open parasol, while his hands were held together behind his back.

He ought to say something. "Did you enjoy your day?"

"Very much." There was a slight quiver in her voice.

"You know, Caroline." Rob glanced sideways at her as they walked around the corner of the house on to the lawn. "I respect you immensely."

She did nothing to acknowledge his comment.

He liked her hair. It was in a loose knot and a whole swathe of it had been left to fall and curl across her shoulder and over her bosom.

"I was thinking, after we saw you in the trap, how much you must have had when you were with the Marquis of Kilbride. It only really occurred to me today what a big step it must have been for you to leave." Perhaps it was not the best of topics to choose, and yet he did not wish to walk in silence and this was what was on his mind. "You gave up a life like Kate's... "

He stopped walking as they neared the open French doors of

69

the morning room. He wished to complete this conversation.

She stopped too, and her hazel eyes widened as they became darker in the shadow of the parasol.

"I want you to know, I admire your courage. To experience such things and then to walk away and leave that life behind." She'd been wrong. She was brave, braver than anyone else he knew.

Her skin pinked across her cheeks, then tears made her eyes appear fluid. "Excuse me…" She turned and then was gone again, his phantom, hurrying towards the house, her fingers clutching her dress to lift the hem.

"You are a damned idiot, Rob," he said aloud, as he followed.

He did not see her in the house, and she was not in the drawing room. He ordered the tea and then went to his room to change out of his riding clothes. She was not downstairs when he returned, nor was she there for dinner.

After dinner, when Mary went up to the nursery to kiss the children goodnight, Rob walked out into the garden with Drew, to drink their port, so Drew might have a cigar.

Rob grasped at their privacy. "I was thinking today about Caroline's marriage. It is no wonder really that her nerves affect her as they do. I mean I know what she went through. I read the details in the paper."

Drew blew smoke up into the cooler night air, then looked at Rob. "You do not know the details. Even I do not. You read the story, which merely scratched at the surface. But for God's sake do not tell her you read anything. I never told her what was printed in the papers. She did not have sight of them at the time. It would have hurt her and she'd been hurt enough, and she would be cut by you speaking of it. She is a private person."

So Rob had noticed. His hand lifted and ran through his hair, then fell.

He was not proud of the conversation he'd started this afternoon. But oddly, the thought made him understand a little more of Caroline. Perhaps her air of wounded pride was not because she had been prideful, but because she was without pride. Perhaps she did not feel proud of her past or herself and that was why embarrassment left her tongue-tied.

"I shall not speak of it," he confirmed to Drew.

He wished, more than anything, to make Caroline feel at ease.

Chapter 9

Caro walked into the nursery after breakfast, knowing that Drew and Mary had gone out for a ride. She'd assumed Robbie had gone too, but he was lying on the floor beside George raining an army of lead soldiers with imaginary cannon fire.

I respect you immensely. Those had been the words he'd used yesterday. *Respect…* When she'd spent the past years feeling shame; feeling like a leech.

But the words and the mention of Albert had thrown her into turmoil, the past rising up before her and memories scurrying through her head, good as well as bad. Yes, she had given up a lot: her home, her self-possession, her position in society. Despite his brutality, she had held her head high, denying in public what happened in private and she had still been looked up to, and she had not felt a burden to Albert… No, that was a lie. Her barren womb had made her a burden to him, and her failure had been a shame she concealed with embarrassment as she'd tried to look confident before others.

She turned to leave. Unsure of what she would say to Robbie. "Caroline."

She turned back. He'd risen from the floor and crossed the room. His long fingers wrapped about her arm to stop her turning away.

His gentle hold reminded her of the way Albert had touched

her in bed.

She pulled her arm free.

"May we speak for a moment?"

I respect you immensely. She lowered her head in agreement.

"We shall return in a moment, George. I wish to speak to your aunt. Have the horses move to the far side and set up a cavalry charge." He lifted his hand so Caro would walk ahead of him. She stopped on the landing, only a few feet away from the nursery door.

Robbie pulled the door closed.

Heat burned in Caro's cheeks when he took a couple of strides towards her. He was nearly a foot taller than her, at least ten inches, and when he moved his athletic physique expressed energy, a love of life, a desire to discover.

His hand lifted as if he might clasp her arm, but then it fell. "Caroline, I'd like to apologise again. I'm sure you shall become bored of hearing me use the word 'sorry' but I wish I had not chosen the topic of conversation I did yesterday. It was crass of me. I am sorry I upset you again. Will you give me another chance?" As he spoke, the hand that had lifted previously rose and swept back his hair, brushing his fringe from his forehead.

"I should have thought before I spoke. Your past is none of my business. Yet I just, well, I wanted you to know that I respect you and I applaud you, and I believe that you must be a lot braver than you think. I see you as a woman full of courage. I did not intend to make you feel uncomfortable. I'll say nothing more on the subject, I swear, only as I said the other day. I hope that by the end of my stay we might be friends, and although I have been making a mull of it, I still have hopes, if you will forgive me?"

She did not really have anything to forgive him for. He'd only mentioned the name of her former husband, it was hardly a crime—and each day she liked Robbie more. He was a kind, good-hearted young man. "You need not ask for my forgiveness. It was not because of you that I became emotional. Your words simply stirred up memories that I ought not to think of. I am sorry I made

73

you feel uncomfortable. You are a guest here. It was rude of me."

"Aun'ie Ca'o! Aun'ie Ca'o!" The nursery door handle rattled.

"Master George! Come back and play, your aunt will be here in a moment."

Caro turned to the door.

Robbie clasped her arm, the gentle touch twisting something in her stomach. "May I ask one thing of you, Caroline? Please do not leave me alone at dinner."

"You cannot be alone. Mary and—"

"Are a couple, and I feel foolish intruding on them every night, as I'm sure you must do when you are here alone. I presume that is why you frequently do not come down, so why not make the most of my presence and have some company?"

"You are a guest. They do not make you feel unwelcome."

"Nor do they you." His tone had dropped and become slightly challenging, but the words were still softly spoken, not threatening.

"Au'nie Ca'o! Play!" George shouted through the wood of the nursery door, as the handle rattled again.

Caro looked at the door then back at Robbie. She had not pulled her arm free. Robbie's touch was soothing. It had been a long time since anyone other than Drew had touched her, and now Robbie continually did so—she was becoming accustomed to his gentle fingers about her arm.

"Shall we take him outside?" Robbie offered. "We could play on the lawn with him; the day is not too hot yet."

She nodded agreement.

He let her go and opened the door. "Are you causing trouble, George?"

"I'm sorry, sir," the nanny said.

"You need not be. We are going to take him outside for a little while, to play in the garden."

Caro smiled at George as his eyes lit up, then he turned and ran across the room, his little legs on a charge.

"My boat!" George pointed to the sailing boat, which was on

74

a shelf above him. He did a little awkward jump. "Play with my boat, Uncle Bobbie?" He looked back at his uncle with a plea.

Robbie crossed the room. "Yes, you shall sail your boat, George. We'll take it out to the pond."

George lifted his arms. Robbie bent to pick him up and held him so that George could take the boat from the shelf.

"Caroline." Robbie indicated for her to walk ahead of them as he came back across the room.

"I have to fetch my bonnet. I will come down soon." She turned and went ahead of them, hurrying down the stairs from the attic. Then she ran along the landing on the second floor to her rooms.

The day was warm, so she did not bother with a shawl, but just picked up a straw bonnet and tied the burgundy ribbons, which secured it beneath her chin. The colour of the ribbons matched the flowers in the pattern on her ivory muslin dress.

Her heart raced as she ran down the stairs, yet it was not from fear, it was from expectation and excitement. *I applaud you. I respect you.* No one had said such things to her.

You must be a lot braver than you think…

Albert had complimented her often when he'd courted her, and during the first year of their marriage, but always for her beauty. Robbie had looked beyond her appearance and considered what was inside, and he'd seen courage.

Courage…

What an odd thing for him to see in her when he'd only known the woman who hid herself away. She smiled as she hurried across the downstairs hall and then she ran lightly through the morning room and out through the French doors into the garden.

She could hear them. George was squealing with excitement, and Robbie's lower tone cheered along with him. When she turned the corner of the second hedge in the parterre gardens, she saw them. Robbie was kneeling at the edge of the pond and George stood beside him with both hands pressed on the stone rim as they blew at the boat. It moved a little, wobbling through the

75

water and sending out ripples.

Caro laughed, the sound bursting from her throat. She could not remember the last time she had laughed. "I see the wind is not really strong enough and so you are making your own."

Robbie looked up, his lips parting in a sudden wide grin and his slate-grey eyes, which were paler in the sunshine, looked full of pleasure. "It is good to hear you laugh, even if it is at our expense. Will you help us blow?" His lips twisted into a wry smile.

"Aun'ie Ca'o," George looked up.

"Are you blowing your boat to make it sail?" She lifted her skirt and knelt on the grass, on the other side of George to Robbie, but as Robbie's hand was settled at George's waist she did not touch George. She leaned onto the stone about the pond and blew at the boat's white sails. George blew too, but he could not purse his lips.

Caro patted his head and laughed at the funny sound he made when he blew. "Who is on your boat, George?"

"Uncle Bahbah and the pi'ates."

Robbie choked mid-blow and laughed more heartily than Caro had done.

Uncle Bahbah was Drew's nickname for the black sheep of Mary's family, Robbie's younger brother Harry.

"Why is Uncle Harry with the pirates, George? What has he done?" Robbie's hand gripped at George's side.

A frown drew a line between George's brows, as though he thought the answer was obvious. "He's been bad, the pi'ates have captu'ed him and then he took ove' the s'ip and now he is the capt'in."

"Well, I am imagining a whole fleet of the Navy's ships coming up behind your pirates, who are ready to save the day, and they shall be captained by your Uncle Robbie."

A humorous, but less exuberant, sound slipped out of Robbie's throat on a low note. "We should have brought your cannons down so we could fire on the pirates."

"We can imagine cannons," Caro dipped her fingers into the

water. "Now, who do you wish to win, George? Are we blowing with all our might for the pirates to get away, or willing the Navy to catch them?"

"The pi'ates get away!"

Robbie looked at Caro with a smile. "He is Drew's son."

"He is, indeed."

"Then we blow."

"We blow."

"Raise the main sail, and pull the yard arm! We need to get away!" Robbie called before he began blowing.

Caro blew too, and the boat began to wobble its way at a snail's pace through the water.

Robbie kept throwing in comments about how Uncle Bahbah and the pirates were preparing to fight. "Draw your swords!"

"But Uncle Robbie is nearly upon them!" Caro cried. "They wish to take the bad pirates to their gaol."

"No! No!" George squealed.

She laughed. "Then blow harder, George. Blow harder."

"And now there's a storm whipping up! It is making my navy ships sail faster." Robbie said, dipping his fingers in the water and stirring it up so that the boat rocked even more. "Blow, George, blow."

"If one of us must rescue it, it will be you who gets his boots wet," she said to Robbie.

He laughed as poor George tried to blow harder and harder, with no effect.

"Uncle Bobbie, Aun'ie Ca'o, blow!"

"I think I owe you a little chivalry. I can be valiant, Caro," Robbie responded, smiling at her, before he turned to blow once more.

He'd not called her "Caro" before; no one did but Drew and Mary. The intimacy of her nickname on his lips touched something inside her and clasped tight. She did feel differently towards him. *Friendship…*

"The storm is coming, George. Tell the pirates to bring down their sails." Robbie said as he stirred up the water rocking the sailing boat, but it was too far out of reach for George to do anything.

"It'll sink, Uncle Bobbie. Stop. Stop the sto'm!"

"Not if they take down their sails. The Navy ships are heavier, they have the cannons, they are more likely to go down! Call out to the pirates, take down your sails!"

"Ta'e down you' sails pi'ates!" George shouted at the boat.

"They are doing it." Caro, cried. "I can see them. Look they are in the rigging, preparing for the storm."

"And the Navy have their cannons ready to fire, and their hatches open, the fools. They'll be caught out." Robbie stirred the water even more and the boat swayed. "Tell the men to come down from the rigging, George, the sea is too wild. Uncle Bahbah is up there too. Tell him to come down."

"Come down, Uncle Bahbah!"

"He is down," Caro said.

"The storm has hit the Navy in full force, the water is sweeping over their decks and it's washing into the gun decks. They are sinking. They are sinking, George. Shout hurrah, the pirates have won."

"Hu'ah!" George shouted, thrusting a fist into the air.

"Hurrah!" Robbie called. Then he looked at Caro. "Are you not pleased, Auntie Caro, why are you not cheering?" It was said with satire, and she smiled, but again something clutched in her middle when she looked at his face.

"Because I think your papa ought to teach you to favour the Navy, George, and I shall tell him so. I would have put those pirates in gaol."

Robbie laughed.

"Pick me up, Uncle Bobbie." George turned and wrapped his arms about Robbie's neck, his interest in the boat gone.

"Bend over, then." Robbie stated as he stood.

George bent over, holding out his hands between his legs. Robbie gripped them and pulled him up so that George spun a somersault in the air. It was a practised manoeuvre, which Robbie must have taught him.

George laughed as Robbie set him on the ground.

Caro closed her mouth on another laugh as her stomach tumbled over. She was laughing in a way she had not done in years, and she was enjoying herself. "You have to rescue George's boat yet..."

"You just wish to watch me get my boots wet, and I cannot afford to have them ruined."

"Then you will have to take them off." Gosh, she could not remember teasing anyone since she and Drew had been children.

He grinned at her. "A perfect solution. Stand up, George." He began pulling off his morning coat. "You may be the bearer of my coat, while I valiantly climb into the pond to rescue your boat from the storm."

Even George grinned as Robbie stripped it off.

He folded his coat. "George put out your arms." George obeyed. "You must stand here, and not let it fall. I do not want grass stains upon it. Conquering heroes should not be covered in grass stains." George looked at him with eyes full of worship.

Caro smiled at George, then looked at Robbie, as he sat on the low stone rim at the edge of the pond, in trousers, shirt and waistcoat. He had a lean waist and narrow hips. Albert had been broader.

Robbie turned back the cuffs of his shirt, revealing the lean, muscular shape of his forearms and the dark hair across his skin.

Caro breathed in. Something twisted in her stomach.

"I do not suppose you would help me with these?" He lifted a booted foot.

She shook her head. She may feel more comfortable with him, but she did not feel comfortable enough to lean over before him and yank at his boot.

He struggled a little, but he had not brought a valet with him so he must take off his own boots every night. It did not take him long.

She looked at George. Robbie had given George a task so he would not run around. It was a wise trick.

"And these are for you, Caro." He held out his boots with a wry smile.

She poked her tongue out at him. When had she last done a thing like that?

George laughed, and she looked down to find him looking up at her. Even he'd noticed the difference in her today. She smiled.

"The hero is rising to the challenge!" Robbie called. "Prepared to get both his trousers and his stockings wet for the sake of your poor boat, George."

Oh, good Lord! She laughed so much her sides ached as he made a great fuss of climbing into the pond. The water came up to his thighs and he waded through it, one hand raised, as though he intended planting a Union Jack and naming it for a territory of Royal Britannia.

"It is rescued!" he cried, when he lifted up George's toy.

"You are stupid, Robbie," Caro breathed as he carried it back.

"Call me Rob, Caro, please. Robbie is so childish, I will never get my brothers and sisters to change, but my friends never call me that."

Friends. Had they achieved that now already? Perhaps not yet, but she truly believed they could become friends. "Let me take the boat, Rob. You may have your boots back."

He smiled. "Thank you." He swapped her the boat for his boots, then put them on the edge of the pond and climbed out. The water had plastered his trousers to his legs.

Physically he was at his peak, so young and beautiful.

He picked up his boots. "May I have my coat, young master coat-keeper?" He held out his hand, George raised his arms and Rob took his coat from them. "And now I think we ought to return to the house. I am soaked and would like a change of clothes, and your mama and papa have probably come back and will be looking for you, George."

Caro gripped George's hand before he could run off. "Come along, then, do you wish to carry your boat?" He nodded, and so the three of them walked back across the lawn with George gripping his boat and Rob carrying his boots, with his coat hanging over his shoulder.

When they reached the house, Rob excused himself and ran upstairs ahead of them, heading to his room, which was on the first floor, displaying the energy and agility that the muscular definition of his body implied as he took the steps two at a time.

Caro followed him, walking more slowly with George.

Chapter 10

Caro had spent her days very differently in the last few weeks. She often played with George and Rob, while Rob thought up silly games. Then in the evenings she dined at the table and afterwards went to the drawing room with Rob, Drew and Mary, where they would either play the pianoforte and sing, or play cards.

It was probably the strangest period of her life because it was the most normal she had ever felt. Rob frequently engaged her in conversation and offered his arm when they walked anywhere together. He also sat beside her at the pianoforte some evenings and would turn the music for her as she played, and on rare occasions, if the song desperately needed a baritone, he would concede and sing with her.

For the first time she did not feel like a parasite, and she was certainly not isolated, she felt a part of life, of a family, and she laughed every day, and smiled often, and most importantly—she was happy. It was a feeling of joy deep inside her.

"Uncle Bobbie!" George complained, gleefully, as his uncle chased after him and captured the running child, wrapping an arm about George and lifting him up by the waist. George's feet kicked as though he was still running.

"I caught this little monkey." Rob turned and grinned at her. "I'm not sure exactly what species it is." George wriggled.

"Aun'ie Caro!" he complained.

They'd taken George for a walk, leaving Mary and Drew to enjoy a little peace with Iris. Their path followed a circular route about the edge of the formal garden, along a woodland wilderness walk. It did not have the orchestrated picturesque views of Albert's vast gardens, but it was quaint and it made Caro feel absorbed in nature. Birds sang from the branches above, and the summer breeze swept through the leaves, which shaded them from the sun, rustling them and making a pretty sound, while bees buzzed and butterflies fluttered through the air, adding more bright colours to the occasional planting that lined the route.

It was a beautiful day.

Rob had left his coat and waistcoat off because the day was so hot. They were used to being informal because of playing with George. He'd rolled his shirt sleeves up too and so, as he carried George under his arm the fine, dark hairs on his forearm showed against his pale skin, and he was sweating, so his shirt stuck to his side and became transparent.

It was a very hot day. It was the best place to be, beneath the trees.

"Put me down, Uncle Bobbie!" George wriggled harder.

"When you can behave, little monkey. You were told not to run."

Rob turned and stopped, waiting for her to catch up. George kicked out, complaining, at Rob's side.

She smiled, her legs slashing at her petticoats and the skirt of her dress. Her bonnet, which hung from her neck by its ribbons, bounced against her back. It was not fair that Rob could strip off layers and she could not. The thought stirred a tight feeling in her stomach.

When she reached him, she ruffled George's hair.

"Aun'ie Ca'o."

Rob swung him round to sit at his hip, and Caro actually glimpsed Rob's skin at his waist as his shirt pulled up.

Rob gripped George's chin and made George look him in the eyes as George clasped Rob's neck. "Now, George Framlington, you are not to run ahead, there is a stream further along. If you tumble into that and drown your mama and papa would string me up. You're to do as you are told or I will not bring you out for a walk again. Do you hear?"

George lifted his chin free, but nodded.

"I wish to hear the promise from your lips. Say it George, *I will not run off*."

George's lower lip wobbled. He hated to be told off, but then he said, "I won't 'un. I p'omise."

"Good boy." Rob patted George's back, then he added more softly. "There's no need for tears. You did wrong. You know you did, but now you are going to do right."

"You may hold my hand," Caroline offered.

"Or ride on my back," Rob added.

"'ide" George chose, already lifting his hands to Rob's neck. Rob shifted him, spinning him to his back as George's arms circled his neck, and then he carried George in a piggyback, with George's legs looped over his arms.

George looked ahead over Rob's shoulder. Caro smiled at them both.

Rob's patience was a wonderful thing.

"You are good with him," she commented when they began walking again.

"I've had enough practice. Remember the size of my family."

"I did not have a close family. We were not like yours."

Rob glanced at her and smiled. "I know. Mary met them. She's spoken of it. She described them as unpleasant."

"She was being polite. But they were not unkind to me. Drew and I were just not wanted and ignored—for understandable reasons. The Marquis did not want Mama's little cuckoos in his nest." She laughed—she was talking to him of things she never spoke of. But they had become friends and friends shared confidences. "I do not even know who my father is. Neither does Drew."

"But the fault was your mother's, not yours. Did the Marquis

84

not recognise that?"

She looked at Rob with a shrug. She had never understood her mother. The woman had not one maternal bone in her body. "Perhaps, but if we were treated as though we did not exist then her infidelity could be ignored. It was Mother's view too. We were mistakes to be disposed of. Fortunately for me, Albert was willing to ignore my birth—or perhaps he did not know. He never mentioned it and neither did I."

"Fortunately… Forgive me if this is ignorant, but what was fortunate about your marriage?"

Caro glanced at him, surprised to hear him speak of it, but she did not feel horror as she might have done a few weeks ago, and she had spoken of it first.

"I'm sorry, it's none of my business." His smile became apologetic.

But it was nice to feel comfortable to talk, and Rob was easy to talk to. He never judged. "It does not matter. You may speak of it. But my marriage was not always bad. I loved him." She still did, in a way. He was the only one who had ever shown her the intensity of feeling that had felt like love, and her body and her soul had never forgotten it—the thing she'd lacked and longed for as a child. Drew may care for her, but it had always felt such a shallow comparison to the infatuation Albert had shown. And she still knew Drew's affection to be a shallow emotion compared to what he felt for Mary… "I was young when I met him and I suppose I idolised him. He was attentive and earnest. He courted me with devotion. We spent hours and hours together before we married, and he was so determined to have me that he threatened to run off with me if the Marquis disagreed. Of course the Marquis did not refuse."

A sound of amusement slipped from her throat when she remembered how happy her mother and the Marquis had been at the news they were to be rid of her so easily.

"Even when we married, though…" She glanced at Rob, to see

him watching and listening. "…things were wonderful, Albert spent hours in my company at the beginning. He never said he loved me, but I thought it was love. Yet in the second year his interest waned, and he began keeping mistresses." Her memories drifted into things she did not want to recall, and she stopped talking as images flashed through her thoughts: strikes, words shouted in her face, the unbearable sensation of failure and loneliness.

"Caro…"

She had stopped walking as well as talking. Her consciousness returned to the woodland walk, the sound of the birds and the sunshine above the trees. Those bad moments and those feelings were behind her. She looked ahead and began walking again. "He spent less and less time with me. He wanted a son and I could not carry a child. In the end I was not good enough for him. Things turned sour and his anger grew worse, and, well… you know the rest," she whispered the last.

They walked a few steps in silence, her gaze focused on the grass pathway.

She glanced at Rob. George was sucking his thumb as his head rested against Rob's shoulder.

An elemental warmth twisted in her stomach—longing. "I am glad I married him. In the first year and the year that he courted me, he made me happy. I was fortunate to have those years. They were the happiest of my life. What I had missed in attention as a child, I received from Albert tenfold, and it felt like heaven then."

"You need more happy years, then," Rob said in answer, as he looked ahead.

"I do not anticipate them…" A lump caught in her throat. She'd never thought of her unhappiness. She had spent years here, angry with herself for her failure to succeed as a wife, disappointed and ashamed. But to be unhappy was unfair on Drew. He'd done so much for her. Yet now Rob was here and she'd discovered what it was to be happy again. She knew how unhappy she'd been.

She swallowed, not looking at Rob, and she did not think he

was looking at her. "Why am I telling you this? I've told all this to no one else, not even Drew." She laughed then, to dispel the melancholy feeling wrapping about her heart.

"I do not know. But I am glad you feel able to. We have truly become friends, haven't we?"

She smiled at him.

"Perhaps I am easy to talk to because I've spent a lifetime listening to my sisters."

She laughed and it was not shallow laughter, it came from her stomach. How absurd. A moment ago she had been remembering the awful muddle she'd made of her life with Albert and then Rob had made her laugh.

Her gaze turned to Rob's shoulder. "George has fallen asleep."

"We're nearly back anyway."

Caro looked ahead. The narrow stream that signalled the end of the woodland walk was a few feet ahead.

Robert navigated it first, carefully stepping onto the flat stone in the middle of the stream. He set one foot on the far bank, left one on the stone, reached an arm behind him, bowing forward to carry George's sleeping weight, then held out a hand to Caro.

Her heartbeat raced, and her breathing fractured when she looked at his bare, slender, long fingers as his hand reached out.

He was being gentlemanly, gallant. It would be ridiculous to refuse the gesture. Yet her hand was bare too. It was too hot for gloves.

It is nothing of consequence.

She clasped his fingers and their warmth and strength closed about her grip, but the feeling of his security grabbed at her soul too when she stepped onto the stone. Her heart thumped as her bosom brushed against his chest briefly.

Heat flared in her cheeks, but there were other sensations too, sensations that recalled memories from her marriage bed.

"Caro…" he said in a low voice, his eyes a very dark grey.

She smiled, ignoring the heat burning in her cheeks and fought

87

a foolish urge to kiss him. Then she stepped on, climbing up onto the far bank, lifting the hem of her dress with her free hand.

He kept hold of her hand and she held him steady as he stepped onto the bank. She met his gaze when he did, her limbs turning to aspic. There was a look in his eyes that she had seen in Albert's long ago, when Albert had courted her—Rob's pupils were wider, and they seemed to glow with a depth that was not normally there.

"George, will fall if you're not careful," she said, letting his hand go.

He smiled. "I'll move him. Just take him for a moment so he does not topple off."

Caro lifted George from his back, and then Rob took him again.

George's head rested against Rob's shoulder, while Rob's arm braced George's back and his hand gripped one of George's legs. He gave Caro another smile. "Do you ride?"

She nodded. She did, but she had not done so for years.

"Then, shall we ride tomorrow? We could ride onto John's land and give the horses their heads."

A gallop. She hadn't ridden since she'd left Albert—she didn't even really know why. But Drew had never offered to accompany her and she'd never asked, nor thought of riding alone. But the thought of it now…

"I would like to."

Chapter 11

"You should come," Rob suggested, leaning back in his chair at the dining table and eyeing Caro with determination as he twisted the stem of his wine glass in his fingers.

She wished to poke her tongue out at him, but she would not before Drew and Mary. Instead her forehead creased into a scowl as she closed her lips on her argument.

"Why not, Caro?" Drew, pushed.

She ignored him.

Drew, Mary and Rob had visited a neighbour's for dinner the night before. She had not joined them, she had become used to Rob being here, and her feelings of discomfort being silent, she did not wish to stir them up again. But now they were trying to persuade her to attend an assembly in Maidstone that they had heard about from Drew's neighbour.

"You will have all three of us with you," Mary urged, quietly.

"You need not even dance, if you do not wish to," Drew stated. "One of us will stay with you."

"I will stay with you," Rob stated, "They will wish to dance with each other."

"We will not," Mary answered, "I can barely persuade him to dance one set, even if it is a waltz. Drew does not *like* dancing."

"It's superfluous," he responded, laughing, "once you have a wife."

"Well, I enjoy it," Mary bit back.

"Then I will dance with you, and Drew can keep Caro company." Rob smiled at his sister.

"Well, I prefer swimming, but I get precious little chance to do that these days." Drew lifted an eyebrow at Mary, who blushed.

"I dare you," Rob said to Caro from across the table.

She shook her head at him. "No, Rob."

"Why?"

"Rob…" she pressed him to be silent.

"Let us talk about this in the comfort of the drawing room over a hand of cards." Drew rose. They all rose then, their chairs scraping on the wooden floor.

Caro walked beside Mary. But then Rob appeared at her other side and gently braced her elbow.

She was used to his touch now. He often held out his arm or his hand for her to take, they'd taken three early-morning rides together in the last week, and when they did he would hold his joined hands in a step for her to mount—and grip her waist to lift her down when they returned.

He leant to her ear and whispered. "I cannot understand what you are so afraid of. It is just a little country dance. Come, and do not dance. I understand you do not like to be touched by strangers, but you might enjoy the company and conversation. Be brave, Caro. I know you are…"

"Rob…" she sighed, willing him to stop pleading.

"You trust me now. You trust Drew and Mary. We would not allow you to feel threatened. If you do, then I will bring you home. I'll even take my own curricle, if you wish, so you may leave at any time."

"You do not understand." She stopped and turned to face him, freeing herself from the distracting grip on her arm.

Drew and Mary walked on.

"I understand that you keep yourself shut in here like a prisoner. You should break out."

Neither Drew nor Mary looked back, leaving them to talk. At first Drew had raised his eyebrows on occasion, when Caro had become more relaxed with Rob, but now it had become commonplace.

"You will come, Caro?" Rob's fingers touched her cheek and turned her gaze to him.

"No."

His thumb brushed the edge of her lips accidently.

Like the first time she'd taken his bare hand and the first time he'd held her waist when he'd lifted her down from a horse, a sudden jolt lanced through her body. She knew what it was – desire. It was the feeling she had learned in her marriage bed, and when she looked at Rob she felt it. He was too beautiful.

"Will you come for my sake?" he asked, his dark eyes glinting in the light of the single candelabra that stood on a cabinet behind her. "You have immense courage. Remember it." His breath caressed her lips. He was so close.

Her gaze held his. His eyes were reassuring, confident and encouraging.

She looked at his lips. She wished to lift to her toes and press her lips against his; there was something invisible within her pulling her to do so. She had imagined it often, ever since they'd crossed the stream, when he'd carried George, and she had thought she'd seen the same pull in his eyes.

That look she'd seen in his eyes then was not there now. She'd thought it desire too, and yet, she wondered if she'd imagined it. She had not seen it in his eyes since, only this open look of like and care.

He was inviting her because he cared…

The thought stirred places in her soul, as his touch moved her physically.

She should go. She should stop locking herself away in her glass gaol, *Do I have the courage?*

Her gaze clung to his. "I will go," *for your sake.* The last words

91

erupted from somewhere within her, but she did not say them. They were foolish, yet true. She wished to be in his company.

His gaze seemed to delve into her.

"Caro! Rob! Are you coming? We've dealt already." Drew's voice stretched back into the hall, echoing about the stairwell.

Rob smiled, cheerfully. There was a charm in his smile and it caught like a stitch in her middle when his hand fell away. "That is settled, then." He cupped her elbow. "Come along, let's tell Drew."

She took a deep breath. *What had she just agreed to?*

When they reached the drawing room, he let go of her. "Caro is coming to the assembly. I have persuaded her."

Drew looked up, his mouth open and his eyebrows lifting. But he said nothing.

For years Drew had encouraged her to broaden her horizons. He would be happy that she was going.

Mary stood. "Oh, I am so glad. We will have fun." She gave Caro a sisterly embrace, full of excitement.

~

The assembly rooms in Maidstone were above the coaching inn, and the area before it tonight was full of carriages when they arrived. They were late because Caro had delayed coming down from her rooms.

Rob had been kicking his heels in the hall for nearly an hour, wondering if he ought to go up. But in the end she'd appeared on the stairs, and he'd had to stop himself from staring as she walked down the last flight.

He'd never seen her in a ball gown. He'd never seen her attend a dance, so of course he had not… But she'd found a dress, or perhaps borrowed one of Mary's. It was teal. The colour set off her golden hair, and as she came closer he noted how well it caught against the colour of her eyes too. The little amber cross necklace she wore rested in the cleft between her breasts.

"You look beautiful," he'd said, and he would have offered his arm, but Drew offered his first, so instead Rob had escorted Mary to the carriage.

A footman opened the carriage door. Drew climbed out and offered his hand to Mary to help her down. Then Drew held his hand out to help Caro. Her shawl slipped from her shoulder a little as she left Rob in the carriage. Her hand was shaking when she pulled her shawl back up. She breathed in deeply as she took Drew's hand and climbed down, and breathed out as her foot touched the ground.

When Rob climbed out, he heard Caro's next shaky intake of air.

She'd been sitting with her head lowered throughout their journey, her bosom lifting and falling with her measured breaths. He'd presumed she'd been fighting her fear, yet now it seemed to be overwhelming her.

When Drew let go of her hand, Rob took it and set her fingers on his bent arm, then pressed his hand over hers. She was shaking and her gaze darted about the carriages and people.

"We are beside you," Rob whispered. Drew looked sideways at them as Mary rested her hand on his arm.

"Caro," Drew encouraged them to walk ahead.

Caro shook her head. "You lead."

"Caro…" Drew's voice expressed concern. It was clear she was not comfortable.

"We will follow you," Rob answered for her.

Drew had commented, only two days ago, on how much Caro had changed, how relaxed she was in Rob's company. Rob had given Drew the same explanation he'd given Caro—it was probably due to him having so many sisters.

It said a great deal, though, that tonight she accepted his support—and she'd only come because he'd urged her. They had grown close. They were friends. He'd had a desire to see her laugh, and he'd achieved that weeks ago, but he still now longed to see her dance even more than he had at the beginning of the summer.

Then it had been a fascinating concept. Now he wished his friend to be able to do as she pleased. To enjoy herself.

Pride swelled in his chest, on her behalf, because she had come this far, and yet he wished her to take more steps.

Drew walked ahead with Mary.

Rob's hand pressed over Caro's, urging her to keep going as they followed.

Caro's fingers curved on his arm, grasping, as they stepped over the threshold of the inn.

"Upstairs, my lord, my lady, sir, ma'am." The doorman directed them to the stairs.

Caro's breathing fractured into short, sharp sounds.

Damn propriety. If others judged, they could go to hell. Rob let his arm fall and clasped her hand in his instead, willing her to be brave as they began to climb the stairs.

Drew glanced back at Caro over his shoulder, offering her a shallow smile. She was not looking up, though, her gaze was on the steps ahead of them, and she did not seem able to notice her surroundings.

Rob nodded at Drew, to say he would help her manage it.

But then she stopped. "I cannot." She looked from Rob to Drew. "I cannot. Take me home. Please."

Rob held her hand more firmly and looked at Drew, who had half-turned. "You go in. I will take Caro back outside for a moment. If she still wishes to go home, I will take her and have the carriage sent back."

Drew looked at Caro, anxiety in his eyes, but she nodded. He smiled slightly, giving his cautious agreement, then turned away.

Voices rose behind them as others began to climb the stairs.

"Rob." Caro's fingers gripped his hand more firmly—clinging. "Please may we go?"

He turned and led her back downstairs, past the group who'd just entered. Her arm trembled, and her breathing became hurried, short gasps for air. It was not a mere lack of confidence, it was a very real terror, the sort of terror he'd seen when one of his younger siblings had woken from a nightmare and were still unsure of what was real and what was not. But he knew Caro's nightmare was not imagined; it had been real in the past.

"We will walk this way," he said, as they stepped back out into the night. The air was warm, humid and heavy.

She drew in a deep breath as he walked her away from the carriages.

A little further along the street the shadows cast by the moon dropped back into the churchyard. If they walked there it would be silent and they would remain undisturbed, and unobserved, while Caro had chance to calm herself.

Rob's heart thumped hard, and compassion gripped tight in his chest as he walked with her. "This way." He led her through the wrought-iron gate onto the stone pathway leading towards the church.

Once they were in there, the darkness consumed them, but it seemed to ease Caro, her hold on his hand softened and her breathing slowed.

"Caro…"

She did not answer and he could not really see her face.

"If I remember rightly, there is a stone bench over there. Shall we sit for a while?"

"My dress, Rob. I would not wish to ruin it."

Of course, that was foolish, the stone seat would be soiled. "At least let's move further back from the street, then." He was suddenly very aware that drawing her out here, alone, in the darkness, was perhaps the wrong thing to have done. People might make assumptions and gossip. But she was a divorced woman with some freedom, not a young, sheltered woman. But even so, he did not wish to damage her reputation. It would be better if they were out of sight.

His fingers threaded through hers and he walked backward, pulling her slowly with him, relief swaying over him. At least she felt better. "Tell me why you became distressed?"

"It is irrational."

Once they were on the far side of the ornate stone porch, they stood in a patch of moonlight and she looked at him with eyes that expressed an inability to understand or control how she felt. Fragility hung in the air about her, as her small hand held his, her fingers woven between his.

"Remember that I am the man you may tell things to, even if you have never spoken of them before. You told me you loved Kilbride. I did not judge. Explain this to me. It will help, I'm sure."

"I do not even know why myself."

"Then tell me what happens. Tell me what you think. How you feel."

"It is just panic. Not even fear. But I suppose it is fear. It's the thought of being surrounded and hemmed in, and… Then I see images from the past, flashes, moments of memory. But it's not the memories that make it unbearable, but the feelings that accompany them."

"What feelings?" His fingers squeezed hers in encouragement

"Rejection," she said, quietly, her gaze falling to look at the stone pavement. "I suppose that is what I fear, rejection, humiliation—cruelty."

"Caro…" Compassion lanced through his chest and his fingers lifted to her chin. She was so, slender and delicate.

He did not know if he lowered his head further or if Caro rose to her toes, but by some action their lips touched. Hers pressed against his, gently.

He hadn't kissed a woman for over a year, but then he'd never really kissed a woman, not a woman like Caro. He'd kissed barmaids when he'd been at college, before he'd realised what those women really wished for, but no more than that.

Caro felt different, her lips were soft and gentle, tentative not urgent.

The barmaids he'd kissed had been seeking payment, or escape from a life of service—Caro sought nothing but the press of his lips against hers.

Her mouth opened against his lips.

The barmaids used to thrust their tongues into his mouth as they pressed against him, desperately searching for opportunities of escape. Once his eyes had been opened to the way of society, of class and rank, he'd never let those women degrade themselves with him again.

He stepped closer, his hand slipping to Caro's nape, as need raced through his stomach.

Her arms came up about his neck as he tentatively pressed his tongue into her mouth.

His other hand braced her waist gently and her tongue stroked over his and danced around his elegantly.

The sensation in his stomach hardened, fisted and grasped at his groin too.

Her fingers combed into his hair, splaying across his scalp, bracing his head, as their tongues continued their exquisite dance.

He sighed into her mouth, the sound leaking from his throat, as he held her more firmly. He'd never had emotions like this for a woman. The desire to lay her back and do far more than kiss her was a hard pull inside him. But it was wrong.

He broke the kiss and looked down at her. The sound of their breaths filled the night air.

"Caro…" What the hell had he done, had he just made a muddle of this? "I'm sorry."

She said nothing as her hands slipped from his hair. He held them. He had to make her understand that she need not feel afraid, so she could be free. "No harm will come to you here. You have my word. Drew is well respected. You will not be rejected or ill-treated."

"I know my fear is irrational. I told you. I am not rejected by your family but I—"

"Then you must learn to believe it. I am here with you and I will not let you be rejected or harmed. I know you have courage. You are capable of this."

~

Courage... He'd used that word to her before. He was the only person who had, and perhaps he'd enchanted her when they'd kissed, because she truly felt strong. "Will you stay with me?"

"Of course I will. There is no question of that."

She pulled one of her hands from his and touched his cheek. The moonlight coloured his features silver, making his hair, his eyes and eyelashes darker.

He was young, beautiful, strong-natured, good-hearted—and he had kissed her.

Emotions played through her nerves, but they were not fear and panic, it was anticipation and longing that made her feel shaky—desire.

"Shall we return, then?"

No. She did not wish to return. She wished to stay here hidden in the darkness and kiss him, but she could not ask for that. "Yes." Her fingers dropped from his cheek and her heart beat more strongly as they turned and began walking from the churchyard.

He walked briskly, as though he feared she might renege and his grip on her hand pulled her with him.

When they left the security of the dark churchyard, he let go of her hand and glanced at her, offering his arm instead. She held it firmly, her senses absorbing the strength of his lean muscle beneath his evening coat.

His hand lay over hers, applying a slight pressure as they walked on. She looked ahead at the inn's door.

She still did not feel panic, her consciousness was on Rob's arm and his hand over hers, as a desperate longing to experience a marriage bed again raged through her blood.

He slowed when they reached the carriages, then navigated her through a group of people who were arriving. At the entrance, the doorman bowed and lifted a hand, encouraging them to progress. Caro gripped Rob's arm tighter as they crossed the threshold.

"As I said, you have courage, be brave," he whispered as they climbed the stairs. She did not want his words of comfort; she wanted his kiss. It had been different to Albert's, a genteel connection, respectful and considerate. Albert had kissed with force and intensity.

As they climbed the stairs her memories were not flashes from the past but flashes from moments ago in the churchyard. At the top of the stairs, he shepherded her into the busy assembly rooms. It was crowded with people, dancing and talking at the edges of the room, as a quartet played music on a dais at the far end of the hall.

Her chest tightened and awareness of her surroundings overtook any other thought. Rob's hand lifted from hers and then his arm dropped. Her heart leapt to the pace of a canter.

"Your brother is over there, look. Remember your courage. Remember you have survived far worse than a simple assembly dance."

Drew was in the corner to the left of the door. She took a breath and felt Rob's hand hover at her lower back as she began to walk. He did not touch her, yet his hand protected her, ensuring no one might bump into her.

Drew watched her progress, a smile lifting his lips slightly. He'd been waiting for her, she could see, hoping she would find the courage to come in.

Relief lay an invisible cloak over her shoulders when she reached him, and Rob stood to one side of her, while Drew moved closer and protected her from the other side, as she stood with her back facing the wall.

"How are you?" Drew had been her sole comfort for years, she'd always looked to him for reassurance, and yet today his words stirred no feeling. It was Rob's comfort she'd clung to.

She nodded, although in truth her nerves were as tight as a

copper coil and she was fighting the urge to run.

Drew took one of her hands and squeezed it gently. "Bravo, Caro."

"I think Caro could do with a drink," Rob said. "Do you wish to come with me to the refreshment table?" *Rather than be left here without him.* He was so thoughtful.

"We'll join you," Mary answered.

They walked about the dancers, but when they reached the refreshments, Rob refused to let Caro take the lemonade. "No, drink this." He handed her a glass of the rum punch. "For a little added courage."

Drew passed Mary one too and she lifted her glass in a toast, smiling at Caro. "To first steps."

"To putting on a brave face," Drew answered, lifting his glass.

"To dancing," Rob concluded, touching his glass to Caro's before emptying it in one swallow.

She shook her head at his suggestion.

He leant to her ear. "I dare you."

She shook her head again, but a smile caught her lips before she took a sip from her glass. The liquor flowed into her blood a moment later, warm and strong.

"Well, Mary and I shall dance the next," Drew stated, "As I have come, I may as well indulge her." He looked at Mary. "If you will indulge me, of course, sweetheart."

"Of course I will. I shall not pass on such an opportunity."

They smiled at each other, but then Drew looked at Caro. "If you will be happy here with Robbie?"

Her answering smile was to reassure him. "Go and make Mary happy. You deserve some fun."

Drew took Mary's hand as the music came to a close and they turned to find a set to join.

"Is dancing fun, then?"

Caro looked at Rob and her smile fell. She took another sip from her glass.

"You said, fun," he pressed. "If you think it fun, you must enjoy it…"

She shook her head and lifted her glass to her lips once more. Rob's fingers settled beneath it and tipped it higher. "A little more courage, I think. I shall have to get my brother Harry to make a drinker of you."

She laughed despite herself, having taken an enforced gulp. A moment later she felt the heat of it in her limbs, making them a little heavier and more relaxed.

"I watched you at my brother's, at John's, at the party before I came to Drew's, you watched people dancing, you watched me dancing as if you would like to dance, so why do you not?"

"Rob…." She could not explain.

"Tell me."

But this was Rob, who never ceased pushing until she did explain.

"I do not wish to be stared at, to become a spectacle, and make a fool of myself."

"People might stare, but it would only be because you are beautiful. But that is not the heart of your issue, is it?"

Her blood heated with the knowledge that he thought her beautiful, but his comment had not been flirtatious, he'd said it with a factual tone.

She took another sip of her punch, then placed the glass down. She did not want to drink too much. "My mother used to drink excessively. I have never been comfortable with liquor." Caro changed the subject, clutching at anything to stop him seeking to persuade her. "I think it was an excess of alcohol that brought Drew and me into the world. I think she knows who Drew's father is, but I think she cannot even remember mine." It was a throwaway comment because she was panicking once more, and yet she realised she had perhaps given away too much of herself.

Pity caught in his eyes.

"Do not pity me for that. I came to terms with it long ago."

"Then, what should I pity you for? What harm is there in telling me why you feel you cannot dance?" He was too perceptive and too forceful.

She picked up the glass again and drank the last of the punch. Then glared at him. "I feel trapped, I cannot be who I wish to be. I cannot do the things I want to do because I'm bound by the past—kept captive by it. I feel as though I have a glass prison cell about me, but it is of my own making."

"Then break it. Dance the next with me."

"Rob—"

"*I cannot…*" He mimicked her voice. "Only because you will not. But half an hour ago you believed you could not walk into this room. At the beginning of the summer you could not abide being in a room with me. You can do anything you wish. Dance."

"You do not understand."

"You have just told me it is you yourself who has created this gaol. You have had the courage to escape far worse. You may tell me tomorrow or the next day, or the day after that why your gaoler still has a hold over you, but tonight… dance."

Can I? Everything he said was true.

Her heart thumped against her ribs. *Could it be so simple?*

The tempo of the music changed as the country dance came to a close and a waltz began.

Rob offered his hand. "I dare you to dance with me."

He was a beautiful young man—and cruel and wonderful. His smile glinted in his eyes.

"Caro," he said more formally, with a slight bow. "May I have the honour of this waltz?"

"You are a fool," she answered.

"Perhaps."

Oh, she had feelings for him. They consumed her when he smiled.

She accepted his hand, and he drew her away from the refreshment table, then lifted their joined hands and formed the hold of the dance as his other hand came about her. When he spun her out onto the floor, she was not aware of anyone else—it was only Rob in the room.

His hand and his fingers, at her back, steered her through the steps.

She'd always loved to dance. Then why had she not done so for years?

Because it was self-punishment, for failing her husband so terribly. But surely she'd done enough penance for the loss of her children. Perhaps now, Rob was right, she might let herself live again.

Guilt cut at her. Yet she could still love and mourn her lost children and not hide or deprive herself of the basic elements of life—dancing. She was dancing.

She looked into Rob's eyes and forgot about anything except the music, the touch of his hands and the look in his eyes.

He did not speak, and she was glad he did not because it would have broken the magic. She was building new glass walls, ones about a palace in the sky. She smiled as the music skipped through her soul. It was a wonderful feeling; she had always loved dancing.

She was breathless when it came to an end, and stupidly disappointed as Rob walked her to the edge of the room, where they met Mary and Drew.

"Caro…" Drew said with emotion. "Will you dance the next with me? I shall willing make a cake of myself no matter what the dance is, if only to see you smile like that again."

She actually laughed at him, the fear and the panic were not there; her restraints had gone.

After she'd danced with Drew, the physician who'd treated Mary through two pregnancies asked Caro to dance. Rob and Drew looked at her meaningfully, willing her to accept. Caro knew him, she had drunk tea with him at the house. She smiled and accepted his hand, though hers trembled, but as they danced her nerves eased. It was a fast, jolly dance and she glanced at Rob often. He was dancing with Mary, but he kept glancing over and smiling at her too. He had given her the courage to achieve this.

She was returned to Drew's side, flushed and smiling. He stood beside a man she did not know. "Caroline, this is Mr Slade, he rents one of my farms. Mr Slade, this is my sister, Lady Framlington."

The farmer bowed. "Would you care to dance with me, ma'am?"

Caro's skin heated by a degree. Had he come to wait with Drew so he might ask? But it was merely a dance, it was what people did—she had forgotten so much of life.

"Indeed." She offered her hand.

It became the pattern of the evening. She did not sit down. Each time a dance ended, another gentleman was introduced to her, and she danced with her brother and with Rob again too.

When they travelled home in Drew's carriage, it was two in the morning, and she was tired and quiet, as a melee of emotions fought within her chest. But happiness was the first, that and hope, pride and wonder. But perhaps the pride was not for herself, yet for Rob. He had given her the courage; she would not have found it without him.

She was wonderfully, physically exhausted, yet she did not think she would be capable of sleep.

She looked from the dark landscape outside the window to Mary and Drew. Drew smiled at her, a gleeful smile, his hand clasping Mary's, and drawing it onto his thigh.

He shook his head at her a little, as if in wonder. She had surprised him, but she had surprised herself.

She looked at Rob. He was sitting beside her, staring out of the window. She wished to hold his hand, but the gesture would be inappropriate. Even more, though, she wished to lean against his shoulder.

She wondered what he was thinking, if the memory of their kiss was still a gentle heat in his blood as it was in hers.

"It was a wonderful evening," Mary said.

They all looked at her. "It was, indeed," Drew agreed, and he usually hated such affairs.

Caro said nothing. She felt as if words might break her new glass castle in the air.

~

Rob leant back against the squabs in the carriage and returned his gaze to the outside, watching clouds cast their shadows across the moonlit fields. He was intensely aware of the heat radiating from Caro's thigh, so close to his.

They had shared a kiss…

He'd not danced with anyone other than Caro and Mary; he'd not liked to in case Caro had needed him. But that had meant he'd had an entire evening to watch her. He'd become a little addicted.

Weeks ago his uncle had asked him what his weakness was. Perhaps his weakness was Caro. All night his thoughts had hovered on the feel of her mouth.

When they reached home, Drew handed Mary and Caro down, and Caro held Drew's arm when they walked up to the first floor.

Rob walked behind them, speaking with Mary.

"I shall retire immediately, if you do not mind?" Caro said to them all.

"I will too," Mary agreed.

"Then I shall retire as well," Drew stated.

"Goodnight, then," Rob responded, he was not tired. He would be unable to sleep. He kissed Mary's cheek as Caro climbed the stairs, and nodded at Drew before they turned to their rooms.

He looked at a footman. "I shall go to the library. You may retire." He picked up a candelabra and took it with him as he walked back downstairs.

In the library he stripped off his coat and his waistcoat and set them over the back of a chair, then pulled off his cravat and poured himself a glass of whiskey before occupying an armchair.

He shut his eyes and let his head fall back.

What had he done? Kissed her…

Bastard.

His blood hummed. Even now, the thought of that kiss made his groin heavy. He was thirsty, but not for the liquor, or any other liquid. It was a thirst to learn more, to find out how things might feel with Caro. He had always had morals. Always.

But God! I am tempted.

Would she be horrified if she knew what he thought?

He lifted his head and opened his eyes, then sipped the whiskey, seeking to regain the reins on his feelings. He'd never found it hard before; he'd never even been tempted. He'd been kissed by the barmaids, but no more. Their brash attitude had never appealed to him, and unlike Harry he'd never sought sexual experiences as trophies of his manhood.

But Caro had not kissed him out of the need those women felt, or for any other reason than their lips had come together. It had merely been a response to a friendship and closeness, which had been weaving about them for weeks. He'd asked for friendship, and he'd called her a friend, but he had known for days that it was becoming more than that. He did not feel a softness in his chest, or a tightness in his gut when he was with his friends.

When they'd waltzed he'd felt the muscle in Caro's back shifting with her movements and her smaller hand in his with a sense of awe.

The door swung open. He looked up. All of the servants ought to be in bed.

It was his phantom. Caro. An apparition in a silk robe that was a deep red. Her blonde hair was plaited and hung across one shoulder. But there were wisps of golden curls left about her face. They gave her a halo.

His gaze dropped to her toes, which peeked from beneath the hem of her white nightdress, that hung lower than the red robe which she wore over it.

Something lanced through his groin. Was it lust? An emotion

Harry spoke of that Rob had never felt.

"Caro?" He rose, although he half-expected her not to be real—he'd drunk more than usual tonight as he'd watched her.

But she was real. "Rob." She came further into the room, her hands clasped together at her waist, and stood a few feet away. "I could not sleep and I heard you tell the footman you were coming downstairs. I wanted to say thank you." She gave him a smile that made her glow.

"It is yourself you have to thank. You found the courage to break the invisible walls around you."

"But I would not have done it without your persuasion."

Her eyes shone in the light of the candelabra, looking at him through pale eyelashes.

He could not help himself. He lifted a hand, morals and self-discipline deserting him. He wished her closer. "Caro."

She walked towards him, seeming to float like the phantom he'd first thought she was, and then his hands were at her waist and hers lay on his shoulders.

He was a little in his cups, the whiskey burned in his blood and heat clasped at his groin. *Thirst.* For more than liquor. "I think you ought to go back to your room."

"Why?"

He shook his head. "You do not wish to know."

"Tell me." She was speaking as though this was the same as her fear. It was not.

"Caro, go back upstairs, please. I'm feeling very weak tonight." His words urged her and yet his whiskey-guided hands still gripped her waist.

He was a bastard.

"Weak?" she breathed, looking at him with confusion.

He did not warn her again as lust reared its head and roared through him. Yes, he was weak tonight and now he understood what Harry spoke of.

This time, undoubtedly, the lead came from him. His lips

touched hers as his hand braced the back of her head, while his other slipped to the curve of her lower back. His tongue pressed into her mouth in a firm, bold stroke.

Her mouth opened wider, compliant, and her hands told him she was willing as they slipped into his hair, bracing his head as she'd done in the churchyard.

He drew her closer, so her body pressed against his as his tongue danced with hers. His blood pulsed, heavy in his veins, as lust clutched in his groin, hardening as she pressed against him, rather than pushing him away.

The hunger inside him pulled and thrust, fighting for him to hold her more tightly, to be as close as he could come to her. *Lust.*

She broke the kiss. "Rob." Her fingers combed through his hair.

"Caro." He did not understand this, and his conscience cried out when she pulled his lips back to hers. But he did not heed it, he did not care for it anymore. He wanted to be closer still.

His hands clasped her bottom, sinking into her soft flesh through the material of her robe and her nightgown as his erection pushed against her stomach, trapped between them. It throbbed to do far more than touch. "Caro," he breathed into her mouth, perhaps for permission, he hardly knew; he'd never done this, had never been like this.

His breathing became rapid as he slid one hand back up across the thin silk of her robe to grip her breast. It filled his hand, the weight of it resting in his palm. She had full, round breasts.

She broke the kiss, but probably because he'd stopped kissing her. Her fingers came forward and cupped his cheeks, cradling his jaw as his gaze met hers, her eyes saying, *it is all right, you may touch me.*

Giddy from the lust and the whiskey in his blood, his hazy gaze held on to the amber in her eyes as his fingers tightened and kneaded her flesh. Her nipple protruded into his palm.

"Why do you not speak?" He wanted her to stop him, because he'd drunk too much to stop himself.

"I do not wish to shatter this."

His gaze fell to the hollow at the heart of her clavicle, where he could see her pulse flickering. The amber cross that hung below it lifted when she breathed in. Surely she ought to be panicking, but she was not.

Damn it. Damn conscience and morals, and doing right. He let go of her breast and lifted his hand, then touched where her pulse flickered. It rose in tempo.

His fingers crept beneath the loose fabric of her silk robe and her cotton nightdress.

A breath left her lips and stirred his fringe when his fingers pushed her robe and nightdress off her shoulder. They hung a little down her arm when his fingers dipped within, cupping her warm flesh gently. The weight and texture of her breast gripped at his soul, and the peak of her nipple was a call to his senses, soft like velvet and yet hard. She shivered when his thumb played with it, brushing across it.

God help him. With other women he'd had resilience like iron, but Caro.

She was his vice.

Her fingers slid to the back of his head and urged him to bend down.

Temptation and longing flared through his blood as if she had knocked over a lantern and the oil had spilled out, in full flame. He lowered his head and lifted her breast to his mouth, exploring, discovering the texture. He cradled her nipple on his tongue and sucked, then bit it gently with his teeth. Then he let his tongue dance with it, sweeping about the silk and velvet textures.

Her fingers ran over his back, her touch brushing over his thin cotton shirt. Then she began pulling it from the waistband of his trousers.

It was as though a fever burned between them. He was not alone in his new addiction.

Her fingers touched his skin and lust yelled. No woman had

ever touched his skin beneath his clothes. He straightened up to kiss her once more, his tongue pressing into her mouth as his hand kneaded her breast and hers swept across his back underneath his shirt.

A soft sound of pleasure seeped from her mouth into his.

Every nerve, every sinew in his body ached to do much more than they were. Instinct screamed in his ears. He wished to press her back, lay her down and lift her nightdress. Both his hands returned to grip her buttocks, holding her against him and her warm, soft breasts pressed against his shirt, moist from his adoration, as his erection pressed against her stomach.

She was pliant and supple.

She broke the kiss. "Rob." His name asked for more, it asked for everything his instinct willed.

Yet he had not run that mad.

She is Drew's sister!

Damn it! What was he doing?

He released her instantly, as if his hands had been burned. Perhaps they had. Most vices he'd learned to keep away from because he'd been burnt by them once. His gaze fell to the beautiful ripe curve of her breast, and her deep-pink nipple, which protruded above the white cotton of her nightdress.

He swallowed back the lump of longing in his throat. He refused to regret what he'd done—what they'd done. He lifted the cotton over her breast, then lifted the silk too and covered her.

She was breathing heavily, her bosom rising and falling with each breath. Her hands gripped his waist beneath his shirt. "Why have you stopped?" Fear hovered in her eyes.

Rejection.

It was not rejection.

He gripped her head, so she could not look away from him. "It is not what you think. I should not be touching you. Yet I warned you I was weak. The kiss, earlier... I am a man... I have instincts. I am sorry... I have been drinking and this should not have happened."

She stepped back, slipping from his fingers as colour flushed her face. Then she turned and fled.

Damn! "Caro."

~

The mist of lust was swept away. *This should not have happened...*

As Caro had walked downstairs, she'd told herself it was only to say thank you. Yet in her heart she'd known that was a lie. She'd hoped Rob would make love to her. The night had been so wonderful. She'd wanted someone to share her happiness with, to feel close to. She wished to renew the experiences of her marriage bed.

Yet now. *Oh Lord.* She could feel her blush, even though she was in the dark, alone, as she climbed the stairs back up to her rooms.

"Caro!" Rob called from below.

People might stare, but it would only be because you look beautiful... I am a man...

Had she misread everything? Had he really not wished to kiss or touch her?

"Caro!"

I have instincts...

Albert had spoken of a man's appetites. A man's instinct was to crave. Albert had said his desires were crafted by nature and not even choosey. He'd claimed he was unable to control his physical urge for women.

She'd gone to Rob in her nightdress, flaunted herself and teased his instincts, and he had felt unable to control his response.

Oh, she was a fool. Rob would think badly of her.

Yet Albert had been wrong in one thing—some men could say no.

"Caro!"

But how mortifying. She had offered him her body and he'd

111

rejected it.

"Caro, come back here!"

Her bare feet brushed on the wood as she hurried up the last few steps to the second floor, her fingers slipping across the wooden banister.

Chapter 12

Rob came down to breakfast late. Caro looked up. They had finished eating; she was now simply talking to Mary while she drank a second cup of chocolate. Drew was reading his paper.

Rob's absence had been a gaping hole in the start of her day. She'd missed him smiling at her from across the table, and Mary had missed him too. She'd looked at the clock several times, a frown creasing her brow, and Drew had glanced at the door every time one of the footmen entered as his fingers had tapped idly, and impatiently, on the tablecloth.

They would all miss Rob when he left and now they all smiled at him. Life after he'd gone would seem very bleak. She could feel that, even as she noticed the heat of a blush touch her cheeks.

She had kissed him twice last night and the second time he'd bid her stop.

Her gaze fell to her cup of chocolate.

Perhaps she ought to go to the nursery, but then she had so little time left with him she did not really wish to hide away again.

"Are you feeling unwell?" Mary asked.

"I could not sleep, and I probably drank more of the punch than I should." Rob sat down.

"And my whiskey decanter had to be replenished significantly this morning," Drew mocked.

"That too."

Caro looked up. He was pale.

"Coffee for my brother-in-law," Drew ordered, "and bring up a fresh pot. That must be cold."

When a footman offered Rob bacon, he lifted a hand. "No, thank you." Then he smiled across the table at Caro, colour tainting his cheeks.

He was embarrassed by their encounter too.

She wished to laugh suddenly. He had not rejected her. His eyes still held their warmth. Of course he had not. He'd said he had not. *It is not what you think. I should not be touching you...* He had merely been righteous and a gentleman. She thought of how many times he'd called her name into the darkness, asking her to go back.

She was judging him by Albert's standards and he was not Albert.

He'd stopped her out of common-sense and kindness.

Rob was a sensible, good man, and if he'd let her continue, this morning he would not feel ill from an over-indulgence of drink, but from remorse and shame.

Last night, when she'd spoken of her glass gaol, he'd said, *Then break it.* He'd made it seem so simple. She had built the walls and last night she had smashed them. She could choose to sulk now and hide in her rooms again, or she might simply forget that she'd given in to lust for a handsome young man, and continue regardless.

She chose the latter.

She was going to apologise to him and forget her foolishness, but not forget her courage.

"You are looking green, Rob." Drew teased him.

Rob rejected the kedgeree with another lifted hand.

"You have to eat," Drew said, "the after-effects of an excess of alcohol must be fed. Ham and eggs, William. My brother-in-law needs a hearty meal to fill his tender stomach." Drew waved the

114

footman off to fetch it.

"I am unused to this," Rob answered. "I think all I need is silence and I admit I am at fault."

Rob's gaze caught on Caro's and apologised. His words had not been about drink.

She smiled tentatively. He was holding himself accountable. But she must say sorry. She had gone downstairs half-dressed, and she had not left when he'd asked her to.

Mary rose and took the fresh pot of coffee from a footman. She poured a cup for Rob. "I am putting sugar in it. It will help your headache."

Rob glanced at her. "Thank you and forgive me if I am poor company today."

Drew laughed, with no deference for Rob's request for silence.

"I'm glad you find my suffering amusing."

"It is only the start of what is to come, little brother," Drew answered. "You need to improve your stamina if you intend running with the London set for a few years before you settle. If you get drunk too easily you'll lose a fortune playing cards."

"Then I shall continue to pass, both on the liquor and the cards."

Drew looked back at his paper with a smirk.

Rob's gaze turned to Caro, and his eyebrows lifted, the look saying, *am I forgiven?*

Yes, of course he was. For a moment their gazes held, as his blue-grey eyes shone in the morning light. Then he looked down as a full plate was set before him.

"Oh." Drew cleared his throat suddenly as he sat more upright in his chair.

Caro looked over. He was looking at her with concern and compassion.

A frown pulled at her brow.

"Caro," he said with an ominous pitch. "There is something here that I do not know if you will wish to see, but as it is here I have to point it out to you."

"What?" What on earth could be in the paper that would interest her?

"Do you wish to see?"

No. Yes. "Drew, just tell me." She rose, to look for herself.

"Here." He pointed to a small announcement.

The Marquis of Kilbride is pleased to announce the birth of his son, William Edward Albert.

Albert had remarried over a year ago. Of course she had known his wife would bear him children. She had known this would come.

Drew looked up at her.

She shook her head, trying to appear as though pain had not lanced through her breast. It should not hurt. But it did.

She retook her seat, choosing not to run and hide and she ignored the fact that they all watched her. "May I have another cup of chocolate?"

Valour was the better course. Albert had moved on, and she must too.

Looking first at Drew, she smiled, then passed her smile to Rob and Mary, making nothing of what was ripping her apart internally.

She reached for the fresh cup of chocolate and sipped from it.

"What was it?" Rob asked her.

"Nothing," she answered, in a voice that urged him not to ask again.

He looked at Drew. But Drew just shook his head, respecting her choice, and then he turned the page and commented on a horse-racing article.

Caro turned to Mary and returned to the conversation they had been sharing on current fashions before Rob had walked in, trying to hide the emotion screaming inside her, but it was too hard.

As soon as she finished her chocolate she rose, "Forgive me." She turned and left the table as tears gathered in a lump in her throat.

~

When Caro walked from the room, Rob's gaze followed her. She'd neither said nor done anything obvious to imply that what Drew had shown her had upset her, and yet he knew it had. He knew her too well. His gaze turned to Drew, his thumping headache forgotten, and he looked the question without speaking.

Drew folded the paper and passed it over. "Announcements."

Rob opened it up and looked through the pages, while Mary rose and walked about the table to look over his shoulder.

He found the page and scanned it. Kilbride's name jumped out. "An heir," Rob said aloud.

Mary, who had leant forward, straightened and looked at Drew. "Should I find her and sit with her this morning?"

Drew shook his head. "Let her do as she wishes. She will come to terms with it."

But Rob did not think she would want to be alone. He stood. She had been lonely. "I'll ask her if she wishes to go for a walk with George, or ride."

"Leave her, Rob, there is no need." Drew said.

"It is kind of you to offer, Rob, but Andrew knows her best," Mary added.

But Drew did not. Caro had told Rob things Drew did not know. No matter how much Rob regretted what had happened last night, or how much he'd sworn to himself while he'd drunk himself into a stupor that he would stay out of her way in future, he could not let her endure this alone.

"I shall go back upstairs and lie down, then."

They gave him sympathetic looks.

Rob wondered how much Drew's influence had hindered Caro and not helped her. The way Drew sought to help her was to disregard her anxiety, yet although Rob thought that she must disregard it to recover, he did not condone leaving her to simply endure it, as Drew did.

Rob did not go to his room. He left the house. He knew where she would be. In the gardens.

She was sitting on the lip of the pond, one hand gripping the stone, while the other played in the water making patterns with the ripples. When he walked closer she looked up at the sky. It was another intensely hot day, but the air felt fresher because it had rained during the night.

"Caro?"

She jumped and then stood up.

"Rob." Her voice sounded calm, but there were tear stains on her cheeks.

She wiped them away with her sleeve.

"I'm sorry about last night. It was wrong of me—" he began, but she interrupted.

"You have nothing to apologise for. It was wrong of me to come down in my nightdress, and you asked me to leave…" Her chin lifted as if in denial of any censure.

Caro had pride in reams as well as courage, and that was why she was afraid of rejection, because she had once been a marchioness.

If she deserved nothing else, she deserved honesty from him. "I should not lie. I am not wholly sorry. I'd been sitting there longing to do those things with you. I've thought you beautiful for weeks, then last night you shone, and I'd had too much to drink. My resolve broke. It does not normally. That is what I am sorry for."

The depth in her eyes grew with a bewildered expression as her eyes turned gold in the morning sunshine. "I cannot accept your apology." She shook her head. The heat of a blush rose in his cheeks as she continued. "It was my fault. I was emotional, I'd enjoyed the evening, and I presented myself in a state that must have… Well, Albert told me about men's instincts. That you cannot control—"

A deep splinter of a laugh erupted from Rob's throat, hurting his head.

She hit his arm. "Do not laugh at me."

"I am not laughing at you, I am laughing at him. Your husband was an ass. A man may control himself. Did I not say stop last night? I have never had a problem saying an emphatic no before that. The problem last night was that I did not wish to and I'm sorry because it was neither right, nor fair of me to take advantage of our friendship, and I was not rejecting you, if you still think that. I do not even particularly regret what we did, and yet I know it was wrong, and so I apologise."

The depth in her eyes changed again as she stepped closer to him while a wood pigeon called from the corner of the garden. "Then I still do not accept your apology. I do not regret it, either." Her hands lifted and braced his head, her fingers slipping into his hair. Then her fingers urged him to bend. He complied, still intoxicated from last night. It felt like a dream as she rose to her toes.

"Let me be sorry for this," she said against his lips.

Her lips pressed against his.

Ah damn. He was not sorry at all. His tongue pushed into her mouth as she gripped his nape and his shoulder.

His hands held her bottom, but after a few moments he broke the kiss. This was not the time, nor the place. But he said over her lips. "You are forgiven."

"So are you," she answered, holding his gaze.

His forehead fell against hers. "Caro, I know, Drew showed me the paper."

A flush coloured her skin. He'd found her crying, and she'd said once that she'd loved Kilbride. Was she embarrassed that he knew? Or embarrassed by her emotions?

"It does not matter." She turned away, letting him go as he let her go. She walked to the flower border.

"Does it not?"

"No." She admired an ornamental daisy as though it were the crown jewels, then walked on along the border with her back to him.

He followed. "Was it a blow? I know you were crying here."

"No."

"Caro," he caught hold of her elbow to stop her walking, but

119

she did not turn back "I know it has upset you, so why lie? This is me. You may speak."

She still did not turn.

He stepped forward and wrapped his arms around her waist from behind, holding her still and offering the comfort she claimed she did not need, yet she leaned back against him.

"Tell me. How does it feel? Do you hurt?"

Her hands settled over his. "Yes. But I should not, should I? Envy is a destructive feeling. But I wanted a child. He divorced me because I could not give him one. That was the reason his anger began."

"Why he hit you?" God, the man was not an ass, he was a bastard.

She nodded, looking up at the sky, not him. He kissed her temple.

"I left him because of the violence, yet he divorced me so he might find a wife who would give him an heir. He has his son now and what do I have? I can never have a child."

His arms tightened a little as he held her, but he did not know what to say to offer comfort. Platitudes would be pointless, so he simply kept holding her and offered physical comfort kissing her temple again.

She turned in his arms and her hands clung at his waist. Then she lifted to her toes. "I will say sorry now," she whispered before she kissed him.

Last night he'd been gripped by lust in the darkness and the candlelight, with liquor flowing in his veins, but in the daylight it had become a gentle pull. There was no urgency. He merely wished to give her comfort and indulge in these new sensations. He was not sorry they had taken this turn in their friendship.

But it was still neither the time nor the place. He broke the kiss and held her head, looking into her eyes. She was so delicate. "You are forgiven."

She smiled.

"Would you like to go up to the nursery? Perhaps we could play with George. You are not without a family, Caro, and George and Iris may ease the ache."

Her forehead pressed into the crook of his neck. "I cannot believe you even understand that there is an ache… Thank you." Her words seeped through his neckcloth as warmth.

"Shall we go up to the nursery?" he repeated.

"Yes," she pulled away from him. "I would like to see George. Perhaps we could bring him down to the drawing room to play, and I would like to hold Iris."

"Come, then." He took her hand and turned, then pulled her back across the lawn.

It was entirely foolish to become attached to her, and yet if all they did was kiss, and if all he did was offer comfort, what harm was there?

When the house came into view he dropped her hand.

They walked in, talking jovially of the assembly the night before, and climbed the stairs to the nursery. When they reached it, Drew and Mary were there also, and George was in the process of using his papa as a climbing frame, full of energy, but when he saw Rob he ran over so he might be lifted up and tumbled.

Mary came over to Caro and set Iris into Caro's arms. That was the comfort that Caro needed most, simply to hold a child. What Rob had told her outside was true, she did have a family. Drew had given her this. But Rob could understand her need for something of her own, it was why he was here, because he was tired of being dependent on his family and looking to create an independent life. He knew Caro would have her own life, too, if she could. Perhaps she would have smashed her glass prison cell years ago if she'd had money to help her step out of it.

He had the money to begin to build his own life if he wished to use it. John had given him that, but the whole idea of using his family to fulfil his great plan made his skin crawl with discomfort.

Chapter 13

Rob lifted his arm, offering it Caro. "Will you walk in the garden with me?"

Caro lay her hand on the sleeve of his evening coat. The evening was warm and yet it was not the cooler air that beckoned but the privacy of the gardens.

She looked up and caught the smile that hovered in his eyes.

The summer heat had built for two days and become endless. Caro had spent those days inside, out of the sun, with the children, in the nursery, with the windows wide open to bring in the breeze as she'd tried to soothe the pain inside her.

She'd played with George and read to him to help him sleep, and sat in the chair rocking Iris while both the children slept. If Mary, Drew or Rob took George from the nursery, then she sat alone singing to Iris.

But in the evenings...

Her evenings were her time with Rob. He only had a few days left, and she wished to capture as many of these precious last moments as she could.

Yet every time she looked at him, her chest tightened. What would she do when he'd gone?

The thought kept whispering through her head. She refused to fret, though. She would worry once he'd gone, not when he was here. Fretting would spoil the time they had left and she was enjoying his company too much for that.

Her fingers gripped his arm gently as they walked out through the French doors.

They found a moment of privacy to kiss at least once an evening: in the hours of dusk, when Mary and Drew were saying goodnight to the children, or as now in the moments after dinner, when Drew and Mary checked that George had gone to sleep.

Each kiss began with an apology and ended with forgiveness, perhaps because Rob knew as much as she did that they ought not to be kissing. Yet it was as if she was possessed by something, something that pulled her to him. She was constantly aware of him whenever they stood or sat in the same room.

As they turned about the end of the first hedge of the parterre gardens, his arm dropped and instead he caught hold of her hand and pulled her into a run. She laughed as they raced deeper into the gardens.

When he pulled her around the third hedge, into the garden with the pond where they had played with George's boat, Caro was breathless.

Rob's fingers clasped her waist and pressed her back against the prickly clipped branches of the yew hedge. "I will say sorry now, Caro."

"You are forgiven," she answered as her arms wrapped about his neck. Then they were kissing again, and she lost herself in the intoxication.

One of his hands lifted and his fingers curled and trailed slowly down the column of her neck.

Rob always touched her tenderly, but since the night in the library, he had not touched her intimately. She supposed that since he would leave soon it was sensible, and yet she longed to be irrational.

He kissed her temple. She nipped at the skin of his jaw above his neck cloth.

"Caro," he said into the air, laughing. "Stop."

She did not, she sucked his neck just beneath his jaw as he looked up at the sky, but then his fingers gripped her chin and lifted her head so he could kiss her again. His warm lips pressed over hers and his tongue delved into her open mouth.

Her fingers clasped his evening coat at his waist.

"Caro! Rob!"

Rob pulled away from her, red staining his cheeks.

"Mary and I thought we would play cards! Where are you?" Drew's voice resonated through the hedges.

Rob cursed quietly.

Caro's heart raced, along with her breathing.

"Caro! Rob!"

"You go," Rob whispered. "I have a small predicament. Tell him I went back to the house."

Caro laughed, doing what she had never done with him and running a fingertip up the line of his erection. "It is not small." She turned away and left him, sending him a smile across her shoulder.

"Caro!"

She ran about the hedge and discovered Drew in the next garden, only a few steps away from discovering them. "Oh, sorry," she said trying to catch her breath and calm her heart. "I walked out as far as the woodland path, it's such a beautiful night."

"Where is Rob?"

"He went back."

Drew looked at her a little oddly, but she gripped his arm and turned him around, her mind still in Rob's arms behind the hedge.

~

As they played cards, Caro sat facing Rob, a smile on her lips. They were partnering each other and they'd won every hand. She only had to look at him and he seemed to know which suit he should lay. Humour danced in his dark eyes.

Because it was hot and humid, Rob and Drew had stripped off their evening coats and rolled up their sleeves.

Rob's dark-brown fringe fell forward as he leaned to play a card. When he leant back he slid a little down in the chair, slouching slightly. The pose gave him an endearing quality. His dark eyelashes lowered, cloaking his gaze as he looked at his cards. Then his slender, long fingers pulled out a card and moved it to another place in his hand. The muscle in his forearm shifted beneath the dark hair covering his skin.

"Caro, it is your turn." Drew prompted.

She leaned forward and laid the queen of hearts. "I claim the trick."

"Oh," Mary huffed, throwing away the two of spades.

Rob glanced up and laughed, his dark-blue eyes glinting as Caro gathered the cards to her.

"How do you two do it?" Drew complained, "Have you established some code. I have been watching you and I can see none."

Heat flooded Caro's skin. She hoped he had not noticed how much she'd been watching Rob.

"You are getting too good at this," Mary complained.

Caro looked up and laid the five of spades. "Hearts are trumps again." She knew neither Drew nor Mary had any.

Drew and Mary sat in mirrored poses, both sitting upright and leaning towards the table, with their feet tucked beneath their chairs.

Mary lay the seven of spades.

Caro slid down a little and slipped her foot from her shoe then touched Rob's leg with her toes.

He glanced at her through his dark eyelashes and smiled as she slipped her foot back into her shoe. Then he sat upright, pulling his legs out of reach, but his gaze hovered on her as he lay the king of spades.

"Damn you, you have it again." Drew threw away the knave of diamonds.

Rob gathered up their cards and pushed them across the table to her. Her fingers touched his when she took them and the contact lanced through her in a spiral, twisting down through her stomach.

She longed for more than kisses. It had been a long time since she'd shared Albert's bed and Rob was to leave in three days.

The house would feel empty when he'd gone, and she would be alone in her rooms and feel like a parasite once more.

She would not urge him to stay, she had told herself that a dozen times. He had a life to lead. She could not trap him here. But she longed to lay with him just once, to know how it would feel to lay with him. To have a memory to keep. It had been too long since she'd experienced the bliss of a marriage bed.

But what then?

She thrust the thought aside. She refused to think of consequence. He'd taught her that she could do what she wished.

I am not a virgin. What harm would there be in it?

"Caro," Drew prompted, "your turn."

Her attention focused on the cards he and Rob had laid. She chose one that unfortunately Mary beat. It was the first trick they'd lost. Caro smiled apologetically at Rob. He'd been watching her.

Mary and Drew celebrated their victory by Drew leaning across the table and pulling her over for a kiss.

Chapter 14

Rob was seated at the breakfast table, answering Drew's numerous questions on his plans, but he kept glancing at Caro. He could not help himself. He was leaving tomorrow. "I have a letter confirming they are expecting me at Pembroke House." He took a deep breath when Drew nodded at his answer.

A part of him did not wish to leave, and yet he could hardly stay, and he did not even wish to, really. His friends were already in London, his life would begin there. His own life, not the one funded by his father or his brother. He'd shared his desire to go into politics with his friends and they'd all pledged to support him. When he went to London he intended to recruit them to help him find a parliamentary seat he might have a chance of winning, and then he would use them to help his campaign to persuade the local men to vote for him.

Yet now there was Caro to leave behind…

She had not looked at him this morning

His heart thumped as he watched her drink a sip of chocolate.

"I used to live in rooms in the Albany. They were nothing fancy, but they were suitable. I can give you a letter of introduction if you wish?"

Rob looked at Drew and laughed. "And a letter from you would obtain me entry… Forgive me, but as I recall you were heavily in debt and behind on your payments. I do not think your reference would help."

Drew laughed too. "Perhaps not."

Caro chose another roll and began buttering it, as though she was not even aware of the conversation.

Rob was to initially stay in John's London property, but from there he intended to search for an apartment suitable for a bachelor. He did not really wish to stay at John's, living on even more of John's largesse, but when he was there at least he would have the house to himself.

Five weeks ago he'd been excited. Yet now there was Caro… Confusion marred the exuberance he ought to feel, and guilt rested heavily in his stomach. It was a tug of war. He did not wish to leave her, yet he did not wish to stay, and there was no option in between.

He hoped he had not hurt her. The numerous apologies and forgiveness they'd shared ran through his head.

He hoped she understood.

"I could ask my friends to help you find somewhere if you wish?"

Rob sighed and looked back at Drew. He liked Drew; he thought of him as a brother, but Rob did not need mollycoddling. That was what he wished to escape.

"Thank you for the offer, but I am one and twenty. I am capable of finding somewhere to live. I will manage on my own, just as well as you did at my age."

Drew laughed again. "Sorry, it is just you are Mary's little brother and you seem like mine. But at your age I suppose I would not have welcomed anyone's intrusion either. Yet if you need us we are only a couple of hours away, and you may visit whenever you wish. You need not even give us a warning."

Rob smiled as if he were grateful, yet he would not come here, not now, because he had let himself become too close to Caro. He could not simply visit.

"Caro." He looked at her. "Do you wish to ride out somewhere today?" He should speak to her. He should apologise again and say a private goodbye.

"It is a bit hot for the horses," Drew commented, "They'll be run ragged in yards. It's too humid. You should have gone earlier."

"But we can ride out directly after tea, in the late afternoon. It will be cooler by then." Rob kept his gaze on Caro.

She did not look up.

"Caro? What do you say, do you wish to go?"

Her gaze finally lifted and her eyes were gold. "Yes. That would be nice."

He gave her a conciliatory smile, then beckoned the butler to poor him more coffee.

~

Caro watched Rob beckon the butler. It was his last day.

Her heart felt like stone, it hung so heavily in her chest. Tomorrow it would crack. But she couldn't help herself. She still wished to spend these last hours with him.

She'd been unable to look at him during breakfast—afraid tears would catch her out. But as the morning progressed she found an excuse to be wherever he was. He smiled at her often.

Mary suggested they eat a picnic outside beneath the plain tree at luncheon.

Caro sat with Mary and watched Rob as he and Drew played cricket with George in the shade. Rob threw the ball to George's bat, while Drew helped George hit it further than he could alone.

While they ate, Rob sat near Caro, speaking with Mary as George climbed onto his lap. George was going to miss Rob too.

Rob took Iris from Mary once she'd been fed and walked about with her until she fell asleep against his shoulder. Then he walked back up to the house, with Mary, to take Iris up to the nursery.

He was close to Mary. He would come to visit again. Yet what if that were awkward—if he came to visit Mary and did not wish to see her?

"You are going to miss him."

Caro looked at Drew. He was sitting beside her, his back resting against the tree trunk, while George lay on top of Drew's legs asleep, with a thumb pressed in his mouth.

"Yes. I am grateful to him. He forced me to face the things I have been hiding from and helped me feel normal again. I feel less like a leech with Rob here."

"A leech…" Drew frowned, his fingers brushing through George's hair.

"I am a parasite. I am completely reliant on you. I do not enjoy it and I'm sure given the choice, you and Mary would rather be alone."

"We would not. Ask Mary. She does not think that. You are no parasite, Caro. You may remove that notion from your head. You are my sister, a part of my family. We love you, and the children adore you. You are welcome for as long as you wish to be here. This is your home as much as it is mine."

But it was not. It was his home. It still felt as though she was lodging here. She looked across the lawn. "It was how Rob persuaded me to dine with you. He said that he felt awkward when it was just the two of you. That is how Rob sees things too."

"But, as you well know, he only said it to get you downstairs. He did not say it to make you feel uncomfortable when he has gone."

"I feel uncomfortable anyway. I did not need him to tell me that I do."

"Caro…" Drew's fingers touched hers. "Do not condemn yourself about living in my home. You are welcome here—very welcome."

"I know, Drew. I'm sorry. I am grateful for all you do for me. But I will miss Rob. I do not feel so like an interloper with him here."

"I'll talk to Mary. If you are happy to receive company, perhaps we should invite people here more regularly, so you may establish your own social life and then you will not feel so awkward with us."

She gripped the hand that had reached out to her. "Thank you. I would like that."

~

When the hour came for their ride and Caro walked into the stable courtyard, Rob was tightening the saddle's strap underneath the horse that Caro was to ride.

His throat dried when he saw her.

She wore a dark-blue riding habit that was tight over her bosom and trim at her waist. It looked new. He'd not seen it before. He hoped it meant she would continue to ride when he left.

He straightened up as she walked towards him, her legs kicking out her skirt. She must be sweltering wrapped up within the layers of velvet and undergarments. It was long past midday but the air was still heavy with heat. He had not even worn his morning coat, nor gloves or a hat, and he'd even rolled up his sleeves to his elbows.

She had, at least, left her hat off too and her hair was pinned up in one big, swirling knot at the back, with a few stray curls framing her face.

"Caro." They'd spoken very little all day.

She would miss him. But then he would miss her.

Does she wish to ask me to stay?

The unspoken question hung in the air as she reached him. He respected her more for not asking. He could not make that choice.

He bent and clasped his hands together, to form a step. She lifted her skirt and placed the sole of her boot in his palms, then gripped his shoulders and pressed down onto his hands. He boosted her up into the saddle.

For a moment he laid his hand on her thigh, gently bracing her while she settled and took her reins.

He left her in the care of the groom, then, and mounted his own horse.

His carriage horses whinnied in their stalls.

Perhaps he should have taken her out in his curricle. They could have talked more easily, but they probably both needed the release of a gallop across the fields.

He looked at Caro and smiled as he tapped his heels and rocked his pelvis forward to set the horse into a walk. She drew alongside him.

Over the last weeks they'd found numerous topics on which to converse, but now he could think of nothing to say.

When they left the courtyard Rob noticed the colour of the sky in the distance, it was a hazy brown-grey. It looked as though the hot weather was about to break, but a good rainfall would freshen the air and it would make it easier for him to travel tomorrow.

He looked at Caro. She must be so hot in her habit. "I feel sorry for you riding in a habit in this heat. I have heard some women ride in breeches."

She glanced at him, smiling. "I would not."

He laughed. No, he could not imagine it. She was too delicate for such rash behaviour. *I will miss her.*

He should regret their kisses, but he did not. He would not forget this summer. It felt as though he had laid the foundations of his life. He'd been content here in a way he'd never been before… All they had left was this, an hour alone, and one evening with Drew and Mary, and then this summer would be over.

The tug of war burst into life in his chest: sadness because he would be leaving here and leaving Caro, and excitement because tomorrow he would ride to London to begin his journey to discover where his life would take him. The future was a canvas for him to paint. He could not regret his need to leave any more than he did not regret his time with Caro. He'd respected her, admired her, and then he had discovered a bond he'd known with no other woman—it was so much more than friendship. So the time they had left was time to be savoured before they must say goodbye.

Caro lifted into a trot and led the way along the drive. She turned to the left when they reached the road, heading towards the home farm.

There was nothing to say and so they rode in silence, in single file, on the edge of the road, as occasional carts passed.

When they reached the farm, they had a choice: to follow a track into the woods, which was on Drew's land, or to turn into the home farm pasture fields which led on to John's land. Caro rode on through the farmyard, then urged her horse to jump the gate into the field.

Rob kicked his heels and urged his horse to follow. Once he'd leapt the gate, he pulled up. She had stopped on the far side.

"I want to ride on the Duke's land. I want to gallop."

He nodded and kicked his heels again when she set off into a canter. They could not gallop on the farm land. It would scare the cattle and the sheep.

The perfume from her hair carried on the warm air and grasped at his senses as she took the lead. Lavender. Her pace created a breeze and so he rode close to her.

Her arms looked even more slender than normal in the dark habit.

Their horses' hooves thudded on the ground, a rhythmic sound that filled the humid, dense air.

The sky was becoming the colour of worn, stained linen, but Caro showed no sign that she wished to turn back.

They rode parallel to the wood on the other side of the rough stone wall that enclosed the field. In places, the wood was the boundary between John's and Drew's land, and the wooden gate ahead of them that had been put in when Drew and Mary had brought the land, led from Drew's pastures onto John's parkland.

Caro rode ahead and bent to open the gate rather than jump it.

It was unlike her to lead him on to John's land. He'd always opened the gate before, but then they'd ridden this way several times.

He leaned down and pulled the gate closed behind them.

She was already kicking her heel to urge the mare she rode

133

into a gallop. He followed, giving his stallion its head, balancing on the stirrups and hovering above his saddle.

They were riding through the parkland on which John's deer herd grazed, but the deer were not in view.

He did not race, but kept a pace behind her, in case her mare hit a rabbit hole and came down.

The air felt even denser here. Their horses cut through it as the sky above them became a broad sheet of stained linen. Still neither of them held back. He did not have the heart to end their ride and clearly Caro did not wish to.

Their hoof beats struck the ground, hard and heavy; a deep sound muffled by the turf as they sent clods of grass and soil flying in their wake.

They still hadn't spoken and yet just to be beside her, sharing a moment of freedom, felt good. He'd given this to her; she had not ridden for years until he'd invited her.

An unmistakable rumble of thunder shook the air. He hadn't seen the lightning but it must have been there somewhere in the distance. It would be a death wish to keep the horses out in a thunderstorm.

He leaned across and gripped Caro's reins, pulling his own too, but he only gripped them for an instant to slow her, then he left her to pull to a halt as he managed his own horse.

"We'll turn and head back to the woods. Hopefully the horses will not be spooked there and we can shelter."

The sky was no longer a linen colour. It was angry, dark and ominous. But there was still that brown hue to it that said there was thunder in the air.

Caro spun her mare around and headed for the wood. He thought she would smile at him, but she did not. She merely stirred the mare into a gallop again as if she tried to outrun him, yet he thought perhaps it was not to race, but to escape the emotion of their goodbye. These were their last moments alone together.

Another clap of thunder roared through the sky.

Caro's horse whinnied and reared its head, slowing suddenly, but Caro held her seat and tried to calm it. The animals were more sensitive. They must be able to smell and feel the storm in the air.

"Steady," he urged Caro when she pressed on, but she didn't ride any slower.

A bright light split the sky above them, stretching from behind them as the air vibrated with a deep growl.

He gripped his reins hard and held his horse steady as it made a sound of discomfort.

Caro held her horse firmly, but a muscle flickered in her animal's neck when another flash lit up the sky to their left. The thunder cracked a couple of moments later.

His horse thrust its head up against the bit. "It's fine, boy. Keep calm." Rob patted the animal's neck.

They raced over the grass heading towards the wall. The quickest way into the woods was to jump it.

They were nearing the wall when the next flash came from their right. The thunder was fast on the back of it, and it sounded as though the sky splintered. Both animals missed a stride, their forelegs landing out of rhythm, but he and Caro urged them on regardless, and Rob prayed there would be no thunder as they jumped.

A large drop of rain fell on his crown, then a second on his shoulder, and a third on his arm. Then there were too many to count. It was as though the rain had been shaken out of the cloud, and now it poured down, drenching his hair and his clothing.

They had a dozen yards left to ride when the rain turned to hail. Sharp balls of ice dropped like stones, stinging and cold. He pressed ahead, lifting his stallion's head and jumping the wall.

He looked over as he leaned back when his horse landed. Caro was a pace behind him and she flew over the wall in a perfect jump.

They had about four strides before they hit the woodland. They both pulled on their reins as the hail turned back into rain.

Caro was soaked. Her hair clung to her head and her face,

while her wet habit defined every curve of her body. The rain dripped from her nose and her chin. Her mare moved restlessly, fractious. "Jump down, Caro." Rob was nervous the animal would shy and unseat her.

His stallion side-stepped, just as uncomfortable.

He lifted a leg over his saddle, then jumped down to the grass, while Caro slid off her saddle and dropped to the ground.

Another flash split the sky above of them and, almost immediately, the thunder shook the air. Caro's mare reared and she fought to keep a hold of the reins.

He gripped her hand to help her, then caught hold of the reins closer to the animal's bit. He left the animal to Caro to keep steady once it had calmed.

A sharp wind swept at the treetops and the branches swayed, spooking the horses even more, while the rain still poured down on them.

He was soaked. His cotton shirt was translucent, revealing the hair that covered his chest beneath it.

"Come on." He led the way into the woods. "It should only be a few yards through the undergrowth and then we should pick up the track."

Under the trees the rain did not fall so heavily but dripped onto them from the canopy of leaves.

When they reached the track, another flash brightened the sky, and a minute or so later the thunder shook the trees. The animals tugged on their reins. He stopped and turned to calm his horse. Caro stroked her mare's muzzle and whispered to it.

Rob looked around. "Is there anywhere to take shelter here?" They were miles away from the house.

"There's an old charcoal-burner's cottage somewhere in the woods. It's never used now. It's somewhere off the track, but I don't know where."

"Come on, then, let us try to find it. Right or left?"

"Left. I would guess it would be nearer the pastures."

It was still raining. A shower of raindrops tumbled from the rustling leaves, blown down by the wind. He shook his head, shaking the water from his hair like a dog.

"It's there. Look. I see it." Caro pointed further along the track.

He could see it through the trees. It was just a small, white-washed single-storey hut.

A flash brightened the sky, and then it was as if the sky had been torn open as the thunder cracked and shook the trees. His horse tried to rear, but Rob held it tight while Caro settled her mare.

"Come on, fellow, keep going." Rob led his stallion into the clearing before the hut.

There was a lean-to on the side of it, which was broad enough to stable the horses. He walked his stallion over to it. The animals would at least be out of the rain, and perhaps feel more secure. He tied his reins onto a wooden post in the frame. Water dripped from his hair as he released the girth strap under the horse's belly, then pulled off the saddle. Then he turned to release the girth strap on Caro's horse.

He lifted the saddle off her mare while she secured the animal's reins.

When she'd finished, she stood to one side, out of the way of the horses, her arms clutched across her chest.

"Let's go inside." He held her arm, led her back out into the rain and around to the front door of the hut. The door swung open when he pushed it. He urged Caro to go in first.

The hut had a dirt floor, and there was only a single cot-like bed and a small table in the room. The fireplace stood empty. It was a simple labourer's hut.

Caro's eyes were wide as she looked around. She turned to him and breathed in heavily.

The sharp, sudden thirst he'd become used to with her gripped at his throat as she lifted to her toes. Her fingers clasped the back of his neck to pull his head down. "I apologise to you now," she said against his lips.

"You're forgiven," he said in the moment before their kiss began. This would most likely be their last kiss. He would treasure these moments with Caro for his whole life.

She pressed against him, her tongue dancing around his with more urgency than it had before.

His hands slid down the back of her wet habit and braced her bottom, holding her against him. The damp, heavy velvet crushing in his fingers.

Another flash and another clap of thunder shook the hut, but it did not matter now that they were in the shelter.

Her arms wrapped about his neck.

The heaviness in his groin solidified and his erection pressed against his trousers and her stomach.

He kneaded her bottom through the layers of cloth as the thirst he'd known the night she'd come to the library raged in his blood. Yet today he'd had no liquor. Perhaps his intoxication had only ever been due to Caro.

She broke the kiss and looked into his eyes. Hers shone like deep, light amber. "Touch me." As she spoke she pulled at the damp cotton either side of his stomach, trying to free his shirt from his trousers.

Lust screamed for far more. He cupped her breast. It filled his palm and his fingers splayed as he kneaded the damp cloth and her flesh beneath it, remembering the feel of soft skin, as his mouth pressed down on hers.

Her fingers tugged at his soaked shirt and pulled it from his trousers. Then her fingers touched his waist, holding on in a way that said the words she had not spoken, *don't go.*

She broke their kiss again. "May we lie down?"

Yes. All he wished to do was lay her back and move between her legs, but that would be wrong, he was leaving within hours.

He kissed her temple, then nodded, silenced by thoughts he should not consider.

"Would you help me remove the coat of my habit, it's

uncomfortable." She was breathing heavily and her hands were shaking as she began freeing buttons. He took over the task, then helped her peel it off.

She wore only a chemise beneath it. She must have left off her corset due to the heat. Her chemise was wet too; it clung to her dark-pink nipples and stuck to the curves of her breasts.

A sensation tore through his chest to his stomach, then grasped in his groin. It was lust... Harry's addiction.

Rob's was Caro.

He leaned forward, gripped the back of her neck and kissed her hard as he backed her towards the bed, his tongue thrusting into her mouth.

"Wait." She stopped him as they reached the rustic wooden frame, and freed the small buttons at the front of her chemise too. When she'd finished it hung open, revealing the amber cross she wore and the first curve of each breast.

When she lay down the little cross slid over her skin. "You have held back and not touched me since the night of the dance. I do not wish you to hold back. Touch me as you did then." He stood over her as she lifted her skirt to make it easier for him to lie between her legs. The bed was only wide enough for them to lie together.

Once her skirt was above her knees, she caught hold of his hand and pulled him down, bringing his hand to her breast. "This is what I want."

Need clasped tight in his chest as he gently brushed the wet cotton aside and looked at the swell of her bosom.

He knelt between her parted legs on the stiff, uneven straw mattress.

His imagination cried out for him to do a hundred different things as he leant forward and held her breast, then brought her nipple to his mouth while his hair dripped water onto her skin.

Her breast had become cold.

She sighed into the air above his head.

Her fingertips ran across his back and combed through his

damp hair.

Outside, another flash lit up the sky, but the rumble of thunder came long after.

He sucked her breast, nipping it with his teeth, then licking, revelling in the textures.

She arched beneath him.

"Rob, take off your shirt. It's wet and uncomfortable."

Her words broke him from a trance. He let her nipple slip from his mouth, before straightening up to kneel between her thighs, looking down at her.

It still poured with rain outside.

His bottom rested on the heels of his boots, as he pulled his shirt off and left it on the end of the bed. Caro lay before him, with her chemise parted over her breasts, and her thighs parted beneath her skirt. She offered herself like a sacrificial gift. He leant forward, gripping the straw mattress beside her shoulders and pressed his lips onto hers.

Her breasts brushed against the hair on his chest, part soft skin and part wet cotton.

His hand cradled her head and the other clasped the flesh of one breast while their tongues caressed and played.

His instincts—the dry need in his throat and lust in his groin—called his mouth back to her breast. Her body lifted, pressing up as he caught her nipple on his tongue, then sucked it fiercely.

Caro's fingers ran over his back and then down to the waist-band of his trousers. The tips of her fingers slipped beneath it as she pressed her hips up against his erection, sounds of enjoyment breaking from her throat.

The lust and thirst inside him gathered like the storm. He let her nipple slip from his mouth, raised himself up and stared down at her as her hips fell back to the mattress. "We should cease this."

"No." Her head shook, crushing her damp, darkened, golden hair against the mattress while her eyes begged him to continue.

"It can be nothing more than this."

Her lips and her nipples had become a deeper pink.

"I know, but I don't ask you to hold back and yet you do?"

"Because I have a conscience and I believe in holding fast to morals."

"Forget them." Her eyes were liquid, pools of emotion. "Just this once. These are our last moments, we will not have this chance again." … She was part naked beneath him and he was half naked above her.

His body cried out for him to listen and let go.

Her hand reached down between them and freed a button that secured his flap. He caught hold of her hand to stop her freeing the next.

Her eyes had looked at what she was doing, but now she looked at him. "Let me. Let us…"

He breathed out heavily.

Lust was a drug, it was heady and confusing; it made his blood thick and his skin hot and his mind a pulp.

"Let me, Rob, there will be no harm done. I am not an innocent, young woman." Her words pierced through his chest, but he would not tell her why.

I am innocent…

The sound of the rain on the roof filled his consciousness as he breathed hard while his idealistic nature fought against the thirst grasping at the back of his throat.

"Let go. It is what I desperately want. Let us have this memory."

He eased the grip on her hand and it slipped away to free the next button on his trousers, and the next. He felt in pain, conquered. He could not fight this anymore. He did not wish to.

Her hand clasped his flesh as her gaze held his. He'd dreamed of such things since their night in the library and woken up amidst sweat-dampened sheets.

He leant forward, lowered his head, and kissed her as her small hand held him tighter and slid up, then down.

She was so fragile and slender beneath him.

Her thumb brushed across his tip and his whole body jolted. *Damn.* He did not wish to hold back. He thrust into her hand, sliding through her fingers, then withdrew from them, while his breath released into her mouth.

Her other hand began raising her skirt.

He took over the task, wondering how far they would let this go. He cupped her bottom through the thin layer of her damp underwear as he thrust through her fingers again and again, the heat in his blood rising, and the pulp in his brain thickening, confusing his thoughts.

"Take off my underwear."

How far did she wish him to go?

He broke their kiss and his forehead fell against hers, as he clung to sanity, with his eyes closed... "Would you have me be entirely indecent?"

"Yes." Her fingers held him, as though she treasured him.

He opened his eyes and lifted his head.

Her gaze begged. "Just this once."

His heart pounded like a piston in his chest.

Just this once. His body ached for it.

He knelt onto his heels once more, his erection bouncing as his trousers hung open. The dryness of the carnal thirst clutched at the back of his throat with desperation.

He leant and pulled loose the ribbon which secured her drawers, then she began sliding them off her hips. He gripped the wet cotton covering her thighs and pulled it away, taking her drawers off her legs as she raised them to allow it, and stripped them off over her short boots.

When he looked at her, a breath left her lips.

She was perfect. The dark-blue velvet of her skirt was bunched up about her waist, and the contrast between her golden curls and her pale legs was beautiful.

The back of his fingers ran up her inner thigh as he remained kneeling before her, stripped to the waist, with his trousers loose and his flesh exposed. He touched her between her legs, exploring with the tips of his fingers.

She closed her eyes.

He dipped his fingertips within her; she was hot and moist. He slid two fingers deeper within, and she sighed, her mouth opening. It remained open as he withdrew his fingers, then pushed them in once more in a gentle stroke.

"What happens when I visit here again?" he said, as his fingers moved within her and his body longed for what might come next "When I visit John or Mary? How will we be with one another after this?"

Her eyes opened. They still begged him. "We will be friends. But I do not wish to think of it now. I have no expectation beyond this. I am not asking you to stay. I know you cannot. I do not even expect loyalty. I know you have a life to live. I just want this, Rob. I have missed it since my marriage ended, and I care for you, and I want to experience this with you."

Cared for… He cared for her too. But care was not the hard, elemental feeling gripping in his gut. That was lust. Hs fingers played with her. "I cannot make promises—" This did not feel honourable, and yet she was offering herself and he had senti-mental feelings too, something had fermented like yeast between them in the summer and now it was intoxicating.

"I am not asking for promises."

His fingers slid out of her and he watched the movement, then slid his fingers back within her warmth.

"This is what you will do in town. You will have affairs there, before you settle. So why not now, with me?"

She was still trying to persuade him, but he no longer needed to be persuaded.

His fingers worked more steadily as he watched what he did, she closed her eyes and arched upward, her breasts rocking. Then she bowed back and pushed her hips up towards his intrusion.

Weeks ago he'd hoped to see her laugh and wished to see her

dance, he had seen how happy she was then, and now this… This was in a league beyond happiness; this was ecstasy.

He leant and kissed her between the legs, he'd never imagined a woman could look so pretty and delicate there. His hands held her thighs. They were made of the softest flesh, but the flesh between her legs was silk and velvet.

Her fingers could not reach him. Instead she touched herself, her fingertips playing around his tongue. He kissed one of her fingers, then kissed her flesh, then sucked her fingertip when she offered it to him to taste.

Chapter 15

She'd begged outrageously, as though she had no pride. She did not even know herself, she was behaving so badly. But she'd watched him all day, longing to feel like this. She'd missed this and she wished to make a memory with Rob.

The look in his eyes confused her as he lifted up, then came down over her. His eyes dark.

He kissed her again, his tongue slipping into her mouth then withdrawing. Then his lips brushed over hers while his fingers stroked between her legs and slid inside her. She reached down and clasped him, as she'd done before, a feeling of satisfaction and longing racing in her blood; her body recalled all the sensations of lying with a man.

He kissed the edge of her lips, her cheek and then her neck. "You're beautiful," he said against her skin.

He had no need to say it. She knew he thought it. His touch and his eyes had said it a dozen times.

This felt as it had with Albert in the beginning. Rob's physical expression spoke of utter adoration. Yet it was different, because Rob's touch was so tender and gentle. Albert had never been gentle.

A storm gathered in her blood—and she could enjoy this without guilt because Rob was a good man. She had no need to berate her body. He was beautiful inside as well as outwardly. She had no need to feel shame because she was failing in her marriage, or fear that she might fail again and displease… This was only about this physical moment of escape to ecstasy.

She pressed the heels of her boots into the lumpy mattress and thrust up against his invasion as her fingers gripped him more firmly and licked her dry lips.

He gently bit the skin covering her shoulder as she tilted back her head, arching against him. Warmth and longing… spiralled through her, to the place where his fingers stroked her.

Albert had taught her what men liked. She knew how to please Rob and she knew how to please herself. She let go of him and felt where his fingers invaded, gathering her moisture and then her fingers spread it over his tip. Rob shuddered as a groan escaped his throat.

What happens when I come here again?

It would probably be nothing. He would find another woman, and any affection he held for her would wither, as Albert's affection had. She was cherishing this moment. She would probably never lie with a man again, and any fear of future embarrassment would not hold her back.

Each time this endearing young man came here she would have this moment to remember.

She focused on every sensation he engendered, pressing her heels into the mattress and pushing up against the invasion of his fingers. She had longed for this for years. Her bed had been the loneliest place since her marriage had ended.

~

Rob's mind was a fog of dense emotions and his blood ran heavily in his veins. It thickened like the air before the storm.

He appreciated every essence of Caro, the salty taste of her skin, the moist silk between her thighs, the sound of her whimpers of pleasure, and the scent of her heated skin. It was not only lust

146

that led him on, there were other emotions warring in his chest—respect, admiration and love, perhaps.

But love was a foolish thing to feel; this could be nothing. *You will have affairs there, before you settle. So why not now, with me?* He had never thought about setting up an intrigue with a woman—it would be immoral and damage his political aims.

This was immoral and would damage his political aims if it were ever discovered… Perhaps lust had made him insane, and yet he did not try to stop.

The muscle in her thighs shivered and the brush of her fingers egged him on as she touched herself, gathering more moisture to share with him. He knelt up, pulling away so she could not reach to touch him. He did not wish his end to be in her hand.

She smiled, then shut her eyes, and touched herself.

He amended his rhythm to match hers, watching her fingers, and watching his own enter her vivid pink flesh, pushing in, then pulling out.

Her body jolted when his fingers reached their full extent inside her, and her mouth opened, releasing a breathy sound of gratitude. His fingers withdrew then slid back, seeking the spot that had made her gasp.

She clasped his wrist as a sharp sound escaped her throat, and then her body pulsed about his fingers as the heat inside her broke into fluid. She bit her lip and her back arched, her head pressing into the mattress.

His fingers slid out of her, then ran along her inner thigh until they reached her stocking top, leaving a trail of her moisture.

He gripped the mattress beside her hips and leant to lick the trail of moisture from her thigh, then moved his hands, walking them up the bed either side of her until they pressed into the uneven straw in the mattress beside her shoulders.

The air between them was as humid as it had been before the storm.

She opened her eyes. His gaze held hers.

"Come into me."

He'd intended to, he was simply savouring the moment. Her damp skirt was bunched at her middle, and her chemise parted, open at her breasts, and she still wore her stockings and boots.

Will she think me gauche?

His heartbeat echoed in his head and his groin.

Caro had truly been a phantom when he'd come to Drew's; she had only shown people a shadow of herself. This strong, vibrant, passionate woman was the one who'd been hiding within her glass walls.

The mattress dented as the heels of her boots pressed down and her pelvis lifted, urging him to continue. Her hands gripped his shoulders.

God, he would never be able to come to John's and ride out and not think of this. He looked down and rested himself against her silk-soft skin, ready to press in, then looked up. "Caro."

Her eyes opened.

"I will apologise now." But saying that was not enough, this was not a kiss. "There will be no going back from this, if you regret, will you forgive—"

"I will not regret," she breathed up at him, "and you have my forgiveness now."

Ah damn. He was no better than his brother and his cousins at heart.

He pressed into her. It was a swift, glorious glide as his sensitive tip was absorbed in her heat.

He withdrew, then thrust back inside her, looking down to watch. The muscles in his thighs and his buttocks worked as he moved. It was like baptism, like being ducked beneath the water.

He looked back up at her eyes. She had been watching him, looking at him with the wonder that he felt for her.

He pressed in more firmly, pushing to the hilt.

A slight sound escaped her throat.

He withdrew, then did the same again.

There was another sound.

She liked the movement; that was what her sounds expressed. In the last weeks he'd helped her, encouraged her to learn how to be free and do as she wished—now he'd become her pupil.

She cried out as her fingers clasped his buttocks and urged him to move more vigorously. He did as she encouraged, sinking into her with heavy strokes that hit her pelvis and rocked her breasts.

Her eyes were shining and her lips swollen, a vivid red.

Her breaths stirred the hairs over his chest as he pushed into her and the air left her lungs every time he invaded her.

She bit her lip.

He lowered his head and nipped it too, with his lips not his teeth.

She laughed, as he continued moving, her hands moving up and down his arms, and over his chest, then down to his abdomen following the arrow of narrowing hair, to his stomach.

Her fingertips touched his innards, not just his skin. He felt her in his bones and in his blood.

"Move faster." Her feet lifted and her boots gripped the back of his thighs over his trousers.

He moved more heavily and more swiftly. Her eyes shut, her head pressing back onto the mattress,

"Ah." The sound from her lips was heavier and sharper too. "Oh."

It was blissful. Beautiful. The movement clawed at him, the pressure of her boots on his thighs, and her fingernails grasping at his shoulders. He looked down and watched himself be buried within her. Sensations quickened inside him, gripping in the pit of his stomach. His storm was going to break. His breath came in the same pattern of shallow pants as hers, and there was sweat on his skin.

"Ah," Caro cried out, her warmth flooding about him, as her body pulled at his, urging him for something more, something natural.

A long breath dragged into his lungs as heat clenched within his groin, catching a hold of him, squeezing hard and pulling his muscles taught. *Oh Lord!* He spilled his soul inside her. *The devil.*

He shut his eyes and held on as the sensation spun through his blood, tangling up about each nerve, it was as though a tide swilled within his limbs. It captured hold of everything and held him away from the world.

Hell.

But it was not hell it was heaven—although hell would probably be where he would be going for doing this.

He breathed heavily and his arms shook as he tried not to collapse like a fool on top of her.

Her fingers stroked his fringe from his brow. It fell back.

He withdrew, let his weight fall and lay half over her, breathing heavily, as her fingers continued to comb through his hair. He should have withdrawn earlier and protected her from the possibility of a child.

He lay still, his mind full of pulp, trying to make sense of the things he'd done and felt.

Emotion tied tight knots in his chest, emotion that did not feel as though it was to do with the sensations he'd enjoyed as they'd played.

Perhaps this was love?

~

Caro lay still, pinned down by Rob's weight, spent and exhilarated, listening to his breathing slow, while she combed her fingers through his hair. She was a lucky woman, to have won the attentions of such a beautiful, honourable young man.

He'd taught her so much about herself.

She had revered the physical love she'd shared with Albert; held it up and placed it on a pedestal and looked up to it as the most perfect part of her life, because in their bed he'd always been her lover, absorbed in her and attentive. She had even used it as a reference to put her current life under a shadow of guilt and shame. She had felt that all the failings of her marriage were hers. She had lost the children. She had not satisfied him enough in their bed that he had gone to others...

Then she'd discovered Rob and he'd cut through the shadows that surrounded her—a ray of sunshine.

And now he'd taught her what it truly was to be cared for and appreciated in a physical sense.

The emotion in Rob's eyes had been deep with respect and compassion. She'd said at the beginning that she cared for him—he cared for her too, she had seen it. Albert had never cared, his eyes had only ever held a shallow look of lust. All he'd ever cared for was her body. Rob cared for her...

She looked at Rob's bent head and his steady breaths pressed his chest against her breasts.

I love you.

It was a fact, merely that. It could be nothing more than this. She had not asked for promises; she did not intend to. This was only a moment they had claimed in time. But she would hold it to her heart for the rest of her life.

Chapter 16

Rob twisted to his side, his shoulder pressing into the mattress beside hers, his hand slipping to rest at her waist, while his legs remained tangled up with hers. The straw in the mattress was uncomfortable and the thing smelt musty. Now that lust had left him he saw the entire cottage differently. It was dirty and sordid. They had lain here and done this on a soiled mattress, half-clothed, without even removing their boots.

He was no better than Harry.

He would have tumbled over and lain on his back but the narrow bed was not wide enough. Instead he pressed a kiss against her cheek, then grasped the waist of his trousers and climbed up off her, trying not to hurt or crush her as he did so.

Perhaps the scene was sordid, but her body was still beautiful. As she lay there half naked, sensations hummed and skipped through his blood.

His gaze lifted to the window. The rain had ceased and it looked as if the storm had passed over long ago. Mary and Drew would be awaiting them for dinner and wondering where they were.

"We had better go back." He looked down at her. His tongue itched to apologise and yet he had apologised before they'd begun and she'd forgiven him and said she would not regret it, nor ask him to make her any promises. There was nothing else for him to say.

Yet, he wished to make promises, they hovered on his tongue too.

He secured his trousers as she sat up.

But before she had chance to rise and restore her clothing, he leant and cupped her face with one palm. She lifted her mouth and he kissed her lips. "I love you," he said as he pulled away, "but I cannot—" The words had slipped from his mouth. He half believed them. They were the only way to express the sentiment inside him, and it had seemed so wrong to say nothing of his feelings after what they'd done.

"I have no expectation. I am not asking you to make promises you will not keep."

"I wish to make them, though." That was true. They burned in his throat. He did not wish to merely walk away. She was in his blood now. In his brain and in his bones.

"You said yourself you could not."

"I have nowhere to live, no livelihood—" He was questioning himself… He ached to make promises. Promises he could see no possibility of keeping. This had never been a part of his plan. He'd never intended to seek a wife.

"You are young and your life is ahead of you. I love you also, but I do not want this to take your life away from you. I expect nothing."

He held her gaze. What could he say? He wished to say more, to do more. He did not wish to leave her. The emotion cutting his chest in half had to be love. "Will you come to town with Drew and Mary in September? They will come for the autumn, they always do. Come with them. If you think you can cope. You would have to attend the entertainments, though, otherwise it would seem strange. Yet if you think you could, I would like you to be there. I do not want to leave you behind. But I cannot stay here and I cannot visit often. I need to be in town. I wish to become a politician, Caro. I have told no one in my family because it is something I wish to do without their help. You must not speak of it, please, and yet to achieve it, I must make connections in

153

London. I cannot stay here."

"You will make a wonderful politician, Rob, and perhaps a prime minister one day, and I will watch your success and be proud of you. I will say nothing to Mary or Drew, and I know you must go."

"But will you come to London?"

She looked at him for a long moment, as his fingers pressed against her soft cheek, pleading as much as she had pleaded for him to join with her. He wished her to come desperately—perhaps this was love…

It would take her courage and yet if she would not come, her feelings could not be as strong as his.

"Yes, I will come."

Gratitude, joy and pain ripped through him. He truly did not want to leave her, but now he would see her again in weeks, and perhaps, once he'd found the niche he searched for in the House of Commons, this might become something right and permanent, and less sordid.

"And you will write," he urged as his hand slipped from her cheek, and he reached for his shirt.

"No, it would be misunderstood. I am a divorced woman. If I write to a young bachelor even Drew would question it, and what would your family think?"

He pulled his wet shirt over his head, then slid it down. "They are your family too. You have no other."

The enormity of what they'd done washed over him. She ought to be like a sister to him, like a cousin. This had been wrong. Yet he did not care what his family thought. It was their choice. *I will not regret.* She had said those words with conviction, he did not regret either, and perhaps it would be something more, but for now it had to be their secret. He did not fear for himself but he would not risk his family's ill opinion being cast on her.

He'd thought himself no better than Harry when the lust had left him, but… No. He was not like Harry. Harry had definitely never thought about making a woman his wife after he'd bedded her and certainly Harry did not give a damn whether she was respected.

He looked at Caro as she struggled with the tiny buttons to secure her chemise.

"Then I will write things in letters to my sister, meant for you, and you will know to whom they are written, even though she will not."

Caro smiled as he reached for her drawers. "And I will ask her to mention me in her letters, and say things on my behalf."

His heart clenched hard in his chest, releasing a deep ache into his blood. Harry would have thought him a fool for saying that he loved her, but Rob did not think it a lie.

~

When Caro walked over the threshold of the house an hour later, her clothes rumpled and still damp, Rob held her hand in his, clasped behind her back.

It was a true home-coming, the first Caro had known in a very long time. It felt as it had done when she'd come to Albert's home from the church after her wedding in the little church on his estate, only this time there was no fear of what was to come in the marriage bed. This time her blood was alive and fresh from the marriage bed. She was still a little intoxicated from the feelings and she probably gazed at Rob with wonder and adoration when she glanced up at him in the moment before they let each other go.

She loved him. She was in no doubt.

And he'd said, *I love you.*

Yet she did not believe that.

He was honourable, kind and good, and he cared for her, she saw those things, but he was too young and elemental to be in love with her, there was too much in his life to draw him away from her. He'd said the words because he knew he ought to think them, and say them, in the wake of what they'd done. But she'd not needed to hear them.

155

She may have fallen for him, but she was not foolish enough to believe in a fairytale. She had learned how false they were from Albert. This time she was holding on to truth and not dreaming of happy endings, but merely enjoying what she had known—a moment of heaven.

Then tomorrow, when he left, she would refuse to be maudlin. She would see him in London in a few weeks because he had invited her there, and when she saw him she would remember this and treasure the memory, without hope for more, and learn to live a life where she might watch him, and recall it, without feeling regret.

Mary walked briskly into the hall from the morning room, a moment after they'd let each other go.

Heat flared beneath Caro's skin, a blush probably rising.

"I'm so glad you're back. We were worried. Drew was considering setting up a search party. Even poor George wondered where you'd got to when I tucked him in. We feared one of your horses had bolted or shied and one of you was hurt, waiting for us to find you… and you are soaked…"

"We sheltered in the charcoal-burners hut, and waited until the rain passed," Rob answered

And probably a good half an hour after that. She had not even noticed when the rain had stopped.

"Go to your rooms. I'll have baths sent up," Mary ordered. "The kitchen has the water ready. We expected you to arrive bedraggled. We will eat as soon as you come down, and it is your last night, Rob, so hurry—"

"So the wanderers have returned." Drew stood at the top of the stairs. "You owe my son a kiss goodnight, both of you. I've been sitting with him because he cannot sleep for wondering why he's not received a kiss from Auntie Caro or a story from his Uncle Rob."

"I'll come up, now. Was he scared by the storm?" Caro lifted her heavy, damp skirt and crossed the room to begin climbing the stairs. She had been selfish today.

156

"No, he thought it entertaining. I suppose you two had a lark, riding through it." The last was directed at Rob, yet even so the heat in Caro's cheeks intensified. She could not look Drew in the eyes for fear of giving herself away.

"Caro's horse panicked when a bolt struck overhead and mine shied. But we headed into the wood and dismounted, we are both unharmed."

She thanked God for Rob's choice of words. He did not think himself harmed by her selfishness then.

"And you have returned whole."

But that she was not, she had left a little piece of herself back in that hut, and another piece of her was held by Rob, and it would leave tomorrow. She walked past Drew and turned towards the next flight of stairs.

"I'll come and say goodnight to George, too."

Caro glanced down as Rob looked up, and he smiled at her. It turned her stomach to aspic.

Rob looked at Drew as Rob began ascending. "After all, it is the last night that I can."

Rob's words pressed like a little knife into her chest.

Chapter 17

Caro watched Rob throughout dinner and during the quiet evening in the drawing room that followed. They did not play cards, it was his last evening, and so Drew and Mary talked to him about his plans, and about their family, while Caro sat in silence.

She longed for a moment to speak to him privately as all the feelings that he'd engendered in the day still played through her nerves and ran in her blood. They shared a secret and occasionally he would glance at her and she would see their secret in his eyes.

Mary made him promise to look after himself, then suggested they retire as he was to leave early. They all stood.

Yet Caro did not want the evening to end. Tomorrow he was going. She wished today could last forever.

Her heart pounded as they walked from the room, and it felt as heavy as lead as she walked upstairs to her bedchamber while Mary and Drew said goodnight to Rob on the first floor landing where their rooms were.

Caro let the maid undress her and brush out her hair, then crawled into bed and lay on her side. Memories, images and feelings played through her head, as though he was with her and touched her now.

She had never expected to feel those things again, and this summer she'd laughed with him, danced with him and then lain with him. He would go, but he would leave behind a woman whom he'd helped to find herself again.

Her heart ached. It would break tomorrow. But he'd taught her that she could choose how to respond, she could mourn and shut herself away, or she could keep living as though nothing had changed. She would keep living because she'd promised him that doing what they'd done would not affect their future.

But she hadn't lost him yet. He was still in a room downstairs.

She sat up and threw the sheets back. They still had tonight. Why was she lying here in sorrow when she could be with him?

Her footfalls were soft as she walked over the floorboards, gripping her cotton nightgown and lifting the hem. It was dark, but she knew the house well enough to find her way.

The stairs creaked when she walked down them, her hand on the rail, but no one would hear. Drew's and Mary's rooms were at the farthest end of the first-floor landing.

Her hand followed the rail of the staircase. Then her fingertips trailed along the wall as she walked in the dark, trying to find the bedchambers.

The room Rob had been staying in was the first door on the opposite side to Mary's and Drew's.

She felt the doorframe and her hand fell to touch the brass doorknob.

Her heart skipped in a rhythm akin to the steps of a vigorous country dance when she knocked gently.

It must be barely half an hour since they'd retired. She hoped he was still awake.

~

A slight rap on wood pulled Rob into consciousness. He'd been thinking about Caro and drifting into sleep. The enormity of his day was a weight on his chest. But there was a tight pain in his groin too, as memories had played through his head.

159

The sound came again. Someone was knocking on his bedroom door.

He sat up, the sheet covering him slid to his waist. The air was not as warm since the storm had passed, but he had still come to bed naked—it was too hot for clothing.

The knock struck a little harder. "Rob." His name was whispered through the wood.

Caro.

"Come in," he called back.

The door creaked as it opened. He turned in the bed, rubbing his forehead as he tried to wake up. The room was pitch black, the night was cloudy and there was no light from the moon.

"Where are you?"

"Here, Caro."

Her soft footsteps and the sound of shifting cotton came towards him.

He ought to get up and cover himself, but he would be scrabbling about in the dark.

"I could not sleep," she whispered. "Do you mind?"

"No." He'd spent the entire evening sensing her watching him, aware they only had hours left. "I'm glad." He was, he refused to heed the guilt that lanced through his chest.

"But you were sleeping."

"Only lightly. I was tired."

"Do you wish me to go?"

"No," he stood up as he heard her before him, the sheet slipping over his skin, and he reached out, blindly.

He touched her shoulder.

"Rob." She took another step and came into his arms.

His fingers ran over her hair, it was loose, flowing down her back.

Her hair brushed against his chest as his head lowered and his lips found hers.

All evening his conscience had been challenging him, condemning him, and yet here he was again, looking into the eyes

160

of lust, faced with a trial. Lust won. He did not care for morals and idealism with Caro. He wished for another moment of bliss.

He gripped her nightgown and lifted it off over her head.

This time they were both entirely naked and yet it was too dark to see.

"Lay on the bed," he urged, his hand slipping over her naked hip. She moved beneath his touch, and his hand followed as they guided each other in the dark.

She smelt of lavender and the perfume lingered in the air as she moved.

He touched her leg to get his bearings and found the soft flesh of her inner thigh.

He sighed when her legs moved, opening for him. Then he knelt on the bed. The mattress dipped, rocking her leg and he imagined the sway of her breasts.

The memories from their moments in the cramped bed in that shabby hut flooded him in waves. His erection brushed her hip as he leant to kiss her and gripped one of her breasts. There was something very different about learning her body in the dark. It made his senses more alive. He let his fingertips run over every curve, gently tracing her body, drawing it in his memory and holding it firm. He wished to remember every detail of her when he'd gone.

In the early summer he'd watched her and seen something within her he didn't think others saw. Now he knew everything that no one else saw.

He'd always felt thirst with her, but now he felt hunger. His stomach was empty. His body had become a vacuum that wished to devour her. He wanted her with a lust that was all-consuming.

"I love you," he said the words over her mouth before pressing a kiss against her jaw. He was still unsure of the words, and yet they were the words on his tongue. They wished to be said.

"And I love you." Her echo of them lifted into the air above his head, with a depth of emotion that implied utter truth. They

161

stirred like a spoon in his soul.

His kisses followed the path of his fingers, learning her body with his lips and his tongue. Then he said against her breast. "I shall not apologise, not now or after, this is what we both wish for."

"Yes."

When his kisses ran across her stomach, he swept his tongue into her navel.

She sighed as he kissed below it, then trailed his tongue over the line of her hip bone, where it pushed against her soft skin.

His fingers skimmed over the skin of her thighs and he lowered his head and kissed the tender flesh there.

When he licked the velvety skin between her legs, she gripped his hair and arched up with a breathless sound of agreement.

His fingers ran down her leg to her heel, then he lifted her foot. Her foot pulled loose from his hand and her leg rested on his shoulder.

He was learning from her again.

"Rob." Her hands clutched his hair tighter and she rocked up against his tongue as it dipped within her and drew out, while his hand ran up the back of her raised thigh. Then he slid his fingers into her and used them as he had done at the hut, only when they withdrew he licked them and licked her.

"Rob." Her hips rocked against him in the rhythm of intercourse, as her fingers clung in his hair.

The tip of his tongue teased the little bead at the head of her flesh, which she'd touched in the hut.

A choked sound escaped her mouth, then a little groan as he did it again. His lips closed about it, and he kissed it, as his fingers worked. The sounds from her mouth slipped to the shallow pants of breath she had succumbed to at the end of their time in the hut. She was close to the little death.

"Will you suck me there?"

If she could see him in the daylight she might have seen him blush, to be told how to do this, and yet she had been married,

162

she knew more than him, and if he was to learn, let him learn from her. But God, it cut to think of her with someone else. He would not.

His lips closed about her and he sucked as he'd sucked her nipple.

"Ah." Her cry was harsh and long, as she broke onto his fingers, throbbing on the tip of his tongue.

When he rose up, over her, he felt like a king. There was no other feeling like this. Her hands gripped his shoulders as his hands pressed into the soft mattress either side of her.

He was baptised again when he sank into her, dipping his whole body beneath the water.

Caro made slight sounds as he moved, and her fractured breathing and shallow cries filled his room.

He moved swiftly and then slowly, pushing hard to a deep depth and then pressing in in shallow pulses, before rocking into her in a slow, long movement. He was learning—discovering every sense and sensation in the darkness—and all the time her hands ran over him and whimpers of breath left her lips as she broke beneath him and continued to pour fluid about him.

He was creating the foundation of their future. When she came to town in the autumn he hoped to have begun to fulfil his plan, and then he would make arrangements, even if it was to bind themselves with an engagement until he could offer her more. But until then they had this to hold on to.

Her thighs gripped at his hips and her bare feet brushed over the back of his legs as her body arched into another spasm of release.

His weight still in his palms, he leant and found her head was turned. He pressed a kiss on her cheek. She turned her mouth to him and said against his lips. "I love you so much." The words seemed to echo through his soul, her voice was full of throaty emotion.

"I love you also." His response was flatter, and yet, in that moment, he was certain the words were true.

163

He rose up and thrust more heavily into her, his pelvis striking hers. Then he withdrew fully and thrust hard again. Her breaths and shallow sounds became little cries each time he entered her as he felt the storm sweep in about him, gathering in heat and heaviness, and tension, clasping in every muscle. Three last hard thrusts and then he pulled out of her and broke onto her stomach, pushing himself against her and breathing hard. He felt as if he stood beneath a waterfall, only the waterfall ran inside him, pouring through him.

When he returned from heaven, he rested his forehead against hers, his breathing hard and fractured.

"I love you very much also." It was true. He kissed her temple then tumbled to his back, his senses rioting and clamouring. He was utterly relaxed and sleep claimed him as Caro's head made a pillow of his shoulder. Her arm came over his chest and her leg slipped over his thigh.

Chapter 18

Rob woke as the grey light of dawn leaked through the curtains. Caro lay in his bed. She lay half across him, her head resting against his neck.

He breathed in and smelled the lavender perfume in her hair. Her hair was a darker, duller blonde in the half-light. He soaked up the feel of her as the room lightened in slow degrees.

But she could not stay. The servants would be waking.

His fingers brushed across her cheek. "Caro."

She didn't wake. He leaned up a little and let her slide from his shoulder, then pressed a kiss on her lips. "Caro."

Her eyelids flickered, then lifted.

His thumb brushed her cheek. "Good morning, sweetheart."

Her eyes were pools of liquid and her fingers came up and touched his cheek. "You are so beautiful."

"You are more so, especially half asleep." His fingers brushed beneath her chin. She blushed. "I love your eyes, Caro, they turn gold in daylight, but in the candlelight they're like amber."

She smiled.

"You may not believe it but I saw this for us at John's at the beginning of the summer. I saw you then and I saw a remarkable woman, a woman I wished to see laugh and dance, and now—"

"You will go to town and meet a hundred other women and

165

forget me."

"I will never forget you." She'd said she did not want promises and he needed to begin to fulfil his plan and make a living for himself before he would make them. If he made promises now he would become dependent on his income from John. He wanted a place for himself in Parliament, to make his own name in the world. To have some influence for the good of society. He had nothing to give her but his body at this moment. He was a penniless, dependent, no one. He would not offer her that. He brushed a lock of hair back from her brow.

Her eyes softened and then her gaze fell to his lips in an invitation.

"Caro, you need to go back to your room, darling, the servants will be up."

She sighed.

He laughed. "Much as I would love an encore too, you know it would be foolish. I know you do not want to be seen sneaking from my room."

"No." She began to rise, so he had to lift up, but he sensed sadness settle over her. He grasped her wrist. Stopping her.

Her pulse raced beneath his thumb.

"We will see each other in the autumn. It is only a few weeks until September."

She smiled at him. "I know. I am being selfish and wishing you need not go."

She slipped from his hold, rose and picked up her nightgown from the floor. He watched her place it over her head in silence.

Everything he ought to say was locked in his throat. He could not stay, and, Lord, if he proposed to her now where could he offer her for a home? A room in one of John's homes… That life would kill him.

The fabric sheathed her body.

He climbed from the bed, stood up and gripped her hands. "This will be our private goodbye. I will not be able to say it properly later, but you will know this is want I want to say before I go. I have fallen in love with you—"

"You will forget me the minute you reach town." It was as though she fought against his expression of his feelings. As though she was afraid to believe him. But she'd told him once that she'd thought her husband had loved her, and that his affection had died.

"I will not forget you and I shall look forward to seeing you when you come. You will still come?"

"Yes."

"Then trust me until then at least." He'd never experienced this before, he had no idea how deep his feelings ran compared to others, whether they would stand the test of time, and yet he did believe himself in love with her. The emotion inside him was in his heart and his soul, not just his groin and his gut.

She nodded, but her eyes shone with tears. He brushed one away with his thumb as it slipped from her eyelashes. "I will miss you."

"I will miss you too."

The light within the room had become white. She ought to leave him. But he would have no other chance to kiss her again. He clasped her head and brought her lips to his. They kissed for moments as she gripped his shoulders while his fingers ran into her hair.

He broke the kiss, promising her the only things he could. "I will write in hidden words to Mary, and you will come to town, and we will see each other then."

"We will," she nodded. But then her forehead fell against his shoulder in a silent plea that said *don't go*.

His arms wrapped around her and he held her for a moment more but, "Sweetheart, you need to leave."

"I know." She lifted her head, rose to her toes, and kissed his lips. "When I say goodbye later, I will want to kiss you but you'll know I cannot."

He nodded, tears gathering in his throat. This decision to come to Mary and Drew's had changed his life.

"I will go."

"I will see you downstairs in a while."

"Yes,"

She did not move, though.

He pressed another swift kiss on her lips. "Go, or I will have to carry you back to your room, and then if anyone sees us we would surely be damned."

She laughed, though it was a hollow sound. Then, at last, she turned away and crossed the room, the fabric of her nightgown whispering about her. When she reached the door she looked back. "Goodbye, Rob."

"I will see you soon downstairs, and listen for my words in Mary's letters."

She nodded, then turned, opened the door and left him. He sat down on the bed and rested his head in his hands, trying to get used to the thoughts in his mind and the feelings in his body. His life had changed entirely in hours. He would have to marry her, regardless of anything else. Morally he would never be able to live with himself if he did not. But there was emotion and affection between them, there was no doubt of that, and he felt it as love now, but their weeks of separation would be a test of that.

A test for both of them, because surely she could be no more certain than him that her feelings had not been affected by their intimacy, and yet she had said "I love you" last night in such a way that he'd believed it without doubt.

He was suddenly afraid of hurting her. He couldn't marry her and not show the affection and love she deserved.

Damn, he was tying himself in knots.

He did love her. Love was the emotion burning in his chest. He would explore all else when she came to London, when he would be in a better position to make choices over their future.

Chapter 19

Rob kept looking at Caro throughout breakfast and her gaze continually caught on his. Each time heat crept into her cheeks and she looked away.

Drew talked to her as he might any other morning, but this morning she could not find more than a single word to answer, so she responded with yes or no, or any slight acknowledgement, while her heart began to crack.

When they finished breakfast and the clock on the mantel rang out ten strikes, Rob and Mary stood. They left the room together as Drew rose.

When Drew walked past Caro his hand settled on her shoulder and squeezed it gently, then he leant to say, "You will miss him, but we will speak once he's gone and think of ways to draw you more into the local community. You need more friends, Caro. Things won't go back to the way they were."

She looked up and nodded. Then she stood and hugged him, as she had probably not done for years. She had three other half-brothers, but none of them had spoken to her since she'd been a child. But Drew had looked after her for most of her life; even as children he'd been the one she'd turned to.

She longed to be able to share with him how she felt, but that would put Rob in an impossible situation. Yet Rob had left a legacy.

Drew was right, she needed to be amongst people. She could not go back to feeling as she had done, she was reliant upon Drew but she need no longer be an emotional chain about his neck.

"Thank you." She pressed a kiss on his cheek.

"Mary and I do love you, you know. We do not begrudge you a thing."

"I know."

When they walked out into the hall her hand rested on his arm.

She clutched it more firmly when she saw the footmen carrying Rob's luggage out to his curricle.

"Papa! An'ie Ca'o!" She looked up. George was pulling on a nursery maid's hand as she walked him downstairs.

"Steady, George, you'll pull Lily over and then you will both topple down the stairs." Drew's arm slipped from Caro's grip. He crossed the room and met them on about the fourth step from the bottom, then caught his son up. "Come along, you little rogue."

"My Lord." Caro glanced up to see their nanny carrying Iris down.

"Come along, then, let us go outside and say goodbye to Uncle Robbie," Drew said to George.

Caro let Drew and the nanny walk ahead, her heart kicking. She did not want Rob to go.

He was speaking with Mary, watching as his luggage was loaded.

"Uncle Bobbie!"

Rob looked at George as Drew set George on his feet. Then Rob dropped to one knee, unmindful of the dirty gravel as George charged the short distance into his uncle's arms. Rob hugged him with a generosity and affection that was utterly at odds with his age. None of his male cousins of a similar age gave any regard to the young children. Rob was different, perhaps because he'd never known pain or hurt, or hardship, so he could be open without fear. But his cousins knew nothing of any of those things either and they had grown up self-centred and hedonistic.

It was that difference in him that had drawn her to him first.

When he stood he lifted George with him and looked at her. She smiled as her skin heated, then she looked at Drew instead.

"Will you come back, Uncle Bobbie?"

"Sometime," Rob answered, Caro looked at him again. His fingers tousled George's hair. "Or…" Rob looked at Drew, "Will I see him when you come to town in the autumn. Are you intending to come this year? I know you usually do."

"Probably, although we've not discussed it," Drew answered.

"We will, otherwise we have to wait until Christmas to see everyone," Mary concluded, as she took Iris from the nanny. "I want to see Mama and Papa, Andrew."

"Then we will," Drew said, with a note of humour.

"I suggested to Caro yesterday, that if you do, she should consider coming. It would be the final boundary broken if she did." Rob was looking at Drew, but his words were for her, he was tying her into their agreement.

It touched her to know he genuinely wanted her to go.

His gaze shifted from Drew to her and he smiled again.

Heat flooded her cheeks.

He looked at Mary and Iris and carried George over to join them. George's arm gripped about Rob's neck.

"Goodbye, little one," Rob touched Iris's cheek as she looked up at him. Then he leaned to kiss Mary's cheek. "Mary."

"If you need anything, Rob, you know you are always welcome here."

"I know." He straightened up.

"Would you like to pat my horses one last time, George?"

"Yes," George's voice brimmed with excitement.

Caro moved closer when Rob turned, as though she were metal and pulled by a magnet. Mary passed Iris back to the nanny.

Rob's presence had lit this house up; they were all going to miss him but Caro knew she would miss him the most. Her heart cracked a little more as she watched him lift George so he could pet the horses.

A groom held the horses' heads and the one George patted whinnied, shaking out its mane after George had stroked it, while the other pawed the ground.

"I like you' ho'ses," George said as he patted its neck.

"They are rather fine, aren't they?" Rob patted the animal's neck too, more firmly.

But his matching pair of horses only reminded Caro that away from here he led a young man's life. What she had said to him had been true. She had not wished for promises, she expected him to leave here and forget her, and she would not be bitter or hurt, she'd had this summer with him, and she'd shared his bed.

Drew walked forward and held out his hands to take George.

George transferred to his papa and clung about Drew's neck instead.

When Rob was gone she would hide her sorrow with the children as she'd always done. It would pass.

Mary stepped forward and hugged Rob, wrapping her arms about her brother's neck. Then she pressed a kiss on his cheek before letting him go. "Thank you for coming to stay, we have all enjoyed your company. I will miss you."

"Thank you for inviting me. It has felt like my own home for the summer."

Mary smiled and Rob turned to Drew.

"Goodbye." Drew stated, holding out a hand.

Rob shook it. "Goodbye. Thank you for your company, you have kept me entertained."

Drew laughed and patted Rob's shoulder.

Caro's heart thumped hard in her chest. It felt as though it would burst. This parting was too painful.

"Caro," he said, turning to look at her. She stepped forward. This was their very last moment. Her mind filled with the things he'd spoken to her this morning that he could not say here.

"Goodbye," she said in a quiet voice.

He gripped her hand and squeezed it for an instant, then he

bowed and lifted it to his lips, and the kiss on the back of her fingers seemed long, but it was probably only a moment. When he straightened he looked into her eyes. "Thank you for allowing me to come to know you."

She swallowed back the tears catching in her throat. "Thank you for giving me the courage to do more than I have done in years."

"The courage was always yours. You did not need me to show it to you."

Heat burned her skin. He let her hand go. "Goodbye."

She nodded, no longer able to speak. Her heart was going to shatter.

He turned and climbed up into his carriage. So athletic.

Her heart climbed up there with him.

He flicked the straps, setting the horses into a walk and lifted one hand.

"Goodbye." Mary and Drew called.

Caro waved.

Then they all stood there watching as he sped the horses up into a trot and the carriage rolled on down the drive. Her heart shattered the moment he passed out of sight, but she could not reveal her feelings and so she swallowed hard.

Mary's arm slipped through Caro's. "Would you like to sit outside with Iris and me?" She looked at Drew and George as Drew walked ahead. "Perhaps we could even persuade Papa to sit with us, George, and read us all a story?

Drew glanced over his shoulder. "Perhaps I may. Seeing as it is such a fine day and I fancy sitting beneath a tree. So are we calling for lemonade, then?"

"Hu'ah!" George cheered.

Mary laughed.

Rob had gone, and everything would slip back to how it had been. The hole he'd left would heal up. Except she would not let it go back to exactly how it had been. She intended to live differently, to meet and speak to people, and build a life for herself that would make her less of a burden on Drew and help her feel more self-respect.

When Mary let Caro's arm go to take Iris from the nursery maid, Caro glanced along the drive. She could feel the distance growing between them. *Goodbye, I love you, Rob, but I shall not hold you to anything. I am just glad that you came and you helped me, and that you gave me so much of yourself.*

"Caro." Drew called from the doorway.

She turned and forced a smile as she climbed the steps back into her old life. But not her old self.

She had felt ashamed and blamed herself for Albert's affection withering. This time she held no expectation of Rob's feelings lasting, and so she would not be hurt when they died, or transferred to another woman. She would merely hold onto the moments he'd been wholly hers, in memories.

Chapter 20

Rob's hands shook a little as they held the straps, when he steered his horses out of Drew's gateway and onto the road. He felt like a heel, and ashamed. He ought to turn back and make promises to her—offer to marry her, even if he had to say their engagement might be long. Yet he could not stand to do it, because he had too much pride. He did not have anything to offer her yet. He had his plan to fulfil and then he would be a man suitable to offer her marriage. But first he must make his name, do something of worth, and make a place for them in society.

But he had made himself a hypocrite he could no longer condemn Harry. At least Harry took his pleasures with the sort of woman who knew exactly where they stood. Harry only ever slept with women he paid. Harry did not defile genteel women. Rob had taken his pleasure within the very heart of his family. His father would kill him if he knew he'd done this and made no promise.

Yet he did intend to make a promise, once he was set up. But God, she'd been a marchioness, how could he offer her the hand of a gentleman who lived off his brother? He could not. He had to wait until he was independent from his family.

He missed her already, missed her quiet presence and her silent watching. His heart throbbed in his chest as memories of the past hours played through his head.

He had touched a woman—lain with a woman…

He flicked the reins and stirred his animals into a gallop so his mind might focus on that and not the eclectic clutter of emotions roiling inside him.

He'd come to Drew's confused about how to fulfil his plan for the future. He left there tied up in knots. His options had narrowed. Whatever he did, he must choose to do it quickly, and he must earn money enough that would enable him to keep a wife. Politicians did not earn money, unless they allowed themselves to be bribed. He had no intention of doing that. Perhaps his whole plan needed to be rethought…

He breathed heavily. He'd done wrong and he must face the consequences that had not seemed to matter in the hut yesterday, or in the dark.

"Hey. Hey." He whipped up the horses and raced them on.

She has been a marchioness! *What on earth will persuade her to accept me even if I do offer?*

~

When Rob pulled up before Pembroke House, John's town residence, a porter opened the door and came out to greet him, and a moment later two grooms came about to manage his horses. He left the curricle for them to take around to the stables.

"Sir." The porter bowed. "I hope you will find all to your liking. We have made both the family drawing room and the morning room ready, they are at your disposal and if you require anything, please ask."

Rob nodded, lifting off his hat. "I'm sure that will be fine, thank you." He followed the porter back up the steps and within the huge marble-lined hall three footmen stood in a line on the black-and-white chequered floor.

"Sir." They all bowed at once. Rob nodded.

He looked back at the porter, "Which room am I in? I shall change and take luncheon in the morning room and then I will go out."

"Smith will show you up, sir, and I will have your luggage brought up directly."

Two of the footmen walked away, while the third lifted a hand. "This way, sir."

Rob trailed through his brother's giant house, following the man. All the artefacts John and their grandfather had brought back from the grand tour, the busts, and even the portraits on the walls, were covered up under dustsheets.

Only a small part of the house had been opened up for Rob's use because he did not need it all and John's army of servants had travelled with him to whatever estate he was currently visiting, so there was no butler to direct anything, merely the housekeeper and a few maids and footmen, who were left to keep things in order until John came back.

It only made things more obvious to Rob that his life, as it stood, was not one he could invite Caro to join him in.

Once he'd changed he ate alone, with one footman serving, and then he went downstairs and told the porter not to bother ordering his carriage, he would walk to his club.

Walking through London felt a little surreal, though, when he'd become so used to the quieter life in the country, and the fresh air—and Caro.

Her face hovered in his mind's eye as he made his way through the people and traffic, as she'd looked this morning when they'd said goodbye in his room. He saw her with her hair down and her eyes bright. He remembered the colour of them in sunlight.

He and his friends had not joined White's, the club his entire family belonged to, instead they'd joined Brooks's, at Rob's urging. When Rob sought his seat in the House of Commons he intended to stand for the Whig party, who were aligned to Brooks's club. His brother and his uncles spoke out for the Tories in the House of Lords, and White's was full of men with that political view.

Choosing Brooks's had been his first step towards establishing an independence from his family. He would no longer walk in the shadow of his brother or his cousins. At Brooks's he might be his own man, not be judged by, and compared to, the others, and develop a network to help him find a seat in Parliament.

It was quite a momentous thing, though, to walk up the steps and give his name. "Mr Rob Marlow." The doorman stepped aside. It felt like taking a passage into manhood. He was now a member here and accepted in this masculine world of London's elite clubs and, most importantly, in his own right, not as a brother, nephew or cousin of his family.

He glanced about the room, his heart beating in a steady rhythm.

"Would you care for a drink, sir?"

Rob looked at the footman. "Yes, coffee, thank you."

"Rob!" He turned to see his friends, they were in a corner behind him. A sense of relief ran through him. It felt as though he'd been lost and now he'd come back home into a place he understood.

"Hello." They stood as he approached. He had a group of seven friends, who were close. They were similar to him, none debauched like Harry, none fighters, none gamblers and none of them drank to any excess—and yet now he'd set himself apart because he'd lain with a woman, a dependent of his family—a woman he ought to have left alone.

A soft pain twisted in his stomach and he breathed heavily as he sat with them, feeling colour rise beneath his skin and guilt draw its mark on his soul.

"So what will you do, Rob, have you made plans over the summer, what seat are we aiming for?" Patrick asked.

Rob shook his head. No he'd been foolish and idle. "No, but I must start, I need to find rooms still too. I'm at John's currently."

"I shall come with you tomorrow, if you like, it should be easy enough to find somewhere that will do. We are all settled," Patrick offered

Rob nodded.

"I will help you too," Arthur volunteered.

"Thank you." It would be a first step, and he must take things a step at a time, but he had to think hard and find a clear route to fulfil his plan that would enable him to keep Caro in a condition which befitted a former marchioness, and one that would not hurt his pride and allow him to have an impact on the lives of those less fortunate than him, because that was how he wished to leave his mark on this world.

When he returned to John's it was about eleven at night and yet, as he walked through the door, he said to the porter, "Where might I find a quill and paper?"

"In the library, sir."

That too was shrouded in dust covers, but Rob walked over to John's desk and lifted the cover off. There were drawers down either side of the desk. He opened the first; it was ledgers. When he opened another beneath it he shut it immediately when he saw explicit images of Kate. John's drawing could be too good, then, at times. He smiled. Kate would probably smack her husband if she knew he kept such things in his desk.

Rob moved to the far side, and in the top drawer found a blank sheet, a quill and ink. He sat down and wrote to Mary, only in truth it was not Mary he was writing to.

He told her he'd arrived in town safely, and that he'd already met his friends and was to begin searching for a place to live tomorrow, and then he wrote for Caro, *I enjoyed my summer weeks with you, they were halcyon days that I will always remember and treasure.* Then he told Mary to pass on his greetings and good wishes to Drew and Caro, and to kiss the children for him. He thought of kissing Caro when he signed his name, and of all the times he, or she, had asked for forgiveness and the other had given it. Yet he did not really think they'd known how much forgiveness they would need. He'd not truly foreseen how much it would affect him, or his life.

~

"I enjoyed my summer weeks with you, they were halcyon days that I will always remember and treasure. Please pass my greetings and good wishes on to Drew and Caro, and kiss the children for me. Your loving brother and their loving uncle, Rob."

Caro watched as Mary smiled at Drew and then folded the letter. "It was kind of him to write and let me know he arrived safely. I must admit, I had not expected to hear so soon."

Had he written not for Mary's sake but for Caro's, to tell her that he'd arrived there and was still thinking of her? Caro's heart pumped hard in her chest. Her mind and her heart clung to the words, *remember* and *treasure*. She hoped that those words were for her, and that they were true.

Drew smiled, and looked at Caro, then Mary. "So who shall we invite to dine with us? Who would you like to get to know, Caro? We have to continue to expand your world."

She swallowed. Fear was there, creeping up on her, but she knew that if she refused to accept it then she could do as she wished. "I would like to know some other women who live locally… I would like friends beyond this house."

"Well, then, I know of two spinsters who are your age who live together," Mary answered, "and we will invite Mr Slade and Dr Palmer. We will need another man, Drew?"

"I shall ask Mark. He will turn up to escort you, so you may be with someone you know."

Drew's friend from college was someone she'd always felt comfortable with.

"And we should ask two couples, to round off the group, otherwise people will think we are matchmaking," Mary said.

Caro nodded, she would hate that, and Drew and Mary ought to be able to use such things to invite their friends here. "The Martins then and the Baxters," Drew stated.

"Well, then, our first dinner party is arranged. Will you come and help me write the invitations, Caro? We may choose the menu together too."

~

"There is another letter from your brother, Mary." Drew tossed it across the table. "One thing we may not accuse him of is not keeping us appraised of his affairs."

He was joking.

Caro's gaze followed its path and she watched Mary break the seal and open it, her heart skipping through a country dance.

Rob had kept his promise and written comments in his letters, which Mary had taken to reading aloud over breakfast. The second letter had arrived a week after he'd left, when he'd said that he had to write "because he missed them all". Caro had sensed the sentence was written to her.

In the following weeks, through his letters, she'd learned that he'd found accommodation, invested some of his income, and was spending much of his time with friends, bare-knuckle fighting, fencing, shooting and looking over horses, and she knew he dined at his club. He'd said nothing of his pursuit to find a seat in the House of Commons, though. But he'd said he did not want Mary and Drew to know, and so she'd not asked Mary to enquire about it. She had simply listened out for the lines within his tales that were written for her. He would say things like, "and then I remembered when Caro and I were caught by that storm." Telling her, he had not forgotten.

She'd not forgotten either, and nor had she retreated back into her glass gaol. She had deliberately continued pushing boundaries, socialising among the local community, making her own friends. She'd befriended the two spinsters who Mary had invited to join them for their first dinner party, and now she was in the habit of taking luncheon with them twice a week. Which left Drew and Mary time alone.

"He says he has not seen John, even though John is in town…" Mary looked up at Drew.

"I am sure he prefers the company of his friends over a brother."

Caro smiled, because that would be Drew's answer. His friends had been more brotherly to them both than their brothers had ever been.

Mary lowered her head to read. "I am very much looking forward to you all coming to town. We shall have to take George to the park. I know John is here already, but I have not seen him. Yet it heralds your arrival and so I am now looking forward to it even more. I am currently thinking of the night we attended the assembly rooms, the first night Caro danced, and I am looking forward to challenging her to dance at some grand ball."

Caro smiled again, thinking of their moments in the churchyard. She was unsure what she hoped for when she went to town. She'd had no expectation that he would feel the same, even though he'd spoken to her in his letters, and yet he did still remember, and he'd left her in no doubt he wished to see her.

She wished to see him.

"I gather from all you have said that Caro is still recovering from her fear and so I hope she will be happy to come and willing to accept my challenge. Tell Drew I saw Mark Harper, he said he'd visited you recently and noticed the change in Caro. It was good to hear the children are well, and that little Iris is sitting up. They grow so fast, don't they? I'm glad you are bringing the children to town so I will see them. Give them a kiss from me, and say my hello to Drew, and send my fond regards to Caro, and tell her she must be prepared to dance. Your adoring brother, Rob." Mary folded the paper and smiled at Caro.

Drew smiled at her too.

Tears clutched at the back of her throat. She nodded and stood. "I must leave, I want to look about Isabella's garden before we take luncheon."

"Enjoy your day," Drew stated.

She nodded, then walked from the room, her heart racing and the hall misting. Rob had said nice things, and her tears were foolish, yet she was terrified.

He still had feelings for her, his words said so. Feelings that would die in the future. Feelings that may have already faded a little. Feelings that might fade entirely when he saw her again. After all, during their summer here he'd been isolated from his friends. In town he might see her differently. Yet when he wrote like that, hope and longing filled her.

She was setting herself up for more pain. She had promised herself she would not believe in fairytales again. When she went to London her heart would break all over again if she allowed herself to believe that she might be loved. Love like that was not accessible to her. She could not have children… Albert had been far more adamant about his affection than Rob in the beginning, and even that affection had died. Yet Rob had said he'd loved her, and the affection in his eyes had been more tender than Albert's ever had.

She forced the thought away, as she'd forced the pain away over the weeks since Rob had left, and clung to the words he hid within his letters. But what would happen when the words stopped… She must think that they would stop. She could not let herself hope for any more. The words would stop at some point. Maybe even after the autumn. There could be nothing more than this between them, when she could not bear children.

She took a breath, told a footman to have the trap Drew had bought her made ready, then hurried upstairs to fetch a bonnet.

She would not fret, she would continue as she was and go to London in a fortnight, and remember the summer with fondness, then come home and carry on, and allow him to forget her. She had promised him she expected nothing from him. She would honour her promise.

Chapter 21

The street was full of noise and bustle, the sound was intense, vendors shouting out their wares from the kerb, the clop of horses' hooves on cobbles and the rumble of iron-rimmed carriage wheels. There seemed to be people and vehicles everywhere in London. She'd forgotten all of this, this haste and clamour. Her anxiety thrived like a living, breathing monster as she pressed back into the squabs of Drew's carriage.

She turned her gaze away from the window and looked at Drew. He smiled.

George was curled into his side asleep and Mary was seated beside him sleeping too, with Iris also asleep in her arms.

Caro sighed. A part of her was still not certain she should have come, this was probably stupid, and yet Rob had continued to speak to her in his letters, and so she had come, as she'd promised.

But she had been happy in the months since he'd left, or perhaps a better word would be content, and so if she came and he turned his back, it would hurt and spoil the memories she'd clung to. She did not wish them spoiled.

Many things they'd done and said in the summer had played through her head as she'd travelled, and his last words in a letter had run through her mind too. *I am so glad you are coming up to town, and that Caro is coming too. I will look forward to seeing you all at John's.*

Her eyes turned to look from the window again.

They were going to stay at the Duke of Pembroke's townhouse. She'd never visited before. She'd not been to town since she'd run away, slipping out through the back of the dressmaker's shop, with Drew, three and a half years before. She was terrified. Terrified not only of the noise and the open space and being at social events with many people, but of meeting people she'd known in her former life.

As the carriage rolled on through London's busy streets, her palms grew damp and cold.

Albert would be in town, sitting in the House of Lords. Of course she'd known that when she'd said she would come. It was testimony to how much she wished to see Rob.

Pain and fear twisted in her stomach when she thought of Albert. They were nearing his house—foolishly there were still other feelings. Her heart remembered loving him. It refused to forget. She remembered Rob's eyes, and his touch on that narrow bed in the dirty hut. That was what she wished to hold close. Her memories of her marriage bed were false.

Drew leant forward and squeezed her hand. "You will have a dozen or more people about you, Caro, at all times. You will not be at risk. Besides, Kilbride has moved on. I do not think he will give you another thought."

No, yet why did that hurt more than it eased her fear.

She nodded as Drew let go of her hand and sat back.

But she could not simply set aside three years of her life. There was no relief in hearing that Albert would not think of her. Her life had been left empty when she'd left him, bearing the guilt and shame of failing to make her husband happy, and failing to fulfil her duty to bear him children. His life had carried on regardless.

But now her life had begun to continue, because of Rob…

If she had to face Albert in a room full of people, she hoped Rob would be with her, and she hoped Albert would ignore her,

185

because if he did anything else she would not know what to do.

Her heart beat in time with the rhythm of the horses' hooves as the carriage turned into one of the busiest streets near where she'd used to live. They passed the dressmaker's from which she'd run.

A sadness crept over her soul when she looked. She'd not known that day how much her life would change, or how it would make her feel.

They turned into the street where she'd once lived and she saw the vast house that had been hers to manage.

Was Albert within?

"Caro," Drew said drawing her eyes to him, deliberately. "I am not sure who will be there, when we get to John's. Often in the afternoon a number of the family call. Sometimes there are also other callers." It was a warning, preparing her to be thrown into the deep.

But she was more accustomed to people now, yet not large crowds.

She nodded, although her heart thumped so hard she feared she'd collapse as it rang in her ears.

The carriage rumbled on into Regent Street, and then she saw the Duke of Pembroke's Palladian property set back from the road.

Her vision darkened. She closed her eyes and breathed deeply. She did not wish to faint.

Would Rob be here to greet them?

She pictured him on the night of the assembly and remembered how he'd talked her through her fear. That had been the first time they'd kissed.

As the carriage pulled to a halt, Drew lifted his son on to his lap. George woke and made a whimpering sound as he stretched and yawned.

Mary woke, looking sleepy-eyed. Drew smiled at her, with love in his eyes. Jealousy pierced Caro's heart, which was entirely wrong, because she was happy for her brother.

When a footman opened the door, Drew climbed down first,

George clinging to his neck and balancing on his arm. Then he turned back and held a hand out to help Mary down. When he let her go he lifted his hand to help Caro.

She felt exactly as she had done on the stairs leading to that assembly hall months before, but she'd learned courage and she had faith in herself. She could walk through glass walls. She did not let them trap her in anymore.

"Come," Drew offered his free arm, as George clung to him, and Mary climbed the steps ahead of them holding Iris.

Caro gripped Drew's arm, clutching at the support he gave.

"I warn you I do not feel well," she whispered as they climbed the steps, "I feel a little faint."

"I know," he answered in a solid tone, "you are as white as a sheet, Caro."

"I am pathetic, aren't I?" she whispered.

"Nonsense! What you are is brave. I never thought I would see you return to town when you let your fear control you. But we both know this is only the beginning. It will take considerable courage for you to go on. But you will not fail at this first hurdle. You have developed too much strength for that. Now you have set your mind to putting your past aside, you can achieve anything. You can do this, and you know it too."

The hall was huge, and cold, both in appearance and in temperature. The floor was black and white squares of marble, but the walls were giant structures of white marble, and the stairs were a pale stone.

"His Grace is expecting your arrival, Lady Framlington," the butler was saying to Mary.

Mary looked over her shoulder and smiled before turning to climb the stairs to the first floor.

Caro lifted her chin, instilling her spine with steel. Drew was right. Rob had taught her that. She had once been a marchioness, she was equal to this family, and she had broken free from her glass gaol. She would not go back.

As they climbed the shallow stairs behind Mary, Caro heard voices spilling from somewhere on the first floor.

When they reached the landing, which was a clutter of objects, antiques, family busts and portraits, Mary was already entering a room further along. Exclamations followed her, the sound of people fussing over Iris.

Before Caro and Drew reached the room, though, the Duchess of Pembroke appeared and she hurried the few steps to greet them. "Drew, Caroline, how lovely to see you, and little George. Are you tired, sweetheart?" She brushed George's cheek with her fingertips, as he buried his head against Drew's shoulder. She looked up at Caro. "Would you like me to show you to your room, Caroline? So you might go there whenever you wish. Then if you feel uncomfortable at all you may disappear."

Caro swallowed. The Duchess was being kind, yet... "Thank you, but I am happy to wait until Mary and Drew retire to dress for dinner…" She did not even want the chance of an escape. She needed to believe that there was no escape; she had to achieve this. As Rob had said, if they were to be able to see each other while she was in town she had to socialise.

Yet the drawing room was full, just as Pembroke Place was each summer and at Christmas.

The Duke of Pembroke approached them as they entered, smiling broadly at Drew. "Welcome. Was your journey comfortable?"

"We deliberately chose the hour when the children would be sleeping. Hence the silence, George is not truly awake yet." Drew lifted his arm, meaning she had to let go of it, and he ruffled George's hair, while George gave his uncle a sheepish look then buried his face in Drew's cravat.

"Paul?" George said in a muffled voice.

"Is in the nursery," the Duke, John, answered. "I'm sure your Papa will take you up in a while." He patted George's shoulder then looked at Caro. "Caroline, this is an honour. Katherine and I are very glad you chose to come."

With a determination she forced upon herself, Caro lifted her hand. If she was to be brave she must simply be brave.

He looked at it for a moment, surprised, but then held it gently and bowed.

"Thank you for inviting me."

"Well, to us you are merely a member of the family and you must feel at home here." He let her hand go. "Ask for anything you need, and do exactly as you wish." He smiled. Caro smiled in return. "Take a seat. There is tea if you wish for a cup. Katherine." he called across the room. The Duchess, who had been drawn into another conversation, turned back. "Tea, for Caroline and Drew."

"Of course, come with me."

Caro looked about the room, quickly glancing over its occupants. Rob was not here. Her throat dried. She had hoped he would be waiting for them.

As she and Drew walked across the room with Kate, Caro longed to ask, *is Robbie due to call today?* and yet she did not have the confidence. She feared they would think her interest odd.

~

Rob leapt down from his curricle, his heart pumping hard.

John's grooms held the horses' heads and so Rob left his animals in their hands and turned to go in.

He slipped off his riding gloves as he climbed the steps. They were coming today and Mary had said they would arrive late afternoon. A chilly autumn breeze swept at his long coat as he waited until the door opened. It was a footman—not Finch, the butler. He must be upstairs.

The weeks since he'd left Drew's had felt long and he'd thought of Caro constantly. She could be yards away from him now.

He jogged upstairs, having left his hat, outdoor coat and gloves with the footman.

He was still in love with her, and so it felt very strange to not have spoken to her for weeks, not even in writing.

Yet he still had no route to fulfil his plan. What he'd discovered was that to even enter to run for a seat he needed money, and he needed money for his campaign for votes, and even if he won the seat, he would then need money to support himself while he sat in the House of Commons. All he'd done so far was invest some of his income from John in his Uncle Robert's business properties. But that had felt traitorous to himself, because if he was to stand up and speak for the working class, how could he do so when he lived off his family? No matter that that was what the majority of those in the House of Commons did, he wished to be different.

So now his plan was suspended until he could find himself an alternative income. He'd spent some hours with John's man of business to see if any aspect of the administration of estates might inspire him. But if he were to sit in Parliament he could not undertake a position that required his constant presence. Yet he'd said nothing to John of that when John had offered him the experience in a letter.

So to date he'd amused himself with horses, looking over them at Tattersall's, walked about museums, boxed, fenced and fired pistols in Mantons, rather than commit to anything he did not wish to do. He was still fixed upon his plan, he simply needed to work out his route to achieving it. He needed a position that would give him an income but did not require his presence.

He might have thought about breeding horses, but his father's friend Lord Forth, who bred them, had told him months ago that he did not have an eye for a good race horse. It was like everything, John was better at it, or his father had been better at it, or another member of his family was…

"Master Robert," Finch, John's butler welcomed Rob on the landing before the drawing room. "Do you wish me to announce you?"

"Has my sister arrived?" His heart pumped excitement and expectation into his blood as he awaited the answer.

"Indeed, sir, a little more than half an hour ago."

"Thank you. There's no need for an announcement." Rob walked on past him. He heard many voices. He could not pick Caro's out.

What if her feelings had changed?

His heart beat more violently when he walked into the room.

Mary had said in her letters that Caro had been doing more. She'd joined their party when they entertained and had begun visiting with Mary, as well as visiting two local women alone. She had friends.

If her feelings were changed…

If they were changed then he would always remember the time they'd spent together in the summer, and be grateful that Caro had been his first. But in his experience absence had made his heart grow fonder. He longed to see her. As he walked into the room, his gaze ignored everybody else and looked for her.

She was wearing mauve and her blonde hair was pinned up high, although a swirl had been left to hang to her nape and then curled across one shoulder. Her presence pierced his chest, as though a sword had run him through. She was even more beautiful and more delicate in appearance than he remembered.

"Robbie," his aunt Penny exclaimed. She was the first to notice him. "Oh, how good to see you. You do not normally come."

No, he rarely called. He had his own rooms, and coming to London had been about escaping his family not visiting them daily. He spent his days with his friends, if he had no other pursuit.

"Aunt Penny." He bowed, to say hello.

"How are you?" Rob's uncle Richard joined them. "Have you found your chosen occupation?"

Rob shook his head. It was questions like that which made him choose to avoid these afternoons of social chatter. He was still keeping what he wished to do with his life to himself.

~

"Robbie."

Caro looked across the room the moment Penny said his name, and she'd been speaking, but then she could not think what to say. She looked to Mary for help as the image of Rob standing there, tall and athletic, gripped at her heart.

Her mind threw all sorts of images at her, memories from the summer.

"Excuse me," Mary said rising. "I wish to greet, Rob."

Caro rose too, automatically—pulled towards him—then she realised she'd said nothing and it might look odd, but she could not sit again. "Excuse me."

She followed Mary across the room.

Rob was standing with his aunt and uncle.

He looked at Mary first as she walked before Caro, but then he glanced at Caro, and smiled for her. His eyes said so much more than a smile. They said he'd not forgotten her at all and that if he could he would say he loved her.

After a heartbeat's length he looked away.

"Oh, Rob, I am pleased to see you." Mary hugged him. "How are you? It feels like an age since you stayed with us. George will be over the moon, and you will not recognise Iris, she's grown so much, but I took them up to the nursery."

He pressed a kiss on Mary's cheek, saying something Caro could not hear. Then when he pulled away his eyes turned to Caro again. It looked as though he soaked her up as she absorbed him too. It had been so long.

"Caro."

She stepped forward, longing to hug him and kiss his lips. Instead she lifted her hand. He gripped it and bowed quite low as he pressed his lips against the back of her fingers. The kiss was extremely gentle, and his hold seemed to treasure her. His feelings were unchanged, she knew it.

"I cannot believe you made it here," he said, as his head lifted, his hand clinging to hers. "Yet I'm glad to see you have." He looked at Mary. "She is impressive, isn't she?"

"Very," Mary said looking at her. "Andrew and I are very proud of you, Caro."

Rob squeezed Caro's hand gently, then let go.

Love welled up within her. There was no doubt left, she did love him, she could not feel as she did if it was not love, and he still cared for her. As in the summer, she would not think of future, only now.

"I could do with a cup of tea, Caro, would you pour me one?" It was a ploy to separate them from the others as the tea urn stood on a table against the far wall. "And perhaps you would take me up to the nursery afterwards so I might see George, Mary"

"Or, better still, I will go and fetch him down," Mary answered, "He will not want to miss you. I'll go now."

When Mary walked away, Rob caught hold of Caro's elbow and gently turned her towards the urn. "Let us fetch that tea," he said aloud, but then in a lower voice, as they walked across the room, he said, "How are you? I have missed you."

She glanced up at him, smiling. "I did not realise you had a devious streak, Rob Marlow. Perhaps you would take me to the nursery, indeed… you knew Mary would go and fetch him."

"I missed you too, Rob," he mocked. "I am really glad you called today. I wanted to see you."

She looked up at him and her smile broadened. If anyone watched them they must see that there was something between them, but she did not think people were looking. "I have, I am, and I did, or rather, I do, yet I would guess you do not really want a cup of tea."

"Guilty," he laughed gently. "But as we are now at the tea urn, you had better pour me one."

She laughed as she picked up a cup.

"How are you anyway, truly? Mary told me that you have been going out more and that you've made friends."

"Yes, Isabella and Pauline. They are sisters. They live in a house together in Maidstone. But I think it is good for Drew too, because it gives Mary and Drew time alone." She tipped milk into his cup.

"And what does it give you?" he said when he took the cup from her hand.

"Companionship, I am able to be myself with them."

He smiled at her. "Were you yourself with me in the summer."

"Towards the end, yes."

He looked into her eyes. "I still feel the same."

She swallowed as the words twisted inside her. "I feel the same too."

"May we go driving one afternoon, but not until next week. I would not want to draw attention to it. Until then, I'm afraid we will have to endure the crowd."

She nodded. "That would be nice. Yet I can cope with a crowd if you are within it."

He gave her a broad smile and she longed to reach her arms around his neck and hold him. But mostly to feel him hold her. "When we arrived, I felt as I did at the assembly. I wished you were here."

"But you coped regardless." His gaze searched hers.

"Yes, because I knew I would see you, and now I have."

"Do you think anyone would notice if I stole you away."

"Mary is coming back, to bring George to see you."

"We should have gone up," he said quietly, but then he glanced beyond her, and whispered through the edge of his mouth. "Your brother is behind you and approaching. Drew, how are you?" Rob said the last louder.

Drew's arm settled on Caro's shoulders, in gentle reassurance. "I did not think I would ever see Caro in town again."

Rob looked at her. "Well, she is here."

"And I think it is with thanks to you," Drew acknowledged.

"Uncle Bobbie!"

Caro turned as Rob did, to see Mary set George down, and then the little scoundrel ran across the room.

"Tyke!" Rob answered in mocking humour, bending down to pick George up. "Little rogue. Have you been good since I left?" Rob lifted him high.

"Very good."

"And you have learned your "r"s"

"Yes, but I think you will always be Uncle Bobbie." Mary answered.

"Robbie, I hope you will not rush off. It is so rare that you call. Will you stay to dinner?" Kate approached.

Rob smiled. "Thank you, I would like to, yes."

Caro's heart ached in response, she was to have his company for a few hours, then.

"I'm afraid that I've started a riot in the nursery, Kate." Mary said. "All the children wish to come down because I have let George come."

"I will tell Finch to send word that they may. No one will mind. It is only that the toys are there for them to play with."

There was no further opportunity for private conversation after that, they were constantly surrounded by his family, and in the evening the number was too small for them to find any opportunities to slip away. It was only Mary and Drew and the Duke and Duchess, and then Caro and Rob.

Yet she was able to sit beside Rob at dinner because the others were couples and after dinner they entertained each other in pairs at the pianoforte. Drew turned Mary's pages with an amused smile as she played and sang, but then Caro and Rob sang a perfect harmony, sitting close together, while Caro played and Rob flipped the music sheets over. The Duke and Duchess outshone them, though, the Duke had a powerful, pitch-perfect voice.

It was eleven when Rob stood. "I suppose I ought to leave."

Everyone stood. He kissed Mary's cheek and then Kate's, shook the Duke's hand, then Drew's, and then he turned to Caro. She wished he might kiss her cheek, but she was not family. Instead he took her hand and bowed slightly as he pressed a kiss on to the back of her fingers. "Goodnight, Caro."

"Goodnight Rob."

Their parting was impersonal, and yet she sensed that he felt as she did, that he would kiss her if he could.

When he let her hand go he looked at Kate.

"Where will you be tomorrow evening? Are you going out?"

"To a parliamentary dinner," John answered, "Business, I'm afraid,"

"And we have been invited to dine with Lord Brooke," Mary answered, "Caro is joining us."

"We thought it an opportunity for Caro to test her wings," Drew added. "As she has known Brooke from childhood, Caro will find it easier there, with only Brooke and his new wife."

She did not particularly wish to attend, because she would be with couples, but Rob could hardly invite himself along.

He smiled at her, with understanding, as though he wished that he could.

"Well perhaps I will see you the night after." Rob concluded, looking at Mary.

"That is Pickford's ball," Kate answered. "If you cannot acquire yourself an invitation then call here in the afternoon and arrange to come with us."

"I'll come with you. It's easier than trying to wheedle one." Rob answered, glancing at Kate.

Warmth flowed into Caro's blood. He would be with her when she attended her first society event, and she would be on his arm because they would be a six.

"Well, I will be off, goodnight all." He bowed, then nodded slightly at Caro, smiling before he turned away and walked from the room. Her heart left with him.

Chapter 22

Having to wait a day, a night and another day to see Caro, was like having an itch in his blood that could not be scratched. Yet he never normally called upon John, and it would look odd if he spent hour after hour here. So he'd waited until the night he'd agreed to accompany them. But as he stood outside, waiting for the door of Pembroke House to open, he hoped for an opportunity to speak with Caro alone; an open, seeping wound wept inside him for an opportunity to kiss her.

His friends had all found it highly amusing that he'd chosen to attend an event with his family over sitting in the club with them. He did not normally attend balls and such, yet he'd used the firm excuse that Mary was his closest sister and he wished to spend some time with her. He had not even mentioned Caro's name, to avoid their speculation.

Finch opened the door and stepped back, the others were already gathered in the hall. Rob smiled at John and Kate as he stepped in.

He'd heard from his mother today. His parents were coming to town in a fortnight, which would curb his ability to spend time with Caro further. They would notice if he acted oddly, and so he had two weeks to make the most of her presence here.

"Did you bring your curricle?" John asked, looking out through the door before it was closed.

"No, I walked, seeing as we were using your carriage. I thought it pointless bringing my horses."

"Are your rooms close to here, then?" Caro asked.

He turned. Her appearance winded him with a fist in the stomach. She was clothed in amber satin, which hugged her generous bosom and then her narrow waist, before widening to flow over her hips and down to the floor like fluid. The dress spoke of her fragility, as the short sleeves and bodice displayed her slender arms and narrow shoulders, but also her beautiful cleavage, where the little amber cross nestled.

He bowed to her. "They are not that close, a half-hour's walk, but I do not mind it."

"Let us go, then, now Rob is here," John stated.

Rob stepped towards Caro. He did not wish Drew offering his arm first, he wished to escort Caro not Mary. It was why he was here.

He lifted his arm. Caro's hand settled upon it. "Thank you."

A rightness filled his soul.

His fingers covered her slender and smaller hand as he looked down and mouthed, *you look beautiful.*

She smiled, and mouthed back, *so do you.*

This was real. Since the summer it had felt surreal, but, no, this was very real; she was here with him, in town, flesh and bone, and he felt the same.

In the carriage, she sat between himself and Drew, and he sensed her anxiety building. He longed to take up her hand, but he did not, for fear that John might think it strange.

When they arrived and the carriage drew to a halt, he leapt down first and lifted his hand to help Caro down. She waited in the carriage, though, and it was Mary who took his hand, then John climbed down and helped Kate before Drew came and helped Caro.

Drew would have held on to her hand, and left Rob to take Mary in, but Caro intervened.

"You walk with Mary. Rob will escort me."

Drew looked at them both, glancing from one to the other.

Rob smiled. "I do not mind."

Drew nodded letting Caro's fingers go, before turning to Mary. Rob lifted his arm and Caro laid her fingers on it.

"You are nervous…" he whispered as the others walked ahead.

"Terrified," she answered.

"You will cope."

"I will, with you here… Do you think Albert will be here?"

He glanced at her as they climbed the stone steps to the open door. "He may be, I suppose. But if he is here, that is the final step. You will be wholly free of your fear once you've crossed it."

"Will I?" She looked as though she did not believe it.

If she baulked tonight, there was nowhere else he might take her, not before the eyes of elite society. She was throwing herself into the deep this evening. It was brave of her, and he respected her courage a dozen times more.

"If this is awful, you may remember that I am doing this for you." She breathed up at him in a whisper.

For him… To see him. It expressed how much she felt for him.

"Thank you, but it will not be awful. Breathe slowly." Their quiet conversation ceased as Drew and Mary stopped ahead of them and waited.

Rob nodded at Drew, telling him that Caro was struggling.

"Caro, if you need to go, tell us, we may leave, at any point."

She gave Drew a slight, nervous nod as her fingers gripped Rob's arm over tightly.

She stood stiffly when they waited in the receiving line.

John and Kate were introduced to the Earl of Pickford, then Drew and Mary and then Rob stepped forward, leading Caro.

A rush of pride and adoration raced through his blood when Caro lifted her hand for Pickford to take.

"It has been a while, Caroline."

Rob was thrown by Pickford's use of her name.

"Indeed," was all she answered, before she turned to his wife.

"Lady Pickford." Caro curtsied.

"Lady Framlington."

A frown furrowed Rob's brow, as he greeted Pickford. Why would the man use Caro's first name and his wife not? A bitter taste filled Rob's mouth—jealousy.

"How do you know him?" Rob questioned in the moment before they turned to the others.

"Rob, I knew everyone. I was a marchioness. I have held and attended dozens of balls and numerous parliamentary dinners. He was, is, an ally of Albert's. I had forgotten until I saw his face. Yet it means Albert will be here."

Rob's heart pumped, hers must be thumping like a drum.

He looked at Drew, who was watching them.

"Will you dance the first with me?" she asked.

Rob looked down at Caro, clearly her fear had forced her to forget caution. She should not ask, and yet friends danced, him dancing with her would be nothing out of the ordinary and no one beyond Drew and Mary had heard her ask.

He nodded. "Yes, but it will not be this dance, I believe it has just begun. It will have to be the next."

"I will dance the set after that with you, Caro. Dancing will keep your mind off other things," Drew offered.

"You dance now, Caroline?" They all looked up to realise John had heard.

Her lips pursed, yet she nodded. Pride became a firm spear lodged in Rob's chest. It was a far better feeling than jealousy, and yet it seemed that love amplified every emotion.

"Then may I have your hand for the next after Drew," John asked.

"Yes."

Rob saw his uncle Richard on the far side of the room, with his uncle Robert. John led their group across the room to join the others.

Rob glanced around. He could not see the Marquis of Kilbride.

But then Kilbride was shorter than the majority of Rob's family, he might hide more easily amongst the crowd.

"He is here," Caro whispered, her fingers clawing into Rob's arm. "I have just seen him walk into an anteroom."

"Well, then, at least he is not in the same room as us."

Her eyes were wide and dark.

"Are you sure you wish to dance?"

"I will not look like a coward before him."

Drew cleared his throat behind them as they reached the family group. Rob looked back. Drew had noted Kilbride's presence too.

"Shall I fetch you a drink, Caro, it may calm your nerves," Rob offered.

"Do not leave me," she whispered in the moment before they were swamped by his family. A round of greetings followed and Rob moved a little away so his attention would not be noticed.

The women fussed over the new, more confident Caro, while people commented on his unexpected attendance.

When the dance ended, after a short applause, muffled by the gloves the dancers wore, the orchestra struck up a new tune and Rob returned to Caro. "We are dancing, I believe." He bowed slightly, ignoring their audience. He did not realise how much he'd longed to dance with her again until she lay her fingers on his arm. The touch was gentle as they walked out on to the floor.

"Overwhelmed?" he asked.

"Absolutely," she answered.

Her bosom lifted, pressing against her bodice when she took a breath, and then it fell.

He held her hand, aiding her to her position in a long set. It trembled in his fingers.

"It will be easier by the next ball."

"I am not convinced. I am terrified Albert will speak to me."

"The anteroom he walked into is the card room. He will probably be there a while. You may forget about him."

"I will try. I shall look at you and not think of him." She smiled for him.

He smiled back.

"Oh, and you have not told me yet, and said nothing in your letters. What of your great plan to tackle politics? You only mentioned it at the last moment and you told me nothing—"

The music began, though, ending their conversation, meaning nor could he tell her now. But suddenly he longed to share his hopes for the future with her. He hoped, too, she would be included in them. "I will tell you when we go out for our carriage ride."

Rob took three steps back to join the line of men, and faced her.

He was ready to commence the country dance, as a ripple passed about the room. It was sound and movement. People turning to whisper and speak to others. They looked at Caro and then they looked away and spoke, and eyes widened with disbelief before heads turned, and fans fluttered. The volume of their whispers was an audible wave.

Rob smiled at Caro. She stood a yard beyond his reach.

She had noticed, but her chin lifted in defiance and she looked at some point on the wall across the room, beyond him, denying their comments, whatever they were.

It had never occurred to him that it would be like this for her. He'd not imagined that people would recognise her so easily, and yet, as she'd said earlier, she had been a marchioness, near the peak of the elite—of course she would be known. She must have stood in receiving lines welcoming all these people in the past.

In contrast, he doubted the majority of the room even knew with whom she danced. It was another reminder of how hard he would need to work to have his aims reach fruition through Parliament.

Yet perhaps it had been wrong of him to bring her to town.

~

The music began. Caro breathed out with relief and took the first steps of the country dance, her eyes on Rob as her heart beat with the knowledge that Albert was only yards away.

Rob spoke as they moved past one another, but she did not catch his words, her mind had turned to chaos. All she could think of was not muddling her steps and she let her mind be filled with the music and not those who stared.

Yet when the dance came to a close, the room and the people crowded back in upon her. Rob gripped her elbow. "Save me the supper dance. I'll not hover by you when you return to the family, but I will not be far away in case you need me. Simply give me some sign."

Before she even reached the family Drew came forward to take her hand for the next dance. When Rob let her arm go and moved away the loss clasped in her stomach, but she'd been brave without him for weeks at home, she could be so here. Her chin lifted a little as she smiled at Drew, denying the looks of all those staring at her.

Drew turned to take her back amongst the dancers and Caro looked across the room, her heart skipping along to the dance already. On the far side of the room she saw Albert walk out from the card room, his hand rubbing his jaw as he walked.

It was a gesture that had once been so familiar to her it made her dizzy. He looked the same, exactly the same. Warmth flooded her skin.

She looked at Drew, but then something pulled her to glance back.

Albert stood at the edge of the crowd about the dancers, and his eyes scanned those on the floor. Someone had told him she was here. He was looking for her.

The rhythm of her heartbeat pulsed at her throat, where his hands had wrapped about her neck. Yet she still felt emotion from him—an echo of love. There was still feeling in her soul that longed.

Why? Why could she not free herself entirely of the past?

Albert's gaze ran across the dancers.

She did not look away as she took up her position in the set. She refused to look weak. She was not his wife now. He had no power over her. She wondered if his new wife was here. What was he like with her? Was he brutal and violent towards her?

"Caro." Drew called her attention to him.

Albert stood behind him. Drew did not know he was there.

She looked at her brother and yet beyond him she could still see Albert. Their gazes met across the room, his eyes a deep, dark brown. She had looked into those eyes when they had shared a bed.

She loved Rob, but that was a different feeling; that was founded on admiration and gratitude. It was gentle—and like a new flower opening. What she felt for Albert was hard and needy—and broken. Yet he had owned her heart first and he'd not let it go for years, so how might she give it wholly to Rob, when it could never be quite whole.

He never loved you. She looked away. She had learned true care and affection from Rob, things that Albert had never shown. It had never been love on Albert's part. Her heart had been fooled and given itself away blindly.

Her love for Albert had always felt needy, it had been all about need for her. She had so longed for a man's love to fill the void her parents had left in her childhood. She had allowed Albert to step in and stomp all over her affections.

There was the guilt again. Guilt because he'd not loved her when she'd done nothing but love him, as her parents had not loved her, and so there must be something wrong on her part. Shame swept over her in a wave. Shame that her lack of ability to bear children had made Albert hate her so much he'd beaten her. Guilt that she could still have cherished and loved a man, who treated her so badly, because she craved so much for the attentions and the mimicked love he'd shown her in their bed—but then she had continually hoped that her love might win over his.

Drew stepped forward and took her hand as the dance began, his eyes watching her expression. He was concerned for her, protective.

When she completed a turn, she looked for Rob. He was in conversation with his uncle and his fringe tumbled forward over his eyes when he leant to listen to something his uncle said. But then, as if he sensed her looking, he straightened and looked across the room, his fingers brushing his fringe back.

When he saw her watching, a smile twisted his lips for an instant.

She focused on Drew after that, and the music, and the steps.

When the dance came to an end, Drew lifted his arm. Caro laid her hand on it. "Albert is behind you, he's watching."

Drew glanced over his shoulder, then looked back at her. "How long has he been watching you?"

"Since the beginning of the dance."

Caro stole another glance in Albert's direction as the dancers moved, swapping partners or returning to the edge of the room.

A blonde woman walked up to Albert and touched his arm, then lifted to her toes and whispered something in his ear. He smiled—the benevolent smile he'd often bestowed on Caro in the first year of their marriage. It meant he was willing to concede to something, a gift, a new dress or an outing.

Was that his new wife? She was younger than Caro, full of youth and smiles. She did not look beaten or brutalised, and yet she was a mother.

"Caroline." She turned to find the Duke of Pembroke bowing before her. Of course she had agreed to dance with him too. Four months ago she'd known him far better than his younger brother. She had lived with him for a while before Drew had purchased his property, and now they were neighbours. Yet she'd never even let him touch her hand, and she'd barely said a dozen words to him in all those years. It was testament to how high the glass walls of her prison cell had been, and she'd set them about herself for love of the man across the room who had a new wife and a child, and had never cared for her.

She held out her hand and the Duke took it. He walked with her onto the floor. He was not at all like Rob, Rob was a man who opened his heart and let a person see what was within, but the Duke was more reserved, cautious, he held himself at a distance, and it was even in the touch of his fingers.

"I'm sorry to increase your woes, Caroline, but you may wish to know that your family have arrived."

She shut her eyes for an instant. Rob had said if she endured this step then she would have faced every fear, and he could not have been more right. She did not look for them; she had no interest. They had not looked for her since she'd run away from town.

After she'd danced with the Duke, she danced with one of his cousins and one of his uncles and then, at last, the chords of the supper dance began. It was a waltz.

Relief gripped at every sense when Rob came to lead her out, and when he held her…

"You are very pale," Rob stated as he began to turn her.

"Albert has been watching me most of the evening."

"I know, Caro, I have been watching him."

"My parents are here too."

"Yes, I heard, Mary pointed it out to Drew."

"Have you heard what people are saying?"

"Only that they had not expected to see you in town again. You have defied their perceptions. I believe you have defied Kilbride's too."

"And from your voice, you think that a good thing."

"And from yours, you think it is not."

No. She longed for Drew's quiet home and the children, and the peace. "No, I would happily walk from the room and not return and let them think what they like. I am happy at Drew's. I prefer it there."

His eyes suddenly became a dozen shades darker. "I enjoyed it there also in the summer, I'd prefer to be there too, then we might have slipped away into the garden and I could kiss you and forget all these people. But we cannot do that and so let us enjoy what we might have, this moment. I feel as though I have waited a century to have you in my arms again, and now you are, even if it is before a crowd of hundreds."

She smiled, her lips parting as she held his warm gaze and forgot their audience entirely. She had longed to be with him too.

"I will take you driving the day after tomorrow. I cannot wait until next week. But we must appear to be no more than friends and so I will not accompany you tomorrow night, but Drew will be with you, so you need not be afraid without me, and we will look forward to the day after…"

She nodded. He was using this moment to say as much as he could, because he could not speak before his family.

"I will call early to visit the children and spend the morning with them, then stay for luncheon, and in the afternoon I will propose a drive. It will look as though it wasn't planned. They know we are friends; I hope Drew will not think it odd. But when you come driving with me wear a broad-rimmed bonnet."

"Because you are ashamed of being seen with me?" she smiled.

"Because I do not want your reputation challenged. People will see you with a younger man and think you fast. People do not know me, Caro, I do not attend these sorts of things normally, and I will not see more judgement heaped upon you."

"Thank you." She said the words, not sure that she truly was thankful; in his arms, looking up at him, she did not care what others thought.

"Did I say how beautiful you look?"

"You did,"

"You do not regret…" he said then, his expression suddenly looking serious.

She longed to stop dancing and kiss him. "I do not regret anything that happened between us, Rob."

"Neither do I. I had thought perhaps I did, when I first came to town, because I can promise you nothing still, Caro, and I felt guilty. But now you are here and I see you, I can only see what I long for."

"You need not have felt guilty. I told you I did not expect promises—"

"Then where do you see this progressing?" His gaze looked into her eyes, searching for the answer.

"I cannot say, can it not just be?"

"I wish to do right by you in the future, as I ought to, but I am in no position to offer for you. I have no living—"

"Rob, I do not expect it."

The music slowed, and Rob turned her with a flourish. Then he leant to her ear, "Well, you ought to expect it, you have my heart. You may know that now, at least."

"And you have mine," she whispered back, even though she knew that Albert still had a grip upon it. But in Rob's arms, she could not think of Albert.

"Will you wait until I am able to offer, then?"

She had told herself she would only think of now. She had promised him she had no expectations. Yet seeing Albert had helped her see how much more happiness might be found with Rob. "Yes." Oh she had not hoped. She had not dared build up such dreams, and yet he was speaking of marriage. Could she truly be married again?

He looked beyond her and his expression changed.

She turned following his gaze. He was looking at Albert. "Rob. Stop glowering, you are as bad as Drew and I thought you did not wish to give us away."

His gaze fell to her and he smiled. "Caro, darling, my entire family are glowering at him. It will not give my interest away."

When they walked across the room to join his family, she saw that it was true. Every man in the group stared at Albert.

"Well, I wish they would not, it will not help, it will make his interest more obvious, and it will only rile him, and it is none of their concern."

"You are their concern because you are under Drew's care. I have told you before you're an honorary member of my family."

Rob's tone was flat and factual. "Will you sit beside me to eat supper? That will not be misconstrued, it is expected as we have danced this set."

"Yes." She would like that.

They sat amongst his family, with Drew on her other side, about a large table, and so there was no more chance for private conversation.

Albert sat across the room beside the blonde woman he'd spoken to, amongst his friends, and every time Caro looked up he was looking at her. Although it was not a hostile stare, but nor was it the open interest he had looked at her with when he'd courted her.

Perhaps she was an embarrassment he'd wished to keep hidden.

"Is that his wife?" she asked of Drew, when Drew looked up and caught him watching, then glowered.

Albert ignored Drew's look, as he had ignored all the others.

Drew turned and smiled at her, "Yes, and pray, please say you do not care."

"I do not." That was such a lie. That woman had born him the child Caro could not and envy breathed deep within her blood.

"Do you never speak to your parents?" Rob asked, looking at them both.

He had waded onto ground that should not be traversed.

"Our mother," Drew began pointedly, marking the fact that the Marquis was not their parent, "does not care to acknowledge our existence. I gave up trying to gain her notice years ago."

"I never sought to obtain it and she never gave it," Caro responded.

"I only asked because I was surprised they have not spoken to Caro, as she has been so long away from town."

"We are not surprised." Drew answered, in a petulant tone.

"Would they not even speak if they passed you in a street? Even your mother?" Rob's eyebrows lifted.

"She would cross over it, in fact she has done it," Drew answered.

"I see," Rob stated.

"I'm sure you do not," Drew responded.

Mary's fingers gripped Drew's, and she leaned around him. "We do not speak of them, Rob, they are naught to do with us."

Caro could not dance with Rob again. They had danced the two sets that polite society allowed, and so she danced the first after supper with Drew, then another with the Duke and from then on she danced with Rob's wider family, as they ensured no one else might ask.

When it came time to leave, it was Rob who laid her cloak on her shoulders and held her fingers as she climbed up into the carriage, and then he sat beside her, his thigh against hers.

His brother had agreed to drop him at his rooms, and when they stopped he smiled at her, then he looked about everyone. "Goodnight." He said before he climbed out and the footman shut the door behind him.

It had been the most impersonal parting.

Her thoughts clung to the moment of their waltz. *"Will you wait until I am able to offer, then?"* *"Yes."*

Chapter 23

The day after the Earl of Pickford's ball, after the family had eaten luncheon, a stream of unexpected visitors began calling on the Duke and Duchess of Pembroke. Caro watched them arriving from the drawing room. Carriage after carriage came.

They had not called to see either Kate or John, they had called to stare at the fallen marchioness. Drew had shown her a column in the paper that morning, and it had recorded her return to public life. *It was noted last evening that the cast-off Marchioness of K dared show her face in town and all eyes were upon the Marquis, yet his were upon her.*

Caro's skin had heated, but she was glad Drew had shown her. It was better that she knew what was said about her than that she lived in ignorance.

John had called it nonsense. While both Kate and Mary had advised her to think nothing of it, or Kilbride.

She had been surprised, though, when she'd not thought of it last night, nor of Albert. She'd expected to lie awake thinking of him, but instead she'd fallen asleep remembering her waltz with Rob, and during the day all she thought of was that tomorrow he'd said he would call early and then ask her to drive out with him.

She nodded as people spoke, and asked polite questions. But her thoughts were not in the room with them. Not because she was anxious at all, simply because she did not care that they were here. Few of the callers stayed longer than half an hour, and she was never in the room without Mary and Kate, and so the day was entirely bearable, yet exhausting.

When the clock chimed four, the last caller left and Caro fell back in the armchair, sighing.

Mary laughed.

Caro smiled at her. "May I cry off this evening?" The family were going to a musical evening. Rob would not be there and so there was no need for her to go. "After today I would rather stay here, if you do not mind?"

Mary rose and crossed the room, then pressed a hand on Caro's shoulder. "Why would we mind? Of course we do not. Remain here as you wish and rest."

"I shall retire now, then, if you will excuse me, Kate. May I take a simple supper in my rooms?" Caro stood.

"Of course, Caroline."

~

Rob had slept restlessly. His friends had teased him in the evening, wondering over the cause of his absences when he'd said he would be busy all of the following day.

"Is it a woman?" Tarquin had accused. "It is the only reason I imagine you might be drawn into ballrooms and drawing rooms."

"It is not," Rob had denied. But perhaps his skin had coloured because his friends had captured the theme.

"I think it is too," Arthur agreed.

"Who is it?" Stephen asked.

"No one. There is no woman." Thank God he'd been in Brooks's and not White's, where someone within his family might have heard.

"I think he lies," Patrick had teased. "You should be careful of this political reputation you wish to build if you are consorting with other men's wives."

"If any of you spread such a stupid rumour…" A threat hung in his words, but that was so unlike him, in itself, it probably gave the depth of his emotion away, and confirmed their assumption that it was a woman who was pulling him away from progressing his plan.

"Then he will take us down to Manton's and put us at the end of the shooting range as targets," Tarquin laughed.

"Yet, I still think it true," Thomas had thrown his t'pence in.

Rob had made a face at him. "But it is not and so please do not repeat your foolish thoughts." He had never lied in his life until he'd begun this thing with Caro. It was not only his plan her presence in London was leading astray, it was his morals too.

Memories of the twice he'd lain with her whispered in his head.

He had sinned with her in the summer, and he wished to commit sin with her again.

He swallowed against a dry throat as he knocked on the door of John's opulent town house. He would be alone with her today, he hoped, and he hoped they would have an opportunity to become intimate again.

Finch opened the door. "Master Marlow." He bowed.

Rob walked in. "Is anyone free."

"Their Graces have just broken their fast. The Duke is in the library, sir, and Lord Framlington is out visiting, however the Duchess and Lady Framlington are in the drawing room."

He presumed Caro was too. "Thank you, Finch, I'll show myself up."

He handed Finch his hat and gloves, then ran upstairs, taking the shallow stone steps two at a time, his heart thumping with an eagerness to see her.

When he walked into the drawing room, before he even said good morning, he asked, "Where is Caro?"

Mary stood up to greet him, smiling broadly. "She has not come down. She is not feeling well. I think things are taking a toll on her."

"We had a considerable number of callers yesterday. Or, rather, poor Caroline did and she chose to keep to her room last evening," Kate clarified.

"I cannot blame her, Rob, she spent the entire afternoon playing exhibit."

I should have been here. He wished to go to her room. The words hovered on his tongue, but of course he could not.

Instead he walked forward and kissed Mary's cheek, then Kate's. "I called early so I might see the children."

Mary smiled, "I will call for them." She crossed the room and pulled the bell rope, while Kate waved a hand encouraging him to sit.

"We are planning an outing." Kate sat forward in her chair. "Will you join us? We are asking all the family. We thought to take the children out somewhere and give them some space to run."

"When?"

"In a fortnight, when Mama and Papa are in town," Mary answered as she came to sit next to him on the sofa.

"Rob."

He rose and turned as Caro walked into the room, his heart flooding with a violin tune. He crossed the room and clasped her hands. She had dark circles beneath her eyes and she looked pale. "Mary said you were not well."

"I was tired. I did not sleep. Forgive me for not coming down, Kate."

He remembered himself as she looked at Kate, and let Caro's hands go.

"I understand entirely," Kate responded.

"I was going to go up and visit the children, but then I heard Rob arrive."

She'd come down to see him, then.

He returned to his seat, as she sat in an armchair near Kate.

"I have called to see the children."

She smiled at him.

He felt awkward and tongue-tied suddenly.

When the elder children were brought down from the nursery, George, Paul, and John's second, David, who was the same age as George. They vied for Rob's attention and so Rob let his concentration and energy be absorbed by them while the women talked and planned their family outing.

John was still in his library when it came time to eat luncheon, and so they ate in the morning room with the children.

As they finished, Rob looked at Caro. "You look as though you could do with some fresh air, Caro, and perhaps it may be an idea to escape the house before the calling hour. Why not come driving with me? We could go to the Tower. Have you been?"

She was sitting at the table with George on her lap. She looked up. "No, I have never been."

"Well that's it, then. We will go for a drive, in the opposite direction to Hyde Park, and ride out to the Tower and you will get some air and feel better."

A smile parted her lips slightly. "I would like that, thank you, Rob."

He looked at Mary. She was smiling at him too. She had seen nothing odd in his offer. "You do not mind if I steal her away for the afternoon?"

"Not at all, it will be good for you, Caro. George, come here poppet."

"Go fetch your bonnet," Rob nodded to Caro, meaningfully. "I'll await you in the hall."

She handed George to Mary, then rose and smiled again before leaving the room.

He said goodbye to the children, Mary and Kate, then left them and went downstairs.

When he waited for a footman to fetch his hat and gloves, and for John's grooms to bring his curricle around. He knocked on the library door.

"Come," John called in his ducal voice.

Rob opened the door, but he did not step in. "I just thought I would say hello. I have been visiting the children, but I'm leaving now. I'm taking Caro out to escape the callers."

John lifted a hand and smiled. He was in a meeting with Phillip, Kate's brother, John's business man. "Hello and goodbye, then."

Rob smiled at John, then Phillip. "Yes. Goodbye." He lifted a hand, then shut the door as Caro hurried downstairs.

If anyone beyond the servants had seen her haste they would guess there was something between them. Her smile was broad and excitement glittered in her eyes. She no longer looked tired. But John's servants did not know Caro. They had barely seen her for years, they would not know the expression was unusual for her.

She wore a moss-green pelisse and a matching broad-rimmed bonnet, with white rose buds decorating it and she also wore kid-leather gloves and a thin cream silk scarf.

He smiled at her as Finch crossed to pass him his gloves and hat. "We will be a while. If anyone calls to speak to Lady Framlington let them know she is out for the afternoon." He offered his arm to Caro, and then the door was opened and they were stepping out.

He had her at last.

His fingers pressed over hers as they lay on his arm, while jubilation skipped through his blood.

He handed her up into his curricle as the grooms held the horses, then he walked about the far side and climbed up himself.

When he took the reins he glanced at her. "I suppose this is nothing new to you. You must have ridden in Kilbride's or Drew's curricles."

"No, actually." The sunlight caught in her eyes, making them gleam gold. "Never."

"This will be a treat, then. Except we cannot go particularly fast in London. I should have taken you out when I stayed at Drew's; I could have shown you how fast my horses can fly."

"They may be fast, but I am sure they cannot fly."

"Very well, I admit they cannot, but it feels as though they can

216

when you are going at a gallop and racing through the wind."

He flicked the reins, set the horses into a trot and once they were a distance from the grooms, he glanced at her. "Caro, we can go to the Tower if you like, or we can go to my apartment?" He could see nothing but the rim of her bonnet. "Caro…"

Her head turned. "I have seen the Tower a dozen times, Rob."

"My apartment then…" *God.* His heart pumped with the power of a piston thrust. He drove through the back streets, avoiding the routes society preferred. They passed a couple of carriages, with occupants they might know, but her bonnet kept her hidden and he doubted anyone would be interested in who he had beside him. It was the rest of his family who were important. He was insignificant to the elite of London, a mere relation, unheard of as yet.

When they reached the stables where he kept his curricle he slowed the horses to a walk, then halted them. He threw the ribbons to a groom when he jumped down, and walked about the curricle to help Caro descend. He did not take her hand, but gripped her waist.

She kept her head lowered, demurely, keeping her face hidden within her bonnet.

They walked out from the mews and crossed the street, holding hands.

His apartment had a private staircase.

When they reached the black-painted door, he took the key from his pocket. His hand shook as he turned it in the lock. He ought not to be doing this.

She swept past him, her perfume hovering in the air. Lavender. He remembered the smell from their night in the dark. When he shut the door behind them and threw the bolt, she was running upstairs.

He followed her, hurrying too, and at the top, as she stood before his door, he caught hold of her. She lifted her head at the same moment he lowered his, ducking beneath her bonnet. "You must accept my apology now," he said over her lips, "for this and

217

much more."

"You are forgiven."

When their lips met it was as though he had spent his last weeks in a desert and Caro was water, their mouths opened and their tongues danced. "I love you," he said as he pulled away and opened the door to his rooms.

She paid no attention to the small amount of purposeful furniture in his sitting room, but reached to his shoulders, urging him to remove his morning coat. He pulled the ribbons of her bonnet loose before he conceded, and then as she tugged at the knot of his cravat, he released the buttons at the front of her pelisse.

When he was clothed in his shirt and his trousers only, and she in her dress, the buttons undone to her stomach, he gripped the back of her head and kissed her once more, pressing her back against the wall.

Her lips were swollen and her pupils wide and bright when he let her go.

She tipped her head back against the plaster and breathed in, as if she'd been dying of thirst too and sighed out her relief.

"How are you, Caro? I have been in agony waiting to get you alone like this." He slipped his fingers beneath the shoulders of her dress to take it off her.

"I missed you yesterday."

Her dress fell to floor and she stepped out of it.

"I know, Mary told me about your callers. I wish I had been there. I will be there tomorrow. Turn."

She turned her back so he might unlace her corset. "If you had been, you could not have helped, or held my hand as I wished."

"No, but I would have been in the room, and you would have known I was there." She tipped her head back onto his shoulder as her corset fell to the floor.

His hands crept over her stomach, running across the cotton of her chemise. Then he gripped her full breasts through the garment as he kissed her neck.

She sighed into the air.

They ought not to be here, and yet no one knew they were, it was as if they were not. They were in a secret world.

He turned her and kissed her again, then held her hand and led her to his bedchamber. A single chest of drawers and a wardrobe stood against one wall, and the bed against another. She did not look at them, she looked at him.

"Shall I light a fire?"

"No, we will be warm enough beneath the covers.

"Sit on the bed and I'll take off your boots." He unlaced her walking boots. Her feet were tiny and slender; they fit in the length of his hand. He stripped off her stockings too, rolling them down her pale legs. "Take off your chemise and your drawers and slip beneath the covers, while I take off my boots, before you become cold."

It was not yet winter, and odd days were still warm, but today was colder.

He sat on the edge of the bed, yanking at his boots, watching her.

She slid off her drawers first, beneath her chemise, but then she lifted that off. Her body was feminine curves and pale skin—beautiful. She lifted the covers and slid beneath, smiling at him.

His boot dropped to the floor. He removed the other and then stood and stripped off his trousers, underwear and stockings. Then, finally, he lifted his shirt off over his head.

When he joined her in the bed, his heart ran, pounding through his chest.

He was to be intimate with her again, in daylight, when he might see her body. He'd thought he loved her before today, but today… it was amplified a dozen times.

~

When Rob lifted the covers and lay beside her, Caro shivered. The sheets were cold. "Warm me up."

219

"Yes, m'lady." He laughed against her neck as his hand ran over her hip, then upwards. He cupped her breast and kneaded it. She rolled to her back as his head lowered and, despite the cold, her arms lifted above the covers as he began to suck her breast. His mouth was warm.

She clasped his shoulders and let every sensation seep into her blood.

The bed smelt of him.

She pressed her head back into the pillow.

His teeth caught her nipple and bit gently. "Ah."

He laughed, but then he licked it, before kissing across her middle and over her stomach. She lay back and breathed slowly.

Sunlight poured through the narrow window. It looked out across the street, but she could see the blue sky above the houses.

His fingers touched between her legs.

"Oh."

"I have dreamed of this so many times," Rob whispered against her stomach, before he moved down the bed and she opened her legs for him and shut her eyes.

"I have dreamed of it too."

He held her thighs gently as his lips, tongue and teeth caressed her.

Her body arched against him. She was not cold anymore. Her hips undulated as he worked, and her mind was completely lost in the sensations of adoration. The amber cross on her necklace slid across her throat as she moved. She died her little death on his tongue, and felt her body fall into the soft bed that smelt of him.

Then he was above her, looking down at her, his legs between hers and his body poised over hers. "Caro," he said, in a voice of utter adoration. "I have wanted you constantly since you came to town."

Her fingers brushed his fringe from his brow. "You have me now."

"Yes." He pressed into her, and she grasped his shoulders.

It was paradise.

Her breasts rocked with his movements, as he watched her body. It was their first time unclothed in the light.

"I love you," she said. He looked so young sometimes.

His lips twisted when he looked up, and then, his palms pressing into the mattress beside her shoulders he moved more vigorously. She lifted her legs.

His hips brushed against her inner thighs as he continued moving.

She raised her arms and gripped the iron struts at the head of his bed.

He moved more aggressively still. He had truly been longing for this.

She bit her lip and shut her eyes, letting him invade her with as much force as he wished, but his roughness was still unlike Albert's because if she looked into his eyes she would see the gentleness and emotion in Rob's.

He was looking down at where they joined, biting his upper lip, as he fought to avoid his release for as long as he might.

No he was not Albert.

"Oh." A sensation caught inside her, as he struck the sensitive spot between her legs. "Yes, continue like that." She said into the air, her body involuntarily arching. "Ah!" She cried out when she fell and the release rushed through her veins.

He looked at her with a smile and moved more aggressively, seeking his own completion, but when it came he withdrew and let himself pulse across her stomach, the warm sticky liquid settling there, as a muscle flickered in his cheek.

He'd had no need to be cautious, she could not carry children, and he knew that. It was another sign of his thoughtfulness.

He rolled away, collapsing beside her. "My conscience knows I should not have let this begin, I have no life to offer you yet, but I cannot regret it."

"You need not," she said in return, her body satisfied and her

221

heart full. "Tell me about your hopes in politics…"

"My hopes…" He laughed.

"Yes. You said you had a plan. Tell me about it…"

"I wish to make a difference in the world. To be influential. I want to speak out for the working class. For those who need a voice but have no power to speak in Parliament. They have no right to vote. They need a voice."

It was such a Rob-like statement, she smiled to herself.

He rolled towards her, looking at her, and his fingers ran across her cheek before he tucked the strands of her hair behind her ear. "There are numerous women who live in poverty and are forced to do things which they do not wish to do. I would free them from that life if I can. And I wish to free men from being controlled by their employers' greed. I wish to force employers into paying a fair wage. The current system favours the wealthy too much. They are allowed, within the law, to grind those who earn them their money into the ground. It is not right."

Respect and admiration swelled inside Caro, as Rob rolled to lie on his back. She turned to rest her head on his chest. "I am glad someone like you wishes to give them a voice. It will be a good voice. You are a man of compassion."

Albert sat in the House of Lords. She had heard him practise his speeches—he'd only ever spoken for the bills that made the rich, richer, and the landowners more secure.

Rob was so different. He cared not only about her, but for right and goodness. He was a good man. And she had feared he would forget her before coming to town, that had been folly, a foolish construction created by the history of her past. Rob was a good man who would not treat her lightly—her heart and head must learn that he was not Albert.

"My family would call it idealism, not compassion." He laughed slightly as his hand lifted and tucked behind his head. "But perhaps it is idealism. I had not realised how much money I will need to achieve this dream of speaking for the poor. Which in itself makes

222

the whole thing a farce."

"Your brother—"

"Do not say it." His hand slipped from beneath his head and rested on her hair. "How may I speak for the working class if I am living off my family? Yes, and before you say this too, I know a dozen others do it, but I am not them."

"No," Caro rolled onto her stomach, her fingers pressing onto his chest as she met his gaze. "You are not like them, you are passionate and compassionate and I love you."

~

The clock in the other room chimed four.

Caro brushed a hand across Rob's shoulder to wake him. They had lain in bed all afternoon, and they had made love twice, on the second occasion she'd touched him and aroused him once more, then used her mouth and ridden him, sitting astride his hips and watching the adoration in his eyes as his palms had lain on her thighs, his thumbs brushing over the inner surface.

But now it was time to go back.

"It is four, Rob."

His dark-grey eyes opened and looked at her. He smiled. "Sorry, I have so little time to spend with you and I fall asleep."

"I fell asleep too." It was the first time she'd slept deeply for days.

His fingers brushed her cheek. "But now I must give you up again. At least I think the dark circles that were beneath your eyes when I picked you up have gone."

"You have a way with compliments, Rob Marlow." She turned and began to rise, feeling him move, rolling to his side.

She looked back to see he'd rested his head on a palm, while the sheet settled low over his hip. The athletic definition of his torso was visible. It had been visible to her throughout their love-making, along with the dark dusting of hair across the centre of his chest.

"You are beautiful, you know you are, you do not need my

compliments, but if you wish for them, then what I notice more is your eyes when they turn gold in the sunlight."

She did not know what to say, the look in his eyes said hers were gold now. What she saw in his was adulation.

She rose and picked up her chemise from the floor.

"Caro." He stood behind her. His hands gripped her waist and pulled her back against him. Then he spoke into her hair. "I wish us to be married. I have nothing to offer you yet, but I wish it so, as soon as it can be. As soon as we do not need to rely on John or Papa."

The words slid through her soul. She wished for it too.

He kissed her earlobe. "But I do not want to say anything to anyone yet. Let us hold this as our secret. If my family know, then they will prevent us from escaping like this. We will act as friends before them, and be lovers when we are alone."

She nodded. She understood. She hoped for a future, yet what she valued most were these moments with him.

"Yes." She turned and kissed his lips briefly, then pulled free and bent to pick up her drawers and her stockings, then she began to dress.

He turned away to dress too. "I will call more, though. After yesterday I do not want to leave you facing any of those harpies alone."

Chapter 24

Rob slept well, the scents of sex and Caro seeping from his sheets into his soul. He was in love and as much of a slave to sex as Harry. The euphoria of release still glowed within his muscles and echoed through his nerves. He had not found the route to fulfil the plan he'd mapped out for his life before the summer and yet he'd found one constant for his life. Caro.

They would be wed, and until then he would have moments such as yesterday to hold close.

But he must strive harder to find the living that would enable him to take up a seat in the House of Commons. He could not endure being beholden to John for much longer, and he needed to support Caro.

In the afternoon, he sat in his brother's drawing room and wished the day were yesterday, when he and Caro had been in his bed. Instead he listened to the droning conversation of numerous female callers, all of whom ogled poor Caro.

He knew none of them, but when he was introduced he paid attention to their names. He would need allies at this level of society to achieve the political career he wished for; once he had his seat any bills he presented must be supported by others to win a vote, and some wives were able to influence their husbands. He did not attempt to participate in the inane conversation about frippery and fanciful ideas, though, he left that to Mary, Kate and Drew to manage, while he sat in silence trying to solve the puzzle of his life—how to earn a living to enable him to do what he wished.

But his reluctant brain refused to be led, and instead focused on images from the summer. The feel of Caro's hand about his as they'd ascended the stairs to that assembly hall. Their first kiss in that dark churchyard.

Sighing he uncrossed his legs, shifted in the chair and crossed them again in the opposite direction.

An image of Caro, damp and half naked, hovered in his head.

She glanced across at him as she spoke to someone near where he sat. These women would think him churlish, but for the moment he did not care. Let them think as they wished. She had come to town for him, and he was here for her. They both only endured these people so they might sit in the same room, with their desire unnoticed.

"Tea, Rob." Mary held a cup out to him. "You look bored. I'm surprised you came today."

He smiled at her, then noticed John walking across the room. He'd not even seen his brother come in. John took a seat beside Rob, once everyone in the room had ceased bowing and scraping, and leaned on the arm of his chair. "I would have thought you'd have better things to do than this, especially as you spent yesterday alone with the women. Were there no trips to look over horses, or some sporting activity to entertain you?"

"Were they the sort of pursuits you followed when you were on your grand tour?"

Mary walked away, leaving them to talk. It was very rarely that he spoke to John alone.

"No, I had one pursuit at your age, women. But I know you have far more self-restraint than I."

I did. "Unlike Harry," he responded with the words John would expect him to say.

"Quite. But perhaps I was as bad as Harry, in my way. My first paramour was Caroline and Drew's elder sister."

The fact punched Rob in the gut. He had not known that. "Lady Ponsonby…"

"She has not made a play for you?"

"God no." Rob shook his head, wondering why the hell John was speaking to him of such things.

"She likes young men. In fact she has a passion for them, but only while they are young. In my innocence, I fell for her charm. It took me until I met Katherine to realise that it had never been true affection, merely a craving for the wares she traded in. Like wine and the throw of a dice, sex is a drug of sorts, and women tempt you and then they trap you. You are right to avoid such things. I admire your discipline, but I would keep on your guard now you are in town."

Rob smiled, closed-lipped, trying not to let John see how untimely his warning was. He was no longer innocent, nor self-righteous and he liked the new drug he'd discovered. Even now their encounter yesterday warmed his blood, as though the ashes still glowed.

"So, what have you been up to? Do you need your time filled? I could put some work your way."

Rob sipped his tea.

When John had first come back from abroad, before he'd married Kate, he'd taken Rob to Tattersall's with him to buy his first horses and a carriage. Rob had been thrilled to acquire his older brother's attention. Now he did not particularly care for it. "Thank you, but no thank you. I appreciated you letting me sit with Phillip, but I want to forge my own path, when I decide what it is I want to do."

"That is understandable, Rob, and admirable. I am only glad the income I give you is allowing you the time to consider your choice."

A bitter taste burned the back of Rob's throat.

John's smile suddenly twisted sideways. "Do I annoy you with my largesse?"

Rob smiled too, ignoring the discomfort and taking his brother's gestures for what they were—kindness. "A little, I admit. There is no fulfilment in living on your charity." *Especially when I wish to help those who have no rich relatives to turn to. I would prefer not to make myself a hypocrite.*

"You wish to be independent. I appreciate that. But all I've given you is a foothold, Rob. Accept it for what it is, a gift. I have no intention of undermining you. I merely wish to see you, and the others, share in my wealth. You are my brother. Drew has made himself on the sum from Mary's dowry. He purchased his property with it, but it is he who manages his estate and has achieved the profits. He was not too proud to take it. Do you think him a lesser man?"

Rob turned towards John. Of course he did not.

"I know you do not. So why do you think yourself a lesser man because you live on my money. Did you know your papa's property was bought with Mama's dowry?"

Rob shook his head.

"It is no sin, Rob."

"I mean no insult to you, it is just…" He did not wish to upset John, but nor did he wish to speak of his aims yet. He would speak at the time he knew how to achieve them without John's help.

"I am not insulted. I can imagine how difficult it must be to carve your own path in the world behind a brother who is a duke. But you will find your way. Simply use what I give you to help you achieve it."

"I do not mean to seem ungrateful."

"I was your age once. I do know the need to be your own man. Why do you think I spent so long abroad? Had I come home Grandpapa would have had his hooks in me. However, I still lived on the allowance he provided, and I was not ashamed to do so."

"Are you telling me to stop sulking?"

John laughed, "Perhaps. Was that all I needed to say?"

"I was not sulking. I was thinking. I am still considering my profession."

"Very well, keep thinking. But while you do, give yourself permission to be young. You are far too sober at times. I know you well enough to know you have a vision for yourself, with some high ideal you wish to aim for, and neither Papa nor I wish to pin you down. All we wish for is to see you content."

"Your Grace. Lady Newbury."

John looked away and stood as another visitor was shown into the room. Of course it was up to John to help Kate welcome their new guest.

But John's discussion on the subject was not over.

Rob travelled with the others to his Aunt Penny's and Uncle Richard's for an extended family dinner, and at the table the subject of conversation turned to, "What might Rob do?" He was not even sure who began it, but every gentleman about him at his aunt's table had something to say, hurling suggestions into the mix.

Rob was not impressed. If they wished to interfere, he would rather avoid his family. His innards twisted with embarrassment. He knew what he wished to do, but his cousins were at the table, so he would certainly not speak about it here.

He was sure colour burned in his cheeks.

He did not look at Caro as the conversation progressed, but kept his gaze on his glass of wine, or his plate, despite the fact that he sensed her gaze rest on him. He was glad he had failed to secure her a place at his side. He'd escorted one of his younger female cousins in to dine, having been in the wrong place at the moment supper was announced.

Rob felt his blush intensify when his cousin Gregory commented. Gregory was the Earl of Preston's heir. He was a year older than Rob. Then Frederick, the heir to the Duke of Bradford, said something else and laughed. Frederick, another of his cousins, was six months Rob's senior.

They had never been close to Rob, they were closer to riotous and outrageous Harry. Rob had actively avoided them at Eton and then at Oxford.

It was not amusing to have his life discussed by them.

"We are heading out to the clubs after dinner, Rob, for a game of Farrow. Join us. Then you could leave what to do to chance…" Greg called from along the table, then laughed.

"You were always too much of a prude at school." Fred added to the conversation, descending into the open digs Rob was used to from them. He'd heard enough of them in his school years, but not before the rest of his family, and not before Caro.

They lived off their fathers and they were the exact example of why he did not wish to live off John, and why he wished to be far more than like them.

He would prefer to be a prude and have morals and ideals than live as they did. "Thank you, but no." Others were having conversations about the table; Rob's words cut over them.

"I spent most of my time at the races when I was your age. That is what led me into breeding horses," Forth, his father's close friend, stated. He was seated across the table, beside Caro. Rob glanced at him, avoiding looking at her.

"Have you thought of breeding horses?" Rob's uncle Richard suggested from the head of the table, highlighting that the conversation now included everyone.

Rob wished to rise and throw his napkin down, and thank them all for their interest, but then tell them to mind their own damned affairs. "Forth says I do not have the right eye." God, he was glad his father was not here to add another voice to this condescending crowd, he had persistently been inquiring after Rob's intent in letters. Yet it certainly gave Rob no desire to speak of his true intent, else that would be picked to pieces too.

"I did not say that," Forth denied. "I did say you do not have an eye for picking race horses, the mares you selected would have done well enough if you were looking for working stock. In fact they would have been an excellent choice."

Drew lifted his hand. "I am going to a market in Spitalfields in a couple of days, Rob. You may come with me and test your eye again."

The look Drew threw Rob, said, "*say yes and we will shut them up*".

"Thank you, Drew. Yes. I accept." Rob's pitch was blunt, and it said stop, enough, and if they did not hear it they were fools.

Greg smiled before lifting his glass. Rob wondered if he or Fred had begun the conversation for their amusement, at his expense. It meant it was not only John who'd noticed his dislike of being kept. The thought itched. He did not wish to be judged against others in his family. What he wished to do, he wished to do for others who did not have the opportunities his family were born to. Let those people judge him.

He sighed and reached for his glass.

~

Rob's cousin Gregory escorted Caro into the drawing room after dinner. The gentlemen had decided to drink their port among the women, rather than exclude them.

Gregory was brash and bold and laughed easily, at his own humour. He was the complete opposite of Rob, who'd spent the entire evening looking uncomfortable and willing himself into the background. She had not noticed that in the summer, before he'd stayed at Mary and Drew's, but among his family, he was more silent in nature, and he did not overly engage with them.

She did not have to endure Gregory's company for long. As soon as they entered the drawing room, he made his excuses and then he and another of Rob's cousins left.

"Caro, will you be my partner for a game of whist?" Mary called.

Caro agreed as the party broke into small groups. Some stood talking in huddles and someone played the pianoforte, while other young women gathered about it, and there were three tables that developed into card games. But as Mary dealt, Caro noticed that

Rob had not joined a group. He stood on his own, his buttocks leaning against a mahogany chest, as he cradled a glass of port in one hand.

He looked as though he was brooding. He'd been impatient with the conversation about him at the table, and she wondered if that was the cause. Yet even in the carriage he'd been quieter, and this afternoon she'd seen him talking to his brother, while a frown had played on his brow.

With Mary and Drew, he was happy and talkative, but amongst the rest of his family, including John, his confidence seemed to ebb.

She played half a dozen rounds with Mary, and they won four of them, but then she bowed out. "I need the retiring room, forgive me." She rose as Mary called for one of her cousins to play in Caro's stead.

When Caro returned to the drawing room Rob was standing in the same place, with the same closed-off posture, though a footman had refilled his port.

"A penny for them," she said as she approached him.

He looked at her and smiled. "Have you come to tell me to stop sulking too?"

"Are you sulking?"

"Probably." He laughed, at his own expense.

No he was nothing like his cousin.

He drained his glass and set it down on the chest, before sliding his hands into his pockets.

"Who thought you were sulking?"

"My brother, this afternoon, and my entire family, I think."

"Why?"

"Did you not hear them at dinner? You do not have your family, so it may be in bad taste for me to complain to you, but on occasion having a family that cares about you is as bad as having one that does not care at all. They all wish to tell me what to do with my life. I am not allowed a single independent thought. If I do not take their advice or rely upon them, then I am in the wrong,

232

and I cannot really complain because I am dependent on John. Yet it does not mean I have to like it and it is why I will not tell the truth about my aims. They would all seek to control them." He laughed at the end of his stream of words, his eyes glittering. "I am sulking, aren't I?"

She wished to wrap her arms about his middle and hold him. "Or perhaps it is just that you have a greater conscience."

"Is it too much to ask, to be a bloody independent man?"

She shook her head as her fingers touched his upper arm. "It is not too much and you are only one and twenty. There is plenty of time to fulfil your plan."

"One and twenty..." he said looking at her. "I hope you do not think that means I am too young to know my own mind."

"I did not say that, and I do not think it."

"No? What age are you, Caro? I have no idea."

"Seven and twenty." She saw no reason not to answer; it was better that he knew the truth. She had known it from the first. "Does it change things between us?" she said more quietly.

"No. My mother is four years older than my father. Did you know that?"

"Robbie, Caroline..." She had not known, of course, but their private conversation was brought to a close as his Aunt Penny joined them with Lady Forth. Caro's fingers slipped from his arm as she turned and smiled at them.

"I am having a ball the day after tomorrow, Robbie," Lady Forth stated, "Will you come? Your mother will never forgive me if I do not persuade you. They are returning to town earlier than planned so they might attend and they will wish to see you."

Caroline looked at Rob. His expression hardened, but he nodded.

He was truly out of sorts tonight.

She wished they were alone. She wished for the time to speak with him for longer. But she could not have either and so she stood near him, as he'd sat near her in the day, a silent support, as his aunts attempted to cheer him.

"I wished Alethea to come to town and have her debut at the ball, but she had a chill, and insisted on staying at home with Susan."

"Is Alethea well now?" Rob asked.

"Yes, yet when Alethea began recovering then poor Susan came down with the chill and has a mild fever."

"It is nothing serious—"

"If it was serious I would be at home with my daughters, Robbie dear. No, she will recover very soon, I'm sure." She touched Rob's arm in a gesture of affection. "There is one thing I do not worry over for my ball, and that is that people will not attend. It is a given when the Pembrokes are invited. There are so many branches of the family, and you are all so influential, so many of you have titles. The House of Lords is full of descendants from the Pembroke line." Lady Forth laughed.

Caro felt the penny she had offered to trade with Rob earlier tumble through her thoughts.

She understood.

He was a descendent of the Pembrokes, yet he had no influence. His father was a second son, and Rob was the eldest, his father's heir, and yet he had no title. He felt inferior, the weight of comparison must hang over him when he was among his family.

She looked at him, as he nodded at something Lady Forth said.

That was why he felt so strongly that he needed to prove his worth. He wished to feel equal.

You are equal in my eyes. He was worth a dozen of his cousins. None of them would have taken the time to help her as he'd done. None of them would have cared. She doubted any of them would even bother visiting one of their sisters, certainly they would not play with her children, let alone wish to change the world to help those who were treated badly and impoverished. They were far too fixated on self-indulgence.

So was another reason for his discomfort at the table his self-indulgent, titled cousins, who had been there listening to the others advising him on how to lead his life?

She wished to hold his hand and tell him she understood. She was born a bastard, after all, and for three years she'd lived as a dependent of Drew's—she, more than anyone, knew how it felt to be the odd one out.

Chapter 25

Rob avoided his family for a day. He'd not been able to bring himself to call at Pembroke House, even though he knew Caro must have endured more scrutiny. Yet she'd managed well enough the day he'd sat with her and he could not suffer any more condescending support from his family.

Instead he'd gone to the club and dined with his friends, only to face a barrage of questions from them. Tarquin had persisted with his theory that Rob had a woman, and when Rob had said he would be attending a ball, a few of them had threatened to obtain invitations to discover who it was. Fortunately the chances of them getting in were low. Like him they were untitled, and the majority held no relationship to anyone in high society.

When he climbed the steps to the front door of John's town house the following evening, it was with a measure of guilt. Caro's presence here was making him distance himself from the only true allies he had in his life, his friends. Yet if there was a choice to be made, he would choose her. But the fact that he was here again said that. His friends would have to endure another evening without his company—and any hopes of progressing his plans would have to wait until another day.

Finch opened the door. "Master Robert, the family are preparing for dinner, I am not sure who is in the drawing room."

He'd come at five deliberately. The callers would have left, and Rob guessed his parents were here now, but he hoped that people were dressing for dinner and that somehow he might capture a moment alone with Caro.

When he reached the drawing room that seemed unlikely. His mother and Mary were there with his father, Drew and John.

"Rob!" His mother crossed the room and embraced him, her arms wrapping about his neck.

"Rob." His father came to welcome Rob too. He had not seen them since the beginning of the summer, and yet he'd spent months away from them for years, ever since he'd begun at Eton.

When his mother let him go, his father hugged him too, and patted his back.

"You have been eating properly?"

"Yes, Mama. I am well. I wrote and told you. I have a small apartment, but I generally eat in the club."

She smiled at him, clearly pleased to see him.

They were a large family, but he'd never doubted he was loved. He'd said to Caro a day ago that sometimes it was as bad to have a family who cared as it was to have a family who did not, but that had been crass. He could not compare his upbringing to Caro's and Drew's; he'd lacked nothing.

He did appreciate his family. It was just that their interfering was excessive and controlling, but he knew it was led by kindness, and it was funny that he saw his friends as allies but his family as a nuisance. Perhaps he ought to begin to look for the positives in his connections. Their influence would help him win more allies in the House of Commons, if he could convert them to his philanthropist views.

"How are you getting along, son?"

"Very well, Papa."

"You are happy?"

"Yes."

"He is doing what young men do, Papa, when they finally have

237

their freedom—enjoying himself and staying away from us," John stated behind them.

Rob slid his hands into his pockets as his father turned.

But John looked at Rob. "They were the same with me, when I returned from abroad, fussing. Annoying isn't it? To be treated like a child, when you are anything but."

Rob gave his brother a close-lipped smile.

"Well, you are my children," his mother said. "And I am proud of you all for who you've become, but I still worry over you. It is a mother's task."

Her words were false flattery where he was concerned, though. He'd become nothing as yet.

She glanced back at him. "John said you were coming. I'm glad you've arrived early. Your sisters are dining upstairs with the young ones as we're going out. They will want to see you, Rob. Will you go up?"

He wondered if Caro would be there, with Kate, but he could hardly ask. He could go, though. "I'll go now," he stated.

He nodded at his father before leaving.

He jogged up the stairs to the nursery floor, his heart pumping hard. The lively conversation of the girls echoed along the hall. All his brothers were in school, and so it was only the girls, and the pitch was always higher. He heard Kate's quieter tones as he knocked on the door.

"Enter." Kate called.

There was a general melee within the room. The girls were playing with Paul and David, and fussing over Iris and Hestia.

"Robbie!" Jemima, his youngest sister, ran to him and clasped his waist. Then Georgiana, the next in age, hugged his midriff from the other side. While Jenny and Helen, who were sixteen and seventeen, came to express their greeting. After Jemima and Georgiana let him go, Jenny and then Helen kissed his cheek.

Helen could have come out this summer, but she'd chosen to wait until she could share the experience with Jenny.

"Robbie." Jemima said again.

"How are you poppet?" Rob tussled her hair.

"Hungry," she answered, lifting her arms to say pick me up. "Have you seen the babies?" He caught her beneath the arms and lifted her. She was getting too big for this, but she was still a tactile child, and she was the baby of his family, so they all spoiled her.

Jemima's arms wrapped about his neck, and her long legs gripped his midriff. He saw Caro then. He had not noticed her because she was sitting in a chair holding Iris, who was asleep.

She smiled.

"Where is George?"

"Asleep. Drew and Mary took him to the park this afternoon with your mother and father. He is exhausted."

"You may see him tomorrow," Kate stated. "We have brought the picnic forward as the weather was so good today. We hope it will still be so tomorrow. Are you able to come? We're going to drive out to Windsor, to the meadows by the Thames."

He nodded. Wondering what his friends might say when he was busy for another day. "I have nothing planned I cannot cancel."

Jemima played with his fringe, brushing it back from his forehead, and then watching it fall down again. It did not bother him. He was used to being petted by his sisters.

"How are you?"

"Have you been having fun?" Helen and Jenny asked simultaneously.

"If you will excuse me, Rob, I'll have another place set for dinner." Kate stood and gave her daughter, who was a little older than Iris, to a nursery maid. "I presume you are dining with us?"

He nodded. "Yes, thank you. I came early to see mother and father."

She nodded, then left the room.

"I'll put Iris down," Caro stood too, then turned to carry her to the younger children's bed chamber.

Rob sat down, with Jemima on his lap, and then told his older

239

sisters a little about his life in town. It had been very unfair to complain about his life; his sisters would never have an opportunity to live independently. They must marry and be dependent on a husband, or remain dependent on whoever within the family might keep them.

He thought of Caro. Of Caro calling herself a parasite.

She ought to be angry at him for his sulking, yet she'd not seemed angry.

When Caro returned she had not only set Iris down but changed for dinner. He asked Jemima to get up, "We ought to go down, Caro." She nodded as he stood.

"Goodnight then, girls."

"Goodnight, Robbie." Helen kissed his cheek.

"Goodnight." He received another kiss from Jenny, and then one from Georgiana, followed by Jemima. He bent down and let Jemima wrap her arms about his neck again. She tried to hang on to him.

He held her forearms and slid them free, laughing. "I have to go, Jemima. Mama and Papa, and, John and Kate will be waiting. I will see you tomorrow."

She gave him a disappointed smile.

"Goodnight all," he said finally, and turned to Caro. "Come along, before they hold me hostage." He gripped her elbow and saw Helen note it, her eyebrows lifting. Of course, they would not know that Caro had changed.

He merely threw her one last smile before he left.

When they walked from the room, his heart raced at the revelation that they would have a few moments alone.

He shut the door, looked along the hall and then, when he saw it was clear, his hand braced the back of Caro's neck and pulled her mouth to his. Her lips parted, and then the kiss became far more than he'd intended as her hands clasped his coat at his waist.

After a few minutes he broke the kiss and rested his forehead against hers. "I'm sorry that I did not call yesterday or this afternoon. Were you upset with me? Did you have to endure many visitors?"

"Not too many, but I missed you."

He caught hold of her hand and turned her to the stairs, but he had to let her go then, the steps were too narrow to walk two abreast.

"You must forgive me for sulking too, and for claiming that my family are remotely comparable to yours. I know they are not. It was crass of me to say it."

"I do not mind that you did not come. I do not expect you to order your life by me, and I understand."

"Understand…"

"How you feel." Caro glanced back as she reached the bottom step. Then she waited to walk beside him as they turned onto the next flight down to the first floor.

His brow creased. "How do I feel?"

"Inferior." His step hesitated, before his foot landed on the first stair.

Caro stopped and turned to look at him. "I can understand because it is how I felt when I was young amongst my brothers and sisters, and since I have lived with Drew it is how I have felt amongst your family."

He took both her hands. "You need not feel like that."

"Nor do you, yet you do feel it."

Damn.

Inferior? The word cut him to the quick. "I have never thought of it as that. I have always known I had my pride, yet… Inferior is a very bitter-tasting word. It makes me feel self-pitying. I do not think I like it, if that is what I am."

"It does not have a very nice taste, does it, and it's burned my tongue since the day your brother collected me from the little cottage Drew had hidden me in and took me to Pembroke Place." She actually laughed. "But I think I am recovered."

"Do you think I should be recovered?"

"I think you should be comfortable to just be who you are. You have great plans, and you should go ahead and fulfil them and be as idealistic as you wish." Her hazel eyes looked at him, as her words struck him in the gut.

No, he was not comfortable with who he was among his family. He was inferior amongst his older cousins. It was a simple fact, and the truth was he had not shared his aims with anyone, to avoid their judgement. Yet… *is that the true reason I wish to make a difference, to make something of myself and make myself equal, not to help those who need help*? The question and the uncertainty it ignited settled heavily on his shoulders. All he managed to say was, "Sorry." Because the feelings would not leave him.

He let her hands go, turned and began descending again, thoughts flying around in his head. *Inferior… Uncomfortable with himself…* They were harsh words.

The dinner gong rang as they reached the first floor. Rob lifted his arm for Caro to take.

"Have I made you angry?" she whispered.

He glanced at her and smiled. "No, just thoughtful. I should not feel as you described. I have no real cause to."

Before they entered the drawing room to join the others, he said. "Save a waltz for me tonight: two if you can."

She nodded and then Rob let his arm fall as he encouraged her to walk ahead.

Over dinner Caro participated in the conversation as much as anyone. It was only Kate and John, Mary and Drew, and his mother and father, and so she must feel comfortable… *bloody word*. But certainly she seemed happy, and his mother smiled at her and kept her talking, while his father watched a little bemused by Caro's participation.

When they gathered in the hall, awaiting the carriage, as the only single male, Rob took the opportunity to escort Caro, and took her cloak from a footman to then rest it on her shoulders. She smiled over her shoulder at him. Rob caught his father's gaze when she looked away.

His eyebrows lifted. *Caroline is letting you help her…*

Rob smiled. *Yes.*

When Caro took his arm, his mother bestowed a smile of approval on them both. He nodded at her to walk ahead with his father. His parents were to share John's carriage; he'd agreed to ride in Drew's with Caro.

Chapter 26

When they reached the Forths' there was a queue of carriages waiting to deposit their passengers. Theirs crept along slowly, continually stopping to stand as the next carriage unloaded. As they waited Drew discussed the cattle market he wished to take Rob to.

When their carriage pulled level with the portico of the Forths' town house, a footman opened the door and bent to lower the step, then lifted his hand to Caro. It was raining a light drizzle. Rob stepped down behind her and lifted the hood of her cloak over her hair.

They climbed the steps ahead of Drew and Mary. Her heart beat steadily and yet it was not unbearable or uncontrollable; she could still breathe. Her fingers did clutch his coat sleeve rather than lie on it, however.

"You'll cope. I'm here," he whispered as they crossed the threshold.

She nodded. She truly felt as though she would. She did not fear for herself at all any more. Yet there was a sudden churning in her stomach as she faced the receiving line and the ballroom full of people. John and Kate were already, walking into the ballroom with Rob's parents.

"Lady Caroline Framlington and Mister Robert Marlow." The footman introduced them as if the Forths would not know. Caro curtsied. "Caroline, Robbie," the Forths acknowledged.

"It is such a shame Alethea could not have come to town this year," Robbie commented, "I would have liked to see her make her debut."

Lady Forth smiled. "I think she would have come if Henry could be here, despite her illness, when Henry is ready to make his debut at balls then I think Alethea will."

"Lord and Lady Framlington!" the butler said behind them as Caro and Rob walked on into the ballroom.

There were a hundred spinning dancers beneath the thousands of shimmering prisms of light dangling in the chandeliers above them, and the room was crammed with people five deep about its edge. Voices and laughter rose above the notes of the string quartet. The air became close about her.

People looked at her as she and Rob walked on. "Do you want to dance immediately? If so, it is probably better I do not lead you, as I led you first the other night, but Drew will—"

"Are you well?" Drew touched her arm.

Caro looked back. "I would like to dance, I think."

He nodded and left Mary to stand with Rob as he took her hand. The music and the need to follow steps captured her errant thoughts and tied them down again, as she held his gaze and forgot about her audience.

"Kilbride is here," Drew stated as he passed her in the pattern of the dance.

"Where?"

"In the corner, to the left of the door. He is watching you again."

She glanced across and her gaze caught his. She looked away. Her heartbeat racing. Why was he watching?

"Ignore him."

Yes, she fully intended to try to, and yet it was disconcerting because for over three years of her life he'd been everything to her. The amber cross resting between her breasts whispered its presence.

When the dance came to an end, Drew walked her back to

where the Pembrokes' extended family had gathered.

Rob was speaking with one of his aunts and Mary stood beside her father. He turned and took Caro's hand, then bowed over it, with an odd expression. "I am thrilled to see you looking so much brighter, Caroline. Ellen and I have both felt for you over the years. I cannot believe the transformation."

Heat flared in her cheeks, and that sense of inferiority burned beneath her skin, and yet that was not what he thought, she knew that.

He let go of her hand. She bobbed a shallow curtsy. "I have conquered my fear, with thanks to your son. Rob helped me in the summer."

"I know, Mary told us, and yet I had not imagined it to be so much of a transformation. Congratulations. You have always held my admiration, but now it is far greater. Do you think you might bring yourself to dance with me?"

"Thank you, yes." She smiled. Rob's eyes came from Edward; they were the exact same colour, and Rob's smile was similar to his father's too.

Edward lifted his arm for her to take and led her onto the floor to join a set for a country dance.

Caro saw Rob join a set too, with one of his female cousins.

Caro was breathless when the dance ended, yet only from exertion.

Edward walked her back as Rob walked back too. Rob smiled at her then he looked at Drew as they both returned to where Drew and Mary stood. "Two of your friends are here. Could you ask them to dance with Caro? I think she ought to keep dancing. It makes her feel easier."

Drew's eyebrows lifted and Edward coughed, then laughed before turning away. Rob's female cousin was speaking with Mary and fortunately had not heard.

"Rob…" she breathed. It was true and yet it was not his place—

"Apparently I must be told how to help my sister," Drew looked at Mary as she finished her conversation and her cousin turned away. "I am to seek out Brooke and ask him to escort Caro in a dance. Will you accompany me? Caro, you ought to stay here among the family." He looked at Rob. "Surprisingly I am sensible enough to know that."

"I have upset him," Rob said as Drew walked away.

"I think so, but I am dependent upon him, and he has cared for me since we were young. He thinks of me as his responsibility."

Rob smiled as the notes of a waltz began, then he bowed over her hand. "May I have this dance?"

"Yes."

They did not talk as they danced. She just looked into his eyes as he spun her. There was a light in them that spoke of his feelings, as the gentle pressure of his hand at her back did too.

She smiled.

"I love you," he whispered in the last moments of the dance. She could not reply as the music stopped. But she squeezed his forearm once he'd lifted it.

When he took her back to his family, Drew stood there with Mary and his friend, Lord Brooke.

"Here is Peter, Caro, fetched as ordered to lead you into a dance." There was something odd in Drew's eyes, something that questioned as Peter laughed.

She offered Peter her hand.

"I would have come to offer without being ordered, Caro."

She smiled at him. She had known Peter since he was fifteen, when he and Drew had left school. "Thank you, Peter. I am grateful."

When he led her out to the floor, she asked, "Where is your wife?"

"With Harry and his wife. You have stolen me away from her, but Harry is minding her until I return, and then I am under orders to take you back there and have Harry dance with you."

"You are such loyal friends."

He laughed again, and they laughed through a lot of the dance as he joked with her when they passed in the movements.

When the dance came to end she excused herself. "I need the retiring room, Peter, would you let Harry know? I will be back soon."

He nodded and bowed slightly.

She had to weave through the crowd at the edge of the room to find her way back out to the hall, and then she hurried up to the first floor. Mary's maid was there.

Caro hurried back downstairs too. She did not wish to miss the next dance. Rob had been right, she felt much more comfortable when she concentrated on dancing. She pushed her way through those who stood about the edge of room. They were all looking towards the dancing and talking and so it was not easy to find a path.

Her arm was clasped in a firm hold as she passed through another gap.

It had been years, and yet she knew. "Albert."

"Caro. Will you allow me this dance?"

He did not bow or show her any respect.

He did not love me.

She wished to pull her arm free, but people about them were watching. His grip pulled her from the crowd and out onto the floor. It was a waltz.

She shivered as his arm came about her, a dozen memories of his hand lifting to strike her scattering through her head. She swallowed against the feelings tying up in her chest. It was not fear, it was another echo of her broken heart.

His hand held hers, in the firm, possessive way he had of touching her, and then he turned her. The scent of his cologne dragged her back through the years.

"That young boy you came in with is staring at you. Is there something between the two of you?"

He was talking as though he was still her husband—as though he had a right to judge those who danced with her. He did not.

She looked into his brown eyes. There was no depth, none of the open emotion that she saw in Rob's eyes.

"Is there?" Albert pressed.

She shook her head, as heat rose in her skin.

"Who is he? Is he one of Wiltshire's sons? He must be one of the Pembrokes. But which line?" A threat hung in his tone. God knew she was used to that pitch. It sent tremors dancing up her spine.

She swallowed against the dryness in her throat, and yet if she was to keep Rob from this, it was better for her to speak. "He is the younger brother of my sister-in-law, and they are all watching you, not just him."

He said nothing for a moment, watching her as she looked about the room, while he turned her. It was true, all of Rob's family watched.

She hoped they realised she had not chosen this.

Her heart raced.

"You are looking beautiful, Caro, but then you always did." Her gaze spun to Albert. There was still no sentiment in his eyes. Perhaps even in the beginning it had just been words.

But the increased pulsing of her heart was not all fear. He still had a harsh handsomeness. The intensity in his looks still wrapped a charm around her. Other memories crept into her heart, of their moments in bed—the moments in which he had convinced her he cared.

"You are not interested in that boy, are you? You could have me back, Caro, if you wished."

She gasped, and he looked down at her bosom as it pressed against her dress, then his gaze lifted and hesitated on the amber cross before lifting to look into her eyes. "You always did enjoy bed sport."

Colour burned beneath her skin. That he knew made it sordid.

"You could become my mistress and we could be as we were—"

"Congratulations on the birth of your son." Caro looked away as he turned her. "Is the Marchioness here?"

He leant close to her ear, his hand sliding a little further across her back. An image of him leaning over her, shouting in her face thrust into her mind.

"She is in the card room. She does not trouble herself over my paramours."

"I am glad you found a wife who gave you the son you wished for."

"I have a dull wife, who provides sons but does not warm my bed. You knew how to please me there."

She swallowed against the dryness in her throat. She wished to run. "But I was never enough. Leave me alone. I want nothing to do with you."

She looked beyond Albert's shoulder, at Rob. He stood at the front of his family group, with his arms folded over his chest. He was ready to move if Albert hurt her. He would risk everyone knowing his feelings. She could see it. He was her dark angel. His dark-blue eyes flashed a warning of retribution.

Albert spun her sharply. She looked back at the man who was more like a devil. His eyes stared into hers for understanding. He was looking for ways to persuade her to let him back into her bed.

She was not a fool; nothing would succeed. She did not love him anymore.

What they'd had had been flawed and broken from the start, and now it was past. For the first time she felt truly free of him. She did not love him, she loved Rob more than she had ever loved Albert.

When the music ceased Albert let her go and stepped back, then bowed formally, as though it had merely been a conciliatory dance. The eyes watching them followed him when he walked away.

Her hands trembled as she turned to leave the floor. But pride raged within her regardless. She had danced with him and held her head high, and he had begged her for her return, and she had rejected him. She clasped her hands together to hide their shaking. She longed to walk to Rob, but the whole room would notice it and think it odd, and so she walked to Drew.

Tears gathered in her throat in the aftermath of the storm, they hurt as if Albert's hand clasped her neck and tried to stop her from breathing and the amber necklace at her throat burned into her skin. Yet beneath that turmoil of emotion was still the pride in herself that she had faced him and withstood.

But she still now felt a need for some air and solitude, and yet she would not walk from the room and let Albert think he had chased her from society. She had returned and she was not going to let him think he had scared her away.

Drew's fingers caught her elbow as soon as she reached the group, and he steered her further away from the floor amongst the family. They surrounded her as if to provide a curtain of privacy.

"Do you wish to leave?" Drew whispered. She leaned on his grip, and his strength, because for the moment she had none.

"No, I have to stay. I will not let him think he has made me run, nor let him see he can disturb me. I have to dance and make it look as though all is well."

"Refreshments, then." He'd slipped back into the fiercely protective Drew of years ago.

She nodded.

The Pembroke family cleared a path for them as they walked out, and then walked about the edge of the floor. Eyes all about the room traced her movements. She sensed Rob's over them all. Drew led her to a table filled with glasses of champagne, and she took one from a footman. The glass trembled as she lifted it to her lips, trying to stand stiffly and appear as though she and Drew were merely taking a rest from the dancing.

"I'm sorry I was not watching."

"You could have done nothing. He stopped me when I returned from the withdrawing room. I should not have gone alone."

Her eyes looked past Drew's shoulder. Rob walked into the room, but he was not alone, he was with his father and Mary. Yet beyond him there were dozens of people walking through.

It had been the supper dance.

"May we sit?" she whispered, terrified her legs would give way.

Drew's fingers held her arm again. "Come." He nodded at Mary as she walked closer. She smiled as they turned to occupy a table for them all.

"Forgive me. I am still a little shaky," she said to Mary as she sat down. Then she looked up. Rob's eyes were pools of concern. He longed to take her away and speak to her, and offer comfort, she could see it there.

"I will fetch you something to eat, Caro. Mary." Drew touched Caro's shoulder.

"I'll come with you and help carry the plates." Rob stated.

"I will fetch you something to eat, Ellen." Edward withdrew a chair for Ellen.

It was as if they had all been shaken up.

Sipping her champagne, Caro watched the entrance to the room, but Albert did not come in and nor did his wife.

"I think Kilbride has gone. I've not seen him," Drew said when he sat down beside her, and put a plate before her. Rob gave a plate to Mary then sat down opposite Caro.

Mary and her mother began talking of the children, sweeping aside what had happened.

When Caro had eaten half her food, Rob's Uncle Richard strode across the room to their table and leant down. "Kilbride has gone."

Relief swept through her, even though Richard had probably made things worse if he had forced Albert to go.

She looked at Rob. He smiled at her, his eyebrows lifting to say, *are you well?*

She shook her head slightly. She longed to go and if Albert was not here it would not matter if she left. She turned to Drew as the notes of a country dance began. "Would you dance with me now, and then ask Rob to take me home?"

"I will, but I will take you home, Caro."

"I do not wish to spoil Mary's evening; she rarely has the chance to see her parents. Rob will not mind."

Drew's hazel eyes gained a dozen leagues in depth, but then he stood and walked to the other side of the table. He pressed a hand on Rob's shoulder and leant to his ear. Then he returned and lifted his hand for her to take.

"You cannot leave with Rob alone," he stated through the edge of his lips as they walked to the floor, we will all leave. Mary and I will come with the two of you. If you left with Rob alone, people would notice you both gone and come to other conclusions."

She swallowed against the bitter lump in her throat at his harsh warning, and yet, of course, he was right.

At the end of the dance they walked over to Rob's family and said their goodbyes. Rob was not amongst them.

Then Drew walked across the room with her and Mary to say goodnight to the Forths.

She curtsied and told them not to worry when they apologised about Albert. Then she walked out into the hall. For the first time in an hour Caro felt able to breathe. Rob was there. He held her cloak in his hands as a footman held Mary's.

He smiled at her, a smile that said, *how are you?* Once more. *Better now I am close to you.*

His hands trembled as he set her cloak on her shoulders, and when she turned to take his arm there was another look in his eyes, a look she had often seen in Drew's—a burning need to protect and defend.

Chapter 27

In the carriage ride home, Drew offered to drop Rob at his apartment, but he declined. His heart still hit against his ribs in a sharp rhythm. He would not be able to sleep unless he had a chance to speak with Caro.

Anger seethed in his blood. It was difficult not to clench his hands into fists. He wished he could have walked onto that floor and thrown a fist at Kilbride, several fists. Yet he was angry with himself too. Why had he not been watching?

Caro's thigh was near his and he could feel her trembling still. Why had he not been close enough to prevent it?

"I'm sorry, Caro." Drew stated. "I should have been looking and ensured you came back to Mary."

"I'm sorry too," Rob stated. "If I had seen him approach you, I would have stopped him."

Drew made a low sound of frustration in the back of his throat.

"It was no one's fault," Caro answered.

"How did he get hold of you?" Drew asked.

"I left Peter to use the retiring room and when I returned Albert was in my path. When I passed through the crowd, he caught a hold of my arm. I could not extricate myself without causing a scene, and neither of you could have gripped my other arm and begun a tug of war." She glanced at Rob, then looked at Drew.

"I could have waited in the hall for you to come down, and then he would not have been able to stop you," Rob stated, the need to be her protector burned in his blood.

"And the entire place may have noted such a thing and rumours would have begun," Drew barked. "It is I who needs to stand with Caro, Rob."

A sigh left Caro's lips.

It was the second time Drew had snapped at Rob tonight, and his unspoken words were *stay away, she is my responsibility.*

Yet she ought to be mine.

"What did he say? Did he threaten you?" Rob longed to hold her hand at least, to offer comfort.

She shook her head. "Albert speaks with actions, not threats." A shaky breath pulled into her lungs. "He asked me to become his mistress."

"No!" *The bastard.* What a thing to say!

"Caro." Mary sounded horrified, and she leant across the carriage to briefly clasp Caro's hand.

"I would like to hit him." Drew stated bluntly, his right hand gripping into a fist and banging on his thigh.

"I think he truly thought I might accept. He was always arrogant. He claimed he is unhappy with his wife, but I think perhaps it may simply be because he liked to control me, and now he has no control over me, he wishes to claim it back."

Rob could not look at her anymore, instead he looked out of the window into the dark streets beyond the carriage. He could not protect her fully unless they announced an engagement. Perhaps they ought to do it…

When they reached Pembroke House, Drew offered Rob a drink as they walked up to the drawing room, and once he was there poured one for Caro too. "Drink this," he stated as he handed it to her.

Her hand shook as she took it.

Drew was watching her with a look of remorse on his face, a

look that said he wished he could wrap Caro up and protect her from the world. But that was what Drew had done for years; it had not been the answer. Caro was now dealing with her past in the way it ought to have been dealt with.

But my marriage was not always bad. I loved him. She had told Rob that in the summer.

Rob wondered what she'd thought when Kilbride made his offer.

Envy pricked his skin. As she'd danced with Kilbride, Rob had watched them. They'd looked well together. He wondered what people thought of him and Caro.

He wished to speak to her alone, but Drew did not retire, even when Mary did, so when the clock struck one, Rob stood. Caro must be tired, she must wish to sleep, and he assumed Drew had no intention of leaving the two of them alone.

"I'll take my leave. I shall see you tomorrow."

Drew nodded. "Shall I call for a carriage?"

"No, I will walk. I am comfortable to do so, and it will clear my head," *and dispel some of my anger*. He was too emotional tonight; he could not hide his concern for Caro.

Caro stood.

He took her hand. "Goodnight, I hope that what happened this evening does not disturb your sleep."

He leant to kiss her cheek, as he might kiss one of his sisters. "Goodnight."

Her skin darkened. He could not see the redness in the candle-light, yet he knew it was a blush.

When he let her hand go, he smiled and bowed slightly, then he turned to look at Drew. "Goodnight."

"Rob," was all Drew said.

Rob walked from the room. It would be a dark, cold walk home tonight; he did not have an outdoor coat.

~

The candle in the room flickered as Rob left and shut the door. Caro looked at Drew. She had hoped he would leave them alone, but he had not. She'd hoped if he'd left her alone with Rob that Rob might be able to come to her room. She longed for Rob's comfort in her bed tonight.

"Sit down again, Caro," Drew said with a weary note.

She did sit because there was something odd about Drew's voice, and his eyes held a strange look of disappointment. "Why?"

"I need to speak to you. Give me your glass and I'll pour you another."

She picked it up from a table and gave it to him. At least the liquor would help her sleep. She did not think she would sleep without it.

He returned to her bearing two glasses. He gave hers back to her and she sipped from it when he sat.

He swallowed a mouthful from his own glass, but did not speak.

"What is it, Drew?"

He held his glass in both hands, sitting forward in the chair. "God, Caro, I do not know how to say this to you."

"Say what?"

He swallowed, although he had not taken another sip, and looked down at the floor, then he looked up and met her gaze. "He is infatuated with you. It is obvious to me. It must be visible to others too."

"Who?"

"Rob." He held her gaze as the word struck.

She sipped from her glass, the brandy burned her throat as a blush burned beneath her skin.

"What is between you? Is there something?"

She shook her head, not looking at Drew but looking at her glass.

"Caro," he said in an impatient, impassioned tone. "I am not a fool. I have eyes. He rarely looks away from you when we are out, and he does not in general dance, which is not unusual for a young man, and yet he takes pains to dance with you. Then tonight he

257

deems to tell me how I ought to care for you. I was glad of your friendship with him in the summer, glad that he has helped you, but, Caro, how far has it gone?"

She looked at him, confused, the heat in her cheeks burning harder.

"How far, Caro?"

She shook her head, unwilling to discuss what was private.

One hand left his glass and lifted to swipe through his hair. "I have no idea how to say this to my sister. But Mary and Rob are not like us. They have not been brought up to endure shallow hearts. They have never felt cold inside and unloved… Damn… I am not explaining myself well, am I? But damn it all to hell, Caro, I hope you have not been behaving like Elizabeth."

"Elizabeth…" their eldest sister.

"Yes. But it seems there is only one way to say this to you. Have you seduced him, lain with him? Mary's bloody brother."

"I… I…," she stuttered.

"Rob is not like our family, nor is Mary. They do not have affairs. Rob's reputation is well known. He does not dally with women. His cousins tease him about his morality."

"I did not intend—"

"If you have slept with him, as far as I'm aware, you would be his first. Are you his first? Have you been playing games with the boy? If so, you will hurt him."

Drew's words cut, slicing though her middle. "He is not a boy, and I am not playing games with him."

"Aren't you? He is one and twenty, with no property of his own. He is uncertain of what he wishes to do, and even when he decides, he will need to work for five years or more to earn enough to purchase somewhere, and he is fiercely independent. That is very important to him."

She did not know what to say.

"You came to town to see him, did you not?"

She did not answer.

"His cousins have begun talking about his odd behaviour. They are speaking about him in the club he does not go to, so he will not know. Your name has not yet been linked to it, but it will be soon if you continue this and it will break him."

She sipped the brandy because her throat was so dry.

"What happened when you went for that long drive when I was out?"

She blushed. It was as though he'd slapped her. "It is not what you think."

"I concede he is not a boy and I know the two of you discovered a friendship in the summer, but it should have gone no further. If you are his first, such a thing engenders emotion and Rob is a young man with high morals. If you have lain with him, he will feel obligated to marry you."

Caro swallowed and bit her lip, nausea rolling through her stomach. She wished to deny everything Drew said, yet it was true.

"I do not doubt he is now in love with you. It is in his every look. It will be a bloody mortal wound to him if you end it. But I urge you to do it, even though it will cut him now. Give the lad space and time, Caro, let him grow up and find his feet. If there is really something between you it will last the years. Do not snatch the poor man straight from the cradle."

"It is hardly the cradle," she breathed. *If she had been his first, why had he not said so?* Their moments in that empty cottage returned. She had urged.

Did I seduce him?

She met Drew's gaze. "I did not—"

"You have done more than nothing with him. Your face says so."

"I have not seduced him, we—"

"Who kissed who first? In fact, you need not even answer, because I know it would not have been him. His morals are too high. It began with a kiss and then…"

She had not known that night who kissed who first. But she had gone to the library, and she had gone to his room the second time they'd been intimate. He would never have come to her.

Her fingers pressed to her collarbone at the base of her neck. She had begun it.

"You look white; you did not know that he was innocent, did you?"

She shook her head.

"Drink some more of the brandy."

He leaned back in his seat, watching her and finished his drink in one swallow.

She felt sick.

"You will have to explain to him that now is not the right moment for you, that it is better to have time, because if you say it is because of him, he will be mortified, Caro."

She nodded, numb.

"I cannot believe that you have done this, and with Mary's brother, of all people." He rose, then, and walked across the room, to leave his glass on the side. Then he turned back. "I will retire. I had hoped, Caro… I had always thought… That you were not like the others in our family, and yet this… Did you learn nothing from their barbaric ways?"

He turned, and walked from the room.

Caro stood.

She had agreed to marry Rob, but Drew was right, his feelings might be infatuation. If she had been his first…

Drew left the door open.

Caro blew out the candles, which burned in a candelabra on the mantle. Then she walked across the room and blew out those in the candelabra that stood on a table on the far side of the room. Then she walked out into the hall. A footman waited near the stairs.

She ignored him and climbed the stairs towards her room, her limbs heavy. Rob had not chosen to do the things they'd done; she'd urged him.

Seduced. Trapped. He'd called the word inferior, bitter, and said it sounded like self-pity. The words Drew had used were a dozen times worse. They made her sound predatory and cruel. She had not been that. That had not been her intent.

Once the maid had helped her undress, and left, Caro looked at herself in the mirror and saw the amber cross hanging at her throat. It had been the one thing she'd clung to from Albert. He'd given it to her when they'd first wed and she'd never removed it. It was a memory of happier times.

With shaky fingers she released the clasp, then left the chain and the pendant on the chest of drawers. She needed no reminder now. She had no wish for memories of Albert. She had no feelings left for him. The feelings and memories she wished to cling to were for Rob.

When she lay down in bed, in her nightgown, between the cold sheets, she wrapped her arms across her chest and wept, feeling a dozen times lonelier than she'd done before. She did not wish to be in the wrong. She loved Rob. All she wished for was for his love in return. But had her craving for love made her take advantage of an offer of friendship?

Oh, she had believed in Rob's love. He'd convinced her wholly since she'd come to town, that it was real and lasting, and yet… Her knowledge of love was so shallow, how could she tell? She had been wrong about Albert, and Albert had been the only person to show her any depth of emotion beyond the brotherly love Drew had always offered her.

Then all she could do was trust in Drew's judgement. Another tear ran onto her cheek.

Chapter 28

When Rob approached his brother's lavish town house, it was with an intent. He'd come to participate in the picnic, and yet he'd equally come to speak to Caro. He wished to announce their engagement. It was the only way he might have the right to care for her openly. They might need to be engaged for years, it might restrict how easily they could slip away, and yet he could not stand to be in the position he'd been in last night. He could not watch her with Kilbride and do nothing.

He'd spent the night awake, with nausea rolling through his stomach.

I will feel better once I've seen her.

He'd wished for a night with her. He'd wished to hold her, to know that she was safe in his arms. Yet thinking of holding her only reminded him how fragile she felt when he did.

He parked his curricle behind the long line of carriages waiting before the house, let a groom take the ribbons, and jumped down.

When he walked into the drawing room there were numerous members of his extended family filling it up. It looked as though they would be travelling in a dozen carriages.

He saw Caro. She stood in a far corner alone, looking out through a window. She was dressed in lemon yellow. The colour was bright, yet her posture and expression were not.

Perhaps she'd been looking for him, but she did not look at him now he'd come into the room.

He bowed to one of his aunts and said good morning, then spoke to a couple of his female cousins as he worked his way across the room.

Caro looked like a phantom again today. She was overly pale and silent, and she had still not looked away from the window.

When his mother stopped him to speak, he refused to be delayed again. "Forgive me, Mama, but I wish to speak to Caro for a moment before we leave."

His mother gave him a questioning look, but smiled and turned away.

He walked the last few paces, then took Caro's hand from where it had rested across her midriff, bowed over it and pressed it to his lips, not caring what anyone thought. But everyone was probably too focused on their own conversations to pay any attention to him. When he rose he kept a hold of her fingers as she looked at him.

"Caro…"

There was sadness in her eyes and she did not smile.

"You look as though you did not sleep."

She pulled her hand free and looked beyond his shoulder.

Rob glanced back, following her gaze, to see Drew watching them.

He smiled.

An odd sense, like a feeling of premonition, slipped over Rob, an internal shiver. Something seemed wrong.

He looked back at Caro. "Are you very disturbed? I have brought my curricle if you would like to ride with me today? Perhaps we could—"

"It is better we do not, Rob. Phillip has offered already and I accepted."

Phillip… The name was a punch to Rob's chest, in the position of his heart. Yet he merely nodded and turned away, unsure how to respond.

263

Phillip…

"We are all here, so I propose we leave! The carriages are ready!" Kate called across the room.

A stream of his relations, and a stream of conversation, flowed down the stairs. Then, in the hall, there was the bustle of cloaks and coats being put on. Rob watched Caro slip on her straw bonnet. Its yellow ribbon matched her dress. The pelisse she put on was a pale brown.

The front door opened and outside more than a dozen footmen waited to hand them all up.

Instead of Caro, Rob took Jenny and Helen in his curricle, the two of them squeezed in beside him, smiling brightly, wearing bonnets and cloaks, with their hands on their laps. Both of them had acquired new pairs of kid-leather gloves.

Their friendship was so close he could imagine them never settling on husbands because they would not wish to be separated.

He was one of the first to leave. He did not wish to hang about to see Caro with Phillip, but as he drove he could sense her following somewhere behind him, watching his back.

Why had she not wanted to ride with him? It would have been a perfect opportunity. It was only his family here, and they would understand their friendship.

"Are you jealous that Caroline is riding with Phillip? You keep looking back."

Rob looked at Helen, shocked.

"I heard you danced with her," Jenny stated.

"She conquered her discomfort in the summer. She dances now, not just with me."

Jenny smiled. "She is pretty, though, isn't she, and Papa said he thinks she has caught your eye."

"And who did he say this to?" Discomfort twisted in Rob's stomach. Was that the cause of her pulling back?

"To Mama, in their rooms, but I overheard."

"And you thought it wise to repeat it?"

264

"Only to you, and Helen, no one else. Do you like her?"

Yes, a lot. "Jenny. You are not to say anything to anyone and you may tell Papa, if you dare to admit you were eavesdropping, that Caroline and I are friends. We became friends in the summer when I stayed with Mary. There is nothing more."

"Except that she is entirely different, and Mary says that is down to you. And Papa says you are acting oddly."

"It is still only friendship, Jenny, and you will embarrass her if you share this."

"I heard Frederick say you were acting oddly too."

"And you would take his word for that." He did not value the opinion of his arrogant cousins. *Inferior.* That horrible word rattled through his bones. "I am acting as I act." He glanced at Helen, then Jenny. "No more talk of this, and if you hear anyone say it, pray tell them they are wrong."

Yet an hour ago he'd hoped to announce his engagement within the week. *It is better we do not, Rob. Phillip has offered already...*

He looked ahead.

There had been nothing particularly wrong with the words she'd spoken, except maybe, *better not*, but her tone of voice and the look of sadness in her eyes had disturbed him.

"Harry was supposed to be meeting us there," Helen said.

"But Papa stopped his allowance this month, and so he said he could not afford to travel. Did you hear?" Jenny asked.

"Papa is constantly stopping his allowance," Rob answered. When Rob had still been at college he'd had to frequently bail his brother out of debts because he had no income, and yet he continued to spend.

"He broke into his master's room last week for a dare and hung his underwear from the window."

"Yes, that is something Harry would do..."

The conversation continued on the subject of Harry for a little while and then turned to what their other brothers had relayed in letters home.

265

Their procession of carriages was like a ribbon running through the countryside, and when they reached the meadow by the Thames, where Kate had planned for them to eat their picnic, there were already two dozen servants there setting out tables and marquees to keep the women shaded from the sun. The great castle stood on the hill above them and the Thames meandered through the flat meadow beneath it. It was a picturesque place.

He was handing Jenny down when Phillip and Caro arrived. They'd travelled alone and she did not look uncomfortable. She was smiling. Rob looked away before Caro saw him watching. He did not wish to appear as though he cared. But if "inferior" was a word that cut, then jealousy was an emotion that growled.

He helped Helen down and then the two girls walked away to offer to help Kate.

"Robbie!" Jemima cried, as she and Georgiana raced across the grass, the hems of their dresses flying.

"Jemima!" He caught her up and spun her, laughing with her. Then he set her feet back on the ground. He'd always been a favourite of the younger girls, because John had been too distant and too old for them to idolise and so they had picked on him, because he was away from home, doing the things they wished they might do. Of course, Harry rarely gave them any attention, so he could not be admired.

He gripped Jemima's hand and rested his other arm about Georgiana's shoulders as he walked towards the others who'd arrived. They were gathering by a group of blankets the servants had laid out.

Caro walked that way too, with her hand on Phillip's arm. She joined the group first, and began speaking with Kate and John, Rob's mother and father, and Mary and Drew. Mary was holding Iris, and Kate held her youngest, Hestia, while Drew held George, and John carried David. Paul stood beside John, gripping his father's trouser leg.

Rob would have walked to another group, but Jemima pulled

him in their parents' direction.

His heart tugged that way anyway.

"Uncle Bobbie!" George cried, raising his arms.

"George!" Rob called back with a smile on his lips, looking only at the child. Jemima let go of his hand, and he took George from Drew. "You are suitably excited, I see, and ready to tire your mama and papa out."

George grinned. "Tumble."

"In a moment. Let me say good day to everyone first."

"Good day, Mary, Papa, John," he swallowed as he looked, "Phillip." Caro he had already spoken to, so he did not say good day, and yet he ought to say more than a simple good day to Phillip, but the words stuck in his throat. He swallowed again. "How are you, Phillip? Thank you again for letting me sit with you the other week."

He was intensely aware that Caro's fingers still gripped Phillip's arm. It made it impossible to speak with Phillip dispassionately.

"You were welcome, as you know, and if there is any more I might help you with."

Rob nodded, but then his gaze reached to Caro. He could not help it. His gaze asked why she had not wished to travel with him.

There was no answer in her eyes; the amber was blank, like shallow glass.

"Uncle Bobbie tumble…" George begged again.

"It is Uncle Robbie." Paul corrected, looking up at Rob with pale-blue, assessing eyes just like John's, as though he thought George and his exuberance an oddity. Paul was three, yet sometimes he sounded thirty, but he was the heir to a dukedom and was already being schooled.

Still, "inferior" was not a word that Rob would have George feel. "I am Bobbie to George, Paul, and I think I always shall be." He tussled Paul's hair, because Paul ought to be a boy before he became a duke.

George tugged at Rob's hair, calling silently for all of his attention.

"Are you going to show your cousins how you can hit a ball with the bat today? You will have to hope your papa, or grandpapa, or one of your great uncles has brought a bat and ball."

"Uncle John has."

"Ah, well, then we are in luck." Rob laughed, then looked down at Paul.

"Now, if George and I are to play tumble, then I think we should play on the blankets. So if anyone else wishes to play, then they may come with us." The offer was put to Paul, but it was David and Jemima who squealed with excitement.

John set his second son down. Georgiana took David's hand, as Rob set George down. George's little legs raced ahead. Rob followed. It was better to be out of Caro's way until they might speak alone.

The morning progressed, with the men setting up a game of cricket, but because George wished to play, then all the children did, and so it became a game of fathers holding the hands of their children and helping them bat, and then the little ones were lifted off the ground when they needed to run.

George had thought it amusing when Rob had picked him up and run with him. He'd had the giggles for ages.

Rob was exhausted, though, when it came time to eat, and hungry. He'd taken off his coat because he'd grown hot, and it was easier to move without it, although he still wore his waistcoat, but he had also rolled up his shirtsleeves to his elbows.

It was not polite dress for a park and yet all the men in his family had done the same.

George walked beside him, holding his hand, and Drew walked on the other side of George. Caro was sitting on a blanket already, with Mary. She held Iris and Phillip was nowhere in sight.

Rob dropped down onto the blanket, remembering the gathering in the summer, before he'd gone to Mary's, when Caro had darted off into the house. He had not known her at all then.

How different things were now.

When he rested his forearms on his bent-up knees, he could feel her looking. He turned. She'd been looking at his arms, at the one part of him that was unclothed.

They knew each other fully without clothes.

She glanced up and smiled awkwardly, blushing a little, then looked away.

He still had that sense that something was not right.

"Would you like some lemonade, Robbie?" He looked up to accept a glass from Helen, only to see Drew watching him too.

He smiled, and Drew smiled.

"Shall I ask Jenny to fill a plate for you, Robbie?"

He nodded.

Helen looked at Drew. "Would you like one? She could fill a plate for you and George."

"No, I shall go to the buffet and help myself, do not worry."

Helen nodded then moved on, and caught up with Jenny.

"Did you see me hit the ball, Aun'ie Caro?"

"Yes, I did George."

"And we ran."

"I know."

"I hit the ball right across the field."

"I saw. I'm very proud of you."

"You have wonderful patience, Rob" Mary said.

"What is patience, Mama?" George crawled towards her.

"What everyone needs when they are faced with your energy."

Caro and Drew laughed. Rob smiled—he was no longer in a mood to laugh.

"You are good with the children."

Rob looked up, to see his father standing over him, with his mother.

They had come over to sit on the blanket beside the one Mary and Caro had occupied.

Rob turned, so his back would not be to them, and yet, after Jenny's words earlier, he felt uncomfortable with his father being

269

so close.

Helen returned with his plate, and then Drew rose to go and fill a plate for him and Mary, Caro already had a plate beside her.

"Can I have some?" George asked looking at Rob's plate.

"I will bring you something on my plate." Drew answered, before walking away.

Rob held out his plate anyway. "You may take a piece of the cold pie now, but, hush, do not tell your mama."

George gave him a devilish, cheeky little grin that was so like Drew, and then picked the piece of pie up and tumbled backward.

Of course, Mary had heard and seen, but she laughed at Rob's dry humour as George gave her a funny, suspicious look.

"Grandmama." George turned to her to obtain a place of safety to eat his pie. She drew him onto her lap.

"Grandpapa!" Paul shouted, hurrying over to the blanket. "David and I will sit with you."

Rob's father patted the blanket. "Sit here."

Paul settled himself and had David sit next to him between Rob and his father. A footman appeared with a full plate. "Lord Sale." The servants knew the lad would be their bread and butter one day. Was it any wonder his cousins, and men like them, had grown up thinking they had a right to order, and play, with the world? There was Paul, who would be handed everything he needed, and then there was open-hearted, accept-me-as-I-am, George, who would spend his childhood like Rob—unable to compare.

Inferior… Perhaps. He suffered. But whatever the emotion, his experience of such feelings had helped give him the idea and incentive to speak out and fight for the underdog. He still wished to do that. More than anything.

John sat behind his sons, with Kate beside him holding Hestia in her arms, and then Phillip, who'd been with them, walked around to sit beside Caro.

Rob's skin itched and he sighed again quietly.

When Drew returned, as they ate he spoke to Rob's father about stock management, asking questions, and Rob listened, interested. He was to go to the market with Drew in the morning. Farming was an option he'd not yet considered properly. He'd dismissed it because it was what his father did, but that was before he'd realised just how much money he would need to help acquire and then fund a place in Parliament.

"How did you get started," he asked them both, "I mean, I know how you came by the lands, but where did you begin?"

"Are you interested in farming now?" his father prodded, laughing. "You have paid no interest before."

"Perhaps, Papa. I am allowed to explore."

He nodded. "Yes, you are. I'm sorry."

"Most of it, day to day, I leave to others, as you saw when you stayed with us," Drew answered. "But I like to know what is what. I like to be asked for agreement before a decision is made, so that I can learn and so that I feel in control. But I began by asking your father and John what they did."

"And I spent hours with the steward on your uncle's estate, and learnt it all first-hand. If you are interested, Rob," his father said, "your Uncle Robert has a vacant tenancy, the property that used to belong to Aunt Jane's family. I bought it on his behalf when it was sold off years ago. It's a large estate. You would make a fair profit from it. I can ask him about it if you'd like."

"I am able to speak for myself and he has already mentioned it, but I'm sure he'd rather keep it open for Henry? And if not, then one of the others ought to have it, Percy…" Percy was his Uncle Robert's second son.

"Can you imagine Henry farming? I cannot, he would not apply his mind to it any more than Harry would be capable of it—"

"Papa, I am only thinking about farming, I have no idea even if I wish to do it." This was what happened if he mentioned anything to his family. Within a moment it was all planned out for him.

"Well, if you decide you are interested, Robert would let the property to you, willingly, because you are my son and you were

271

named after him, after all."

"It would be another favour, then," Rob answered, quietly, not really for his father's ears as a bitter note cut into his voice.

Inferior. It was the need to be—given to—which had left him with such an emotion. But Caro was right, it was what he felt, and it prevented him from letting people help. He breathed out. It was foolish. If he wished to be a good politician, it was an emotion he needed to let go of. Perhaps he was, in a way, as self-absorbed as his cousins were in their arrogance. *Inferior.* Damn it! It made him feel self-pitying. But he could not simply remove the feeling from within him.

Rob looked at the river flowing across the land in front of them, angry with himself.

"Shall we take the children for a walk along the river bank to see the swans?" It was Caro who spoke. He wondered if she'd been listening to his conversation and sensed his discomfort… Or perhaps it had been Phillip's suggestion. That thought slashed across Rob's chest.

"Yes! Pease!" George shouted. He would do anything if it meant he need not sit still.

"May David and I come, please?" Paul asked.

"Of course you may," Drew stood up and brushed crumbs from his waistcoat.

Rob stood too, hoping his father would not come.

Caro passed Iris to Mary and rose.

"I will walk with you." Phillip stood beside her.

Caro only smiled, expressing no particular pleasure as she took Iris back, so Mary could rise. "I will carry her," Drew stepped forward and took his daughter from Caro's arms.

He looked down at Iris with love and pride in his gaze as she reached up and grasped his fringe.

Pride was very different to inferiority. Pride was to be respected. Inferiority was not. Rob had been mistaken about himself for years.

As Phillip offered his arm to Caro, Paul gripped Rob's hand

and Rob smiled down at him. His mother and father had risen too, but clearly Paul wished to have what George had had, a little of his Uncle Robbie's attention.

George gripped his mother's hand and they all began to walk towards the river. Others in the party followed, his aunts and uncles and their families.

The servants brought bread down to the river, and so they helped the children feed it to the ducks and swans, while Caro walked on with Phillip in conversation.

"George." Paul called, offering some of the bread he held, when George had used all of his.

George took it with a smile. "Thank you."

Hell. Is that not just what John is doing with me—sharing. That is all.

Rob had squatted down to help the children, when he stood he faced Caro. Phillip had moved away and was speaking with Kate.

Caro's lips were closed, there was no full, bright smile for him today, and yet it was as if a smile wished to form, but the sadness he saw held her back.

"Uncle Bobbie." He looked down at George, who'd doubled over and reached his hands through his legs to be somersaulted. When Rob bent to fulfil the task, he caught Drew watching. His gaze was complex, but there was sympathy within it.

Why?

When the carriages were loaded for the journey home, Rob had hoped to swap with Phillip, but Caro had avoided a single moment of private conversation with him, so he'd had no chance to persuade her to find an excuse to ride with him, and so ended up watching her let Phillip take her hand.

When they reached Pembroke House, Rob helped Jenny and Helen down, and entered the hall with everyone else, but he did not stay there as the scene became a melee of servants helping people remove coats and take gloves and hats. He slipped into John's library, found paper, a quill and ink.

The words were bubbling inside him, he could not keep them within any longer.

Dearest Caro

I have wanted to speak with you today, but not had the chance. I want you to know that I wish I could have prevented you enduring that dance with Kilbride last night. I'm sorry I could not. Yet it made me think. There is only one way that I may have the right to be your protector. Drew was right, it is not my responsibility but his. Yet if we were engaged it would give me the right. I wish to tell people what is between us. Let us announce our engagement. If you are in agreement? I am sorry, it may need to be an engagement that lasts years, and yet at least I would know that you are to be mine, and others would know.

He thought of Caro walking with Phillip, of her hand on Phillip's arm, and their heads close as they talked, as the quill hovered over the page, but this was not about Phillip. This was about protecting her from Kilbride.

Yours sincerely and devotedly,

Rob

I love you

He folded the letter, picked up the wax and melted some to seal it.

He would have to take a risk. He would have to give the letter to one of John's servants.

He slipped the letter inside his waistcoat and went out into the hall. The commotion was over, the family had gone upstairs and Finch, the butler, had gone with them. But there was one footman left in the hall, perhaps because Finch had known Rob had gone into the library, it would be unlike Finch to miss anything.

"Would you come in a moment," Rob stated, beckoning him into the library. He did not wish his voice to travel in the hall. "Can you be discrete?"

"Yes, sir."

"I have a letter to be delivered, but you must not let anyone see it, or see you give it to that person."

The footman nodded, his eyes intrigued. "I shall give you thre'pence, but you must swear to me that no one will know."

"I swear, sir."

Rob handed the letter over and then reached into his pocket for the change. The footman slipped the letter inside his waistcoat, and the money in his pocket. "Thank you, sir."

"Deliver it as quickly as you can. I am leaving now. If any of the family ask after me, simply tell them I had other arrangements to attend to."

Chapter 29

Rob had spent a successful morning with Drew looking over the farm stock at the market. Drew had agreed that Rob had an eye for spotting a good breeding animal, and the sellers in the stalls had confirmed it.

Rob's interest had gathered as Drew kept asking, "Which do you think?" Then Rob had considered and pointed animals out, and then afterwards Drew had pointed out what it was about them that actually made them right, but Rob had been correct every time without knowing.

Drew had purchased many of the animals Rob had liked and arranged for them to be transported home. Decisions Rob had made would have a future influence on Drew's estate. Descendants of the animals Rob had picked would be there for George to benefit from. Those thoughts had made Rob feel good, and he'd decided then to share his plan to move into politics with Drew. Of all the men in his family Drew was the one he trusted most not to interfere. Drew's eyebrows had lifted in surprise, but then he'd smiled warmly, slapped Rob's shoulder and offered his support—not with money or possessions, as the rest of Rob's family would have done, but through friendship and the use of his voice.

Rob smiled as they climbed the steps to John's house. Pride in his chest. Pride and not inferiority. But then he'd never felt inferior in Drew's company. That was why he'd gone to Drew's in the summer, and that was good, because he hoped later, or perhaps tomorrow, to ask Drew for Caro's hand in marriage. That had been another influence on his decision to share his plans with Drew.

When he walked upstairs to the drawing room beside Drew, he itched inside to tell Caro about his day, but the drawing room was full of visitors again. Of course, the family had been out yesterday. These people had come to discover what had happened during the dance between the Marquis of Kilbride and the former marchioness. Caro would not speak of it anyway.

Caro glanced at Drew and Rob as they entered, but there was no special smile and no particular look for Rob. In fact, she appeared uncomfortable with his presence as he stood at the edge of the room, accepting a cup of tea, which Mary brought over to him. Caro actively tried not to look at him, and when he made a comment in a conversation she bit her lip for a moment before continuing the discussion, only glancing at him for an instant.

He drank his tea quickly, then chose to leave. He would not achieve a private moment with Caro in this setting, and she seemed confident enough with her callers. But before he left he asked Mary where they were to go that evening and if he might accompany them. He would have a private moment with Caro then, whether she willed it or not. He would drag her from the damned ballroom if he must. He was starting to think that she had, for some reason, taken against him since her incident with Kilbride.

Perhaps she blamed him for not protecting her…

~

Caro's heart pounded out a sharp rhythm, knocking against her ribs as she read Rob's words once more. He wished them to be engaged. To tell everyone.

I know the two of you discovered a friendship in the summer, but it should have gone no further. If you are his first, such a thing engenders emotion, and Rob is a young man with high morals. If you have lain with him, he will feel obligated to marry you.

Oh, she hated to think that Drew's words were true, and yet she knew Rob well enough to realise that he would offer for her from feeling, without thought, because his heart was too full of goodness. Drew was right, Rob could never have allowed himself to lie with her and not offer more, and now she'd come into danger and he wished to do all he could to protect her.

He would give up his youth.

She would be cruel to take it from him. She'd forced him into this, not deliberately, but she'd done it none the less. She should give it back to him. But to do so she would have to persuade him she felt nothing. If he thought she cared, he would not make his choices on his own behalf but for her. She needed to give him the time to find his pathway to fulfil his great plan to change the world for the better. He should have his youth to focus on the things he wished to achieve.

Perhaps, when he was older and he'd gained his seat, and established the respect of others in the House of Commons, then there might be a future for them.

She folded his letter and slipped it into her bodice. She would treasure it. It was her first letter from him.

If there is really something between you it will last the years.

She hoped it would, with all her heart.

Yet she was going to let Rob go because his morals and idealism deserved to be treated like for like. She would let their hearts be bruised and hope that in the future there would be more time together.

She took one last look at herself in the mirror, his words pressing against her breast when she breathed in. She would keep them there forever, in case it was all she had of him.

She turned, then, and walked from the room.

When she walked downstairs, she saw Rob in the hall. He'd called to travel with them as he had every night he'd accompanied them. He still had his hat and gloves on, and he was dressed in his evening black and white. His beauty was starker when he was in evening dress, because of his dark-brown hair and dark-blue eyes. Black seemed to hide the softness in him.

He looked up and watched her as she descended the last few steps, then his eyes followed her movement across the hall. She could see he wished to take her hand.

"Caro." Drew was beside her. He cupped her elbow, stopping her before she might reach Rob. She apologised to Rob with her eyes. *I love you*. But she could not form a smile.

"Are we ready to leave?" John asked.

"We are indeed," Edward answered.

They walked out to the carriages, Drew still holding her arm. But they were to travel as they'd done the other night. Rob was to ride in the same carriage as her.

Drew held her fingers firmly as he helped her up into the carriage, while Rob stood on the pavement behind her. Then Drew handed Mary up before climbing in and then sitting beside Mary. When Rob climbed up he sat beside Caro, but his posture was stiffer than normal.

Her heart thumped as her thigh brushed against his when the carriage rocked as it rolled over the cobbles.

His hands lay on his thighs, his palms flat and fingers spread. She could not look at his face. She knew that he'd recognised something was not right yesterday. Today he'd watched her with a need for explanations in his eyes.

Drew spoke to him about the animals he'd bought and Mary commented. Caro sat in silence.

She turned to look out of the window, into the blackness. It would break her heart entirely to let Rob go.

When they reached the Newcombs' house Rob was the first to jump down from the carriage, but Drew climbed down next and again ensured he was the one who took Caro's hand. Rob helped Mary as Drew held on to Caro as though she was his possession.

He was simply trying to break what was between her and Rob, and yet it was breaking both of them too.

I will miss him.

Rob did not try to speak with her or ask her to dance when they reached the ballroom. Instead he asked one of his cousins to dance.

A sharp pain pierced through her breast as he walked out onto the floor.

He must have felt the same, or worse, when she'd taken Phillip's hand and climbed into his carriage. It had felt wrong and yet she'd tried to look happy all day yesterday, as she'd watched Rob play with the children, remembering everything about him that she loved.

Drew asked her to dance, but Caro declined. For a moment she just wished to hide among the family. She had proved to herself that she could be brave. She needed to prove nothing now; she was only here to speak with Rob.

"Kilbride is across the room and staring at you again," Drew stated in a low voice as he and Mary hovered near her.

She had known. She'd sensed him watching. But it did not matter; she did not care anymore.

"Would you dance with me, Caroline?" John asked when the current dance came to its end. She agreed, because he might be insulted if she said no, and the Duke had been kind to her through the years.

She danced the next three dances too, partnered by her brother, then Rob's father and his uncle Richard.

Rob danced the second with Mary, and the third with his mother, but during the fourth he stood out, at the edge of the room, watching Caro, with his arms folded over his chest. She felt his gaze as heat on her skin.

When Richard returned her to the family group, the notes of a slow waltz stretched through the room.

"Will you dance with me?" Rob stood beside her, his gloved hand lifted, waiting for hers to be set within it.

Love was strange and cruel.

Why had her heart picked another unsuitable man? But one who was unsuitable for entirely the opposite reasons. Albert had been cruel and much older than her; Rob was much younger and had a heart that was as precious as gold, open and kind. She would break it, and perhaps tarnish it forever.

The rush of warmth she felt in his company swirled over her as she took his hand. She could not help loving him.

His dark-blue eyes watched as his fingers closed around hers, in a gesture that said, *I have you at last.*

Her heart skipped a beat and then pumped hard as he walked her to the floor.

"Hello, Caro," he whispered.

It was the strangest thing to say. They had been together for over two hours, they had travelled here together, and yet she understood why he said it. He said it because he was saying hello to the person only he knew, the person she became with him.

"How are you? Are you holding up? Did you receive my letter?"

She nodded and then bit her lip as the pain of tears gathered in her throat.

The music played more strongly and the dance began. He turned her, his hand at her back, steady and strong.

"Have you an answer for me, then? Because your expression is worrying me, and yesterday I felt as though you avoided me."

"I'm sorry," she forced the words from her lips, but no more would come. She bit her lip again to hold back the tears.

"For what?"

She swallowed and took a breath. She had to tell him this and say it in a way that ensured he believed it. "I cannot marry you."

"Why?" His gaze searched hers as his fingers tightened about her hand. "I will wait, though, if you wish. We need not announce our engagement now. Yet I would simply like everyone to know you are mine."

"No, Rob. I mean I cannot marry you at all."

His expression looked as though he'd tasted something bitter.

"I'm sorry."

His gaze left her face and he turned her three or four more times, the muscle in his jaw taut, forming an indent in his cheek. Then he breathed out and broke his hold on her, stepping back and changing his grip on her hand.

They were near the edge of the floor, and near the door out into the hall. He pulled her from the floor into the crowd, but it was not done aggressively. People about them noticed, though, and gazes followed them as Rob walked her into the hall. He let go of her hand and gripped her elbow, steering her away from the eyes that watched them.

The hall was empty bar three footmen. Rob did not even look at them, but turned to the right and opened the first door. It was a small dining room. He shut the door before anyone might follow and find them.

"Cannot…" Was all Rob stated when he let her go.

Her hands clasped together at her waist, as she sought the courage he'd seen in her. "I have changed my mind. What we did was wrong and foolish." She did not wish to be a coward in this. The least she could do for him was to speak to him openly and treat him fairly.

"Why?" There was anger in his voice.

"Because you are so young. You cannot be sure that this is what you wish." Yet he knew he wished to do good for others. But Drew was right, if she had seduced him into loving her, she must let him go and follow the path he'd intended before she'd interfered. His commitment to her could be misguided by physical emotions.

He looked at her as though she was mad, and breathed out a long breath that was not a sigh but an expression of frustration.

Caro stepped forward and touched his arm. "Drew has told me that he thinks you are innocent. Was I your first?" The wounded look in his eyes said it was true.

He shook his head, and yet she could see his skin darkening with a blush in the light of the single candelabra burning in the room. It stood in the middle of the table, its light flickering on the polished wood.

It was true. "Then, don't you see, you will love the first woman you have lain with, of course you will, but it will be a love that is unlikely to last. It may be shallow, not real at all, just a physical feeling."

"That is not how I feel."

"You cannot know, Rob. You have nothing to compare it to."

A muscle flickered in his jaw. "I am one and twenty. I am able to know my own mind. What I feel for you is neither shallow nor purely from the physical act, it is a need that grips in my chest, about my heart. I accept this may be too soon for us, but that does not mean you have to end what we have."

"I'm sorry, but it is better for us both if I do."

"For us both…" His pitch had sharpened and dropped an octave or two. "Why is it better for you? You have changed towards me since you danced with Kilbride? Do you still love him? Is that why you no longer wish for me?"

She longed to shake her head, and yet if that was what he believed, then he would forget her, and he would continue his life without carrying any hope that might affect his choices.

"You need to live your life how you wish. You need to fulfil your dream of helping those more needy than either of us, and it will take time and all of your attention to cut a path in this world to achieve it. I will not be a rope around your neck or a shackle about your ankle, holding you back. Let me go, and you may have the life you ought."

"Let you go to him…" It was said in a low, hurt voice. "Does Drew know this is what you plan to do?"

"I have no plan. I simply know that you and I made a mistake. I'm sorry."

He looked up at the ceiling. His hand lifted and gripped his hair for a moment, then fell. It was as though he searched for the words or an action that might change her mind.

He looked at her again, then, and swallowed hard, his Adam's apple shifting.

He could change nothing.

Hurt, anger and accusations hovered in his eyes, but he did not voice them. "Is there nothing I might say or do?"

She shook her head. "I am sorry that I have hurt you, but in years to come you will see this was the right choice." She hoped in those years he did not find someone else to love, and that they would be together again. *If there is really something between you it will last the years…* Yet she would be over thirty, and Rob would probably see that it had been folly.

"That was condescending of you, Caro. You are speaking to me as though I am a youth. I do not need years to know what I feel. I know it now. So, then, the fault is yours. You do not have enough faith in me, or respect for me." He shook his head, as if in disbelief—or disappointment. "Well, as you deem my love not worthy of you, then I shall not force it, or my presence, on you any longer." He turned away.

She had struck him where it hurt most, slashing at his feelings of inferiority. He had never been inferior to his cousins. He was a superior man, even at the age of one and twenty.

"Rob." She reached out to catch hold of his arm. He pulled it free, merely glancing back.

"Goodbye, Caro."

He turned away again and walked from the room, leaving the door open behind him, and leaving her.

No. It could not end like that. She followed him into the hall, but he was already near the front door. A footman opened it, and then Rob was gone. He'd not even waited for his hat. The door closed behind him.

It was over.

She went to the retiring room and sat so that the Pembrokes' maid might check her hair. She was hollow, numb. Her heart had not broken yet, and yet it felt empty, because he'd gone.

She walked downstairs feeling wraith-like. She had no real idea where she was or who she was anymore. She did not exist without Rob.

Albert stood in the hall below. He'd been speaking to a footman. When he turned to the stairs the footman opened the door and went out.

Caro walked on, ignoring Albert's presence. She did not care about him. He had no meaning in her life. She had no feeling for him: not love, nor fear, nor interest.

"Caro." He grasped her arm and glanced down at her throat and then her bosom before his gaze lifted. He was looking at the absence of the cross he'd given her.

Rob's touch had been gentle to the last. Albert's had been brutal from the first. He'd always gripped her arm over-tightly, even before the beatings had begun. It was his way of saying "you are mine". *Only I am not, not anymore.*

"You will dance with me." It was not a question but a statement, and through his hold on her arm he began steering her back into the ballroom.

Heart-sore and empty she let herself be led.

The orchestra was playing another waltz. Albert clasped her hand and lay his other hand on her back, then began to turn her. It was fast-paced. He spun her aggressively into a turn.

"What is that boy to you?"

"It is none of your concern." Her pitch was as flat and hollow as her heart.

"Have your tastes turned to that of your sister's?"

That was what Drew had accused her of too, of being like Elizabeth. Elizabeth used young men like toys. No, Caro was not like Elizabeth, nor Albert. She'd given herself, not taken.

Feelings were returning to her now: anger, disgust. "I do not wish to dance with you."

"I suppose you would rather be with that child?"

"He is not a child." She would not listen to Albert ridiculing Rob.

"He is barely a man."

Caro stopped, pulling free of Albert's hold, but he clasped her arm as she tried to walk away. "Let me go. You cannot control me now."

He stared at her, time hovering over them. Then finally he let go. It was over. Any involvement with him was at an end. She had let him go from her heart and now she let him go from her head. She was free from memories and fear, from the pain he'd caused her. "Rob Marlow is more of a man than you will ever be," she breathed at him.

Before she turned away, she saw her words strike. Albert's eyes widened, and the line that creased down the centre of his brow when he became angry formed. He was ready to strike her. "You cannot hit me here…"

The sharp, sudden light of thought in his eyes implied his realisation that she was no longer cowed by him. He had no control over her any longer, and he had finally realised it, just as she had.

She turned and walked away.

When she reached Rob's family, the air about them was full of whispers as people spoke behind fans and hands.

"Caro." Drew was there.

"I would like to go home," she said, quietly.

"Now?"

"Yes." Her fingers shook as she touched his arm. He gripped them gently. "Rob has gone. I said what you asked me to, and he has left."

Drew looked at her with sympathy. "It was the right thing to do."

It did not feel right anymore. She was numb no longer, her heart was ripping in two. "I do not wish to go back to Pembroke House. I wish to go home. I cannot stay here. These people are his family. He ought to feel able to visit, and he will not if I am here."

"We cannot go tonight, Caro, it is too late, and it would look odd."

"Caro…" Mary stood beside them.

286

"She wishes to go home, to the estate."

"Oh Caro, I am sorry Lord Kilbride has spoilt this for you."

I do not care about him. The words echoed through her head, and yet as with Rob, it would be easier to let Mary think it.

"We will take you to Pembroke House now and leave first thing tomorrow morning. Mary, will you stay with Caro while I arrange for the carriage to be brought about?"

"Come, we will tell John and Kate," Mary turned her as Drew walked away.

Caro endured a dozen farewells as Mary told her brother, John, her parents and others in the family that they intended to leave town, and through it all the pain in her chest intensified. Her heart was gone and in its place was a hole. Rob held her heart and he'd taken it with him.

Chapter 30

He knew, God, he knew, he'd broken a rule. He'd sinned. He'd lain with a woman and begun an affair. Curses ran through his head as he gritted his teeth on the anger in his blood. He'd known such a thing would be foolish, and yet he'd done it because that woman had been Caro.

He walked quickly, his strides long.

God I have been a fool.

Harry and all of his cousins would laugh at him if they knew he'd lain with a woman, his first, and fallen for her.

You will love the first woman you have lain with, of course you will, but it will be a love that is unlikely to last. It is shallow, not real at all.

That was not true. His feelings were not shallow, they were ripping at his soul. She'd betrayed him. Treated him ill. Good, vulnerable and delicate, beautiful, Caro.

The night was dark, there were no stars, and the moon must be hidden behind a layer of clouds, but there were gas lamps in the streets, and some light from the windows. Yet if he walked past a theatre he ought perhaps to pay for a link boy to light his way. The darkness suited the emotion in his soul, though. His whole life felt shadowed.

He'd begun to see a future for himself this morning, as a tenant farmer. He would not need any capital to begin if he were to rent a farm. He need not borrow from anyone, and he would have a home with it that would house a wife. It would also provide him with an income and a living that might be managed from a distance so that he could sit in Parliament. His plan had developed as he'd spoken with Drew earlier. He'd decided to rent a farm near a place where there would be a vacant seat in the House of Commons, and then he'd stand for it. But without Caro the image was void. Nothing felt right without her. He did not even wish to think about his plans for politics without her.

She might have lived in the country too and never come to town. She need never have faced Kilbride again, and yet she'd not denied that she intended going to him.

Damn. Damn her. Why was she such a fool? Why make that choice?

Because I am inferior.

Bloody hell! He longed to hit someone or something, but instead he released his hands from the fists they'd been curled into for the last half hour and slid his hands into his pockets.

It was cold. He'd dressed believing he would be riding in the carriage; he had no outer coat, and he'd left his hat.

He could not believe that Drew had told her that he'd been a virgin! He'd thought Drew a friend. "Go to hell, you bastard!" Rob said the words aloud.

Inferior. The word rang through him like a bell tolling. It was the truth, and she'd seen it. He was inferior to Kilbride, and inferior to all other men, because he'd saved himself until the moment he'd lain with her.

Damn her.

His footfalls echoed as he walked across an empty street. On the far side the street was so dark he could not even see his feet—in the same way that he could not see his future. For all he knew he had none. Caro had taken hope and happiness from him. If she thought him unworthy, then what cause was there? He could carouse like his cousins and waste John's gifts on wine and women. Who would care? No one within his family, and certainly not Caro.

A sharp pain gripped in his gut. But the problem was that he would care, because behaviour like that was not within him. He would not do that, yet nor would he ever marry. He'd reached out and been burned.

Perhaps he ought to become a bloody monk.

A strangled laugh broke from his throat as he turned a corner.

Crack. Something hard and heavy struck the back of his head and Rob fell. Then a boot smashed into face. He lifted his hands to try and protect his head, but the kicks came too fast, and he was dizzy and disorientated from the first blow.

When he raised his hand, something solid and cold, metal, struck it, and a sharp pain lanced up his arm. Then the same solid implement struck his leg. Bile lurched into his throat as the bone broke. He vomited on the pavement.

"The gentleman said to tell you to leave his possessions alone."

Rob's uninjured arm lowered and a searing pain pulsed through his body from his injured leg. His hand moved instinctively to grip it.

Another hard blow hit his head.

Chapter 31

"Hey! There's a toff over 'ere!"

The shout dragged Rob back from the darkness.

The voice was a heavy working man's pitch.

Where the hell was he?

Rob's head throbbed, as though he'd been struck, and a bitter taste filled his mouth. He'd been attacked… He groaned as he tried to lift his arm and found it swollen and immovable. A violent pain shouted in his head.

"Governor…" The man was squatting or kneeling near him, but Rob could not see, his eyes would not open.

"He's been robbed, he 'as," The woman's voice came from above him.

A moan left Rob's lips. God, he was in so much pain, and his throat was too dry to let him speak about the blood in his mouth.

"It's all right, governor. We'll get you sorted. We'll get you home." The man said.

"Where d' you live, sir? Can you tell us?" the woman coaxed. She'd knelt or squatted down too, and her fingers touched his shoulder.

Rob groaned, thinking through the racket that the pain was making in his head… Not his apartment, no one was there. Nor John's. He did not wish to see Caro. "Bloomsbury Square," he said on his breath. "Lord Barrington… The earl." His chest screamed with pain, and his face, and his shoulders. He felt like every bloody bone was broken.

"Get a cart!" the man shouted, standing.

Four men moved Rob onto a piece of tarpaulin and then they all took a corner and lifted him from the pavement as he cried out in agony. The damned pain roared within him with every jolt. But as they slid him back onto the cart the pain from his leg not only roared but burst, splitting his head with anguish. He fell into darkness as he retched.

~

When Rob woke, someone was dropping something bitter into his mouth. It ran across his tongue. It tasted bloody foul.

He sat up, or tried to, as his hand sought to swipe away whatever it was, but neither his body nor his hand moved as he wished, and a pain-filled groan escaped his lips.

The liquid, whatever it was, spilled on to his chest, soaking through his linen shirt.

"Robbie." A woman's voice, a familiar voice. His Aunt Jane's.

He tried to open his eyes. Only one opened, slightly. A damp cloth settled on his brow.

"Robbie." His Uncle Robert.

He tried to sit up again, pressing an elbow into the mattress. The world span full circle and bile rose in his throat.

"Do not move. Lie down." His aunt's cool fingers rested on his shoulder. He caught a glimpse of her through his half-open eye.

His uncle came forward. "You were set upon by footpads last night. Some people found you this morning and brought you here. Just stay still, Robbie, you are a mess. I'll send for your parents. They are at John's, but the men who brought you here said you gave this address."

He thought Rob confused.

"Do not worry." His uncle's hand cupped the side of Rob's bruised face, "They will come—"

"No." It hurt to say the word, his lips were swollen and his jaw bruised. "Do not tell them…" He would not have Caro know of this. How would this look? He could not even protect himself. It would only solidify her view of him, too young to care for himself, let alone her. Inferior. That bitter word. She would pity him and he would not endure that.

"Rob." His uncle leant forward, his fingers slipping into the open palm of Rob's right hand, as his thumb gently touched the back. Even with the lightness of his touch, Rob flinched. His hand was bruised too. "I have sent for a surgeon. You've been badly beaten. But your mother will never speak to me again if I do not tell her that her son has been hurt. They need to know. You will not be healed for weeks."

"Then tell them, but they must tell no one else."

"Rob…" Jane breathed in complaint.

"No one else."

"Your brother—" his uncle began.

"No one," Rob cried on a note of pain, leaning upward.

His aunt pressed her hand to his arm. "Lie back, Robert will do as you wish."

He let go of Rob's hand. "I will go to John's myself and ensure the news is not shared."

Uncle Robert was Rob's favourite uncle. When the old Duke had been alive, before John had inherited, Rob's family had stayed here when his parents came to town, when Rob had been a child. Rob had always felt less out of place here. Uncle Robert's heir, Henry, was younger than Rob, and unrelated to Rob's Pembroke cousins on his mother's side.

As his uncle walked away, his aunt pressed a hand on his arm. "Drink some of this laudanum. It will ease the pain until the surgeon comes, and it will make it easier when he sets your hand and leg."

Sets…

Heaviness and burning resonated from one side.

"Let me lift your head a little." Her palm settled beneath his head.

He flinched as her fingers touched a wound.

"Sorry, can you open your lips a little more?"

His jaw was stiff and his lips felt triple the size, but he did so. Jane tipped a spoonful of the bitter medicine onto his tongue. He swallowed.

"All will be well," Jane said quietly. "Lie back and rest. Your mama and papa will be here soon." She sounded bewildered by his desire to be here and not at John's. She could not understand. But then, Rob did not wish her to.

He shut his eyes. In moments the darkness and the drowsiness from the medicine claimed him.

~

"Son…"

Rob opened his eyes and moved. In one eye his vision was clearer, yet the other was still swollen shut.

"No do not try to sit up, Rob." His father was sitting beside the bed.

"What happened?"

Rob tried to shrug, but instead he flinched with pain.

"Never mind," his father said quietly. "Your eyes are black. You look like hell. Do you want me to get a mirror and show you?"

"How awful I look… No." His throat was dry and his voice rasping.

"The doctor thinks they cracked four of your ribs, and he has splinted your hand and your thigh. Both are badly broken."

And Rob had not even woken… Jane must have given him a large dose of laudanum.

"You will not be exploring your future for a while," his father said in dry, bitter humour.

Rob lowered his head in a slight nod.

"Your mother and I will stay here with you."

A laboured breath drew past Rob's lips as he tried to shake his head.

His father's hand lay on his shoulder. "Your uncle told me you do not want the others to know, yet your mother took one look at you and has gone outside to weep rather than cry before you. She will not leave your side once she has recovered from her tears."

He did not wish his mother upset, not due to him.

The door opened. Rob looked across the room. It was her. She held a handkerchief and her eyes glistened with tears as she sniffed.

He moved to rise again, but his father pressed his shoulder, urging him to stay still.

She cried, a sob escaping her lips, as his father rose from the chair and let her sit.

"I do not know what to say to you," she said quietly. "We should not have let you come to London alone."

"He is one and twenty. The lad has a life to begin. You cannot keep him on a leading rein all his life, Ellen. This could have happened at any time. It is nought to do with his age."

Rob shut his eyes.

"Your mother will worry; it is what mother's do, and I will worry, but I will aim to ensure that neither of us smothers you."

Rob looked at them again, his father's hand was on his mother's shoulder.

Rob coughed painfully. His father lifted Rob's head as Jane had done and held his handkerchief to Rob's lips. When he took it away there was blood upon it.

His father looked at it, then crushed it in his hand.

His mother reached for a glass, which stood on the side. "Here." She held it to his lips, as his father lifted his head once more. The water was cool and refreshing. It washed the bitter taste from his mouth.

He shut his eyes when his father lowered his head. Caro's image hovered in his mind's eye, but not the Caro of recent weeks: Caro in the summer, when they had taken the woodland walk with George.

~

Over the next days, whenever Rob woke, someone was there to help him drink or eat, or with whatever else he needed.

Then, as the days progressed, his mother or his aunt would sit and read to him if they were beside him, or his father and uncle would talk, while he drifted in and out of sleep, still sore and bruised and riding on the dizzying relief of laudanum.

Yet the hours he lay sleeping were spent with Caro. In his dreams they were together as they had been in the summer, and as they had been in his rooms.

But after three weeks, he was tired of sleeping and spending the days unaware. He wished to be able to think clearly. He could not lie here forever looking back at what was not to be. When Jane opened the bottle of laudanum on the side, he gripped her wrist to stop her. "No more."

"But you must still be in pain."

"I shall live with it." His face was no longer swollen, though it probably still had dark-purple and yellow stains from the bruising. He'd seen the bruises on his arms and on his sides, and legs, and so he could imagine his face.

In the hours that followed, the pain was overwhelming. Even his blood ached, as he shivered. His mother sat beside him, replacing the damp cloth on his forehead.

"The doctor said you ought to reduce the laudanum slowly," she murmured, for about the sixth time.

He did not care, the drug made him feel half dead. He did not like it. He wished for his awareness back: at least let his mind be free of the splints, even if his body could not be free yet.

His father sat up with him through the night as Rob continued to shiver and drift into sleep, then woke with gruesome visions in his head. And then the visions were not dreams any more but bizarre illusions that he saw when dawn broke. At one point his bed became a carriage, and the horses had been spooked, and it was racing out of control. Then he saw and heard a thunderstorm in the room, and people were gathered in a ballroom whispering in a corner.

It was late, dark, when the visions ceased. It must have been two days since he'd refused the drug. He lay, still staring at the shadows the moonlight cast across the ceiling.

His mother sat in a chair beside his bed, her hand holding his, but she was asleep. He did not move, he did not wish to wake her; so he lay silent, wondering how his life had come to this. He'd walked a steady road forever, never really stumbling, and then he'd stayed with Mary and become someone he did not know. A man, he supposed. What had happened between him and Caro had changed him, and what had happened to him in that dark street had changed him. He saw things through different eyes now.

He slept when dawn broke through the curtains, without dreams, even though there was a constant hum of pain.

When he woke, the clock on the mantel across the room chimed midday and his mother brought him chicken broth to try and eat. He insisted then that she, and Aunt Jane, help him sit up. He had them place pillows behind him and tried to feed himself. He was tired of being an invalid.

His mother set the bowl on a tray on his lap and gave him the spoon. He was right-handed, but his right hand had been broken, and so with a shaky left hand he fed himself. He spilt it a couple of times, but he did not care. He wished to become independent again. His father sat with him in the afternoon, and Rob slept once more. Then his uncle came too, and the two of them talked while Rob lay with his eyes closed and let the sound fill his soul. His father's voice was a part of home.

When he woke the next morning he felt stronger, and his mother brought buttered toast with honey, which had been his favourite as a child. It made him laugh, but laughing hurt his ribs and made him cough.

She pressed a hand over his shoulder as she stood beside him, her eyes telling him he ought to take some laudanum to relieve the pain. He did not. He was glad to be free of the drug and its numbness. He was not comfortable with hiding in oblivion. He would face this and he would survive and heal—*and have revenge.*

When his father arrived with his uncle later, Rob was still sitting up, leaning back on the pillows. "Your mother says you are feeling a little better."

Rob nodded and smiled. "Yes, a little."

"Your friends were asking after you. They caught us as I walked out of White's. I was not sure what to say."

Rob had not even thought of them, of how they would take his disappearance.

"They are concerned about you," his uncle said. "I had not realised what a sound group of young men you have as friends."

"I told them you are well and that you have been staying out of town, fulfilling some duty for me."

"Thank you."

"They asked if it was to do with the availability of a seat?" His father's eyebrows lifted.

Rob did not comment.

"Mary keeps asking after you in her letters—"

"Do not tell her." He gripped his father's arm.

"I have not, Robbie, but she is worried by your silence too."

The thought of Mary brought forth thoughts of Caro. Rob shut his eyes and shut his father and his uncle out, along with the pain and the past.

"I only wish Henry would choose his friends as wisely as you have, Robbie." Robert was merely being kind.

A chair was moved closer to the bed and someone sat down. Rob opened his eyes to see his father sitting there. His uncle crossed the room and then leant against the windowsill.

Rob's father held Rob's left hand. "We have told the family that your mother and I are here to help Jane. They think she is unwell. We have told the children she is too unwell to cope with a houseful and your cousins are staying at John's. So you may see what a web of lies you have had us spinning."

"I'm sorry." His father's grip loosened and Rob pulled his hand free. "What of Drew and Mary?" *What of Caro?* He'd been dying to ask, but he'd not dared. He did not even know how to speak of her without feeling cut.

"Mary and Drew have gone home. They left the day we came here and John has not queried our tale, he is too busy."

"I'm sorry I have taken you from the others."

"Helen and Jenny are there to take care of the younger ones and we have called in on them frequently, twice a day, so they do not feel deserted and of course there is excitement over having their cousins there."

"But, nevertheless, I'm sorry. I would not have taken all of your attention by choice."

"Rob, you are entitled to it. You are my son too. It does not matter that you are grown. We will always be here when you need us."

Rob shook his head a little. The younger ones needed them more. "Did Caro go with Mary and Drew?" *How is she?*

His father's eyebrows lifted as he nodded. "Anyway, I did not come to speak of your brothers and sisters. I came to speak of you. Your uncle and I have a proposal for you. Robert agrees with me about that property. It is the perfect option for you."

Rob closed his eyes. Their conversation at Windsor seemed a lifetime ago. He'd been a different man then.

"Hear us out," his father said.

"Do not think that I am offering you charity," his uncle stated. "I am not. If you take the tenancy you will have to pay the rent from the income you earn from the farms, and keep the property in good condition. Think of it as a business venture. If you manage

299

the estate well, you will be able to make a profit and give your brother back his allowance. I know that will interest you."

It did. But. Rob opened his eyes and looked at his uncle. He had denied their help a hundred times, and yet for the past three weeks he'd been completely reliant upon his uncle's hospitality and kindness. He should be honest and talk of his true plans. If they tried to interfere he would simply ask them not to.

Uncle Robert smiled.

"Although I cannot for the life of me understand why you are so bloody stubborn on that point," Rob's father said. "I cannot see why you must fight so hard to be equal to your brother and your cousins."

"Because I am not equal," Rob breathed in an impatient voice, looking at his father. *I am inferior*. But even though inferiority may have been the beginning it was not the end; it had sparked his idealistic notions, which he hoped one day would make a difference to many people in need of a way to change their lives for the better.

"No. You are a hundred times better than your cousins," his uncle stated. "I wish Henry had a half of your self-possession and conscience. I have faith one day he will grow out of this wild stage, but you, Edward has never needed to hope because you are a man with morals." His uncle laughed then, a deep sound from low in his throat. "Like your father."

Rob's father laughed too. "Well, equally, if Henry is like you, you shall be waiting until he is thirty for the moment that he learns the error of his ways."

Uncle Robert smiled at Rob's father. "I cannot see why you do not understand your son. I remember you bristling when I returned from the continent, so damned restless because I'd taken the responsibility away from you." He looked at Rob. "He was not that much older than you, four and twenty and seething at the prospect of being left adrift with no responsibility unless he answered to me. So, you are not so different from your father.

He ought to understand. Fortunately for me, he met your mother then and that was that. He had his own property and the arrival of your sister to occupy his mind."

Rob smiled. The moments he looked forward to most here were the hours his father and his uncle sat with him and spoke to each other. He'd never listened to them when they were alone without children to interrupt them. It had given him a new insight into his father.

"Admittedly," his father added, laughing again, "I did not like taking your grandfather's money for your mother either. In fact the first time he offered it, I ripped his cheque up." Uncle Robert laughed and amusement stirred in Rob's chest, but it made him cough and the pain from his ribs tore across his chest.

"Lie back. Do not laugh," his father stated dryly. "The difference between me and you is that I have common-sense. I knew I had to keep your mother and John, and therefore it would have been foolish pride to refuse his money." The point was made with a look that said Rob suffered with foolish pride. "You may wish to think harder about the opportunity your uncle is offering you."

Rob breathed out, fighting the pain in his chest, but he wished to speak the truth to his father. "There is an opportunity I have wished to pursue for ages. I have not spoken of it because I knew you, and everyone else, would wish to interfere and I wanted to achieve it without help. I think it important—"

"Robbie—"

"Let me explain, you will understand. I wish to hold a seat in the House of Commons, and not because I have foolish pride, Papa, but because I want to make a difference for those who are less fortunate in this country. I have joined the Whig party, I have made connections already, I simply need an income to support me in order to throw my hat into the ring to win a seat, and then I will need a living that will enable me to attend the House."

His father shook his head, but he was smiling slightly.

"I cannot speak out for the poor, Papa, if I am living on John

301

and have been helped into my position in government by my rich, aristocratic family. How would that seem to the men and women I want to speak out for?"

Uncle Robert lifted his weight from the windowsill. "I'll leave you two in peace. You have weeks to make up your mind about my property, Rob, I will not let the tenancy to anyone until I know if you want it, and as I said before, you have my respect." His uncle smiled in parting.

Once his uncle had left, his father said. "That aim is commendable, Robbie."

"I am not ruling out Uncle Robert's property. I had decided to rent a farm anyway. It is a living that would suit my needs. I see no issue with it being on Uncle Robert's land. But I wish wherever I settle to be in a place where I will be amongst those who I wish to speak for. I would need to find out if there is a seat there I might win."

His father looked as though he did not know how to answer, and his eyes glistened in the sunlight as he reached out and held Rob's hand for a moment. "Then I will cease interfering for now. But perhaps you will allow me to find out from Robert if there are any seats to be won in that area soon."

Rob nodded. He was out of breath and the pain from his ribs lanced through his chest, but beneath the pain was relief. He was glad that he'd shared this with his father, even though the whole idea now felt hollow without Caro's presence in it.

"I've checked on your horses several times and I've told the grooms to exercise them regularly. It will be weeks before you can climb up into a curricle."

Rob sighed, looking up at the ornate plaster on the ceiling.

"I also called at your apartment and collected your post. It is mostly letters your friends have put through the door, seeking to contact you, but there are also two letters from Mary." He withdrew them from an inside pocket and dropped them on the bed, beside Rob's thigh. "You may read them when you are alone."

Rob looked at them, picked them up with his left hand and noted those from Mary, then set them on the chest beside the bed, his heart thumping, in a sharp beat, even at the prospect of hearing news of Caro. Their relationship was not over for him. He doubted it would ever be over. He would always feel a jolt of awareness when he heard her name.

"What happened, Rob?" Rob looked into his father's eyes. They were the same as those that faced Rob in a mirror. "Caroline is entirely different and you two had become close, yet she left the day this happened and I presume she is the reason you want no one to know. Why did you walk home that night and not take the carriage? You left without telling anyone you were going."

Robert shook his head. He was not prepared to speak of it.

"I was young once. I can understand. I still remember the turmoil I went through when I fell for your mother."

Rob still did not answer.

"Did you see the faces of the men who attacked you?"

Rob shook his head. "It was pitch black. They attacked me from behind."

His father shifted forward in his chair and leant his elbows on his knees. "Rob, would Kilbride have had reason to hold against you?"

The gentleman said to tell y'u to leave his possessions alone. Yes.

His father held Rob's arm, probably because he saw the look of revulsion that must have passed across Rob's face.

"You may speak to me. Tell me honestly. I only wish to understand, I will not even tell your mother if you wish me to keep it private, but my conscience is tearing me apart. You are my son. I cannot stand to see you like this and do nothing."

"There is nothing to be done."

"Nothing I might do."

"No, Papa. If and when there is anything to be done about this, then I shall do it myself. I will not hide behind you."

"Rob, I care about you. Your uncles do too. It is not only Robert who respects you. You are highly thought of in the family, more

303

so than half your cousins. I understand why you would not wish for their support in your political cause, but in this… Stop this foolish battle against them. Against us. Your mother and I, and John, want what is best for you, nothing else."

Rob said nothing. His family would take this over and everything would become public… He needed to protect Caro from judgement and slander.

"Was it Kilbride?"

Yet, if it was only his father who knew.

Rob shut his eyes. "You must swear to do nothing."

"It was, then."

"I think so. I think the men were sent by him. They gave me a message which implied it before they left me."

"Then, what is between you and Caroline?"

Rob sighed, pain gripping like a fist grasping about his heart. It was stronger than the pain clasping at his broken leg. Rob opened his eyes and looked at his father. "I asked her to marry me. She refused the night of the Newcomb's ball. We became close in the summer. She came to town because I asked her to. But since the night she danced with Kilbride she changed her demeanour towards me. I think she is still in love with him."

"In love with him!" His father's expression was horror and disgust.

Yes, he supposed that was why Caro had never spoken of her feelings. "She told me in the summer that she loved him even at the point she left him. Love does not play by any rules, Papa."

His father gave him a skewed, bitter smile. "No, and I should know that more than anyone, and yet I must be told by my son not to judge. See what I mean? You earn people's respect, Robbie. But Caroline did not say no to you because of Kilbride. The night you were injured, I presume after you'd gone, she danced with him only to leave him in the middle of the floor, in the middle of the dance, and moments later she asked Drew if they might leave the ball. They left town early the next morning."

Rob said nothing.

"You are young to think of marriage, Robbie."

"That is what Caro said, and yet she had said she loved me. I thought she felt the same as I. I could do nothing else. I wanted to be with her. When she danced with Kilbride the first time, it hurt. I wanted to be able to keep her safe. The only way I could achieve it was to be engaged, and it may have been a long engagement, but then at least I would have been able to treat her as my own in public."

His father's fingers squeezed his arm. "Your mother and I had a rocky start. She refused to marry me and I desperately wished to be able to protect her. I did not leave her. I could not walk away. She changed her mind."

"Caro will not. She said that I think myself inferior, and she was right. I see now that it is that which has made me wish to help those less fortunate than others, and so I do not regret that I have felt it. Yet she said that I should have time to grow up and discover who I am. Her rejection was condescending."

"Or wise... Or kind... Those things are true in a way."

Emotion clasped Rob's throat. He swallowed. "Yet not what I want. I had begun to see myself as a tenant farmer, pursuing a career in politics, with Caro. But without her... Yet it would not be equal to the life she'd lived as Kilbride's wife. She had wealth and luxury, as Kate does, perhaps that is what she wishes to go back to." In the hours he'd spent lying here, he'd considered everything which might have persuaded her to turn back to Kilbride, even conclusions like this that seemed so unlike Caro. He could not understand it—yet his father had said she'd gone back home to Drew's.

"And you think that is what would motivate her. She walked away from that." His father's eyebrows lifted in a mark of disbelief.

"Because he was cruel to her and she had to, not because she wished to. That is why she has been so unhappy all these years, because she has felt lacking. She felt forced to leave. She has mourned for everything she left behind, including him."

"Still, I do not believe Caroline would place her priority on physical things. She has battled with fear for years, yet she came to town to see you, and even endured being in a room with the man she had run from."

Rob sighed. That was all true, and these were just the circling arguments he'd spun in his own head.

"Rob, when she left Kilbride, she went into hiding. Had it not been for John's help she would have stayed hidden for the rest of her life, by choice, and lived a life far below middle-class. I do not think she would be swayed by money, and she is not indifferent to you. You may say what you like, the evidence speaks differently."

"She refused me."

"What she refused was you bemoaning a need to rely on your family. She must have seen that you would have to do so if you married her now. If she knew you wished to make something of yourself, then most likely she said no to allow you a chance to do it."

"I told her we would live on John's allowance if we must..."

"On your allowance. Rob, you have a right to it. John's inheritance came from his grandfather. He was your grandfather too. Why should you not benefit?"

Rob had never thought of it like that. "I told her she was more important than my feelings about accepting help."

"And yet when I proposed an idea the afternoon at Windsor, you expressed your discomfort. She must have doubted your words."

Rob held his father's gaze, a melee of doubt, desire, and despair, warring in his head.

"Perhaps she was afraid that if she married you your desire for independence would resurface at some point; that later you might regret giving up your dreams and blame her."

Rob longed to get up and go and ask her. But if she was afraid of that, it would change nothing. He would not persuade her with words that she was wrong. His better option was to plan his future without her, and later... ask her to marry him again.

306

"The surgeon has said you must lie here for six weeks, and not move that leg, and you must keep it up and put no weight through it for three months. Then you may go and see her and tell her how you feel. She will have had a chance to understand the consequences of her answer. Ask her her reasons for refusing you; suggest waiting for a while. There is no need to rush. Then if you take the opportunity your uncle is offering you, you could agree to speak of an engagement again in a year, you will have made your mark by then and you will know if your feelings are lasting. You have mine and your mother's blessing."

"What if I married her now?"

"I would support you." His father leaned back. "Your life is yours, Rob. I will give advice, but I will try not to lead your life for you; it sounds as though you have it planned out well enough without any help from me. I'll let you rest now and read your letters. Your mother will be here later. If you wish to reply to any of them, let her know. One of us can write whatever it is you wish to say."

Rob nodded, "Thank you. I value your advice." It was a long time since he'd accepted anything from his father.

"We all reach a point when we need to express our independence and stop feeling reliant on our family. I can understand how you have felt. But equally, as your father, I will always wish to give you what support I can, humour me in future, and your mother. Please. I did not have my father and mother at your age, they had already passed away. I would have given anything to have their help. You have mine, Rob, whenever you need it. It hurts me here," he patted his chest over his heart. "That you have not spoken to me before about your political desires."

"I'm sorry." Rob answered. "I should have done." But the moment to speak had never been there. "Yet, I do not want your help with Kilbride. Promise me you will do nothing and say nothing to my uncles. Leave that to me."

His father sighed. "If that is what you wish."

Rob nodded, smiling as his father did.

His father gripped his shoulder briefly, then turned and left.

Rob's gaze turned to Mary's letters, and with his left hand he picked up the first. It had been sent two days after he'd been attacked. He used his splinted right hand to hold the letter steady as he broke the seal.

Rob

We are so sorry we rushed off and missed you, I wanted to say goodbye, and George was intensely angry that he could not. He threw a tantrum in the carriage half the way home. Andrew said that you would understand, but I feared you would think us awful, and Caro too, especially when you two have been so close.

I am sorry we missed you, but you will write to me, won't you? We will probably not come to town again until next spring, so you must not be a stranger, you must come and visit us.

Your loving sister,

Mary

He lifted the second letter and opened that, leaving the first on the sheet covering his thighs.

I wish I had heard from you, I am chastising you constantly for not replying, and yet Andrew keeps telling me you must be busy doing what young men do in town, and I am not to nag you. So do not tell him that I have.

Caro is much changed since we returned. Quiet again, although she does everything she did before we went to town. She visits her friends, in her own little trap with her pony, and she has taken to visiting the local poor. But Andrew is worried about her because she rarely dines with us. Still Andrew and I are seeking to include her when we can, as we have always done.

Write and tell me how you are? What you are up to? It will cheer Caro too, I am sure. And send some word for George, so that he may cease asking me when he will see his Uncle Bobbie next.

The children are well. Iris has discovered how to clap and giggles at us when she does it. It is very sweet. It melts my heart when she does so and Andrew laughs along with her with a twinkle in his eye. You can imagine just how much he is charmed by it. I think she does it so much simply to please him.

Write back to me soon.

Your loving, impatient sister,

Mary

He would not write back. He could not bring himself to do it yet. Perhaps when the wounds Caro had cut were less raw. But not now. He would do as his father had said, and call on her when he was well. He would not know what to say in a letter to Mary. If he implied all was well, Caro would think he did not care, and yet he could not write to Mary and speak of his pain because then he would look weak to Caro. Better to say nothing.

Chapter 32

"Is there still nothing from Rob," Mary stated as Drew sorted through the morning's letters.

He looked up at her, "No, my dear."

"It has been four weeks."

"It is not long for a young man in town, who has himself to think of before his sister."

Mary sighed. "Yet it is not like him. I am worried, Andrew."

Every time Mary spoke of it, a heavy pain settled in Caro's chest. She'd truly hurt him if he'd cut his sister so Caro might hear nothing of him. She was worried too.

"You should go to town and visit him," Mary told Drew, "at least then I would know he is well."

"He is well. Your father has written and told you so. They have seen him. Leave Rob alone, he will not appreciate you fussing over him."

Caro folded her napkin and lay it on her half-full plate. She was not hungry. Her stomach had been nauseous for the weeks since they'd left London. "I am going to retire to the nursery and spend an hour with the children. Then I will call on Isabella and Pauline. I plan to spend the day there."

Drew looked at her and gave her a sympathetic smile. He knew she was the wedge between Mary and her brother, and yet he said nothing.

She nodded. Drew did not know what an awful mess she had made, though.

When she walked upstairs, her hand rested over her stomach and thoughts whispered through her head, words for the child she believed to be within her. She'd had her courses before she'd left for London, but had not had them since, and it must now be six weeks or more since they'd come.

She was not afraid, nor worried, nor panicked, not even concerned. She could not carry a child full term. There was no need to speak of it to anyone. There was no need to worry Rob.

Yet to believe there was a child within her filled the vacant hole in her heart. She'd always longed for a child of her own, and now she would have a child again, if only for a few months. Even though she would never see it in the flesh. It was her child.

In the nursery she sat with Iris on her knee. Iris clapped as George ordered her to. Iris had become another toy to him.

Images of Rob filled Caro's head, as they did frequently. She hoped he was well. She hoped he did not still hurt too much.

His father had written of him and said that he was well. She wondered if he was happy without her. She was not happy without him.

What would he think if he knew they had created a child? She imagined a look of wonder and awe in his eyes. Love. She knew how he looked at George and Iris. Yet there was no point in speaking of it to him. It would only make his heart hurt even more when she lost the child.

~

Caro stood by the window in the nursery looking out onto the gardens where she and Rob had frequently played with George in the summer. It had been six weeks since they'd left town and still Caro's courses had not come, and still Rob had not written to Mary.

Caro was in no doubt she was with child. Her hand constantly hovered near her stomach as she longed to hold it. She had a child. She loved it with all her heart, and at night when she lay in bed she stroked her stomach even though it was still flat, and she sang to the child within it. She wished for it to be happy and know her as much as it might for the months it was alive within her womb. She wished the child to feel her love.

"Caro…"

Caro looked at Mary, who was kneeling on the floor playing spillikins with George.

"We are dining out tomorrow evening. Will you come with us? Andrew would like you to. You should socialise with us, as you did. I am sure it will make you feel better… and there is a dinner dance next week at the Martins'."

"I see my friends, and I see others when I visit those in need."

"You need more company than conversation. You enjoyed dancing at the last assembly, and in town. Come with us, to the dinner dance if not to dine tomorrow."

The dinner dance would probably be no more than a dozen couples. But she felt no desire to go. It was not that she chose to avoid it through fear, merely that she felt no pleasure at the prospect of going, her heart was too wounded to laugh and dance. "I would rather stay here, because that is what I wish, not because I am hiding, Mary."

Here… Caro had almost said, home, but she had more and more become aware that this was not her home, it was Drew's. She longed to be self-reliant as much as Rob had. She longed for somewhere she could make her own. Memories stirred. She had known one place, although then she had been too wounded to appreciate it.

"Very well, but between you and Rob I am worried sick." Mary looked away, her concentration returning to her game with George.

"You need not worry over me."

Mary glanced back up. "But you do not look happy."

312

"I am content, though, and it is enough, and a beginning."

George broke into giggles when the pile of sticks collapsed, which made his sister clap in her crib.

Caro's fingers brushed her stomach. If she were to leave Drew's home, now would be the time. In a few weeks she would need a maid to let out her clothes, if the child lived that long.

The opportunity to speak to Drew did not come until the next day. She did not go down to breakfast because she was feeling nauseous and the smells of the foods turned her stomach, but after Mary and Drew had eaten she asked one of the footmen where to find him.

"In the library, my lady."

She knocked on the door gently. It was where he studied the estate books and read his letters. It meant he was working—and alone.

"Come in."

She opened the door and slipped around it. He sat at a desk that looked out through the window onto the gardens. She smiled. He loved what he'd achieved, his home, his property, but, most importantly, his wife and his family. He deserved to live here with them and not to have a sister hanging about his neck and sucking the life from him.

He stood up swiftly. "How may I help you, Caro?"

When she walked over to him, he gripped both her hands, the gesture saying that he knew why she spent her days so quietly—because of Rob.

"Do you think Rob is truly well," she asked first.

"His father says so. He would have no need to lie to Mary."

"Yet Rob has not written, and we know he is capable of acting before his family."

"His father would see it. I believe he is well, but obviously he prefers to distance himself from the situation and from us now. I understand. It is what I did when Mary left me, if you remember."

"Yes, but you were a fool, and Rob is not."

He laughed. "No, he is the most sensible man I know."

The words shivered through Caro. He was. Rob was wonderful. Her palm lay over her stomach. "Drew, I wish to ask for something."

"Ask."

"Do you still own the cottage in Maidstone? Is it empty?"

He looked struck. "Why?"

"I wish to move there. I would not feel so reliant upon you there, if I might have an allowance. Perhaps you would sell the jewellery that I brought with me when I left Albert. You have never let me touch it, but if you invested the money on my behalf I could live on an income from it. I would not need much, and yet it would allow me to live as I wished, quietly, but independently."

"Where has this come from?"

"Since we went to London I have discovered myself again and I have never liked the person who's lived here. I would rather be my own woman." There she could let her child grow within her too, without fear of others noticing or questioning it. If she was lucky, she had another six to eight weeks to know her child.

"If it will make you happier…"

"It will."

"I own the property, but there are tenants there. I will need to give them four weeks' notice."

Caro nodded. She longed for that dark little cottage suddenly. Perhaps it would hurt to leave George and Iris here, and yet once her child had passed, she would visit them often.

Chapter 33

Rob's mother helped him into a dressing gown, so that Rob could move from the bed to a chair. He was to spend his afternoon there. They had positioned it by the window, with a high stool to put his splinted leg up on. It was the first time he'd been allowed to rise.

She slid the silk carefully over his splinted hand and then pulled it up his arm. The doctor had said the splints could be removed from his hand in two weeks.

"Your father said you asked Caroline to marry you…"

Lord. Rob laughed, on a choke, and coughed as his good hand pressed against his painful ribs. "He said he would not tell you."

"He said you had not asked him not to speak, but that if he told me I must swear not to mention it to anyone, and he asked me not to mention it to you. But I would have known anyway. You said her name more than a dozen times in your sleep when you were taking laudanum."

He sighed as he lowered his arm. "And Papa must have told you that she refused me."

His mother gave him a close-lipped smile as she held the dressing gown so he could put his good arm into the other sleeve.

"He said I should try again. What do you think?"

Her smile parted her lips. "If you feel so much for her, why would you not? But I would counsel, as your father did, that you

315

should not hurry it. Give yourself time. You are young."

He sighed. He did not feel so young anymore. He did not feel young at all. He'd survived a physical and emotional trauma in the last few weeks.

"I will fetch your uncle to help you stand. Papa is at John's with the children."

"I can move without his help. Simply let me set my arm about you."

"Ever belligerent. You know you were not so until you went to school. Since then you have always fought so hard to be independent."

"Because it was easier than fighting to be noticed at home," he winced as he slid across the bed, trying not to jolt his broken leg. "I left the attention-seeking to Harry. He always had a way for it, winding Papa up. I have never been interested in competing with him."

"So you decided to play holier than thou and gloat."

A smile pulled at his lips and a sound of amusement rumbled in his chest as she gripped his arm to help him stand.

He pushed down on the mattress with his good hand and took his weight on his good leg, but what he had not accounted for was that after six weeks' lying on a bed, his good leg was no longer strong enough to take his weight. He fell back and cried out from the pain which jarred his broken leg, his ribs, and his hand as he instinctively tried to grip the mattress.

"I will fetch your uncle."

"Would you pass the water first?" He did not wish to admit to her that he felt shaky and dizzy. He did not wish to be told he ought to stay in bed.

As she picked up the water he stared at the chair. It might as well be a bloody mile away.

"You are so like your father," she said as she handed him the water. "I should have known you would fall for a woman who needed a knight in shining armour."

His eyebrows lifted. "Was Papa that to you, then?" They never spoke of how they'd met.

She smiled as he sipped more water. "He was, yes. I needed saving and he saved me. And yet it took me time to dare to trust that he could."

"Why did you need saving?"

The look she gave him was cautious. "I was not in a good place. I do not like to discuss it, yet I mentioned it only because I understand Caroline far more than anyone else in the family."

"John's father?" he asked.

"No." The sharp pitch of her voice told him not to ask any more. "I will fetch your uncle, and do not decide to make your way to the chair yourself."

He smiled. No, he would not. He was beginning to learn his boundaries.

Uncle Robert returned with her and put his arm beneath Rob's shoulder to help him rise, then let Rob lean heavily on him as he slowly hopped across the room. But each movement sent agony racing through his broken leg. He breathed heavily when he sat down. His uncle stared at him. "Do you wish me to stay?"

"No, Mama may settle me in, and then I will watch the street and perhaps read."

His uncle smiled then left them, while his mother moved his broken leg carefully and set it more comfortably on the stool. Then she fetched a blanket.

"It will take Caroline courage to trust you," she said when she placed the blanket over his legs. "She has experienced pain in her marriage and you are young. But that is no insult. I know you are wise for your age, and sensible. Even John would admit that you have a far more level head on your shoulders than he had at one and twenty. He fled the country to run wild for a few years. You have never been wild."

She stood before him, her hands gripping her waist. "You have always been the one who's made me most proud and I am proud

317

that you helped Caroline. You have made a difference to her life. Now I just wish you happy, and if you find happiness with Caroline I will be glad for both of you. I suppose some people might frown at the difference in your ages, but I do not think it matters. It has never mattered to your father that I am older.

"Shall I fetch you tea? Would you like me to sit with you? I will read to you if you wish."

Rob shook his head. He wanted to sit and think.

She leant and hugged him. Tears glittered in her eyes when she pulled away. "I love you. I pray that you know it."

He smiled, nodding slightly. "Of course I do, Mama."

"I wish this had not happened to you, but then again it has given your father and me some time to spend with you alone. Both John and Mary have told us that they felt a lack of love because there were too many of you, and since then we try hard to spend more time with each of the young ones alone, but that is too late for you."

"I have not felt a lack, Mama, only love. I have always known you and Papa are there if I have need of you."

"And yet until now you have cut your path of independence so you had no cause to need us."

He smiled, "But I need you now. I would like a cup of tea."

She laughed. "Very well, I shall fetch one."

He watched her turn. "I love you too, Mama."

She looked back and smiled.

Strange sensations twisted in his chest. Hope. Love. Longing. They were spurs to act. He would accept Uncle Robert's property and once he could walk he would go and visit Caro and speak to her. He no longer felt trampled and broken, or bitter. Instead a quiet patience breathed inside him. He had to get better and then he would begin his life.

Chapter 34

A knock struck the door from the hall into Caro's bedchamber. She had come to her rooms to lie down because she was tired.

"Who is it?" Caro called as she sat up.

"Drew. May I come in?"

She let her lower legs slip off the bed and sat on the edge. She had not undressed nor lain beneath the covers, yet her hair was probably untidy, but her brother would not care. "Yes, come in."

The handle turned and he came in smiling. "You have a visitor."

Her heart jumped in her chest. Rob.

"Phillip has come to call. I think you must have enchanted him that day at Windsor. He is even bearing a posy of flowers."

"Oh." She did not know what to say.

"Come along, then, get up. I will send a maid to you so you might tidy your hair and feel presentable. He has come a long way, and it was frosty this morning—it is still cold out there. The man's efforts should at least be rewarded."

Caro swallowed against a dry throat when Drew shut the door. Phillip…

She rose and let the maid take down her hair, brush it and then re-pin it, and so it was more than a quarter hour before she walked downstairs. He stood in the drawing room with Drew, and he looked a little anxious.

He picked up the posy of flowers, which must have been raised in a hothouse because they could not have been grown in winter. Yet the Duke, John, whom he worked for, must have hothouses, and Phillip was his business man and managed all of his properties. "I brought you these," he said as he held out his posy of hyacinths.

Caro took them. "Thank you." She lifted them to her nose. They had a strong, sweet scent.

A maid hovered in the room. She must have brought the men some tea because a tray stood on the side. Caro turned to her. "Would you take these to my room and put them in water." The maid bobbed a curtsy, then took the posy. "Thank you," Caro said quietly.

Why had Phillip come?

"I know it is cold, but perhaps we might walk outside for a little while. If we walk briskly it might not be too cold."

She did not answer because she did not know what to say.

"Sorry, was that presumptuous of me? Of course we may sit in here, in the warm, if you would rather…"

"No. I am happy to walk with you. It would be nice to get some fresh air. You will excuse us, Drew?"

"There is no question of it," Drew answered, smiling at her. He looked thrilled, proud, as he did when Iris clapped—as though Caro was his child and she had just managed some great milestone in her life.

"I will ring for a maid to bring down my pelisse and a bonnet."

"And I would take a muff, if you have one. It is very cold."

She smiled at Phillip. She did not dislike him. She had enjoyed his company when they'd travelled together to Windsor, and walked together.

When the maid arrived, Caro told her what to bring, and then Phillip escorted her to the hall.

"How have you been, Caroline? I have wanted to call and I have prevaricated over it because you disappeared so quickly from town. I was not sure all was well, and I did not like to intrude."

320

"All is well." It was. She really did not feel miserable anymore, or distressed. She had a child within her again, and the only space for feelings was happiness. She would not have her emotions impact on her child. If its short life was to be as blessed as it ought to be, then its mother should love it with all her heart—and Caro did.

Phillip held up her brown pelisse as she slipped her arms into the sleeves, and then he set her bonnet on her head, although she tied the ribbons herself, and finally he took the fox-fur muff from the maid and passed it to her.

"You look beautiful," he stated simply, when she was dressed for the outdoors, and then he put on his hat. He still wore his outdoor coat, so he must have wished all along for them to walk outside.

"Thank you."

A footman opened the door.

Phillip's hand lifted. "Please."

She walked ahead, and he followed her out into the cold. Immediately it crept through her clothes.

"I shall not offer my arm, merely because it would mean your hand will become chilled. Pray keep it within your muff." He slipped his into the pockets of his coat. "Which way should we walk?"

"About the house. There is a series of smaller gardens at the rear and a pond."

"That will probably be frozen, I assure you," he stated as they began to walk, "All the lakes I have seen on the journey out here have been so, but perhaps not hard enough to skate upon."

She smiled. "Do you skate? Did you learn as a child?"

"Oh, yes. With John. We were boys, after all, and we had the whole of the Duke's estate to run wild in."

Phillip had grown up near here, he'd told her the day they had spent together at Windsor. His family still lived in a village on John's estate. His father was a local squire.

Phillip was a few years older than her.

As they crossed the lawn towards the first hedge of the parterre gardens he glanced at her. "You will have to forgive me, Caroline. I have never thought of doing this before, and I am a little nervous, and I feel a little foolish."

She did not answer, because what was there to say?

"Since Windsor, I… I have had feelings for you. I enjoyed that day with you considerably."

She nodded, because it would be unkind to make no response, and yet discomfort had slayed her.

"I enjoyed your company particularly, extremely. I feel that we might suit. I called at John's the day after Windsor, because I wished to see you again, but you had already left, and since then I have been debating with myself over whether or not this is madness, and whether or not I should speak, but I think I will drive myself insane if I do not speak."

Oh Lord.

"All I ask for now is that I might call upon you. I work, as you know, but I have Sundays to myself and I may drive out to visit you so we can begin to know one another better. Will you allow me to call on you and court you, Caroline?"

"Oh, Phillip." Embarrassment cut through her. She saw herself walking here with Rob. "I'm sorry—"

Phillip did not let her get further as they turned behind the first high hedge which hid them from the house. In the summer it was where Rob had turned her and pressed her against the hedge. *I ask for your forgiveness…*

"Have I made an idiot of myself?"

Her hand slipped free from the muff and she held his arm as they walked slowly on. "You have not. I am flattered. It is very kind of you to think of me…" *and if it had been a year ago.* Yet a year ago she would never have gone to London. She had only been there because Rob had given her the courage and invited her. "…Yet I am at a juncture in my life where I cannot think of such things. I am moving out of Drew's home this week. I will be living alone in Maidstone, and that is what I wish. I am not looking for a husband."

His fingers pressed over hers as they walked into the garden with the pond at its centre, the pond where she and Rob had helped George sail his boat. It was frozen.

"What of a friend?" Phillip asked, "Might I be that to you now. Is there room for another friend in your life?"

Rob had favoured the word "crass". It would be crass of her to crush the man so cruelly as to not even accept his offer of friendship, and if he hoped in the future that it might become more, then she would manage his feelings then. She had no intention of spending her future with anyone but Rob, and if he did not want her, she would rather spend it alone, which might be the case because Mary had still heard nothing.

"Of course, I can never have too many friends, Phillip, I will gladly accept that offer."

He nodded at her and smiled, then they walked on and he talked of John and Kate. He said that they were currently housing Mary's younger brothers and sisters, and that Mary's parents had been staying elsewhere in town. He said it was unusual for them to be in town at this time of year. It was nearly Christmas and the family were usually at Pembroke Place for Christmas.

Caro did not ask, yet she listened for mention of Rob's name, but nothing was said.

~

Caro glanced about the hall as the footmen carried down another trunk of her clothes. She had three trunks. Far more than she'd arrived with. When she'd run away from her marriage years before she'd left with only the clothes on her back and a handkerchief full of the gifts Albert had given her.

That handkerchief of jewels had now become a fund managed by Drew, from which she might draw income. She was about to become truly self-reliant.

Her heart beat hard. Rob would be proud of her, she hoped. She was proud of herself.

Yet perhaps Rob would never know. Perhaps he did not even read Mary's letters. He certainly did not reply to them.

Pain clenched about her heart, but she pushed it away, because the child was within her and she refused to feel sad.

It is his child too. That thought kept invading over others as the weeks crept on. But to tell him would only cause him pain he need not suffer if he did not know.

She looked at Drew. It was time to say her goodbyes.

George was balanced on Drew's forearm in a seated position, with one arm wrapped about his papa's shoulder while his other hand gripped the lapel of Drew's morning coat. George was tired and his head was pressed against Drew's shoulder. He was grumpy and angry.

"He does not wish to say goodbye to his Auntie Caro, because he does not wish his Auntie Caro to go."

Caro walked forward, lifted to her toes and kissed her brother's cheek as he bent his head so she might. "I love you. You have done so much for me, and I will be forever grateful for the years you have let me feel safe here."

He patted her shoulder. "There will always be a place for you here."

"Thank you." Her fingers ran over George's hair. He looked at her with his head turned sideways. "And you, little man, must be well behaved for your mama and papa, and I will come and visit you." George didn't say anything.

Mary stood beside Drew, holding Iris facing outward so that Iris might watch everything. She hated to be held against anyone's chest now. She wanted to see the world and discover it.

When Caro leant to hug Mary and say goodbye, Iris grasped the ribbon of Caro's bonnet and pulled it loose. Caro kissed Iris's cheek and then kissed Mary's. "Thank you. You have been very kind to me, like a true sister."

Mary smiled. "You may come anytime. You need not send word."

Caro nodded. It was going to be very strange without the children, and yet she had her own to nourish, for however many weeks they had left.

Caro retied her bonnet's ribbons. She was to drive her trap, so she might have a vehicle to continue visiting her friends and to return here anytime she wished.

"Well, I suppose I ought to go." She swallowed back the tears gripping at her throat.

Drew nodded.

"I am going to miss you," Mary said.

"We all are," Drew added, his hand ruffling George's hair.

"I am only half an hour's ride away."

He nodded.

She wiped away the tear that crept from the corner of her eye. "I am leaving your footmen and your groom out in the cold." She laughed. Where was her courage today? She needed a little more of it.

A footman held her hand as she climbed up into the trap, while Drew and Mary stood at the open door. It was too cold outside for the children.

Caro waved, remembering Rob waving to them all in the summer. She had not realised then how much influence he'd had on her life. She would not have made this choice without his support in the summer.

One of Drew's grooms drove a cart behind her as she travelled the distance into Maidstone. Upon it were her trunks and two footmen to lift them into her home when she reached the cottage.

She left the horse and trap in the inn, where Drew had arranged for her to stable them, and then walked to her new home.

When she'd walked along this street with Drew years ago, having fled from Albert hours before, she'd been terrified, afraid of the future and scared of the past catching up with her. Today her greatest feeling was hope. She felt truly free.

How strange was it that the first time she'd come here it was because of one man, who had hurt her, and now, the second time, it was because another man had helped her heal.

She'd come here in the summer last time, and the garden had been full of flowers, but now it was empty. The footmen were already there unloading the cart, and the woman who held the door was her housekeeper, the same woman who had been there years ago, and so Caro did not even feel as though she would be wholly alone. Instead excitement breathed in her chest.

As she walked up the path, she imagined how beautiful it would be in the summer, and her hand settled over her stomach. Her child would never see that, but Caro would talk of it tonight when she went to bed.

Chapter 35

Rob turned his head a little to the right so his uncle's valet could shave the stubble from below his right ear.

He'd begun to feel human again, instead of a patient.

His hand had been freed from its splints. It was stiff and painful, though, and barely usable. He could not grip easily, so he could not shave himself, yet he had some movement in it and he could move himself about with the aid of crutches, or at least from the bed to the chair by the window. He still had the splint on his leg, but that too would be gone soon; the surgeon had agreed to remove it before Christmas. In less than two weeks he might wear trousers again. He was mortally sick of being clothed in a nightshirt and a dressing gown.

The door was being knocked on.

"Come in," Rob called.

"Hello." His father walked into the room, followed by his mother. They were no longer staying with his uncle. Life had to move on, and they had his brothers and sisters to think of. They had returned to John's, but they called upon Rob every afternoon. His cousins had come home too, and so he was hiding here now.

"Good day," Rob acknowledged brightly, without turning his head.

"You sound happy," his mother said.

"I am counting down the days until the damned splints are off my leg."

A towel was wiped about his chin and then his throat. "There you are, sir." The valet bowed.

"Thank you, Archer."

Archer gave Rob another bow and then walked from the room.

His mother's fingers touched his jaw, and she leant and pressed a kiss on his cheek. "You look well."

"Thank you. I feel well bar my damned leg. I am impatient to be in clothes and up."

She smiled as she straightened, then glanced back at his father as his father pulled a chair over so she might sit near Rob. Then he brought a chair closer for himself and sat forward, his elbows resting on his knees and his hands clasped together, as though he had something to say.

He looked at Rob. He did have something to say.

"Jenny and Helen have been asking us numerous questions, Rob, about you, and about why we continue to go out each afternoon when we have only just returned. They are old enough to realise that the whole thing is odd. We wish to tell them."

"No."

"Just think of this from their perspective. We are confusing them and distressing them a little, and you know we have always been honest with you all."

His mother blushed.

"Then wait two weeks. I will stay at John's for Christmas. You may tell him I have had an accident in my curricle, or some such nonsense. I will have no splints and I will be able to climb into a carriage and get to John's. No one need know."

His father sighed. "Very well, I understand you do not wish Caroline to hear of this, so that is what we shall do."

~

The thought of walking had been far easier than the act, and for the first two days of being without splints Rob favoured using the crutches, but he was determined to need no more than a stick by the time he went to John's, which would be Christmas Eve, three days hence. So he forced himself to learn to balance on two sticks and then one.

He found it easiest to hold it close to his leg when he stood, so that he could put his weight through that, and when he walked he felt unsteady. Yet he believed he had established a style that made it look a lot easier than it felt, as long as he held himself straight and did not scrunch, and as long as he did not sigh when he sat down, and the pain was relieved.

When his father came to fetch him on Christmas Eve, Rob was ready. He'd dressed in outdoor clothes. He stood, gripping his stick. His father smiled. "Your mother is awaiting you at John's and I think the girls have a little celebration in mind."

Rob smiled.

"Uncle Robert has taken his family out, so that you may walk downstairs without them seeing."

Rob laughed. He had been holed up here like some criminal hiding out in his uncle's home for the last few weeks. He would be free now, and as he took his first, slow steps he felt as though he was walking into his life. He had signed all the legal papers to take over his uncle's tenancy. All he needed to do was be well enough to travel to Yorkshire. There was a local seat coming up for election the following year. It gave him the time to get settled and to socialise in the local community so he would be known when it came time to campaign.

His father had agreed that in the weeks while Rob continued to recover at John's he would go over everything about crop and animal management, and equally the management of those Rob would need to employ. He wished to be successful at farming as well as in politics. He needed the income, but success there would make him more credible in his political aims too.

It was a very slow descent down the flight of stairs to the ground floor, but Rob refused his father's assistance and managed with the banister and the stick. At least he'd been in a room on the first floor.

Again he felt the impact of the fact he'd been secretly living within his uncle's home, his cousins would have walked within a hundred yards of the door a dozen times a day since they'd returned here. He had never really thought of them. Numerous lies must have been told on his behalf the entire time he'd lain here.

When he reached the hall, a footman opened the door, and then there were more steps down onto the pavement. The carriage waiting there was his father's. A man held the door. Rob handed his stick to his father and gripped the sides to help himself hop up the step, his right leg was still too stiff to climb the narrow, steep carriage step.

Inside he shifted over so his father might sit beside him, and then leaned back against the squabs with a sigh.

"Put your leg up on the far seat," his father ordered.

Rob did so and then gritted his teeth as the carriage jolted into motion and it sent a jolt of pain through his leg. The bone may have set but the tissue about it was still healing.

His father talked of the family, of things his sisters had been doing, of his younger brothers' jubilation when they'd returned from school, of Harry's indifference when he'd come up from college.

Longing settled low in Rob's stomach. He was looking forward to seeing them all. It made what had happened to him seem more distant. Yet he was looking forward to seeing Caro most. "Papa, after the Christmas celebrations have passed, do you think John would mind stabling my curricle and horses? I wish to drive. I will have more freedom then."

His father nodded. "You know John will not mind."

When they reached John's, Rob had barely passed through the door when the madness began. Helen and Jenny came running down the stairs. "Robbie!"

"Now be careful, girls, he has had a fall from his curricle and his leg is injured quite badly, and so you must treat him with care."

More hesitantly, Helen wrapped her arms about his neck and she gripped tight and held him hard. "I am so glad to have you home. Everyone has been wondering what you have been about." She touched a point above his temple. "You have a scar, was that from your fall too?"

"Yes, I hit my head, as well as hurt my leg."

The rest of the children then raced down the stairs in a tide as Rob fought to keep his balance and not appear as though he was in pain.

"Robbie!" They were all excited.

"Now let him through." His father said, "or I will have to send you all away."

If climbing downstairs had been hard, climbing back up a flight was triply so, and it seemed to take an age.

Once he'd prevailed and reached the top, he stopped, breathing heavily and looked along the hall to see Harry standing beside John. They were watching him with eyes that asked questions Rob did not care to answer.

"You cannot have been racing your curricle, I know," Harry stated.

"I was not, the road was icy."

"Did you turn it over?" John asked. "Have you lost your horses? Is it damaged?"

"No, both the curricle and the horses are fine, it was only myself that was damaged. I lost my seat."

"And the horses did not bolt…" Harry queried.

"I do not remember. I was unconscious by that point. Now if I might reach the drawing room, John, I would be very grateful for a chair."

The children chattered as they followed him, walking at the snail's pace he set. His father walked beside them all with a smile hovering on his lips.

Yes, Rob felt good now. His life was beginning anew.

Even when his extended family called to take dinner at John's, Rob did not feel any lower in spirits.

He did not eat with the family in the dining room, but was served his alone in the drawing room so he might rest his leg up on a stool. His cousin Henry came in with Harry, before the women had even risen from the table, and teased him over his stick, saying that his limp made him appear a dozen years older.

When his other first-born cousins returned with the men, Henry proudly told them all Rob was taking over his father's property, on a lease. He made it sound demeaning, but Rob thought of all he hoped to achieve and did not care. He was certain it was something he would enjoy and it would give him an income and that was all that mattered. He did not feel inferior, he felt better than his cousins, because he aimed to achieve far more than them. When he fulfilled his political aims and helped those less fortunate, then any pride he felt would have foundation and be a worthy thing, not shallow, as theirs was.

Chapter 36

Two weeks after the Christmas celebrations had passed, wrapped up in his warmest coat and wearing a new scarlet scarf one of his sisters had made for him for Christmas, Rob drove away from Pembroke House in his curricle. It was nearly four months since he'd seen Caro.

His heart beat steadily. He'd been driving his curricle a short distance every day to get his right hand used to the straps again, and he'd been walking out daily, too, to encourage his leg to heal. But he had not gone anywhere near as far as Drew's property, and it was a long way to travel when he was still unsure of his capability. Yet when his father had urged him to wait at least another week, Rob's answer had been. "Have I not waited long enough?"

The only people who knew he was undertaking the journey were his parents. He'd told no one else. He'd not even written and told Mary of his plans. He wished simply to arrive and discover whatever he did. Largely because he had never been able to find the words he would feel comfortable writing in a letter.

The pace of his heartbeat rose as he turned the curricle on to Drew's drive, remembering when he'd done so in the summer, excited about the opportunities he hoped for, and eager to spend a carefree summer here. That summer had left him bruised and battered, both inside and out, and yet he would not change a moment of it.

The ground was frozen dry, and the sky above him was grey. It had been blue for most of the summer—except during that thunderstorm.

He prayed as he neared the house that Caro would listen to him; that she still felt something for him.

When he pulled on the straps and slowed the curricle, two of Drew's grooms appeared. He stopped before the front door and thanked the men as they gripped the horses' heads, while he picked up his stick and slid across the seat.

In a curricle, getting down was harder than getting up, because if he used his good leg on the step then he would be forced to land on his bad leg and it would buckle. So ignoring the step he slid down.

Pain jolted up from his thigh.

He leaned on to the stick, taking a breath before he moved.

The door opened and Mary flew out. "Oh, you rogue!"

Her arms were about his neck in a moment and then she pressed her lips against his cheek, before gripping him hard again. He grasped her with his free arm, as much to make sure he did not fall as to actually hold her.

"Hello, stranger," she said against his ear. "I have written and written and you have not replied. I thought you were angry with us for disappearing so quickly from London. Then I thought you ill."

"Ow," he whispered when she let him go and then firmly held his healing hand.

"You have a stick. Why? Have you been hurt? Ought I to have been praying for you, not cursing you?"

"I had an accident in my curricle and fell, but I am nearly healed. You must simply be a little gentle with me for a while."

"Why did Papa or Mama not say?"

"I asked them not to fuss. You know how I hate it."

"But you should have told me. I am angry with you again now."

He laughed. They walked slowly back into the house, Mary

hovering beside him.

"You were truly injured."

"I was, yes. But, as I said, I am getting better now."

"Andrew! Andrew!" Mary called through the house, as they stood in the hall. Then she looked at Rob. "I saw you from the nursery. Andrew does not know you are here. Can you manage the stairs? Andrew!"

"Yes, but slowly. You will need to be patient with me." Was Caro still in the nursery? Had she not come down by choice? Did she wish to avoid him?

"Andrew!" Mary called again as Rob moved to the stairs.

A footman came to the hall.

"Where is Lord Framlington, Pip?"

"In the garden, my lady."

"Oh, then would you fetch him? Tell him my brother Rob is here."

The footman disappeared as Rob gripped the banister with his good hand and used his stick to support his other leg, then began climbing the stairs, one slow step at a time.

"We could have taken tea in the library," Mary apologised.

"No, I must not avoid activity. If I am to get back to normal, I must keep my leg moving."

He wished to ask about Caro, and yet he did not want to appear over-eager. But Mary and Drew had travelled their journey with them in the summer, in a way she would expect him to ask. "Where is Caro? Is she in the nursery with George and Iris?"

"Oh, no, you do not know. Of course you do not. Have you even noticed that I have stopped writing because you never reply?"

He shook his head, focusing on the steps, as she walked beside him.

"Well, I did stop writing, and so you cannot know. Caro has left us. She has moved into the cottage Andrew originally bought for her. Yet she came back to spend Christmas with us, and she seems very happy there."

She had been happy. Not missing him, then. Nor regretting her choice.

"Sit down," Mary said, when they reached the drawing room. "I will ring for tea and biscuits. I am sure you must need something to warm you, and I have not even offered to take your coat."

He let her slip it off, then sat in a chair near the fire. The cold had made his leg ache more. "Where is Caro's cottage?" he asked, as Mary pulled the rope to ring for a maid.

"Maidstone. It is about half an hour from here. Oh, George is going to be so happy to see you, and you will not believe it but Iris can already stand, she grips Andrew's fingers and bobs up and down, bending her knees. But George keeps trying to do it with her, and then forgets she cannot stand unless he lets her hold on."

Rob laughed. Yes, he could image George's attention being drawn by something else and him simply letting go.

Rob heard footsteps in the hall. Drew. He would have stood if it were not for his leg.

"Look what the winter breeze has blown in," Mary stated. "The little brother I had thought lost."

Drew smiled broadly as he walked across the room. "Rob." He held out a hand for Rob to take, and when Rob accepted it, Drew held Rob's hand with both of his. "I am glad to see you." Rob winced as Drew jarred his right hand.

"You have a stick…" Drew stated with a frown, when he let go.

"I have explained it to Mary. She will tell you."

A maid arrived. "Tea, please, and cake and biscuits."

Drew went up to the nursery to fetch George then, while Mary filled Rob in on all the news she had not included in her letters, including the fact that Phillip had been calling on Caro.

Rob's heart tumbled through his chest and fell to the soles of his boots, and the breath froze within his lungs. Caro had forgotten him.

Foolishness grasped his shoulders and shook him. He'd travelled here to repeat his offer while she'd been allowing Phillip to court her. Rob was no longer hungry, no matter how sweet the smell of the fresh biscuits.

When George arrived he squealed at the sight of his favourite uncle and ran across the room, then set his hand on Rob's broken leg and climbed up. Rob gritted his teeth, preventing himself from shouting as he moved George to his good leg. "Be careful, George."

Drew and Mary looked at him with concern. He'd not left enough time to come here. He could not hide the severity of his wounds. He had not accounted for the children. George begged for Rob to play tumble.

"I cannot, George, I'm sorry. See I have a stick to walk with for a while." He held it up. Of course George did not understand.

"Would you go up to the nursery and fetch some of Master George's wooden animals so he might play with those with his uncle," Mary asked the maid who had brought the tea. She bobbed a curtsy and left them.

"Here." Mary stood and crossed the room to pick up two biscuits. She gave one to George to avoid a tantrum. Then she gave one to Iris, who was sitting on Drew's lap.

"You must see her stand," Drew stated, putting her down on her feet. With one hand gripping his, the other holding the biscuit, she balanced on unsteady legs.

"That is very clever, Iris." Rob smiled, despite the turmoil inside him. How could he not love his niece and nephew?

He squeezed George. "Perhaps next time I see you I will be well enough to tumble you."

George nodded as he took another bite from his biscuit.

In the summer Rob had come mostly to see the children. Perhaps he'd lost Caro, but he could not cut the children. He would come back sometime, in the future, when his emotional wounds were healed, but not soon. Now he wished to go to Yorkshire, to the property he'd rented, and get as far away from Caro and the fool she'd made of him as he could.

He played with George, for a while, and told Drew about the

property he'd rented. He hoped Caro would hear of it. He wished her to believe he had not been pining for her. Then he said his goodbyes as soon as he was able.

"You will come back soon, won't you, and write?" Mary said when he said his last goodbye in the downstairs hall.

He nodded, knowing he would not come back soon. He would not feel comfortable here, in case Caro called. "I will be up in Yorkshire for a while, getting the estate set up."

She nodded, her eyes saying she was truly concerned for him. He brushed her cheek. "I shall be fine."

She nodded again, tears glinting in her eyes. "I wish you had written and told me you'd been hurt," she whispered. "At least then I might have understood your lack of contact."

"I'm sorry if I scared you, but Papa told you I was well."

"Yes, but now I know he was lying."

Rob smiled gently, then turned to shake Drew's hand. Iris was on his arm and George had wrapped his arms about his papa's leg, bemoaning the fact his uncle must go.

"Caro would have wished to see you."

Rob took a breath, but did not know what to say. If she was letting Phillip court her, then any desire she would have to see him could not be very strong, and he'd no desire to see her if he'd already become nothing to her.

Mary hugged him one last time before he went back out into the cold.

He climbed up into his curricle, then slotted his stick beneath the seat and pretended it did not exist.

~

When Rob reached John's, he left his curricle to John's grooms and told Finch not to tell anyone he'd returned. Then he hobbled upstairs to his room.

It was dusk outside, and gloomy. Without candles the grey light suited his mood, so he left the room unlit.

He struggled to strip off his outer coat, and then his morning coat too, tossing both garments onto an empty chair. Then he sat in another, his elbows resting on his knees and his head bowed, pressing his hands to his face. He'd never felt so despondent in his life. If this was what loving someone did to a person, he wanted no part of it. He wished to forget.

God, he wanted to weep, but it was not really in him to do so. He'd never been the sort for tears; he was the sort for solutions. Tears were tools his brothers and sisters had used to gain his parents' attention, never him. Yet there was no solution to this. Nothing to be done. But live on.

He sat in the chair as the room became darker, dusk turning to night.

A light tap struck the door.

"Rob, I heard you return, it is nearly dinner. Will you come down or would you like to talk up here?"

Damn. His father. "I do not really feel like talking, Papa, or eating. I am tired." Rob's voice was gravelly.

"May I come in, son, just for a moment?"

"If you wish." Rob straightened in his seat, as the door opened. He did not rise. His leg was too painful.

"Shall I light a candle?"

"No."

"Fancy getting foxed?" his father walked about the chair so Rob could see him and lifted the decanter he gripped by the neck in one hand, while his other held up two glasses.

Rob's lips lifted in a weary smile. "Surely, if it is dinner time, you ought to be preparing."

"I think your mother will excuse me, in the circumstances."

His father set one glass down on the arm of Rob's chair and filled it. Then he poured another for himself and sat down beside Rob.

"I got foxed the night your mother refused me. Very drunk," he laughed at the memory. "Then she arrived in the early hours of the morning, when I was four sheets to the wind. She had changed her mind. She wanted me to run off with her and fetch John. I had not known I could sober up so fast."

Rob smiled at him and sipped the liquor. It slid down his throat as heat, and culled some of the pain in his leg, but not the pain in his heart. "Is this supposed to do the trick, then? Is this supposed to conjure her up? It will not work for me. It is really over. Yet I suppose it is better. This way I can get on with my life as I intended, without distraction."

His father's dark eyebrows lifted. He was cast only in black and white as they sat in the moonlight. "I take it she refused you again?"

"I did not even ask. She is walking out with Phillip. Mary said Phillip has been calling on her and she has left Drew's home and now lives alone, in a cottage in Maidstone. I have heard what I needed to hear. Her answer was truly no, and I am sitting here allowing my heart to break in peace. I did not wish to annoy you with it."

His father smiled and leaned forward to grip Rob's forearm for a moment. When his hand slid away he said, "What will you do?"

"What I have planned. But thank God Uncle Robert's property is in Yorkshire; I wish to be as far away from here as it is possible to be. I wish to never see her again. I am only glad she was not there today. I have made myself her dupe."

His father sighed, then sipped from his glass.

"I shall give myself a month to recover fully, and then I will leave for Yorkshire." Rob took a mouthful of the brandy.

"Time," his father stated.

"Time…" Rob questioned.

"Time heals everything. This feeling will pass."

His father could be so bloody prophetic it was annoying. "Well, I wish it would hurry and go. I do not understand the poets who call love sublime, it is not sublime—it is agony."

"Sometimes it is sublime. Sometimes it is agony. That is true, even when the love is for a child there can be periods of agony, such as when you find your son severely beaten."

Rob had grown a hundred times closer to his father in the last months. Yet it was probably the first time in his life he'd spent so much time alone with him.

"Now finish your drink and I will pour you another; until time heals the pain, let the numbness of the brandy absorb it."

They spoke of estate management as they drank, of the things Rob ought to be careful of, and look forward to. Then his father began sharing stories of his failures, and of funny anecdotes he'd heard told by his labourers.

It was two in the morning when his father left.

Rob fell onto the bed without undressing and let the intoxication claim him. He'd felt numb the night he'd walked out of the Newcombs' ball, because losing Caro had felt like losing the middle of himself. It was that which had probably made him deaf to his attackers. He preferred the numbness of alcohol. Perhaps he would become a drinker after all.

Chapter 37

"Lady Caroline, Lord Framlington is here."

Caro stood. "Tell him to come in. I did not hear him knock. Drew!" she shouted into the hall. His footsteps struck the stone tiles in the short hallway.

"Caro," he stepped into the room, slightly hunched to avoid the low ceiling.

She went over to him as the housekeeper disappeared and enveloped him, her arms about his neck, then kissed his cheek. "I am pleased to see you."

"I was here on business, so I thought I would call."

"Well, you are very welcome. Sit down. You may tell me all the gossip. How is George? How is Iris? Beth, would you bring us tea? Will you stay for tea, Drew? I believe Beth has recently made some ginger cake, certainly the whole cottage smells of it."

He smiled as he took a seat and removed his gloves. He must have left his hat in the hall, as he could not have entered wearing it. "George is his normal rascal self, and Iris is getting stronger on her legs. I am convinced she will walk when she will be barely one."

"Well, she is your child. She must have acquired your determination."

"Perhaps. You look well, Caro? Are you still happy here?"

"I am content, very content."

"Then I am happy. Has Phillip called recently?"

"He has, he called on Sunday. He has called every Sunday since I have lived here."

Drew laughed.

"It is nothing to laugh over, and do not give me that expectant look. I have told him not to come back. He believed by calling he would encourage me to think of him romantically. I had told him all I was able to offer was friendship."

"Would a romantic attachment to Phillip be of any harm?"

She had been glad to see Drew, but his words suddenly pierced her, it seemed like betrayal to even think it. "Of course…" she answered breathlessly. "And now I have made it clear to him that it will never be so."

Drew swallowed before he replied, "I did not simply call. There is something I wish to tell you. We had a visitor…"

"Who?"

"Rob."

"Oh." She nearly stood, and her hands clasped together. Rob had been here, a few miles away. "Was he well? Why has he not written?"

"He had an accident in his curricle, he—"

"He was hurt…"

"Yes, his leg seemed badly injured, though he did not tell us what was wrong, but when George wished to play with him, Rob was not capable of it."

"Oh." Her hands held each other more tightly. She did not wish to think of Rob being ill.

"Yet he seems to be recovering from whatever occurred."

"Tea, ma'am." Beth carried in a tray and set it on the table near Caro.

Caro looked up. "Would you pour?" Her hands would shake too much if she tried to.

Beth handed Caro a full cup, then handed Drew one and offered him a plate and some of the gingerbread, before leaving and

343

closing the door.

"Rob said he has taken the tenancy of a property Lord Barrington owns. He is moving to Yorkshire."

"Oh." So many miles away.

"He seemed pleased with the idea."

"Then I'm glad for him. When Mary writes, please ask her to tell him."

Drew nodded.

Would Rob think the comment meant she did not care if he was close or distant?

She sipped her tea, looking at the cup, the conversation no longer flowing.

"He seemed disappointed that you were not there."

She looked up and smiled. "Thank you for the reassurance."

"It was not that. I think he came to see you. Though I would not tell Mary that." He smiled.

"But there is no point in him seeing me, is there? No more point than Phillip visiting."

Drew's eyebrows lifted. "Yet, perhaps next summer Mary and I might ask him if he is willing to have guests."

"That would be cruel, Drew. He did not take it well when I told him there could be nothing between us." As nor had Phillip. *"But, Caroline, how can you know how you might feel in a few weeks or months, and what is the harm in having a gentleman friend…"*

She did not need gentlemen friends. She had the companionship of women, and yet she missed Rob. Her palm pressed over her stomach as she smiled at Drew. "I think it best if you visit him, that I do not. I do not think he would wish me there, and yet he might feel he had to be polite, or, worse, deny Mary so he need not see me."

"Yet he called at our home, and he thought you would be there."

Drew's response passed through her. Had Rob wished to see her? There had not been one single word of communication between them since he'd walked out of the Newcombs' ball four months ago.

344

Tears threatened to fill her eyes, but she shook her head. There was one communication left between them. A child.

"We will talk about it again in the summer," Drew answered. "You may change your mind."

Perhaps. "Is Mary well?"

Drew smiled sympathetically as he let her change the subject.

~

Caro stroked her stomach and sang the nursery rhymes she'd sung to George when he'd been born, her fingers brushing over her cotton nightgown. She shut her eyes. She had visited Isabella and Pauline today. They'd taken a walk through the countryside because the sun had shone so brightly it had tempted them out. She was happy, and yet she was desperate.

Every day she expected to wake up and find blood between her legs. Or even when they had been walking for there to be a sudden pain in her stomach and then for the blood to flow. Any day now she must say goodbye to her child. She had never carried for more than four months.

She breathed in and sang the rhyme again, her palm brushing over the cotton covering her stomach in a circular motion.

She loved her child.

Rob's face hovered in her thoughts. He was the other part of their child. *He had an accident in his curricle.* It had been two weeks since Drew had come bearing that news. The thought had haunted her. She'd wanted to go to Rob a dozen times. But to interfere with his life would be cruel.

There was a fluttering feeling within her stomach.

Her breath caught.

The sensation of movement within her stirred again. She sat up, the covers slipping to her waist. She longed for someone to speak with.

If she had been at Drew's she would have run to Mary without

345

caution. Mary had carried two children—she would know. It was not a sensation Caro had felt before.

Her children had never quickened.

~

Caro pulled the hood of her cloak a little further over her head, though it was almost impossible that anyone might know her. She had travelled to Tunbridge Wells to avoid anyone in Maidstone seeing her.

She crossed the busy street, then stopped before the doctor's house and took a breath. She'd come because she had to know if the sensations inside her were what she believed.

She knocked the fox's head brass door knocker.

The door opened and a woman, who appeared to be the house-keeper, stood there. "May I help you?"

"I have come to visit Dr Marsh. Is he at home?"

Caro stripped off her gloves. The ring on her left finger felt awkward. But she'd put it on because she knew the doctor would ask difficult questions if she did not have a husband.

"I shall see if he is, madam. Is he expecting you?"

Caro grasped a quick breath to calm the beat of her heart. "No, but I am with child and a friend recommended his skills. I have lost other children, you see." The words gripped at her throat. For four days she'd felt the child move, and she'd begun to hope, when hope was insane. She dare not hope, because if she lost the child, then… Yet hope would not be silenced.

"Very well, ma'am. Please take a seat." The woman indicated the chairs against the wall in the hall.

Caro sat as the woman walked away. She hoped the doctor was free because if she had to wait longer she was likely to expire from fretting.

She looked about the hall. It was dark, painted in a deep green, and there were pictures on the wall of landscapes and suchlike.

The door further along the hall that the woman had disappeared behind opened.

Caro stood, her fingers clutching her gloves in both hands.

"You may go in," the woman stated.

Caro feared she might faint as she walked towards his office.

"Mrs…" the doctor asked as he stood.

"Mrs Farnley." The name was completely made up.

"Very well, please sit."

An armchair stood to one side of his desk. Caro gripped the arms and sat down.

"Miss Griggs said you are with child, but you are worried because you have lost previous children."

Caro took a breath. She'd tried so hard not to worry because she wished not to disturb her child, and yet for four days she had done little but worry. "Yes."

"How many miscarriages have you experienced?"

"Five."

His eyebrows lifted.

"I think the child has quickened. I believe I have felt it move. I have always miscarried before four months before, and now I have reached more than that and I think the child is moving, but before I… I wished to know that I am not imagining it. That all is well."

He nodded. "Then let me take a look. If you go through the door there, there is a bed, please undress to your chemise so I might examine your stomach. I will ask Miss Griggs to help you."

She walked into the room and undid the buttons securing her cloak at her chest, then put it over the back of a chair.

A gentle knock sounded at a second door into the room. Caro presumed it was a door from the hallway. "Come in."

Miss Griggs walked into the room.

Caro turned her back. "Would you undo my dress, please?" Caro had had Beth move the buttons on all her dresses to allow for the recent expansion of her waist, although her increase in size was not too noticeable. She trembled as the woman released them and

347

then helped Caro step out of her dress. Then she undid Caro's loosely laced corset, and when Caro sat on the bed she untied and took off Caro's walking boots.

Caro lay back on the bed and pulled her chemise up beneath her bottom, then lay there in silence, waiting, looking at the ceiling.

It was madness to hope.

A heavier knock struck the door from the doctor's office. "Mrs Farnley, may I come in?"

"Yes."

He held a horn-like instrument, the brass trumpet that doctors used to listen for a heartbeat.

He walked towards her smiling. "Have you seen any other doctor?"

"No."

He lifted her chemise over her stomach and slid her drawers down a little. Then his fingers gently pressed down on her skin, moving across it. "All feels well," he stated. "And you said you were past four months. I would agree."

She nodded.

He lifted the brass horn, then pressed it against her stomach, and his ear to the other end.

A flutter stirred in her stomach.

He moved the horn to a new position, lower down, and then listened again. Then his hand pressed on the upper part of the slight bulge as he continued to listen.

He straightened and lifted the horn away from her stomach. "Well, you may have lost children before, but this child certainly sounds healthy. The heartbeat is very strong and the child is indeed moving."

Oh Lord. Lord. Tears gathered in her eyes and distorted the room, and then one ran onto her cheek. She wiped it a way. *I may have a child.* She could no longer contain the hope.

"I will leave you and send Miss Griggs to help you dress."

Caro nodded. Her hands shaking now, not with fear but with hope.

Her child was healthy and moving within her, with a strong heart.

When she walked out into the street she wished to catch a hold of every stranger's arm and say, "I am with child."

When she reached Maidstone, she wished to ride to Drew's and scream her excitement at Mary. But if she were to tell anyone, if the child was to live, then there was only one person she ought to speak of it to. Rob.

Chapter 38

Caro had never travelled in a mail coach before. But it was the only way she felt comfortable travelling to London. She was not confident enough with the ribbons to take the trap, and so at seven in the morning she waited at the Maidstone coaching inn for the mail coach to arrive, her heart racing.

The inn's yard was full of horses and men brushing out the stables and washing off the cobble with buckets of water.

A part of her wished to run back to her quiet cottage, and yet Rob had told her she had courage, and she did have, and today she would use it to take him her news.

I am with child.

The words had filled her head in the days since the doctor had confirmed it.

The child is healthy.

How would Rob react? She knew he would love their child and yet there was no doubt he would be angry with her for not speaking to him before. His moral view of the world would scream at this—it would destroy everything she'd intended for him too. It would steal away his youth. It would not destroy his dreams, though. She would urge him to continue with them and she would support him in them.

A high-pitched horn called from the high street, announcing

the coach's arrival.

"Mind out the way, madam!" a groom called as the coach pulled into the yard through the archway.

Caro stepped back.

Bags were thrown from the top of the coach, and a half a dozen people climbed down from the seats. Caro had purchased a ticket to sit inside. She only hoped there was room.

A groom held the door and a woman stepped out. Luggage was passed down from the back of the carriage. Caro looked at a groom as she stepped forward, holding out her ticket.

He smiled at her and then held her hand so she might climb inside.

A large gentleman slid across to take the window seat, which had been vacant, leaving Caro space to sit between him and a large woman on the far side. The woman nursed a basket on her lap.

The journey was cramped and uncomfortable, and most of her fellow passengers barely talked, except for a priest, who sat opposite and talked incessantly, even though no one listened.

Out of politeness, she nodded at him and smiled in the beginning, but after a while she too turned her head to look out of the window, giving him a view of the brim of her navy bonnet.

It was warmer today and there were buds on the trees. In a few weeks the orchards would be in blossom. She gripped her reticule as it lay on her lap and imagined a baby in her arms in the summer. Her own child.

Would it be as petite as Iris and as active as George?

Each time she thought of it fear grasped her breath.

Would the child live?

The child is healthy.

No matter that he would be angry, she longed to be with Rob, to receive his reassurance, and that was testament to how different Rob was to Albert. She did not fear his anger at all. Rob's anger would be just and gentle, and then she knew he would reassure her. But still, guilt made her nervous. She had hurt him in the autumn…

When she reached the coach station in London, where a dozen carriages were disembarking, Caro's heart beat out the steps of a wild country dance as she took Rob's address from her reticule and related it to the driver of a hackney carriage.

It was strange to be in London alone, to be travelling on paid transport. Some of Rob's family must be here. The Duke, John, had not returned to his estate beside Drew's since the summer, which was unusual.

Caro looked out the window at the passing terraced houses and shops, her heart skipping through steps.

There was his door.

The driver pulled up before it. She sat still, expecting the driver to climb down to help her out. But after a moment when he did not, she supposed he would not, and turned to free the door latch herself, with shaking hands.

The door came open and the driver called down his fare. She looked for the coins in her reticule as she stood on the street, then placed the money in his outstretched hand. He slipped it in his pocket, looking at the street ahead and flicked the reins.

She was truly alone in the middle of London. Either she was as brave as Rob had thought her or she was entirely mad. Perhaps she ought to have brought Beth. But that would have made everything more complicated. She wished to speak with Rob in private. She had to give him this news in confidence, because she knew his reaction would be emotional. There would anger and shock... yet she hoped there was still love. She loved him still.

There was a simple circular knocker on the door. She rapped it thrice, then took a step back. There was no answer. She knocked again. The street was busy, there were shops either side of his apartment and across the street, and carts passed through, as well as the carriages transporting those visiting the shops. There was no answer.

She turned to see a teashop across the road. She would go there. She could take a table in the window and then see when he came home.

Yet an hour later she was still seated at the table looking out. She sighed, two more hours and the mail coach she had a ticket for would leave.

"May I get you anything else, ma'am?"

Caro looked up at the woman who was serving her and nodded. "Another pot." She could not sit here with nothing.

Yet as the woman set the second pot down, Rob walked around the corner at the end of the street. His stride was uneven as he limped a little, and he looked so much paler than he had done, even when she had seen him last in September.

"Forgive me, I forgot an appointment, and I think my friend has let me down," Caro took the money she owed from her purse and a ha'penny for the waitress and left them on the table. Then she went out, the café's doorbell ringing above her head.

~

Rob walked along the street trying to make his bad leg take the same stride as his good one. He was forcing his body to return to normality as fast as he could. But the damn thing still hurt as his right hand did. Yet he was already fencing again with his friends and they had been to the shooting gallery this morning and tested out his grip on a pistol too. It had not influenced his skill to any major degree.

He'd had the deepest conversation he'd ever had with his friends on the first night he'd returned to their club. They had all patted him on the back and then chided him for not merely writing to them and telling them he'd been unwell.

To which he'd replied, "I broke my writing hand."

They had laughed, but still complained that he could have asked someone to do it for him.

Yet then he'd admitted to them that they had been correct about a woman in his life, and that the woman he'd become involved

353

with had refused an offer from him, and he'd not been in any mood to see a soul.

He had then, instead of teasing, received sympathy and understanding and been asked for Caro's name. He'd not given it. Nor had he told them the truth of his injuries: only his father knew that. Yet it had felt good to speak of her to them, to release some of the pressure in his head and his heart that still cried out for the woman, even though she had cut him dead.

The street was busy. It was probably almost two in the afternoon, a little early for London high society to be about, but the perfect time for those who did not live an elitist life.

He'd come to pack up the last of his things in his rooms, so that John's footmen could collect his trunks tomorrow. He was to travel at the weekend. He was to go up to Yorkshire with his uncle in their carriage since it would be too far for him to drive with his aching hand.

A groom was to drive his curricle up behind them, and his luggage would travel with his uncle's.

Rob turned the corner into the street where his apartment was. It was a long while since he'd been here. The man who'd lived here seemed like another person to him.

He continued walking briskly, though his leg could not easily dodge out of the way of those walking towards him.

He glanced up as a dray passed, loaded with barrels. "Oy! Watch where y'u walking!"

When it rolled on there was a woman on the far side of it who was so close she must have been lucky not to lose a foot beneath the heavy iron-rimmed wheels. She wore a navy bonnet, with a broad rim, and a navy cloak, which was dragging its hem in the dirt on the street as she hurried across it.

Foolish woman.

He looked at his door, searching out the key from his pocket. His heart pumped a little harder as an image of the day he'd brought Caro here filled his mind.

"Rob." Delicate fingers touched his shoulder as he leant to unlock the door.

"Bloody hell." He turned and dropped the damned key.

"Sorry." She stepped back.

"Caro." She had been the woman crossing the street. "Good God! You scared the hell out of me…" He looked at her. Why was she here?

Her face was pale, although her cheeks and the tip of her nose were pink, perhaps from the cold.

He gripped both her hands in his and merely stared for a moment as the world continued past them.

"I need to speak with you." Her voice was quiet.

He let her hands go and nodded, then looked down at the key. It might as well be miles away. He would make a fool of himself if he tried to bend and pick it up. His leg did not bend so easily. He looked at her, "Could you pick up the key? I have an injury—"

"Drew told me." She squatted down delicately to collect it. "I have been worried about you since he said." The last words she spoke as she rose up again, and then she placed the key in his open hand.

He swallowed, his throat had become dry. Was that why she'd come, to offer pity? He did not wish for it. He turned and put the key into the lock, then twisted it and turned the handle. It was the last time he would open this door. In a few days he would open another, a door into his new life in Yorkshire.

He held the door for her so she could enter first, followed her upstairs and opened the door to let her pass into his rooms. The scent of lavender hung in the air.

He'd forgotten just how humble his rooms were. "You are lucky to have caught me here. I have not been staying here. I've been staying at John's because of my injured leg. I only came to pack up my things."

The back of her bonnet had been moving as though her gaze had been flying about his room, but now she turned and looked at him. "Drew said you have a property in Yorkshire."

"Yes, my uncle's."

She nodded. He could see in her eyes that she wished to know more and yet she did not ask. "Sit down, Rob."

He did, because the tone of her voice said she had something to say that he would not like to hear. Had she come to tell him she was to marry Phillip? Had she thought, out of courtesy, that she should give him some warning?

She came across the room and sat down in the other armchair before his small hearth. Her hands clasped together on her lap, over her cloak. She had not even undone the ribbons of her bonnet.

"Rob, there is something I have not told you, and you will think it bad of me, and yet you must understand that I have lost children…"

Children… The word echoed in his head.

"I have never carried beyond four months. I had no expectation that it would progress."

Carried….

"I am with child. I am carrying your child. I fell the day we came here. I am beyond four months, and I… I have felt it moving, and seen a doctor who says its heart is strong. I must think now, I must hope, that the child will survive."

Child… His… "Lord." He was paralysed. It was not the news he'd expected. "Mary said you have been walking out with Phillip."

She shook her head. "He asked if he might court me. I said no. Then he asked if he might call on me as a friend and I agreed, but he called with an expectation that it might become something more. It was never that for me. I have now asked him not to call again. I have thought you angry with me, because you did not write to Mary."

"I did not write because I had no idea what to say. I could not say the things I wished and so it was easier to be silent."

"What did you wish to say?"

"That I hated you, for rejecting me, for deeming me too young

356

to know my own mind. But that I love you still. I came to visit the other week, to see you. I intended repeating my offer. But then Mary said you were with Phillip."

"Mary was wrong."

"And you are with child…" The words echoed through his head. "Do they know?"

"No."

"Who does?"

"The doctor, who I gave a false name to, and my housekeeper, who I asked to let out my clothes."

He was to be a father with his own small infant—like Iris. *Good Lord!* His fingers lifted to his forehead, then he realised he still wore his hat. He took it off and leaned forward in his seat, gripping its brim, looking at her hazel eyes. They were a dark amber, in the shade of her bonnet, and the shadows of his room. "Have you been afraid?"

"No. I have not believed the child would live. I have been enjoying every minute of the feel of it within me. But now, now I think it might live. Now I am afraid."

Her eyes glistened with tears.

He set his hat on the floor and then reached out and held her hand.

"You should have written to me."

"And ruined your life for a child that would never be born. No, it would have been wrong and cruel of me."

"It might have made my life, not ruined it. It might make my life."

She shook her head. "No, Drew was right, it was unfair of me to become attached to you."

"Drew, what has Drew to do with anything between us? You have spoken to him about us?" Rob slid forward in his chair.

"He guessed the first night Albert danced with me. You were being too attentive."

He looked down at the small, gloved hand gripped in his.

357

"What did he say?"

"That I must end it."

Rob looked up. "Why?"

"Because you have only just begun your life. You ought to have been left to find the path you wished without the need to think of me."

"Perhaps that would have been better for me, but it was not how things occurred. I was happy, Caro. I was happy to feel responsible for you. I was frustrated by not being able to be responsible for you in public. The night you rejected me I had already decided to take on a property like my uncle's. I wished to provide a home for us, somewhere we could create our own haven away from town and where I could begin my cause in politics." He sighed. "My uncle's property will be our haven now."

She nodded.

They had no choice. She could not reject him. Discomfort crept over Rob. He did not like the idea of their relationship becoming a necessity.

Her gaze held his, her eyes asking him questions she should not need to ask. Yet he would ask them because he was uncertain of her. "Did you love me? Do you now? We must marry anyway, but I would feel better if I thought it something real."

Her hand closed about his, offering reassurance. "Of course I do. I did as Drew asked and yet I hoped you would not forget me. I hoped that perhaps in three years you might come back to me. I did not speak of that because if I let you think it, I knew you would still let your hope of me affect your choices."

"Why would that have been a bad thing?"

She swallowed. She still thought him too young. He could see it in her eyes.

"You say that now, and yet what if in a year or two you realise you made the wrong choice. I'm sorry, I am taking choice from you."

"Do not be foolish. I am sorry, because things should not have gone as far as they did between us. It has affected both our options."

358

"It was I who took things too far in the hut."

"And it was I who brought you here in September, had I not done so…"

"I do not regret it. Not at all. Because I love you, but also because I may have a child. I had no hope of that. I did not think it possible."

"And yet it is, by the looks of it, even though I withdrew."

"Yes," she laughed. "Oh, Rob." Her fingers held his tighter, hurting his right hand and making him flinch a little. "I am full of hope, and there is excitement, but then there is fear."

He lifted her gloved fingers to his lips and kissed the back of them. "Come, we ought to go."

"I have a ticket for the mail coach in an hour."

"Is that how you came here?"

"Yes, I boarded it in Maidstone. That is where I live now."

"Well, you will not return that way. I will take you to Pembroke House. You may sleep there, and then tomorrow I will take you home, and you may show me your cottage."

"Rob—"

"No, not a word against it. We are engaged now, like it or not, Caro. I have the say of things."

She sighed, letting a sound of frustration slip from her throat.

He did not care if she disliked it. He was a little angry with her still. She had rejected him, and then kept this from him, and she still did not believe him trustworthy.

He stood, her hand still in his, so she must rise too.

"Do you not wish to pack, as you came to do?"

"No, I will hardly be going to Yorkshire at the end of the week. We will be getting married in four weeks. I need to be here."

"Would you not rather I travelled to Yorkshire after you. We may be married there."

"You wish me to hide you away? I will not. We will be married in St George's before my family and I will publish the announcement in the papers, before your family. I will be proud to marry

359

you and I'll not have anyone think otherwise."

A tear escaped one of her eyes, but it did not appear to be an unhappy tear. Her forehead would have rested against his shoulder, except that she still wore her bonnet and instead its brim bumped against him. She laughed as her head lifted.

He wiped the tear away with a thumb. "This will be a good thing, I promise. We made each other happy in the summer. We will make each other happy again."

"Simply having a child will make me happy."

He smiled at that. He had learned in the summer, when there had been the news about Kilbride's son, how deep the longing for a child had been within her. Yet she had lost five children.

His fingers touched beneath her chin as her eyes looked into his. "It will be our child, Caro, and it will make me happy too. But having you will make me happy as well. I wish to make you happy also."

"I have always been happy when I am with you."

He looked away, emotion catching in his throat. Things had shifted between them. They could not simply step back into the hours they'd spent together in the summer. "Would you pick up my hat? I forgot to collect it from the floor before I stood up."

She squatted down to collect it and then he brushed off the top of it.

"What did you do to your leg?"

He met her gaze. "I broke the upper bone. It is healed. I need to merely get my leg moving again, and my strength back."

"I'm sorry."

Chapter 39

They walked to Pembroke House and it took half an hour, as Rob had said when she visited in September. He did not offer his arm, but walked beside her, his arms at his sides and hands clenched as though he fought against his limp.

She longed to hold his arm. But she thought it might make it harder for him to walk.

Love swelled within her as they talked. But when she asked him about his accident, his answers became evasive. He asked her not to tell anyone his leg had been broken because he did not like to be fussed over.

He was still stalwart and idealistic. That was what his desire to be married in St George's was about, because he would not do anything less than he ought to.

She did not mind that he was, though. They were good qualities and his determination had helped her break the glass prison she'd created for herself.

She would be proud of him, and their child would be proud of its father.

Her fingers pressed over her stomach, over the slight bump hidden beneath her cloak as she felt a flutter of movement within her.

"You know, they are going to make a fuss," Rob stated when

they reached the Duke's property. "All my family are still here. Because of my accident they did not return home at the end of the autumn season, as they normally would. We will not tell them about the child, though. You do not obviously show. We will keep it our secret."

She nodded. It would probably embarrass him. Yet would they not think her presence in London, and the two of them suddenly arriving, odd?

The butler, Finch, opened the door. "Mr Marlow and Lady Caroline." He bowed, as though it was not at all odd that she'd turned up unexpectedly.

Rob nodded at him and walked past, heading towards the stairs.

Caro longed for Rob to take her hand, but when he reached the stairs he gripped the banister and his limp became more pronounced. He must have been severely hurt. She wished she had been told.

He took her hand at last as they walked along the landing. The sound of conversation called them forward.

A tremor ran through her.

"You need not worry," he said in a low voice.

He seemed different. There was something new in the tone of his voice. More confident.

"Ready?" he asked as they stood outside the drawing room.

"Yes." *No.*

He lifted her fingers to his lips and kissed the back of her glove. Then he led her in, walking straighter, as though he tried to hide his limp.

"I have a visitor," he stated, lifting her hand.

She bobbed a curtsy to the room in general, relieved to see that it was only his close family, his mother and father, and his sisters, and the Duke and Duchess. His mother stood, the look on her face expressing shock.

"You did not say you were travelling today… and you did not take your curricle," his father stated as he stood.

362

"I did not travel, Caro did."

His father threw Rob an odd look. There was a question in his eyes as he smiled.

Rob let her hand go and took off his hat, then set it aside. A footman immediately appeared to pick it up.

His father walked forward.

"Caro and I are engaged to be married," Rob said to the room.

"Robbie!" His sisters, Helen and Jenny, squealed, stood and ran at him.

"Steady," he urged them as their arms wrapped about his middle.

"Congratulations," Kate said to Caro.

"Thank you."

Rob's mother, Ellen, came forward and gripped both of Caro's hands. "Are you happy? But of course you must be, you came to town. I assume you must have come to speak with Robbie."

Caro nodded as the heat of a blush flooded her cheeks. It was not the normal way of things.

"I am more than pleased for you, son." His father embraced Rob as the girls wished Caro well.

The Duke stood before Rob, holding out his hand, as Rob's father took hers.

"Caroline. I am thrilled," he said quietly. "I have thought you a part of our family for a long time, and so I shall not say welcome. I shall be very glad to think of you as a daughter."

"This ought not to be a surprise, I suppose," John said to them both, "after the two of you formed such a friendship in the summer. But I am still surprised."

Rob settled an arm about her shoulders.

"Robbie let Caroline take her bonnet off and come and sit down, you look peaked, Caroline." Ellen smiled at her.

Rob's arm slid from her shoulders, and he turned to pull the ribbons of her bonnet loose as she looked at him. Then he lifted her bonnet from her head and passed it to the footman, who had taken his hat, before beginning to unbutton her cloak.

There were four buttons across her chest and he struggled with them a little, as though his right hand was stiff. He slid her cloak off and passed it to the footman.

Her hand hovered near her stomach, afraid someone might notice the slight curve.

"Helen, would you ring for tea and ask for some warm chocolate too? I think Caroline is in need of a little sustenance." Rob's mother requested. "What time did you set out, Caroline?"

"At seven. But I took tea in a shop, while I was waiting to see Rob."

He sighed, as though he felt responsible for her having not eaten luncheon.

Caro breathed deeply. Rob held her hand. "May we sit?" he said quietly. His limp was much more pronounced when he began to walk. She felt as though she ought to help him.

They sat next to each other on a sofa.

"Mama, you will have to help us. We wish to be married as soon as possible. I am postponing my journey to Yorkshire and I would like the wedding to take place in St George's."

"Then you will have to speak with the vicar, and the banns must be read."

Rob looked at Caro. "I will speak with him tomorrow, before I take you home."

"Yes."

"Kate, I have made a presumption. Caro was due to travel back by mail coach. She has already missed it, I'm afraid. Would you mind finding a room for her here?"

"Of course! She will be welcome. I shall ask Finch to let the housekeeper know and have a room made ready, and another place laid for dinner."

"I'm sorry. I have nothing to wear for dinner."

"Never mind, there are only a few of us, we may be informal. It will not be the first time," John stated, smiling at her. Then he looked at Rob.

They wished her out of the room. They wanted to speak to Rob alone and discover the truth about the sudden engagement. She wished she had insisted on going home.

"Will you have bridesmaids?" Georgiana asked.

"I think not, we will be planning everything in a hurry so that we might travel to Rob's new property. I'm sorry."

"You need not be sorry," Rob said, his hand reaching out to hold hers.

She smiled at him. She would rather be alone with him too.

"Here is some chocolate," his mother stated as she brought some over from a tray a maid had delivered.

Caro took it, her cheeks warm, as pain stabbed at her heart. She felt as though she'd snuck up like a thief to steal Rob from them, having hidden in the heart of their family for years.

~

Caro retired early, rising from the dinner table and excusing herself, too early for Rob to follow without it looking wrong, and once she'd retired, Kate, his mother and sisters rose to leave Rob, his father and John to their port.

"She came to you…" His father stated as soon as the women had gone.

"Yes. She was waiting for me at my apartment."

"You had no idea."

"No." Rob's heart beat out a sharp rhythm, while discomfort leaned heavily on his shoulders. He had not wholly adjusted to the reason she'd been waiting for him. He wished to speak with her… A child… "But this is what I wished for. You know it is."

"Yes," his father sighed, "although I had not imagined it to be so immediate. But we shall be happy for you, and supportive."

John smiled broadly. "Mama will love it. She, at last, has a wedding to plan. She was deprived by Mary and I."

Rob laughed, but it had a bitter note. He did not think his

mother would be so happy when the news was out that he would be a father in mere months. Perhaps he would tell them after the wedding, and let her live in happy ignorance until he and Caro left for Yorkshire.

He swallowed his port.

"You are still so young," his father said, "at least when John surprised us he was older. Yet you have common sense in droves, and I shall trust in that." His father leaned across to top up Rob's glass. They had dispensed with servants, so the conversation would remain private.

Rob covered the glass with his hand. "No, I will retire. Which room is Caro in, John?"

"Your Mama would be horrified if she heard you ask that question," his father answered.

"I only wish to speak with her. I want to ensure she is not distressed. It will have been difficult for her this evening."

"The second floor, on the right, the third door along," John responded.

Rob rose and nodded at them both, before turning to walk out.

"It had better only be to talk!" his father shouted.

Rob turned and smiled. "It is none of your business."

John laughed.

Rob wished for the flexibility in his leg to be able to easily jog upstairs, in case someone came, but he did not have it, and so he painfully and slowly climbed the stairs and found his way to her door. Then he knocked quietly, "Caro."

"Rob…"

"May I come in?"

"Yes."

She'd left a candle burning by the bed, but she was in bed, and the covers were tucked up beneath her chin. She rolled to her side looking at him.

"How are you?"

A worried sound slipped past her lips. "Tired, but I cannot

sleep."

"Why?"

"Because I am so hopeful and yet so scared."

He crossed the room to be near her. "What are you worried over?"

"That I will lose the child and that when your family find out about it they will dislike me."

"You need not worry over my family. The blame will be put on me."

"It will not. Even Drew guessed that I had begun this, because you are too decent."

Rob laughed. "Except that that is not true. You did not force me into anything, Caro."

She smiled at last, slightly. It was the first true smile he'd seen from her today. At the beginning of the summer that was all he'd wished for—to see her smile, dance and laugh. Look what it had become.

"May I share your bed? It will feel lonely if I sleep in my own. All I wish for is to hold you."

She nodded, her plaited hair brushing over the linen.

He began unbuttoning his evening coat.

"You look very handsome in dinner dress. I have missed seeing you wear it."

He smiled. "I have missed you in every setting."

When he wore only his shirt, he snuffed out the candle and then lifted the covers to join her beneath them. The sheets were cold, but Caro was warm. She turned her back to him, and so he lay close behind her and put his arm about her, his hand resting against her stomach, to find hers there, as though it cradled the child.

He kissed the spot behind her ear, then whispered. "Goodnight."

"Goodnight."

Chapter 40

When Caro woke, Rob had gone. She rolled to her other side and smelled the pillow he'd slept on, his cologne had seeped into it.

She rose and called for a maid to help her dress, so she might break her fast with the family. Rob was not at the table when she entered the room. She looked at the clock. It was almost twelve. She had not slept so soundly for months.

"Rob went out riding," his father stated.

It was only his father and mother there. They'd finished eating and were drinking coffee. Perhaps they'd been waiting for her.

"Sit down and eat, Caroline," his mother encouraged.

They talked of her new cottage, not Rob. She'd assumed they were angry, but they did not seem to be.

A rush of cold air swept into the room when the door was opened, and Rob was there, still in his outdoor clothes, which carried the scent of the cold winter air. He walked forward. "I have spoken to the vicar, Caro, the first banns will be read this Sunday. They must be read three times and then we are to be married the following Tuesday. I have also posted an announcement in the paper, which will appear tomorrow, advising the world of our engagement."

He looked at his father. "I have sent word to let Uncle Robert know he may travel without me. Caro and I will follow later."

"Do you think he would leave and miss the wedding? He would not. He will not travel himself when he hears. Your mother and I will call on him today. You are keeping us all in London for an age, Robbie."

He smiled. "Caro, when you are ready, we'll leave. I wish to call into Drew's before taking you home."

"I am ready now. I'll fetch my bonnet and cloak." She rose. "Is that coffee warm, Mama?"

"Yes."

"I shall drink a cup then while I wait for you to come back, Caro."

She smiled when she left the room. She felt as though she'd seen through a window into a future that was now possible for her. Her parents' home had not been like this, nor had her marriage with Albert, and yet her marriage with Rob might include quiet, companionable breakfasts and family dinners.

She felt the same about her marriage as she did about her child: hopeful, excited and yet equally afraid, although she could not even say why she was afraid about her marriage.

Perhaps it was only because they had not really had a chance to talk.

~

When Rob drove up to the front of Drew's house he was suffering from the events of the last hours, shock had settled on his shoulders like a cloak. They had driven out of London in silence, mostly. He hadn't known what to say. He was to be a father, not only a husband. It did not seem real. Yet Caro sat beside him as testimony to the fact that those hours had occurred. He'd not dreamt them.

It was a physical pain to think that she'd known all this time and not spoken, and yet he'd never thought to ask, and so he bore his own guilt.

He'd called at his club after visiting the vicar, only for a few moments, but he'd wished to see his friends before they discovered his whereabouts through an announcement in the paper.

Their disbelief had echoed within him as exclamations rang. "You are too young to hang yourself in a parson's noose."

"But I have heard Kilbride's first wife was a beauty."

"You are insane, Rob."

"I've never seen her, but I have heard she is outstanding."

"I remember the rumours about her when we were at school. How the hell did you win her?"

"The most notorious beauty in London when we were at school"

"She is still a beauty," Rob had informed them, with a smile.

And now he was here to officially ask for her hand in marriage, when the marriage was already arranged.

He handed his reins off to the groom and then slipped down unsteadily. He still could not jump, it jarred his bad leg if he did.

He walked about the curricle, and held Caro's hand as she climbed down.

Behind him the door opened.

"Caro, Rob…" It was Drew himself, with George in his arms.

"Aun'ie Caro! Uncle Bobbie!" George's arms stretched out. Caro covered the distance to him quickly and took George from his father, hugging him tightly. His arms wrapped about her neck and he hugged her too.

In a year, their child would be in her arms.

George turned and held his arms out to Rob.

"I am still not healed, George. I may hold you but if I hold you I cannot walk, my legs are still not up to carrying two."

"Come here, rascal." Drew took George back from Caro.

"Where is Mary?" Caro asked

"Feeding, she will be down in a moment. But, more importantly, why are you here?" He looked from Caro to Rob. "Together…"

"I wish to speak to you alone, if I may?"

"That all sounds very formal, Rob." Drew put George down. "George, take Auntie Caro up to the nursery to show her your new soldiers."

George grinned and gripped Caro's hand, then began pulling her away.

Rob felt a fool. It was far too late for this conversation, but it was the right thing to do.

Drew gave him a nod and lifted a hand, encouraging Rob to go in. "The library…" He suggested when they entered the hall.

"Will Uncle Bobbie play later?" George asked Caro as they climbed the stairs.

"I'm sure he will," Caro answered.

Rob's heart played the beat of a drum as he turned to the library, thinking of their child again.

Drew shut the door behind them. Rob turned to face him. He'd thought Drew his friend, but in town he'd advised Caro to dispose of Rob and his youthful affection.

"What is it?"

"I'm here to ask you for your agreement to me marrying Caro."

Drew's eyebrows shot up. "Where has this come from?"

"I know you know we were together in the summer. Caro has told me what you said. You were wrong. I can support her and I wish to do so. I had John's allowance, but now I also have the tenancy."

"I know you can support her, that was never my complaint." Drew leant his buttocks back against the table and gripped its rim. "But you are one and twenty, it is young to settle—"

"Yes, but that is my choice, and her choice." Rob felt as though his heart was in his throat, choking him. It would be important to Caro that Drew understood.

Drew sighed. "I'm aware that Caro has an attachment to you. I know her feelings, but there is an age difference, and I would not see her hurt. What if, in a year or two, you change your mind about the direction you have chosen for your life?"

"I will not. I have never been fickle. I do not intend to become so."

"Are you certain this is what you want?"

371

"It is what we want."

"Then why not wait for a year or two, as I advised Caro? You would then know for certain and there would be no risk."

"Why can you not believe that I know my own heart and mind now?"

Drew sighed out a breath and gripped the back of his neck with both hands, but then he laughed as his hands fell. "Very well. Probably because I am thinking of myself and my own family and I am not used to the understanding and the depth of feeling within yours."

"I am marrying Caro, Drew. With respect, I am merely asking in order to be polite. You cannot actually say no to me."

Drew laughed again. "And so you have my blessing. I know you can make her happy and keep her happy."

Rob nodded. *I will keep her happy.* It was a mental oath

Drew straightened. "We had better go up to the drawing room. Mary will hate to be the last to know your news."

"I'm afraid she is. Caro has spent the night in town at John's. He and Kate and Mama and Papa know. The announcement will be in the paper tomorrow. The wedding will be at St George's, Tuesday, four weeks hence."

"There is no time for me to adjust to the idea, then, and Mary shall hate you for not having told her your plans first. Especially when it is my sister you have chosen."

Rob smiled.

When they climbed the stairs Drew asked Rob more about the estate he was leasing.

"The mansion that accompanies it is quite large. Caro will be comfortable there, I'm sure."

Drew nodded as they walked into the drawing room. "I'll send a maid up and ask Caro to bring George back down. I'm sure Mary will come down as soon as she is able."

When the maid arrived, Drew turned. "We will have tea and cake, Molly, and would you ask Lady Caroline to come down from the nursery, and George may come too. We have something to celebrate."

"If I leave Caro here, would you and Mary bring her to town in a fortnight, so she will have time to buy everything she needs for the wedding?"

"Of course. I will write to John in the morning. I take it he is there."

"He is, as are Mama and Papa." Rob did not mention why.

"Uncle Bobbie!" George's cry rang out, as he turned the corner and ran into the room, and then straight into Rob's legs, to hug him.

Pain seared up Rob's leg. "Ah, George. Be a little careful. You scoundrel."

"He's missed you," Caro said, looking at Rob with worry in her eyes.

"Let me sit down, then, and I will hold you." Rob took his hat off.

"Give it to me," Caro took it. "I will take it to the footman, and let me take your coat."

She had noticed how difficult Rob was finding things. It made him embarrassed.

"Now you may sit down and play with me, George."

"On the floor."

"On the sofa. I cannot get up and down from the floor yet. Give me a couple of months."

A footman was at the door and Caro passed over Rob's things, then turned back. Rob looked up at her.

"I have two of his new soldiers in my pocket. I brought them down for him to show you, so you do not have to climb two flights of stairs." She held them out and came to give them to him, as George pressed a hand on Rob's bad leg.

"Ow, George, be gentle with me." He held out his hand for the soldiers as George climbed up onto his good leg.

"Uncle Bobbie had a big tumble, George, he hurt himself very badly, so you must be careful."

George nodded, looking at Rob. "Where does it hurt?"

"On this leg here, and this hand." Rob lifted his right hand. George gripped it and kissed it.

"There, it's all better now."

"Thank you." The words slipped from Rob's lips on a whisper while something shot straight through his heart, like a bullet. Damn, he would have his own son or daughter.

He looked up at Caro, but his gaze paused on her stomach before lifting to her face.

They would have a son or daughter.

Her eyes glittered with moisture before she turned away. "I shall pour." She would be doing that in his home, as his wife.

He looked at George's soldiers. "They are rather smart. Their scarlet jackets are very grand."

"Papa bought them."

Rob looked up at Drew. "Good old Papa."

"They are firing their guns," George said.

"Yes."

"Robbie!" Mary swept into the room as excited as her son, "and Caro, and you came together, how wonderful."

"They have some news," Drew stated.

"We do," Rob answered, and he would have stood, but he had George on his lap. "We are engaged."

Mary looked at Caro, her mouth open. She'd truly not seen that this was likely. "You are happy?"

There was a pause before Caro answered, and she looked as though she thought about the answer, then she breathed, "Yes." It was as though she had just discovered it.

Rob laughed. "I hope you are. If you are not, I will be sad."

Caro looked at him. "I am."

"And you, Rob?"

"More than happy." His lips parted, with a smile. He was, truly—just a little in shock. "We are to be married in four weeks." He looked at Caro. "I asked Drew to bring you back to town in a fortnight. You may stay at John's and I will stay at my uncle's. My

374

rooms will have been let. Then you will have chance to purchase a dress and other things for the wedding and some clothes and things for our journey north."

She shook her head as though she would spend nothing.

"Caro, I have plenty of money, you will purchase what you wish." He looked at Mary. "Ensure she has everything she needs."

Mary nodded, beaming. She was not worried about his age at least.

"Will you stay for luncheon? We have not eaten yet."

"Yes, if you are happy to, Caro?"

She nodded. "May I take Iris?"

"Of course." Mary passed her over, then turned to the footman hovering near the door. "Would you tell cook we have two guests?"

After they'd eaten, Rob and Caro dressed for the cold again, and he held her hand as she climbed up into the curricle. Then they waved their goodbye, with arrangements made for Drew to collect Caro in ten days.

When they arrived in Maidstone, Caro directed him to the inn where he could leave his curricle, and then they walked from there.

She gripped his arm and it made movement more difficult, but he ignored that, the feel of her fingers was a balm that outweighed it.

He'd not realised how small her cottage was. It was no more than a hall and room wide, and two rooms in depth. It was a terrace and whitewashed on the outside, while inside it was dark and full of shadows cast by the limited light that came from small squat, square windows.

He took off his hat and ducked beneath the lintel, and then apologised to her housekeeper for keeping Caro in town and frightening the poor women when Caro had not returned.

What surprised him most, though, was Caro's ease in the place. As soon as she walked through the door she seemed brighter and lighter in spirit. "Will you have more tea with me, do you think you can stomach it?"

He laughed, "I will have tea with you, whether I am able to drink it or not, solely for the luxury of sitting with you to do so in your own home."

She looked at her housekeeper. "Tea, then, Beth."

"May I take Beth to Yorkshire with us? We have become close. I would like her about me."

"If she is up to managing a small household of servants rather than a cottage, she may have the post of housekeeper there. I have not appointed one."

"I will ask her when you have gone."

Caro sat down on the edge of the chair opposite his, looking eager.

"You have been happy here, haven't you?"

"I feel free here. I am not at all dependent on Drew; my income is from the jewellery I brought from my marriage."

Inferior. When she'd said it of him, she'd said it of herself too. Why had he not remembered that?

He'd thought she'd rejected him for his inferiority, but that was ridiculous. She was happy in a tiny working man's cottage.

He'd been an ass. Why had he not seen through what she was really afraid of? His youth represented insecurity. She had been unsure of his constancy. She'd said Kilbride had adored her and then his love had died. The evidence from her life was a good reason for her to be wary.

"I'm glad for you."

"I knew you would be." She was smiling broadly. "The day I moved in I longed to be able to tell you because I felt proud, and I knew you would understand and be proud of me."

"I am. But will you regret having to leave?"

Her hand touched her stomach. "No. I would rather be with you. This was only a place for me to live until... I hoped you would come back to me."

"You need never have hoped for it. I did not wish to leave you."

"I'll chase up our tea," she stood, but he caught her wrist as she walked past.

"Caro."

She leaned down and kissed his lips, perhaps understanding the longing that must have shown in his eyes. He turned in the seat and gripped the back of her head, holding her mouth to his for a moment more, then let her go.

She smiled, then turned away.

Chapter 41

Mister Robert Marlow, the Grandson of the 8th Duke of Pembroke and the 10th Earl of Barrington, announces his engagement to Lady Caroline Framlington.

Rob sat in his club reading the announcement and hoped Kilbride had read it.

He'd seen nothing of Kilbride since rising from his sick bed, but this felt like revenge, and if the man crawled out from the woodwork now Rob was not going to back away or hide.

It should not bother him, but the fact that Caro had a history of years with Kilbride itched beneath Rob's skin. He wished he could erase that part of her life. It rankled.

Yet we have a child.

Every time he thought of the child, his heart missed a beat.

"Rob!" Tarquin called him.

Rob looked up to see his most foolish friend pulling up an imaginary noose at the side of his neck.

Rob laughed. "You will be jealous."

"I am jealous." He stated, "I have heard a dozen more rumours about the quality of her beauty, and the perfection of her skin."

"I do not wish you to admire it."

Tarquin laughed.

"The deed is done, then," Roger sat down next to Rob.

"It is." There was no going back and he did not wish to.

~

When his father's hand settled on his shoulder, Rob looked up. "They've arrived."

Rob's thoughts had been drifting—he'd not heard them. He rose, his heart racing with excitement. He smiled. He'd longed to see her. If he could bloody run down the stairs he would, instead he gripped the banister and limped heavily down them, but a little faster than he'd walked down them a week ago. Every week he made small progressions in his health.

John was already in the hall, as were Kate and his mother, and behind him he heard his sisters coming down.

He wished none of them to see or touch Caro before he did. So here was another of the emotions that Caro engendered in him with a strength that was irrational—possessiveness.

Rob's father had always been like a dark, guardian angel at their shoulders. Perhaps Rob would be like that over his children. Or perhaps he would be like George with a bloody new toy and become obsessed with it. He laughed out loud as he mocked himself and tried to hurry his leg.

Caro walked through the door into the hall with Mary. She was wrapped up in the same cloak and bonnet she'd worn when she'd come to him.

Her gaze passed quickly over those in the hall then lifted, looking for him. She smiled broadly when she saw him coming downstairs. He grinned at her. If he'd been fit and healthy he would have run and lifted her off her feet when he reached the hall.

Instead she walked towards him as he descended the last few steps. In his mind he greeted her with a kiss. But he could not do it in reality before his family. Her eyes were gilded by the light in John's hall, and they soaked up his features with a visible thirst.

Forgetting everyone about him, he pulled the ribbons of her bonnet loose and lifted it from her head. "Was your journey good?"

She nodded, but her smile fell, leaving only a slight lilt at the edges of her mouth. She was nervous.

"Let me take your cloak too."

"Thank you."

"Have you a list of all you need to buy in town?"

"I do not wish to spend your money."

"It will be your money too once we are wed. What is mine will be yours, and I have enough. I neither gamble nor drink heavily, as you know, and as I have not really wished to be supported by John, I have a sum saved. I also do not even feel guilty spending it anymore, because, as my father pointed out, John's money was my grandfather's and therefore should I not deserve a share as I was equally his grandson?"

Caro's smile lifted again. "You are a little different from what you used to be. You seem more confident." The words were whispered, as the rest of his family fussed over Mary and Drew and the children.

"Perhaps. I have travelled a little bit of a journey since I fell from my curricle. I was forced to become dependent on my family, and learned to know myself a little better as I lay in bed reflecting on our conversations in the summer and the autumn. Like you, I suppose, I found my freedom to become myself."

She smiled more truly then, with no nervousness in her eyes.

"Caroline, how lovely to see you again." His mother came to welcome her.

He gave Caro's cloak and bonnet to a footman, then turned as his family fussed over her. His mother hugged her. "We are very happy for you both, Caroline."

His father stepped forward and did the same, pressing a parental kiss on Caro's cheek.

John greeted her then, and she dropped a shallow curtsy. "None of that. You will be my sister, so we must be informal. Katherine and I are also very glad for you, and you are very welcome here. We shall take good care of you until the wedding. Katherine has been eagerly looking forward to taking you shopping."

Kate hugged her too.

"We may exhaust you, though, I'm afraid," his mother said, "We have arranged all sorts of visits with trades people to obtain everything we will need. We have so little time, and Rob is insisting we do everything properly."

Caro glanced at him.

His extravagance was for both of them. He wished Caro to have a day to remember, but he wished it for his mother too.

But when his mother would have led Caro upstairs he caught Caro's arm. "Wait." He let his family walk on ahead, then took Caro's hand and walked with her, at his slower pace. "The announcement has appeared in the paper."

"I know. Drew showed me."

"Are you still happy with the idea?" he asked as he took the steps. He did not use the banister, but clasped her hand tighter when he put his weight on his weaker leg. It held.

"I am, but I am terrified too. The future still scares me."

"The future will not be terrifying. It will be as it was in the summer."

She glanced at him. "You have always known what to say to me."

There was that swelling in his chest. Love. To help her like this and have her so close were things his body had craved. That thirsty feeling of the summer was now something deeper, something within his gut and his chest rather than his throat.

"I have been terrified of facing your parents again too. They have not shown it, but I am sure they must not approve."

"They would rather I was older, but they understand that love cannot be chosen. They know we did not plan for this to happen, and they already think of you as a member of the family." His beast of possessiveness quietened as her fingers gripped his more firmly, but perhaps he was holding hers too hard due to the pain from his leg.

"This is the first time I have walked upstairs without using the banister. If I am bruising your hand you must tell me," he whispered, as his family turned towards the drawing room.

"I would not tell you even if you were, because I am glad to help you, but you are not anyway."

~

Rob caught hold of Drew's elbow as they rose from the dinner table. "Might I speak with you?"

Drew looked back and smiled at him. "Of course."

"I mean privately, before we join the women. We can go down to the library."

Drew nodded.

The dining room was full. His wider family had come to John's to take dinner in an informal celebration of Rob's engagement. He'd had his shoulder slapped a dozen or more times, and received various inappropriate comments from his cousins. He'd wished to throw a punch at them on three occasions, but he knew his cousins well enough to realise that if he responded, the teasing would become worse, so he'd left them to their foolishness.

But as he'd eaten he'd been watching Drew and the words Drew had spoken to Caro in the autumn had been stewing in Rob's head.

They descended the stairs in silence. The lower floor was full of shadows as the candles burned on the upper floor only. There were none lit in the library, but the window shutters were turned back and the room was full of moonlight. It reached across the floor in wide strips.

"What is it, little brother?"

It was a name Drew had used for Rob for a long time, ever since he'd married Mary, yet tonight it kicked. "I wish to tell you that you had no right to tell Caro what to do in the autumn. The things you said about me were wrong. You should have let her do as she wished and left us alone. We would have been engaged that week, and she need not have endured worry."

Drew lifted his hands, palm outward. "I meant no offence. I was merely thinking of what was best for you both."

"She had complete faith in me until then, and now she is not certain. She fears that I will have a change of heart, and that is only because you put that in her mind."

Drew's hands fell and his gaze met Rob's. He was a dark shadow, with the moonlight behind him. "Then I am sorry. That was not my intent."

"But you're intent was to meddle, and it was not for good, Drew. You ought to have spoken with me if you were concerned, not to Caro. Fortunately things between us have been resolved regardless. But I wish you to know, in future do not doubt me, and do not stir up emotions that will make Caro afraid. She has endured enough fear, she needs to be able to feel confident."

"I know." A repentant pitch hung in Drew's voice. "I did not say to her what I did from an ill intent."

"I know."

Drew laughed. "Well, then, you have truly grown up, and now I am reprimanded by my sister's future husband."

Rob did not think Caro's sadness or fear amusing.

"Come," Drew clasped Rob's shoulder, "let us join the women. I shall not misjudge you again. You are truly ready to be old."

Rob let Drew lead him from the room, but he was not sure the statement was a compliment. "I may be engaged to your sister, but I am not old, and nor is she. She may be older than me, but she is still young."

"And obviously very charming, to have won such a level-headed man. I am glad for Caro, and I am glad for you, if you are truly content with it, Rob."

Rob stopped walking and Drew's arm slipped from his shoulder. "There is still doubt, *if*, such words will hover in Caro's mind. You know how she is. There is no if. This is what I want. To be with

Caro and to build a home for us, a place she can be certain of. You have no more faith in me than she does."

"I do, it is just our history is different to yours. Doubt, a lack of belief in people, has been bred into us. It is only proof of the opposite that takes it out."

"You will have proof."

"It is Caro who needs it, not I." Drew smiled, and turned to begin climbing the stairs.

Chapter 42

It was almost as if the peace of the past few weeks in Caro's cottage had never existed. The pace of life in town was sweeping those weeks away. It was so much faster, overwhelming.

Mary took Caro shopping for clothes and encouraged her to buy far more than what she needed for the wedding. She said Caro should "buy anything bright and pretty that makes you feel happy, so you might walk into your marriage as though it is spring."

Caro had laughed at that, yet a new marriage, a new life, it was a new beginning for her.

Rob's mother had helped her write all the invitations and then choose flowers for her bouquet and flowers for the church and to adorn the hall for the wedding breakfast. Everything was to be evergreens, including holly, and her bouquet was to be daffodils and tulips.

Then they had considered, with the Duchess of Pembroke's chef, how they might have the bride-cake decorated.

Mary had also convinced Caro that it would be cruel not to allow Rob's younger sisters to act as bridesmaids, and so a colour was decided upon, and a modiste called to measure all of them and agree the style of their dresses.

They'd visited a fabric warehouse to choose the material and swathes of cream silk would now decorate the walls in the ballroom for the wedding breakfast too. In an odd twist of fate it was the warehouse where once she'd met Drew, when she'd been with Albert. It had been there Drew have first told her he had the money to help her leave Albert. It was there her life had begun on the path that had led to Rob.

Her life was a whirl of activity, and if society called on her, to find out about her impending marriage, she did not know because she was never free to be able to speak with callers. She was caught on the crest of a wave, with everything progressing at such a rate of knots she could neither stop it nor control it.

The best time of the day, though, the time she had come to look forward to, was when Rob called to dine with them. They had not attended a single entertainment in the week she'd been here, and so in the evenings they'd sit beside each other at the table and then next to each other in the drawing room as his family talked, or played the pianoforte, or cards.

They'd not spent much time simply talking about themselves in the summer, and so it was good to have time to come to know him better. He talked mostly of the future, of what he'd learned of the property he was taking on, and how to manage the stock and the land, and how he planned to socialise and make a name for himself before the election came. Yet he asked her mostly of the past, not of her first marriage but of her childhood. He asked her about all the things she wished for, as if he planned to make all her wishes come true.

She only wished to be with him and for their child to be born healthy.

They could not be physically close in anyway, because they were among his family constantly, and yet she still felt a physical connection. If he touched her arm a shiver of awareness skimmed through her body, like a ripple on a lake.

She longed for him to be in her bed, not intimately, she would be too worried about the child, but at least to be held by him. But Rob was not staying at John's, so he could not creep down

386

to her room.

She wished he would find a moment to pull her about a corner and kiss her, though, as he'd done in the summer. The lack of kisses made her fear that he was already growing out of his love for her, as Albert had done. The thought hovered at the back of her mind, and in the depths of her heart, no matter how much she tried to push it aside.

~

Caro stood before the long mirror in her room as the maid secured the buttons at the back of her dress. It was the evening their wedding celebrations were to begin; there was a ball. The Duke and Duchess of Pembroke were hosting it here, to celebrate and say farewell to Rob.

She and Rob were to be married the day after tomorrow at twelve and then they would attend the wedding breakfast here, before beginning their journey north.

The whirl of the last few weeks had suddenly seemed to stop spinning today, and she'd spent the afternoon alone, in her room. She was afraid. Terrified. That Rob would cease to love her. That she would lose the child. That she would not cope with this evening. This was not who she was. She wished to be the person who had been happy in her cottage. Yet she still longed to be with Rob and have their child. Only she wanted to be alone with Rob.

We will be soon.

"You are ready, ma'am."

"Thank you," Caro turned and smiled at the maid.

She had to walk downstairs alone. Her hands shook as she left the room. *You have courage, Rob told you so, and he is right.*

The hallways here were so oppressive, with giant gilt-framed portraits and domineering marble busts of numerous previous dukes, who glared at her. She could hear voices downstairs. The servants setting up, the family had agreed to meet in the drawing

387

room. Of course, all of Rob's extended family had returned to London for the wedding, and they were numerous. They filled the house before they even began receiving guests.

She breathed heavily, remembering her old fears.

She only had this night to survive, and then one more day, and the morning of the wedding, and then there would only be Rob.

Rob was seated between his father and his uncle. He stood. She felt like running into his arms. "You look beautiful," he said, as he walked towards her.

"So do you," she breathed. Her longing for a kiss had become a pain hovering in her chest whenever he was close.

He gripped her hand and lifted it so he could kiss the back of her fingers. It was not the same.

He smiled at her. "You have not spoken to some of my cousins yet. Come, help me prove how equal I am." It was a jest, but she was not in the mood for his teasing, or their belligerence. Whether it was right or wrong, she did not like more than half of them. Yet she did like his younger brother Harry. His hair was brown like Rob's and his father's and yet he had the same eyes as Mary and her mother, a very pale blue, and they sparkled with amusement constantly.

"George will be looking to play a game of tumble with his uncle Baba tomorrow morning," Drew stated in a dry voice when he joined them.

Harry grinned.

Rob laughed. "Especially as I have been unable to play rough with him."

"I shall step up to the mark," Harry stated, winking at Caro.

The boy was brash and reckless, although he was hardly a boy anymore. Like Rob he'd grown up in the last few years.

He lifted his glass to Rob, then to her. "I shall see you with George about my neck in the morning, because I have no desire to stay for this bloody ball. I and some of the others are off to find more preferable entertainment."

"Women…" Rob whispered as Harry walked away. "Papa will kill him when he hears he's gone."

"We ought to go downstairs and form the receiving line." John came over and touched Rob's arm.

Rob looked back. "Yes, of course. We will come."

He looked at Caro. "Are you prepared?"

She took a breath, her heart racing. "Not at all."

"You will be fine, as long as Rob is beside you," Drew stated. "I seem to recall you were fine the night of the assembly once you two had gone off outside alone in the dark."

Caro poked her tongue out at Drew for his little jab, as Rob merely smiled and clasped her elbow, turning her away. The Duke was speaking with his mother and father, probably telling them to come down too.

"I wish we could slip away," Caro stated as they left the room. The wave she'd been riding for weeks was breaking, and the roar of it was deafening as she was pulled beneath the foam. She was drowning.

He stopped and turned. No one else was in the hall.

His fingers gripped the back of her neck, his dark eyes gleaming, and then his lips pressed over hers briefly, and yet, just that slight moment filled up her soul, as though his love poured into it. "Only one more day," he said over her lips before turning away as the sound of his parents and brother following came from the drawing room.

His limp had eased a little more in the days she'd been here, and his movement was not so awkward as he descended.

"I have asked the orchestra to play plenty of waltzes. I think my leg might survive those. I do not think it will survive a country dance."

She squeezed his arm gently.

The Duke and Duchess were to stand at the head of the line, as most senior in rank and the hosts, and then his parents, and she was to stand on the end beside Rob. Vulnerability hovered in

389

her nerves.

The rest of his family came down and began filling the ball-room. When the doors opened into the hall for the first time and a breeze swept in, with their first guests. The introductions began. She'd done this a hundred times before with Albert, yet this was so different. She was different. She had been broken and repaired, but she was still fragile.

She curtsied and smiled through three dozen greetings.

"Rob."

"Tarquin." Rob shook a young man's hand firmly. "Caro, this is one of my good friends. Tarquin Holland, meet my wife-to-be, Caroline."

Heat crept into her skin and she curtsied. She presumed Rob's friend had no title, as Rob had not given him one. "Hello."

The man's gaze seemed to pass all over her face before he smiled. Then he nodded at Rob. "I approve."

Rob laughed. Then he smiled at her. "Forgive him, Caro, he does not always realise what an idiot he is."

Caro smiled.

"The others are in the hall stripping off coats, we walked, and it's a bloody cold night." He looked at Caro again suddenly. "Oh, forgive me, I am not used to the presence of women."

"Hello, Rob!"

Caro looked to see another six young men, of Rob's age, lined up to greet the Duke and Duchess and then his parents. One of them had lifted a hand to Rob.

When they reached him, there was more vigorous hand-shaking, and Rob's shoulder was slapped a couple of times. Then he introduced them all at once. "Meet my friends, Caro, Thomas Grey, Christopher Michaels, Roger Price, Patrick Ellis, Stephan Dalton and Arthur Wilson." They walked past her in a line, taking her hand and kissing her fingers and passing her hand onto the next one.

They were nice, and so young, and these were his friends. But they were sensible young men, all of them. She could not imagine any of them sneaking off to a brothel. They were like Rob. Yet he was not like them. They probably spent half their lives at their leisure. He was to be a father in a few months. Now she understood why Drew had been concerned. Yes, she had stolen Rob from another life. It did not make her feel good.

"Might I dance with you? Obviously not the first, that will be Rob's, but another?" Arthur asked.

She nodded. "Of course."

"I think they are all now under your spell," Rob whispered to her as they walked away.

Her smile fell. Seeing his friends had stirred up her fear again. What if he came to regret it all? What if his love died?

The arrival of guests began to thin and the orchestra started playing.

"Go," his mother said to Rob and Caro, "You must dance the first together. We will come and watch you in a moment."

Rob leant to Caro's ear as they broke from the line. "I have not tested out my theory that I am able to dance, so this may end up with the two of us in a heap on the floor."

She laughed and looked up at him as they walked into the middle of the room. "I love you." It was said with a clinging tone she did not like, but her fear had made her speak.

"I love you also." His hand took hers and his other settled at her back.

"You had better keep looking at me and nowhere else because I have never felt more vulnerable in my life."

His lips lifted into a warm smile. "Nor I. Half these people will not have even known who the hell I am until tonight. I preferred it that way, but I suppose I cannot remain inconspicuous if I wish to make the allies I will need in Parliament." He started the first turn, and it was slow, and his movement a little awkward, but he succeeded.

The music swelled, growing in tempo. She glanced about the room as he continued turning her with measured careful steps.

His parents were smiling and looking pleased. She still feared they would be angry once they knew of the child. Guilt pierced her chest as she looked back at Rob, but then over his shoulder she saw his friends watching too, talking to one another, and laughing.

"Yorkshire is a long way from town, will your friends still come there to support you when you begin to campaign?"

"They will come to Yorkshire. I will tempt them with tales of all the ruins to explore. They are not really town people; they would far rather head up to the Lake District and discover the wilderness."

She nodded, but it was more awkward than his movement.

"You are nervous?"

"Far too nervous. So nervous I wish my old fear would return so I had an excuse to run."

"You do not wish that. I'm sorry if this is too much, but it will be over the day after tomorrow, and then we may run together. I know I could have made this easy for you, Caro, had I acquired a special licence, but Mama did not see Mary or John married. I wished to give her this, and I wished to give it to you too. It is right that we begin our marriage with a statement we and others will remember."

He was as always trying to do what was right. "You are man of morals… and I am honoured."

He laughed. "I preferred it when you simply said I love you."

At last others began to dance about them and the floor filled.

She spent most of the evening dancing. Rob's friends took up half the evening, but then she danced with Rob's father and Drew, and then John. She was exhausted as they ate supper and glad that they'd decided not to hold the ball the day before the wedding. She would have been too tired and her feet too tender to walk up the aisle.

"I call for speeches!" Rob's father stood and shouted suddenly.

"I agree!" John shouted, as he walked behind their seat, and then leant to whisper something to Rob.

Rob's uncle, Robert, stood and began telling the room in a

loud voice how he'd been smitten by his little nephew, when Rob was a child… and he poured out anecdotes of Rob's childhood.

Heat touched Caro's cheeks as Rob's skin held a high colour too. He'd not known they'd do this. He looked uncomfortable as John's hand slipped from his shoulder and John moved to sit down.

The speech was ended with glasses being raised and then a gift was brought over from his uncle and aunt. Rob had been given a diamond pin for his cravat and Caro was given a silver comb for her hair.

It was the first of several gifts from his family, as they all wished them well. Caro's gifts were mostly ornaments for her to wear for the wedding.

She was truly touched.

Drew made a speech last, he spoke about Rob's and Caro's relationship in the summer, and said, "Only a man with Rob's humility could have found the path to Caro's heart. To their happiness!"

Another toast was drunk and then Drew and Mary came over. "Here." Mary gave a gift to Rob. It was a pocket watch. "So you might always find the time to come and visit us."

Caro smiled as she freed the ribbon about the box Drew had given her. It was a gold necklace, a narrow chain with a small heart-shaped pendant decorated with three small rubies. She looked up at him. "It's lovely."

"It is to replace another. You have a heart and you deserve to be loved."

Caro fought to form a smile as tears gathered in her eyes. She understood his intent; to tell her to forget the love they'd lacked as children and the love she had lacked in her marriage. He was saying that it was not because of anything to do with her.

The tears ran. He gave her a handkerchief, as he'd done a dozen times before when she'd been married to Albert and cried on his shoulder over her misery.

Happiness was within reach, and yet she was terrified of it breaking.

Rob's arm came about her and he kissed her temple.

"May I dance the next with you?" she looked at Rob as she dabbed her tears away.

He nodded.

"I did not expect your uncles and aunts to be so nice," she said when the music began and he led her to the floor.

He laughed at that. "You have been a part of my family for a long time. Have you never really looked at us?"

She shook her head. "No, I suppose I was too busy hiding." Ignoring their audience entirely, she slipped her arms about his neck and hugged him briefly before letting go and forming the correct hold for the dance.

"My family are an interfering bunch, but you have to love them regardless, niceness, and caring exuberantly, are their best and their worst qualities," he jested.

She longed for the wedding to be over and to have him to herself.

Rob said goodnight to her in the hall, when everyone else had walked upstairs, while his uncle waited outside in the carriage. But there were servants about them, tidying up.

"I want to kiss you," he said before smiling.

"I have wanted to kiss you for days."

"I am tempted to do it even though the servants are here."

She laughed. "Do not ruin my reputation a day before the wedding."

"It is just a day more..."

"Yes, just a day. You had best leave or your uncle and aunt will become impatient."

"Life is cruel, a day is too long. Why did I not make the date for tomorrow, our banns are read."

"Then you have created your own torture."

He laughed and tapped her beneath the chin. "You survived tonight beautifully. I love you. I will see you at the church. Goodnight." He lifted off his hat again for a moment and leant to press a very brief kiss on her lips before he turned to the door.

A footman opened it.

He looked back again and smiled before he left.

She would not to see him tomorrow—today—it was four in the morning. The next time she saw him would be on their wedding day as he stood at the altar and she walked up the aisle.

As she walked up the stairs, her hand rested against her stomach. She had not felt the child move for days, and yet she'd been so busy she'd probably not noticed it. She would sing to it tonight.

~

Pain burnt through Rob's side as he turned away from Caro. His leg was aching like the devil. He'd been standing on it half the night, but it was not from that. It felt as though Caro was torn from him. He would rather not leave; he'd rather stay. But all the arrangements had been made.

The cold night air swept at him as he walked out the door. He wished away the day they had left. He wished they stood at the church and he might whisk her off in a carriage.

Rob looked both ways up the street. It was too dark to see far, the light from gas lamps outside John's bleached out the moonlight. But, even so, he knew he was being watched. He felt it.

The footman before him turned to open the door of his uncle's carriage. Rob had not been fool enough to walk anywhere at night, not since the announcement.

"Come along, Rob, get in, it is chilly sitting here," Aunt Jane complained. He smiled at her and climbed in, putting his weight through his right leg and gripping the handle with his right hand. His right hand was only a vague, whispering pain, his right leg a low grumble, but there was no sharp sudden cry of pain that said "don't stand on me". He was healing.

As he seated himself next to his uncle, Rob's hands curled into fists, the words John had whispered in his ear over supper echoed in his head. *"So that you know, the Marquis of Kilbride has just tried to get himself in."*

Apparently Kilbride had turned up at the door, hoping the footmen would be too awed by his rank to reject him, but they had held fast to the rule that only those with invitations might come in—and refused. Finch had been the one to finally throw the man out.

Rob was angry that Kilbride had even dared try, and yet really it was no surprise, he'd made it clear enough that he still thought of Caro as his.

She was not, though, and he should learn that.

Anger was low in Rob's stomach, another outcome of the emotion loving Caro had brought into his life.

Yet it had felt good, to be the one that John told, to be the one who was seen as the person to protect her. That was what Rob had wished for in the autumn.

Chapter 43

Caro took the lead toy soldier Drew held out and passed it to George. "There, see, we have it, there was no need for so many tears." She'd taken George down to the library, where John, Drew and Edward had gathered, to retrieve George's favourite soldier from Drew's pocket. "Papa only put it in his pocket to keep it safe."

George nodded against her shoulder, with the rescued soldier clutched in his tight little fist.

"...Mister Robert Marlow."

Caro looked up as she stepped out from the open library door. She knew that voice.

"He is not staying here, my lord."

"Then I want to see... Caro!" When Albert saw her, he moved forward. There were three footmen about him and Finch. Caro gripped George tighter, instinctively clasping him to her chest.

"Come here! Come with me!" Albert's barked order told her to move. She backed away as George glanced at the angry red-faced stranger.

"You are not welcome here. I have asked you to leave," Finch said calmly.

Caro backed away two more steps towards the stairs.

One of the footmen turned to open the front door, as two others moved towards Albert as though they planned to push him out, but Albert would not endure that.

She took three steps back as he came forward, taking the advantage of only two men before him to slip past them, and then he was before her, yelling at her and lifting his hand.

She gripped George's head, covering his ears, trying to protect him and not scare him as she stepped away, ducking to avoid a slap, but she stumbled and fell.

"Caroline…"

"Kilbride! What the hell are you doing here?"

"Get out, you bastard!"

The three men came out of the library behind her, with a surge of aggression. In the moment, she fell back, slipping on the first stone stair.

"Ah!" She held onto George, terrified he would be hurt as they tumbled onto the steps. Her hip and elbow hit the stone and George thrust his head back, shouting, as he bumped the side of his face. Caro lay there, nausea twisting through her stomach as George howled in her arms, while John, Edward and the footmen manhandled Albert out the door.

"Caro." Drew was there, and his hand braced her elbow. "Are you hurt?"

Only within. "Bruised, that is all."

"Why did you let him into the hall?" John was shouting at his staff.

"George." Rob's father was there. "Let me take him?"

Caro gave him up willingly. She'd probably been holding him too tightly.

"I bumped my head." George said as tears spilled down his cheeks.

"Can you stand?" Drew asked Caro.

He helped her up, but her hand shook and her legs felt as though they belonged to someone else.

"You put Lady Caroline at risk!" John shouted at the footmen and Finch.

"I will take you upstairs." Drew held her arm.

"May I go to my room?" Mortification swept over her, that Rob's family had seen how violently she'd been treated, that she'd been holding poor George.

"I know, he was a very nasty man," Rob's father said as he walked before them with George.

Caro shook violently as they reached the first floor. John was still shouting downstairs and George's sobs could be heard as his grandfather carried him on to the drawing room. Drew's hand stayed beneath Caro's arm, guiding her towards her room.

She did not try to undress, merely kicked off her shoes and lay down on the bed as Drew looked down at her. She was suddenly terribly tired.

"I am sorry this happened, Caro."

"It is not your fault. It is no one's fault."

"Will you manage here if I go to see George?"

"I shall be fine. I will sleep. I am still tired from last night."

"You're sure?"

"Yes, I had a shock, that is all. I just need to rest."

~

Rob leaned back in his seat and laughed at something one of Uncle Robert's friends had said. Lord Sparks patted his arm in answer. "I am serious, young Robbie. It is no joke. Robert and I have sons who are forever being pulled from brothels in Oxford and then there is you with your desire for politics."

"Although, as I have said before, like father like son. Yet Geoff and I did not trouble ourselves with brothels." Uncle Robert lifted an eyebrow.

Rob laughed again. His uncle would not speak to his son, Henry, like this. In fact, none of his uncles spoke to his cousins like this.

Perhaps his inspiration to help those less lucky in life had come from a base of a sense of inferiority to his cousins, but as a man, and even as a child he'd been their equal. He had been blood, skin and bone too. It was mystifying how fate played with you. If he'd not felt inferior, he would not have chosen the path he had, nor would he now see any man—or woman—he walked past in the street as equal. Simply born into a different situation. The understanding would make him a better politician when his time came.

He had been so cut by Caro calling him inferior, when in fact that had been a blessing, and an awakening of the knowledge that was enabling him to step into a stream of politics his family would have never recommended—but now admired.

He laughed again, but this laughter was directed at himself— equally his cousins had been born into a set of circumstances, the way they behaved, although he still did not approve, had virtually been laid out for them. He must learn to be as tolerant of their circumstances as he was of the poor.

"...I am a much more pleasant man," Uncle Robert finished saying.

"With a son who has taken far too much of your blood."

"So has yours."

Both Lord Sparks and Uncle Robert laughed.

"Excuse me, I need to stretch my leg." Rob stood.

He was not in his own club but in his uncle's, in White's. Uncle Robert's man of business had wanted to meet with Rob and explain the tenancy agreement in person and then Uncle Robert had brought him here for luncheon.

They'd seen nothing of his father or John, but Pembroke House was probably still silent. It had been a late night. He and Uncle Robert had agreed to rise early and get their last day of planning for their journey done. Rob was no longer to ride in his uncle's carriage, but his uncle had offered to hire another for him, so he and Caro might travel up alone. Following his meeting with Uncle Robert's business man, Rob now had the keys to Allington Manor in his pocket. It was the place he would make into a home with Caro.

They were the keys to a new life and he'd gripped them in his hand.

"Marlow."

Rob turned around. He was in the hall. He was not alone, there were two footman and the doors at either end of the hall were open. Yet, even so, an odd sensation raced up Rob's spine, and his memory turned back to the dark and the strikes of a heavy metal bar. "Kilbride. I take it this corridor is a little light, and not empty enough for your messengers and so you came yourself—"

"The Marquis of Kilbride to you, child."

Rob did not answer.

"You cannot have her."

"That is not your choice. Caro is naught to do with you."

"She is mine, she always will be."

"She walked away from you the night you sent your thugs after me. Did that not tell you her view? She is no longer tied to you."

"Robbie…" Rob's uncle Robert walked into the hall.

Kilbride glared at him, then glared at Rob. "You will not have her. What I did to you is nothing compared to what I might do." He walked away then, heading for the outer door as though he planned to leave the club.

Rob breathed out. His uncle's hand lay on his shoulder. "What was that about? What was he speaking of? What did he do to you?"

Rob said nothing. The feelings of that night, the feelings of the following day brimming in his head. But had that threat been towards him or Caro?

His uncle's hand held Rob's shoulder more firmly. "Is what I'm thinking correct?"

Rob shook his head. He would have turned away, but his uncle's grip held firm.

"It was not thieves, was it? The men who left you lying in the street half dead…"

Rob shook his head.

"Do not deny it, Robbie, I heard."

401

"Very well, you are right, but do nothing and say nothing. This for me to resolve."

"Does your father know?"

"Yes, but he is the only one. Mama does not and please tell no one else. They will all wish to be involved and make things worse. I will manage it myself."

Manage it… He had not been doing that. He had been ignoring it.

"Does Caroline know? Have you told her?"

"God, no, it would make me feel like a fool. We'd separated at the time. It would have embarrassed me and now it would worry her."

"I saw you, remember, the embarrassment is his, that he must mutilate a rival to try and keep the interest of a woman. The man is a coward, and why is he interested anyway? He divorced her."

"He might have divorced her, but he does not dislike her, he wants to keep hold of her, like a possession." *Lord*, Rob must forget his own possessiveness.

His uncle sighed. "What am I to do, then?"

"As I said, nothing. We ignore his threats. I have been careful, and Papa has ensured that Caro is always with someone when she has been out. That is what I wish and this is my concern. We will be out of town in a day anyway."

Uncle Robert sighed. "If that is what you want."

"It is."

"Well, then, why do we not go out to Tattersall's and buy you another wedding present. Instead of hiring a carriage to take you north, I shall buy you one, and the horses to go with it."

"That is too much."

"It is not. Remember I owe your father for numerous years of land management."

Rob smiled. But inside there was turmoil. How could he walk away from such a threat when he'd already taken a crippling beating from Kilbride?

~

Caro turned to her back, her arm lifting as she dreamed of a fist flying towards her, and the low, vicious sound of Albert's voice threatening her.

She sat up, breathing hard and sweating. Her dress was damp; it stuck to her skin.

She'd thought the days in which she'd needed to be afraid of Albert's violence passed.

She ran her hand across the slight curve of her stomach, and looked down. She needed to feel the child move. Her dress was a vivid scarlet below her waist, between her legs.

Blood.

Blood...

She rose, her fingers gripping between her legs as if by sheer will she might hold the child in.

Not now, not when she had so much hope.

She rang the bell for a maid, and then returned to the bed and curled about her child, her fingers holding beneath her stomach and her legs curled up and tightly closed.

Why is there blood?

When the maid came it was through sobs that Caro asked her to fetch Mary.

She was losing her child.

"No." Tears crept from her eyes, filling up her eyelashes and running onto the pillow.

Mary's knock was gentle.

"Come in. Please!" Caro's voice was a desperate plea, as though Mary might save the child simply by being in the room.

"Caro, what is it? The maid said you were distressed." Mary came across the room.

"I am with child. But there is blood. I'm losing my child..."

Mary looked pale and confused.

Caro clasped her wrist. "Please help me!"

Mary's free hand covered Caro's. "I will fetch Mama. She will know what to do, and Kate will call the doctor. Lie still."

Tears ran like fingers brushing down Caro's cheeks as Mary left.

Rob's family would all think ill of her now. They would know about the child.

Chapter 44

Rob climbed the steps to his uncle's house in high spirits. He would have jogged up them with an eager stride if he was fit and healthy. But he did not because his leg held him back. He'd enjoyed his day with his uncle. He hoped to enjoy living beside him.

He looked back and smiled at Uncle Robert as they walked into the hall. Jenkins, his uncle's butler, greeted them, bowing slightly. "Lord Marlow is waiting for you in the drawing room, with Lady Barrington, Master Robert, I believe he has an urgent message."

Urgent… Rob headed to the stairs, forcing his weak leg to move as fast as it would.

When Rob walked into the drawing room, his father rose from a chair.

"Papa…"

"Rob, you must come back with me." He looked at Rob's aunt. "Please call for the carriage to be brought about, Jane."

"Why?" Kilbride's threat echoed through Rob's head.

His father walked towards him, gripped his arm and led him back out of the room.

"It is Caroline. Kilbride called this morning. Caroline happened to be in the hall and she was caught up in the footmen trying to get Kilbride out. She fell and she has been bleeding since then. She is afraid she will lose the child. A child, which you failed to mention to us. A child that must be due in less than four months, Robbie."

Heat burned in Rob's cheeks. "You had no need to know. I did not know until she came to town looking for me. I would have told you after we left. I did not wish her to feel embarrassed while we remained in town."

"It is not Caroline who ought to feel embarrassed, a man leads these things."

"Papa, I do not wish to discuss it."

"It is unimportant now, anyway. The only thing of importance is that I get you home. She has been crying for you. Where have you been?"

"At Tattersall's."

"Well, never mind, let us get you there."

Rob swore at his bloody leg as he tried to make it hurry down the damned stairs.

Jenkins opened the door for them. "Tell Uncle Robert, I am going out—"

"I have told your aunt. She will let Robert know."

The carriage was already waiting.

"Get in," his father stated, and then, as soon as the door shut he continued, "I am angry with you. Caroline was under the protection of this family."

"You know I am marrying her for more reasons than the child. I told you I wished to marry Caro before I even knew."

"And it is a good thing, because I am not sure the child will survive."

Rob stared at his father. No. That was nonsense.

"But whether you wished to marry or not, you should not have lain with her. I would have expected this of Harry, not you."

"Things happen, Papa, and this is hardly the time for you to preach morality. This speech is too late, we are to be married tomorrow."

"But I am allowed to express my anger and disappointment."

"I was disappointed in myself at first, and yet I do not regret this child, or that I shall have a lifetime with Caro, and she is thrilled, she has lost…" The words died on his lips, but he forced them out. "She has lost five children. This is the first time she has carried beyond four months. That's why she did not tell me. She expected to lose the child."

It cut into his heart. It was his child that might be lost now.

His father stared at him as the carriage rocked over the cobbles.

Rob could see Caro's eyes as she had looked at him while they'd waltzed last night, wide and bright, shining amber and gold in the bright glow for the chandeliers, and he could see her breaths lift her bodice, and feel the beat of her pulse in her wrist as he gripped her hand.

"Drew said you are the only one who has ever been able to calm Caroline when she is anxious."

"She calms herself. I merely challenge and encourage her to do it. She is more capable than she thinks." Rob's heart pumped hard. "Do you think she will really lose the child?"

"I do not know. Kate had called for her doctor when I left. But your mother said Caro has lost a lot of blood."

She may have already lost the child, then… Rob had wished to protect Caro, he'd not even thought of his child. He'd been at Tattersall's. He'd let Kilbride threaten them this morning.

"What time did Kilbride call?"

"Midday."

Kilbride had called there, distressed Caro and then come to White's and threatened Rob. There was one thing Rob was certain of. Kilbride must learn a lesson. Rob had to extinguish Kilbride's threats.

When they reached John's, without thinking, Rob opened the carriage door and jumped down, pain lanced up his leg but he ignored it, although it made him limp more severely as he hurried up the steps.

Finch opened the door. "Master Robert, Lord Marlow."

Rob did not acknowledge Finch. He looked at his father. "Where

407

is she?"

"In her room, on the first floor, turn to the right and the second door along." His father answered.

Rob climbed the stairs faster than he had done in weeks.

"Drew!"

Drew paced the landing outside Caro's room, his hands fisted.

"How is she?"

"Unwell. Crying. Fearful. But the child's heart is still beating." Drew clasped Rob's arm. "She has lost children."

"I know."

Drew breathed out a sigh. "She has lost five."

"I know." Rob turned to the door, but Drew's grip firmed on his arm.

"I was never sure if she truly miscarried or if Kilbride beat her over something and the miscarriages were a consequence. Certainly after each miscarriage I saw her badly beaten. She fell today when Kilbride called here."

"I know…" Rob's words were uttered on a hard sigh, as the weight of his responsibility caught a firmer hold of him. He'd wished to protect Caro and their child. He'd failed today.

Rob knocked as Drew let him go.

"Your mother and Mary are with her."

When the door opened, Mary stood there. She looked pale, but as soon as she saw Rob she caught hold of his sleeve and pulled him in, closing the door behind him. "Thank God you are here. Caro has been crying for hours and there has been so much blood. She is terrified."

He could hear Caro in the bedchamber next door wailing with her distress.

"The doctor…"

"He left, he had other calls, but he promised to return."

Rob walked ahead. Caro lay under the covers, on her side, curled up and he could see through the creases in the covers that she was gripping her stomach with both her hands. Her hair was a tangle of blonde about her face and when her eyes looked at him they were wide and wild. "Rob."

His name was said in a pained plea.

She reached out a hand. "I am losing it."

He took her hand. He still wore his gloves. "You are not. Not yet. That is not what the doctor has said."

"Rob." Tears flooded her eyes, then ran onto her cheeks.

His mother touched his shoulder. "Let me take your outer things."

He let go of Caro's hand and stripped off his gloves, then gave those and his hat to his mother. Mary helped him remove his coat, and then he removed his morning coat too and handed that to Mary. Then he gave his hand to Caro again. Hers was warm and clammy.

"Here…" His mother pulled up a chair. "Sit, Robbie."

He did sit, although it was as if he fell, his fingers clinging to Caro's. He lifted her fingers to his lips. "Have faith."

"I cannot," she breathed. "I had thought I could survive the loss. I'd thought I would live with it and enjoy my child for the months I felt it within me, but then it held past four months and I hoped, I hoped and now I must lose it. I cannot bear it."

Rob looked back. "Mama, Mary, would you leave us alone, please?"

His mother acquiesced. "Come along, Mary." Mary looked back with concern before they left.

Caro was in bed in her nightdress. By rights he ought not to be here at all, and not alone with her, and yet what did propriety matter when she was already with child and they were to be wed tomorrow.

He kissed the back of her fingertips. She looked so pale.

"I am losing our child," she said more quietly, her fingers clinging to his as though she clung to a cliff.

"Drew told me he was never sure if the loss of your children was due to natural causes or Kilbride. Did Kilbride beat you before

409

you lost the children?"

"Not before the first."

"But the second and third…" *and the fourth and the fifth.*

"I do not remember. He forever found things that were wrong with what I did, and after I miscarried… But what does that matter, there is still blood now." It was said on a wail of distress, and she let go of his hand, as if she no longer trusted him.

"And there is still a heartbeat, Drew said."

He caught her hand back and kissed it again, then rose and leant and kissed her damp cheek. Her skin was salty with tears.

He'd been laughing in White's this morning when she'd been assaulted by Kilbride. He'd been choosing bloody horses when she'd been enduring this.

He held their joined hands to her stomach, willing her to be calm at least. "The child is still within you, you will make it afraid, with all your concern. Relax and lay still, Caro, and for now we will trust in the words of the doctor, not your fear."

A tear slipped from one corner of her eye.

He leant and kissed her lips, then bent and kissed the slight outward curve of her stomach. She did not really show. The child must still be tiny. Yet when he kissed her, something jerked within her.

"Caro." He straightened, elation twisting in his gut and in his voice. "Have you felt the child move?"

"Yes."

"I felt it. Put down your legs, the child is not about to give up its life if it can kick or hit out. We have a fighter, Caro. But then I should never have doubted that; you are a fighter. It must be a girl, then, who takes after her mother."

More tears slipped from her eyes. They rolled into her hair.

"Put down your legs, leave your hand on your stomach, shut your eyes, lie quietly and feel for our daughter's movement. Perhaps she wishes to tell you she is well and you are not to worry."

"But there was so much blood."

"But there is still the heart beat and the feel of the child moving. Shut your eyes, lie quietly and let us see if she will kick again."

His hand spread across the cotton sheet over her stomach, and one of hers spread over his, while the other cradled the child below his. She shut her eyes as he watched their hands.

"Breathe slowly," he said quietly.

She did. Then there was a sudden sharp thrust of movement beneath his hand.

"She moved," Caro whispered.

"She did indeed, as I told you, she seems well."

Then came more tears. "I have been so afraid."

"When there was no need, not yet."

"But I have woken to blood before and then there has been pain and I have lost the child."

"Has there been pain this time?"

"Only back ache."

"Well, then, another sign that this is not the same. The bleeding came hours ago, did it not?"

"But it has continued."

"As much?"

"Not as much."

"I am not a doctor, Caro, but I will hold by anything he says and if he is content the child's heartbeat is strong. I am."

She nodded. Tears of relief now flooding her eyes.

You will not have her, what I did to you is nothing compared to what I might do. Rob heard the words in Kilbride's voice.

He was still unsure who the threat had been for.

He'd suffered at Kilbride's hands once. She had suffered at Kilbride's hands numerous times, and she was such a delicate woman. How had she survived?

But she had not. She had lost five children.

Ah, he really was a fool. Today Kilbride had intervened in Caro's new safe life because Rob had brought her to town and spurred the man, publishing the news of their wedding in the paper. Rob should have acquired a special licence and taken her away to Yorkshire immediately. But he could not turn back time.

Caro's eyes were shut again, and she was breathing slowly as her hands stroked over her stomach, as if calming the child. Her hand occasionally ran over his too as tears slipped from the corners of her eyes.

"Albert did hit me when I was with child, and I remember the second time I lost my child, he'd kicked me in the stomach."

Bile rose at the back of Rob's throat. The night he'd been attacked he'd been kicked in the stomach and the chest, in the ribs and the head. How violent had Kilbride been to her? "He did not kick you now. Drew said you fell and banged your hip."

"Yes."

Her eyes opened. Dark amber looked at him about wide pupils. There were memories in her eyes.

Rob breathed out. He could not imagine how helpless and alone she must have felt, and then how embarrassed to rise up and face the world again, knowing that within her home she was treated with such cruelty. He'd been too embarrassed for her to know of his injuries. He'd hidden them from her. She had hidden years of injuries from the world.

"This child will be loved and it will never know such things. Close your eyes again and try to sleep. Rest is the best thing for both of you. If you sleep, she will sleep."

She nodded.

He sat beside her, his hand on her stomach underneath hers, as her breathing slowed, and the lines of worry on her face eased. But the child did not sleep. The more Caro relaxed, the more he felt their daughter kick, or hit. He was certain it was a girl.

He sat for a while, until he was sure Caro slept, and he stayed for a little longer as the child stilled. He was afraid too. It was not normal to bleed in pregnancy. He'd grown up in a large family, where there was always a woman expecting a child. None of them had bled, as far as he was aware.

Guilt bit at him, and a burning desire to fix everything for Caro, so she need never fear. He could not stop her bleeding. Yet there were other things that he could do.

His fingers slipped from beneath hers, and his lips touched her temple, gently with a kiss. He did not wish to wake her. She needed to sleep.

He left the room and hurried along the hall, his urgency pushing his leg to move faster. "Mama!" He called, his stride uneven.

"Lady Marlow is in the drawing room." Finch must have waited on the landing in case anything was needed.

"Have someone send for the doctor again, Finch." When Rob walked into the drawing room he saw his mother and father, Kate and John and Mary and Drew and all the children. "Mama, would you sit with Caro. She is sleeping and there is something I need to do. I have asked for the doctor to call again. I wish to speak with him. But then I have to go out."

"How is she?" Drew had risen when Rob came into the room.

"Broken-hearted, but the child is kicking within her. I have persuaded her to believe it is safe for now."

Drew looked at his father. "What did I tell you, Papa? Rob has a knack for making her calm."

Rob looked at his father too. "Is Harry here?"

"In bed. I believe he came back about two hours after sunrise."

Rob looked at Kate. "Which room?"

"Second floor, the opposite wing to Caro's, fourth door on the right."

"Thank you," Rob turned away.

"I will walk back with you." He glanced back as his mother set down the tea she'd been drinking and stood.

Caro held his heart gripped in her hand and his mind was left in the room with her. He could not think clearly.

"You are good for her." His mother stated, her fingers slipping about his arm, as they left the room.

"She is good for me,"

"I will not refute it, but comments have been made to your father and I about the difference in your age."

"And you of all people should pay little heed to it. It is of no matter to Caro or me."

"No. But you failed to tell us she is with child, and you are very young to become a father."

"Older than Mary when Mary became a mother, and older than you when you had John."

She sighed. "That is true."

"And Mama, now is not the time to chastise me over a child Caro is terrified of losing. It is too late for judgements."

"Of course, I am happy for you both, if this will make you happy."

"Mama, I did not propose because of the child. You know I proposed before my accident."

"I am not saying that. I do not even know what I am saying..." She sighed. "I am speaking nonsense. I am simply shocked and mourning the loss of another child of mine who is rushing into marriage. It has been a long day and I did not expect this of you." She sighed again. "Yet, Caroline loves you, and you love her..."

They reached the stairs and he turned and held her. "I will not be a loss, Mama. It will be a gain. You will have a new daughter and a grandchild if God is just."

"Yes. I am happy for you. I am just shocked."

He hugged her tightly. This was not about the child or his marriage. She was thinking of him, of the fact she'd nearly lost him a few months ago. He could understand her emotion more now that he had his own child who he feared for. A daughter.

"I'm going to Yorkshire, Mama, not Timbuktu. You may visit us whenever you wish."

She nodded against his shoulder. "I am very proud of you. But you know that."

He'd probably not known a few weeks ago, but he did know now. His mother pulled away. "I told you, I should have known you would fall for a woman who was in need, and rescue her. You are like your father."

"I need to speak with Harry, Mama. If Caro wakes, tell her I will be back soon."

She nodded.

Rob walked upstairs to his brother's room and knocked on the door, emotion rattling around in his chest.

There was no answer.

He opened the door. The shutters were still closed and the room stank of stale liquor. Harry lay naked amidst the sheets, lying on his stomach with his arms above his head and his legs tangled in the sheets.

He'd come home when the servants were already up and preparing breakfast, but he'd still come home drunk.

"Harry!" Rob slapped Harry's bare leg, then turned and went to the window. He opened the shutters and let the daylight in, then turned back to look at the bed again. Harry hadn't moved. "Harry!"

He groaned.

"Come on, for once in your life I need you to do something for me. I have baled you out of a million scrapes. You owe me."

Harry rolled to his back, his forearm covering his eyes. "What are you doing in my room?"

"Waking you up. I need your help."

"You never ask me for help."

"I know, but you are the only person I trust to stand with me in this and I need your canniness and also I need you to swear you will tell no one about what we are doing."

"What are we doing?" Harry had not risen. He still lay in the bed looking up at Rob.

"I am only telling you when you swear."

"Very well, I swear." He sat up and the sheet slipped to his hips.

"We are calling on the Marquis of Kilbride."

"What?"

Harry had probably never paid any attention to Caroline's

history. But then nor had Rob until the summer, and, damn it, if he was taking Harry with him, he ought to let Harry know what he was getting into.

"Kilbride is Caroline's former husband. He used to beat her and now she is carrying my child and terrified of losing it because her former husband called on her and threatened her. And… you must swear your silence."

"I have sworn it."

"I did not fall from my carriage. Kilbride had some thugs who were in his pay beat me."

Harry stood up, the sheet slipping off him entirely. "What?"

"They left me in the street. I had the men that found me take me to Uncle Robert's. If the girls told you Mama and Papa stayed there to look after Aunt Jane it was a lie. They were looking after me. I am not proud of what happened, I was in a mood, walking in the dark, and three of them attacked me with an iron bar."

Harry crossed to a chest of drawers and opened one to pick out a shirt. "I would not judge you for losing a fight with thugs. You could have told me."

"I am going downstairs. I wish to speak to the doctor who saw Caro. I will leave you to dress. As soon as you are clothed come down, and we will go, but I mean it, tell no one. I do not want the family involved. You know how they are, they would all interfere, and I want this to be quiet."

Chapter 45

"I cannot say, Mr Marlow. She has not lost the fluid about the child, which would imply the bleeding is from her womb, where the child is attached. Yet all that I know for certain is that the child is alive, and nothing about its heartbeat infers it is at risk, but tomorrow things might change, there can be no surety."

"We are to be married tomorrow."

The doctor stared at Rob with a pompous look. Of course it was normal to marry and then beget a child. But Rob was not ashamed, he did not care what the man thought, all he wished to know was what the risks were. Would his daughter live?

"I have seen a dozen cases like this, no more. The pregnancy will need to be monitored and Lady Framlington ought to rest as much as possible. There is no evidence from the amount of blood how high the risk is to the child, and yet if she continues to bleed there is a risk to her. A risk that the internal wound might become infected or that she may lose too much blood."

It had not occurred to Rob that Caro might be at risk. "She has lost children before."

"Lady Caroline has told me."

"Her former husband kicked her stomach when she was with child."

"That may have affected her womb, if that is the case. Usually this issue simply arises when a woman has had a number of children—"

"She has had five miscarriages."

The doctor gave him a look that said you are too young to manage this.

Why might a woman have a child from sixteen upward, while a man must be thirty before he wed?

"The cause may be the miscarriages or the violence. I can only treat the symptoms, not the cause."

Rob nodded. He would treat the cause. "Would you call again in the morning and listen for the heartbeat to reassure her, and then will you advise on how her brother might take her to the church."

The man stared at him, the words in his eyes, *she should not go at all*. Yet she was with child. Rob would not delay the date, the wedding needed to occur.

"Thank you, you may go. Send your invoice to me here—"

"The Duke will—"

"I manage my own debts."

The doctor nodded, then turned away.

Rob had a feeling the man was a social climber. He would not have come had it not been the Duchess who'd called for him. In general, he probably chose not to support the mere mortals of the world. It was probably a lance to his ego that he must be paid by a gentleman. It was men like that who Rob wished to make change through new laws. Why should the poor not be treated the same as the rich when it came to such things as medicine?

~

Rob walked out of Pembroke House with Harry. He'd told Mary and his father that he was going out on an errand for medication, having spoken to the doctor. But there was no medicine that would help Caro—except perhaps for her mind to be free from any fear of Kilbride.

418

"Where are we going?" Harry asked as he jogged down the steps while Rob hobbled, although his limp was becoming far less noticeable. He hoped to hide it when they found Kilbride.

"To his home first, and if he is not there to wherever it is we may find him."

"Will your leg hold up if we walk?" Harry gripped Rob's shoulder.

Rob glanced over at him and smiled when Harry's hand slipped away, they were entirely opposite in so many ways and yet there was a closeness between them that ran deeper than a conflict in morals. That was why he'd wished to have Harry with him—they had always been there for each other in times of trouble throughout their school and college years. "It is getting stronger, it would, but we will take a hackney because I wish to be quick, and if he is not at home, I do not want to be walking about London like a fool. Come on, we will walk to the next square and pick one up so no one within the house sees and wonders why we have not used John's carriage."

"This subterfuge is not like you, Rob."

"I have discovered a lot of new things that were unlike me since the summer. Like I can feel jealous, angry and possessive as hell."

His brother laughed. "You…"

"Me," Rob grinned. "Women do that to you. They take you to extremes."

"The women I know only take me to one extreme."

"You only stay with them for a few hours. It is not the same."

"At least I know how to avoid making them pregnant. I would not be fool enough to do that."

"No, you will catch the French disease."

"God, you are so naïve. There is a thing called a condom. It is made of pig's bladder. You use it as a sheath to protect yourself from a whore and having a child."

"Is that all you think of the women you sleep with? Whores."

Harry smiled. "That is what they are, and I am merely paying

419

for the service they offer, as I've told Papa every time he yells at me about it. Better that than I defile young ladies."

"Your morals are twisted."

"And yours are broken. You cannot preach to me now you have impregnated the family's one ward."

Rob lifted a hand to hail a hackney as Harry laughed.

"You should have come to me if you wanted to have sex with her, and I would have told you how to avoid a child."

Rob glanced at Harry as he climbed into the small carriage, and jested. "My younger brother, the font of all knowledge."

"When it comes to bedroom sport, yes, and where you are concerned, definitely, because you knew nothing and look at the position you have landed yourself in."

Harry tumbled into the seat beside Rob, as Rob leant back into the squabs. "I have not landed myself in anything. I wish to be with Caro. It is called love. Admittedly it was unplanned, it evolved, and it has continued evolving. Yet I am still wiser than you, because while you may know all about bedroom sport you know nothing about love."

"I do not wish to know. That knowledge you may keep. John has agreed to pay a commission for me when I am done at Oxford. What will I need with love? It would be a burden to have a wife when I become a captain in a regiment. You may keep your wife. I am happy with my whores."

Rob shook his head. Harry was irresponsible, but unchangeable. He'd endured numerous lectures from their father; none had touched him. He never changed his behaviour. But now Harry's rebellious nature was exactly what Rob needed.

"I have no idea what we will walk into," Rob said more seriously. "I am taking a gamble that with the two of us together, and no space to claim it might be footpads, that Kilbride will not attack us, but I do not know."

"I should have my fists ready, then. Had you told me, I would have brought a knife."

"This will not be a tavern brawl, Harry. I intend to call him out."

"That is against the law and a thing of two decades ago," Harry glared, with a look which said, are you are mad?

"It is that or I ask him to shoot against me at Mantons or I fence with him or spar with him in a club. It would not be the same, and I hope he will be eager enough to shoot me that he will disregard all else."

Amusement growled in Harry's throat when he looked out the far window. "I have had you wrong all these years. You are madder than me." He looked back at Rob. "I cannot believe you wish to make yourself a shooting target."

"I will make myself as small a one as I may."

"And then you are able to fire."

"And then I may fire."

Harry shook his head. "Let us hope that he is a bad shot."

"He has to accept the duel first."

When the hackney pulled up before Kilbride's town mansion, the driver knocked on the roof. Harry climbed down, then held the door for Rob.

"Wait for us." Rob said to the driver as he paid him their fare.

When Rob climbed the steps, he thought of Caro's small feet upon them. She must have climbed these steps the first day she had wed, and many days throughout her marriage. When she had first married, she must have skipped up the steps. She would have been three years younger than him and Kilbride had been nearly thirty. Her steps must have become heavier with the loss of each child, and with each beating.

It was a foolish distortion of society that they believed it acceptable for women to bear the age difference but not men.

Rob knocked on the door, his strike firm. He was determined to hold his ground and force this issue.

The door was answered by a porter, which probably meant that the butler was engaged in the drawing room. Either the Marquis of Kilbride was at home or the Marchioness was.

"We have come to speak with the Marquis in private."

"He is entertaining."

"Perhaps, but this is urgent. You may tell him that Robert Marlow is here."

"And Harry Marlow." Harry grinned as though this was a great lark.

Rob was suddenly swamped by his sense of inferiority. The two of them were nothing compared to the place they stood in. Kilbride had power. The mansion was neither as big as John's nor as showy and yet it was one hundred times larger than the small rooms Rob had rented.

The plaster above them was painted with cherubs and gilded. Caro must have thought herself in heaven when she'd crossed the threshold—only to be transported to hell.

No, he was not inferior; he was better than this man, perhaps not in the measure of possessions, but possessions did not matter, it was what lay in your heart that was the measure of a man. Poor or rich—it made no difference.

"Wait here." The porter walked away and pulled a tassel to call for a servant. A footman appeared from a door beneath the wooden staircase. The porter said something in a low voice, then the man went out as he'd come in, probably to tell Kilbride they were there.

Rob's heart began to knock against his ribs with a heavy beat.

Caro would not wish him to do this. Nor would his father. But Rob was not doing this for Caro, not really, he was doing it for himself, to quieten the possessiveness and protectiveness. He needed to know that Kilbride would not touch them again; that he could keep his family safe. Yet the anger burning low in his stomach was also for revenge, revenge for all of Caro's children this man had killed, and the years of life she'd lost in her glass gaol.

It was madness, though, because if he was caught duelling, Rob would have to flee the country or he'd end up in a real gaol.

…So he would not be caught.

"That child…" Kilbride stated.

422

Rob looked up as the insult echoed about the hall. Harry was looking at him not Kilbride, but Rob focused his attention on "*the monster*". Kilbride stood on the first-floor landing looking down.

"Why have you come?" His hand skimmed along the banister as he began walking down.

That hand had hit Caro many times.

"I will speak when we are in private."

"What can you have to say to me in private that might not be said before my servants?"

"You will discover that."

Kilbride stepped from the bottom stair. He was shorter than Rob by inches, but broader by inches too.

A footman, who had followed Kilbride down, crossed the hall and opened a door. "This way, then. Is that other boy joining us" He flicked a hand at Harry, who grew an extra inch with anger.

Harry had never tolerated mocking. If anyone had said that at school, they would have been on the floor with Harry astride them and a fist in their face.

Rob gripped Harry's coat sleeve for an instant as they walked towards the open door. He wished this to be played on his terms. He did not want Harry's temper flying.

Rob entered the room behind Kilbride, Harry followed, and then behind them the door shut. Rob glanced about the room. The walls were lined with books and in the centre of the room was a round table with a large globe upon it.

Behind Kilbride, above the mantel, was a painting of Venice. Of course, like John and Drew, Kilbride would have done the grand tour.

"Have you come to ask me to play a game with you?"

Rob's temper soared, but he would not allow it to control him. "You might call it that, if you like to play games with pistols. You have set your men on me, beaten Caroline and kicked your defenceless children out of her, and yet you look down on me. I think that strange when you have not been man enough to face me and fight."

Kilbride looked lost for words.

"I am challenging you to a duel."

"That is illegal."

"Who cares? I do not. Are you a coward, then? I am offering you a chance to stand on a field with me and take aim at me. In return I ask you to allow me to do the same. Are you man enough for that?"

Kilbride had stilled; there was no bravado in his expression now. He was racing though his options. Reject the duel and he would look weak, accept and he might die. Did he have the courage? The look in his eyes changed, as though he was weighing up the likelihood of his death, or rather the potential skill of his shot.

"Very well."

Rob wished to yell for joy. He had not wholly believed Kilbride would take the challenge. He'd believed the man a coward. "Then we will meet in the fields before Windsor, on the edge of the river. Tomorrow. At dawn. Turn off the road at the White Swan Inn. We will duel at sunrise."

Rob turned away. There was nothing more to say. Harry pulled the door open himself and they both walked out.

The porter opened the front door.

As they descended the steps outside, Rob almost achieved a jog.

Harry slung an arm about Rob's shoulders, with brotherly pride, before they climbed into the hackney.

Rob glanced at him. "You know this will not be easy. I do not know how good a shot he is, or whether he will simply bring the runners, or whether he will instead send a dozen men to beat us both."

"Then we will take a dozen loaded guns." Harry winked.

Rob laughed.

"And if he brings the runners, we will take one of Uncle Robert's dogs and claim we were merely there for a walk and Kilbride is mad."

"You are mad," Rob answered.

"And I would guess the Marquis of Kilbride has far too much pride not to come himself and alone, so he might do the deed now the challenge has been set. He would know himself a lesser man than the one he calls a child if he does not accept your offer."

"Thank you for coming with me. Your sense of humour and your blind stupidity are just what I need. Anyone else in our family would be telling me to cease this foolish notion."

"Not me," Harry laughed.

Chapter 46

Caro lay in the bed looking pale and weak. She'd woken while Rob had been out and asked after him.

"Have you felt our daughter kick again?" he asked as he walked across the room.

"Your mother said you went out."

Rob looked at his mother, who sat on the far side of the bed. She rose as he looked back down at Caro. "Not for long. I wished to arrange things for tomorrow."

"Will tomorrow happen now?"

"Have you bled any more?"

"No."

"Then we will see what tomorrow brings. I have asked the doctor to call early so he might advise on how we may take you to the church. Perhaps in a bath chair."

A choked sound of humour slipped from her lips and she held her stomach. "Do not make me laugh, it jolts me." Her eyes widened. "She kicked."

"You have decided it is a girl, then" his mother said. She must have been reading aloud to Caro—she held a book with her thumb marking a page.

Caro looked at her. "Rob has decided, and if it is a boy, when it is born, he will hold it against him that his father called him a girl."

Rob laughed, glad to hear her speak of the child living. She held out a hand to him. When he took it he leant to kiss her forehead. "Hello."

"Hello."

"Did you bring me medicine? Your Mama said you went to fetch some."

"I did, a maid will bring it." It was a herbal tea he'd purchased so he might not return empty-handed. "He hoped neither woman said anything to the doctor." Lord, he had turned from an intensely moral man into a man who was entirely immoral—he would lie to her—and today he had threatened to kill a man. But it was a violent man.

He sat down next to her and pressed the back of her fingers to his lips.

"I will leave you alone." His mother smiled.

"I missed you when I woke." Caro said after the door had closed.

He stroked the hair from her brow. "Sorry."

"I wish to marry you tomorrow."

"I wish to marry you too. I am sorry this has happened at all, but I am even more sorry it has happened now."

Her fingers separated and then wove between his as she smiled at him. "I am sorry."

"You have nothing to be sorry for, Caro. Do not apologise for what is not your fault."

He leant his elbows on the bed and pressed the back of her hand to his forehead. The doctor had said he might lose her. He would not allow it to happen.

His free hand lay on top of the covers over her stomach. "Is she kicking now?"

"She has not since I laughed."

He was tired, he'd gone to bed late and risen early.

"Would you read to me for a little while? I feel better then. It stops me thinking. I would guess your mother left the book she was reading next door."

427

"I'll fetch it." He rose, but when he walked into the other room he was besieged by emotions he'd subdued all day: fear, shock, sadness. Tears ran as he walked across the room. He could not stop walking because she would be listening to his footfalls. He wiped the tears away with the cuff of his morning coat, then stripped that off to give himself more time to regain his composure. The book was on a table by a chair. He picked it up. *Frankenstein*. It was an odd choice.

He walked back into the bed chamber. "Why this?"

"It is absorbing, it is filling my mind with other things than my own sorrow."

Then he should read it and let it absorb his thoughts too.

"She is kicking." Caro held her hand out for his.

When he reached her, she took his hand and lay it flat over her stomach. He felt the jolt. "Yes, I feel it." The reassurance slipped through his soul.

"I have sung to her at night, so she knows my voice, but she will not know yours."

"She will learn it now as I read, although I would have picked a less gruesome topic for the first story I read to my daughter."

Caro laughed. "I love you."

"And I love you. Now lie silent and still so our daughter has space to kick, and a chance to hear my voice."

She smiled. Rob felt as if his heart was weeping as he read. He could not bear to lose her. Or their child.

When Drew and Mary came to say goodnight to Caro, Drew's hand settled on Rob's shoulder before Rob had chance to stand. "How are you?"

"Tired and beleaguered. But Caro is happier now we have felt the child move frequently."

Drew smiled. "There is no denying you are good for her." He turned to Caro as she held out a hand to him.

Rob rose and moved out of the way. "Caro, I will go back to my uncle's."

428

He glanced at Drew. "The doctor is to call at nine to assess if Caro is well enough to come to the church and, if so, how best to transport her safely. We wish to be married, but neither of us would risk the child. I will leave that situation for you to solve. Send word to me if she is unable to reach the church and I will come here." He turned to Caro. "But if you are well enough I will see you at eleven at the church."

She nodded.

He leant past Drew and kissed Caro on the lips. Her hand reached to the back of his head and her fingers ran through his hair when he pulled away. "Goodnight."

"Goodnight.

Chapter 47

Rob smiled when Harry opened the door of Pembroke House, but it was a nervous smile. It was still dark and Rob had not gone near the door but waited, seated on his curricle, at the corner of the square.

The servants would know that Harry had crept out, but none of them would question it. No antics were beyond Harry.

Harry ran across the square at a slow jog, then gripped the bar by the steps and leapt up with the energetic ease Rob had known until a few months ago. "Are you ready to slay the dragon?"

"I am indeed."

He'd not slept much last night. His thoughts had been of Caro. She was oblivious to the fact that she might be at risk, and he would not tell her, but for half the night a prayer had run through his head that both Caro and his daughter would live.

He flicked the straps.

As they travelled out of London and the sky began to turn from a very dark blue to a lighter shade. Harry spoke of their cousins and the things they had all got up to in the last few days since they'd been in town for the wedding—mostly racing, drinking heavily and attending brothels.

It was probably the first time Rob had been glad to hear of their nonsense, but Harry's tales of lechery kept Rob's mind from the task, until he turned off the road and drove out into the flat meadows by the wide, meandering river.

Kilbride's carriage was there, emblazoned with his coat of arms, shouting Rob's folly to the world. If they were found out Rob would be thrown into gaol, but Kilbride would probably find some way to pay someone and walk free. Again it was that mark of rich against poor.

Yet oddly Rob was relying on the one thing that had been his former sin. Pride. He hoped Kilbride would continue with the duel honestly because his pride would shame him if he did not stand up to the challenge of a younger man, and that afterwards, when Rob had won, Kilbride's pride would hold him silent because he would not wish to admit to anyone that a younger man had beaten him.

"Hold fast," Harry said when Rob flicked the straps. "Do not rush. Make him wait. Make him sweat."

Rob glanced sideways and smiled at him. Harry was the right companion for this task.

When Rob pulled his curricle up, the sky was a sapphire blue.

Kilbride stood on the far side of his carriage. He looked as though he had been practising with his pistol, warming the gun up. Of course, he would not have warmed up both pistols.

Harry leapt down easily as Rob set the brake and tied off the straps. He climbed down then, forcing his leg to look as normal in movement as he could manage.

The birds sang in the trees near the river. It was a raucous sound of hundreds of high-pitched trills.

"Two boys come out for a game of pistols!" Kilbride called.

The truth hit Rob in the face as Kilbride handled the pistol he'd already selected. The man might have tampered with his guns, or he might even simply be a bloody good shot. If either thing was true then Rob might be dead within the hour. Caro would not thank him.

This was reckless.

Last night he'd shed tears for fear that he might lose her and

431

lose his child, and today he had come to the meadows before the sunrise, on his wedding day, to offer up his own life like a fool.

Yet someone had to teach Kilbride a lesson, and if anyone was to avenge Caro it ought to be Rob. He did not have armies of servants or thousands of pounds to force Kilbride into submission, but he did have himself and his strength of will.

Sunlight spread across the sky from the east.

The only person Kilbride had brought with him was a groom.

"May I see the pistols?" As the man who'd been challenged, according to the old custom, it was Kilbride's right to choose the weapons, but Rob had taken a set of duelling pistols from John's last night and they were stowed beneath his seat on the curricle, in case Kilbride tried to play him false.

The groom opened the lid of a wooden box and offered Rob the gun, which laid on a bed of velvet.

"Thank you." Rob took it and held it up, looking down the barrel and then he opened the mechanism and scanned it, looking for any sign that the metal had been filed to put the shot off. He handed it to Harry who checked it too.

"May I see the other?" He would not lose his life through lack of care.

Kilbride handed it over with a smirk, pulling at his lips. "You do not trust me?"

"You beat a woman black and blue and murder your unborn children and have men attack me from behind in the dark. No I do not trust you."

If it kicked Kilbride when Rob mentioned the children Kilbride had wanted and lost, he did not show it. But there was a tightness in his jaw, which inferred some emotion. Perhaps he'd never considered the fact that his beatings might have killed the children he wanted. But then he had his son now and perhaps he'd never cared for a child, only an heir.

Rob checked the pistol Kilbride had held. It was identical to the other, only warm. Rob gave it to Harry to look at too.

"Give me powder and a bullet," Rob ordered the groom as Harry gave Kilbride his weapon back. "I wish to test that the pistol fires, and warm the gun so that we are on equal ground."

Harry charged the pistol for Rob. Rob took it, aimed at a blade of grass and squeezed the trigger. The fingers of his right hand were still stiff, and it was as if they took a moment to obey the command of his mind. But when the pistol fired and the flash and the puff of smoke declared it, the shot was true, and the bullet raced through the air and sliced through the thin piece of grass.

The bitter smell of the smoke from the pistol burned Rob's throat, as the birds in the trees behind him called out their alarm at the sudden, sharp sound.

He looked at Kilbride. "I am happy with the pistols." He had only ever gambled with money once in his life, and yet now he was about to gamble with his life. Caro would be screaming at him if she knew. But for his sanity, for justice, for his sense of right and wrong, he had to do this.

Harry filled Rob's pistol with powder, then replaced the shot, while Kilbride's groom did the same for his.

Rob took off his hat and gloves and threw them on the ground.

"I will call," Harry said to the groom when they were done. "You may watch and ensure I do it right."

Kilbride walked a few paces further out into the field and Rob followed, the long grass swiping at his boots, while his heart raced, swiping at his ribs.

He would not lose.

Harry had them stand back to back, and Rob felt his greater height against Kilbride's broader frame. Rob had the easier target.

"Take ten paces out."

Rob counted out his strides as Kilbride's groom watched him walk. The sun broke over the horizon. The tip of a golden orb, peeking at the world, sending out rays of red and gold. He counted ten and turned.

The birds were now singing out a greeting to the day. The sound

433

escalated in a huge swell of jumbled noise. Rob hoped he would be alive to see it end. It was his wedding day.

"Lift your pistols and aim," Harry stated, as though he'd carried out this deed a hundred times before. He'd always been theatrical.

Rob faced sideways, looking over his shoulder, holding his body as straight as it was possible to do. A breeze swept his hair from his brow.

"Let my man drop a handkerchief to begin the match!" Kilbride yelled. "When it touches the ground, we fire."

There was no precise way to ensure they fired at the same time; it made little difference how the duel was called. Rob nodded at Harry, who delved into his pocket for a handkerchief and handed it to the groom.

"Prepare!" Harry yelled.

Rob straightened his arm and his right hand held firm, but his fingers were stiff on the trigger. They became stiffer as he waited, the day was cold, and the cold was seeping into his healing bones.

The groom dropped the white square of cloth, and Rob turned his head from the groom to look as the echo of a shot rang across the field. Damn, Kilbride had shot early. Of course, the man would cheat.

A burning whip of pain struck across the side of Rob's head, but Rob had learned pain in the months after the assault. He took aim. He could shoot the man through the heart—Kilbride had not turned well enough to guard it. Or he could shoot him through the head and watch him fall like a wooden puppet. Or he could shoot and let the man live and know that he had been bested by a man he'd called a child. Rob lowered his arm and fired. Kilbride fell.

"Ah!" His scream of pain echoed about the fields, competing with the birds' cries as they took to the air for fear of the gunshots. "You bastard, child."

Rob walked towards Kilbride as the groom ran to help him. "Take his neckcloth off."

Kilbride was writhing on the floor, gripping his right leg, where

Rob had shot through his thigh and most likely broken his bone. Certainly that had been his intent.

"You bloody bastard!" Kilbride yelled.

"I would not shout too much," Harry stated, staring down at Kilbride while the groom unravelled his neck cloth. "You will have everyone come running to see exactly how you were shot by a child."

Rob knelt and took the neckcloth from the groom's hand, before tying it about Kilbride's thigh to stop the flow of blood. There would be a lot more pain when the bullet was dug out of his leg, and still more as he recovered and tried to walk again. "If you think this is in revenge for what you did to me, it is not. It is in revenge for the harm you did to Caro."

"She lost my children. She was a useless, barren wife," Kilbride breathed in a bitter voice.

"Because you kicked half of them out of her. You are no good to live on this earth, and from now on you will cease your threats towards me and my wife and keep away from us."

"If there is one thing my brother is good at," Harry stated, "it is shooting. He never misses a shot. I would not shoot against him in a duel, and nor would any of my cousins. It is a shame you did not bother to find that out. But then you were so busy calling him weak, I should not think you contemplated that he had the power to kill you today. You are lucky that my brother has such high morals. Otherwise…" As Rob stood again, leaving Kilbride on the floor, Harry lifted his booted foot. "He would have shot you here." Harry's heel pressed down on Kilbride's forehead, pushing his head into the ground.

They turned then and walked away. Rob's heart thumped hard in his chest.

"You know, you are bleeding," Harry stated as they climbed up into the curricle.

Gripping the straps with his left hand, Rob saw blood on his hand. Yes, he'd known his wound was bleeding. He'd been ignoring

435

it. "Did you pick up that handkerchief?"

Harry passed it over.

"The bullet only skimmed me." But head wounds bled a lot. The bullet had grazed his cheek and nicked his ear. He pressed the handkerchief against the wound as Harry slid across the seat.

"I'll drive."

If the shot had been a half an inch further over, Rob would have been dead. If he had not turned his head… Kilbride had not aimed to wound, Kilbride had aimed to kill.

Rob leaned back, pressing the handkerchief hard against his wounds.

At least if Kilbride did decide to admit his shame and call for a magistrate, Rob would have evidence that he'd been fired upon too and evidence that Kilbride had attempted murder.

The sky flushed pink as the sun rose higher, but it was clear and bright. "Go to Uncle Robert's. You may get ready with me there. I wish you to stand at the altar with me."

"Me—not one of your friends…"

"I have too many to choose one. I would offend the others."

Harry smiled, "Thank you, I accept that as the honour it is from my righteous older brother."

Rob laughed. "You can hardly call me righteous now."

Harry looked over and laughed too. "True, I take it back. It is no honour at all."

Rob rested a hand on Harry's shoulder. "One day you will understand what it means to have feelings for a woman, and then you will change too and understand what honour means."

"If I change, it must be for the better. Papa would have an apoplexy if I became worse. But I will not marry anyway. I am happy as I am." He glanced at Rob. "But I do think marriage is right for you. I hear them all moaning that Caro is too old and yet I see that she is different and you are different and obviously the two of you are good for one another. I am happy to be your groom's man, and I will celebrate your wedding as if it were my own because I will not have one."

Rob laughed again.

It was nearly nine when they pulled into Bloomsbury Square, where Uncle Robert's town house stood. It was far less ostentatious than John's.

The head groom came around from the mews at the side of the house and stared at the blood on Rob's coat. But then he checked himself and moved to take the horses' heads. "Sorry, sir."

"It is nothing, James, just a nick."

"A nick, a tear, a chunk out of your ear, it is all semantics, it would bleed the same," Harry said as he jumped down, "And you have not seen it in a mirror."

"Are you saying I have lost my ear?"

"No, but a chunk rather than a nick, perhaps."

They left the horses to James and walked towards the door. Rob had left it unlocked when he'd gone out; there was no constant watch, unlike at John's. He turned the handle and went in.

The hall was a dark square, with an oak staircase winding about its edge.

"Let us go up to your room and ring for Uncle Robert's valet. He will know how to stop your wound bleeding."

Archer had been in Uncle Robert's employ for years and he clucked and fussed over the tear in Rob's ear. Harry was right, it was not a nick, it was more like a chunk, and his ear was red. Although Archer succeeded in stopping the blood flow, Rob was not going to be able to hide it. Nor would it be wise to wear a hat—in the church no one would be wearing a hat. He needed only to get there first.

Once he'd cleaned up and changed, and Harry had swapped his morning coat for a clean one borrowed from Rob, they went downstairs to take breakfast with their uncle's family.

"Harry!" Their cousin Henry stood as they entered.

"I did not know you were here, Harry," Uncle Robert stated.

"I came to help prepare Rob for the shackles."

437

Henry laughed as he sat again. He was of the same ilk as Harry. He normally paid little attention to Rob, yet today… "You have hurt your ear, and your cheek."

Uncle Robert and Aunt Jane looked as Rob walked about the table to take a seat, and his cousins' heads all spun.

"How did you do that? You did not have an injury last night," Henry pushed.

"Scissors. I was having my hair cut."

Harry laughed, and then everyone looked at him as he sat down, as if they expected him to explain. He brazenly passed a smile about them all and then smiled at Rob to pass the baton back over.

Rob sat. "What is there to eat? I am starved and I am about to walk to the altar."

"You look nice," his cousin, Julie, leant to whisper.

"Thank you," he whispered back in a conspiratorial way.

"Apart from your ear, though. It is a bit red," Harry said from across the table.

If Rob could have reached he'd have kicked him.

Julie smiled as the footmen surrounded him with different bowls of steaming food. He had an hour left before Caro would approach him along the aisle, and there had been no note received to say he should not meet her there. The doctor would have come and gone, with plenty of time to send word.

Rob helped himself from the bowls held out to him. It looked as though he would be a married man today.

He hoped she was truly well.

When he looked up, after filling his plate, his uncle was still looking at Rob's injured ear. Rob smiled, then returned his attention to his meal.

Chapter 48

Caro's heart played a wild drumbeat as Drew came into her room. "It is time for you to make an honest women of yourself and give your child a legitimate name."

Mary and Rob's mother had helped Caro dress in an ivory gown covered with Belgium lace. It made her feel feminine and beautiful, despite the fact that it had been a struggle to dress without rising, and now Drew had come to carry her down. There had been no more blood and the doctor had said that the heartbeat was still strong and so he'd agreed that she might go to the church. However, he said that she ought to stay off her feet and lie down as much as possible—so everyone was determined to keep her prostrate.

"Rob would have married me months ago, and our daughter would already have her father's name, if you had not deterred us." She lifted her arms and wrapped them about Drew's neck when he bent down.

One of his arms slipped beneath her knees while the other braced her shoulders.

"Ready?" he asked, as she clung about his neck.

"Yes."

"About me deterring you," he said as he carried her from the room, "I am sorry for that. I know now I should have kept my advice to myself. Rob is not me, or like anyone else I have known.

439

You were right, he does not feel trapped or seduced or—"

"But he would not know that, would he? It worries me that he will grow tired of me."

"Rob… No, not Rob."

His eyes smiled at her as he carried her out of the sitting room onto the landing.

"I still fear it, though."

"Then you may enjoy the next fifty years discovering you are wrong. Have you looked at this family? When they marry they commit, and Rob is the most moral of them all."

"But he might stay with me and not love me…" She was speaking from experience.

"Is this what you are thinking on your wedding day, about how in the future he might let you down?" He walked slowly along the landing.

All the former Pembroke Dukes stared at them.

"When I married Mary, I made a muddle of it, you know I did, and that was because I spent so many hours expecting Mary to let me down that I was the one who let her down. Do not do the same. Trust him. You know he loves you. It was visible even in the summer. I thought he would grow out of it, but I had forgotten he was half Pembroke and half Marlow. He will love you all your life, you need have no fear."

Caro smiled. "I hope so."

The hall was clear apart from the servants—everyone was already in carriages on their way to St George's.

"My Lord, my Lady." Finch opened the door.

Drew carried her outside. The sky was blue and the day bright, and it was not overly cold.

A carriage waited for them and another footman held that door open.

"Put me down. I can climb the steps."

"No, Edward is within."

So she was then handed up from Drew to Rob's father and set

on a seat with cushions to lean back upon, prepared so that she could sit sideways. Drew climbed up to sit with Mary and her father on the opposite side of the carriage.

"I feel foolish."

"You should not, Caroline. You look lovely," Rob's father stated.

He must dislike her now he knew about the child. She had stolen Rob from them and given him no choice to back down.

"You do look beautiful," Drew said.

Mary smiled.

The carriage driver kept the horses at a walk, so the carriage would not rock aggressively as they drove the short distance to St George's.

When they passed the tall row of pillars, Caro sat up a little.

The church, which was most fashionable for society weddings, had a Palladian front that made it more like a small palace than a church.

A footman opened the door and Drew immediately climbed down. Then he turned.

"Hold my shoulders." Edward requested as he leaned forward.

She did so, as he lifted her, and then he turned carefully to hand her to Drew, who carried her up the steps to the church as Rob's father helped Mary.

"Set me down," Caro said as they reached the giant, red doors.

"Caro, there is no harm in me carrying you up the aisle."

"Except that I wish to walk, and there are ten dozen people in there who would take great pleasure in gossiping, who know nothing about the child, and will think it odd if I am carried in as an invalid."

He hesitated.

"Set me down and you may walk up the aisle with me and I shall hold your arm. We need not even walk quickly because a bride should walk slowly."

"It is your choice, but Rob will be unhappy with me if I let you come to harm."

"Yet this is the last few moments that I am under your care. I will be glad to be married again, but you have been here for me for years, since we were children. I would like to walk beside you, and for you to feel proud as you let me go, not that I am a burden you are handing over."

"Caro, you have never been a burden. I have cared for you because you are my sister and I love you."

She smiled. "And I love you." A memory of the two of them huddled together inside a wardrobe in a cold, unused guest room in their mother's home, when Caro had perhaps been five, and he not even ten, settled in her thoughts. She could hear the servants calling, to give Drew a whipping for taking fresh bread from the kitchens.

He set her legs down gently. "We will walk very slowly."

She nodded. As children, they had run very fast. She smiled as she gripped his hand, as they had then, and she squeezed his fingers, then let go.

He held out his elbow and she took it. "Are you ready to face the gossips?"

"I think so."

They stepped into the church. Rob's sisters were waiting there to walk behind her, all dressed in pale yellow, and Mary, who came in behind them, gathered them all together, then passed Caro her posy, before setting the bridesmaids in order as the organ played, filling the church with sound. Caro stepped forward, looking ahead. Rob stood in the first pew at the front, with his back to her.

She took a breath and kept walking, praying that it did not harm the child, and praying that this young determined, passionate, moral young man would love her for all of his life.

Mary walked behind Drew and Caro, and behind Mary walked the rest of Rob's sisters, from the smallest to the tallest.

Rob turned to look. His smile lit up the church.

She smiled back and saw moisture glisten in his eyes.

When she reached the altar, Caro turned to hand Mary her

posy, then looked at Rob. His eyes were dark, a thin line of blue about his black pupils. But there was a mark on his cheek, and when he looked at his sisters, she saw a cut in his ear.

I love you, he mouthed, when he looked back at her.

I love you too.

If it was inappropriate at a society wedding to be so affectionate, she did not care, and when Drew passed her hand to Rob, she did not lay her hand on his, but held his.

They recited the words.

"In sickness and in health…"

"For better or worse…"

"I, Caroline Miriam Framlington take thee…"

"I, Robert Marlow take thee…"

"I give you this ring…"

Her heart raced.

"I now pronounce you man and wife… What God has joined together let no man set asunder."

Caro had heard those words before, and the man she'd been joined to was the one who had torn them apart. But this man…

Rob held both her hands, and his eyes glowed as Albert's had never done. This man was pure to the heart.

"How is our daughter?"

"Kicking, but I am to be off my feet as much as I can. Your papa and Drew have carried me here."

"Then I will carry you home."

"You cannot. You have your leg to think of."

"Leave me to worry about it."

"What did you do to your face and your ear?"

He smiled, and a low sound left his throat. "Uncle Robert's valet became a little too eager with his shears when he cut my hair."

"I will tell him off."

"Come. I will carry you down the aisle."

"You cannot. Do not make me argue with you on our wedding day."

443

He laughed.

"We will walk slowly."

"Congratulations," Drew said, as they walked past him. He touched her shoulder.

Drew and Mary, then Harry with Helen, and then all of Rob's family walked back down the aisle behind them as the organ boomed out a dramatic ending to their wedding ceremony. Yet as they reached the doors, Drew caught hold of Rob's elbow. "She should not be on her feet, it is only hours since she bled."

"I may climb into the carriage," Caro answered. "People are watching us and I would rather not appear an invalid." The street was full of common people, who had come to stare at the bride in all her finery.

Rob cupped her elbow as she climbed in, because her hand was full of flowers. Then he took her posy, before making her comfortable on the cushions. Drew shut the door.

The street about the carriage filled up even more as members of the congregation filed out of the Palladian church. They had not all been invited. Many had come just to stare.

"I cannot wait to be away with you." Caro breathed. "Oh." The carriage lurched too sharply into motion and nearly tossed her onto the floor.

Rob braced her, then stood and opened the hatch. "Steadily, for God's sake!"

It was unlike him to shout.

"You should not sit up through the wedding breakfast, anyway. If you wish, we could leave immediately. Our journey is going to be much slower than planned and so there would be no harm in us setting out early. We will make some excuse to our guests."

"You have become wicked," she teased, but her words sent a strange expression across his face.

"Perhaps."

He was not wicked.

As they'd travelled slowly Drew, Mary, his parents and half their

444

guests were already there when they reached Pembroke House. Drew opened their carriage door. "I will carry you, but where would you like to go?"

"You cannot carry my wife over the threshold. I will carry her and we will go to the state drawing room. Caro may lie on a sofa and we will greet the guests, but then we are going to leave. Caro cannot sit through the meal and so we will leave early."

"Your leg…" his father stated.

"Will be fine."

Rob jumped down, although he flinched a little after he landed. "Put your arm about my shoulders." She did so, holding him tighter than she'd held Drew or his father as he lifted her into his arms. He walked steadily, obviously in pain, and yet seeking not to show it.

When they entered the hall there were three dozen guests there: his extended family and others from society who were close to the families or important in status. There was a chorus of cheers, applause and then laughter.

Of course none of them knew he carried her because she was in danger of losing his child.

"Rob, set me on my feet, I will greet them on my feet and then we will leave, we will say we have heard it's snowing in the north and so we wish to begin our journey early, and I promise I will then stay off my feet for the rest of the day."

"It is a glorious day. They will not believe there is snow."

"They cannot know it is a lie, though." She smiled.

He kept a hold of her, attempting to hide his limp and holding her legs more tightly as he took her to the drawing room. He set her down carefully there, as the servants arrived with trays of full glasses.

They formed a receiving line, as they had for the ball two nights before.

Caro's jaw ached from smiling when the last guest passed.

"We will leave now," Rob looked at his mother and father, and John.

They had told their guests as they passed that they did not intend to join them for the meal. "I am sorry you have not quite experienced a normal wedding, Mama."

Her fingers cupped Rob's cheek. "I have had the pleasure of seeing my son stand at an altar and join himself to a woman of his choice, with happiness in his eyes."

Rob smiled, then turned to shake his father's and his brother's hands.

Ellen turned to Caro. "I am very proud of Rob, and I am extremely happy for you both."

"Are you?" Caro said quietly. "I feel that you must think I am an awful woman, that he came to Drew's in the summer and I stole him."

"That you stole…" Ellen smiled and shook her head. "Dearest Caroline, we have watched you live unhappily among us, and I will not lie and say that I was not surprised when Rob decided to settle down so young, yet I can see you are perfect for him. He said to me, when he was ill, that love is not something you choose, and he was right. You need not fear our ill judgement, we have known of his feelings for months and we encouraged him to propose a second time. So you see, you are wrong, we are very happy for you, and glad you make each other happy."

~

Rob's father clasped his hand. "I would speak with you privately before you leave."

"Why?"

"I will tell you when we speak."

"Are you leaving now?" Drew, Mary and Harry joined them as their guests talked and laughed inside the drawing room.

"Mary, would you take Caro to the retiring room?" Rob's father asked, "I am sure she must require it before she travels, and then you may settle her in the carriage, Drew. Rob, Harry and I need to talk."

Rob sighed. If his father had slipped into a managing mood, then their talk was not going to be a fond farewell. Suspicion pricked.

"John will you come? And have a servant ask Robert to join us."

This was to be some family onslaught then.

Rob turned to Caro. He could, of course, refuse to listen, but that would be crass when it was the last day he would see his father in months. The least he could do was hear him out. "Let Drew carry you up to the retiring room. I shall say goodbye to my family."

She nodded.

"Come then, Mrs Marlow." Drew stepped forward and lifted her into his arms.

The name struck Rob in the chest. She was Mrs Marlow, Caroline Marlow. The novelty of it clutched about his heart as he followed his father and John across the chequered marble floor into John's library.

When a footman shut the door behind Harry, Rob's father turned. "What have you two been about?"

John walked past Harry. "You were seen leaving the house before dawn, Harry, and climbing into a curricle which the servants recognised as Robbie's. They did stable it here, Robbie..." John did not seem to miss a damn thing.

"And then you turn up at the church with a wound on your face and ear," his father continued. "I have asked your uncle if it was Archer's fault. He sent his groom home. Archer says that is nonsense. You arrived there grazed and bleeding."

The door behind Rob opened and his uncle Robert came in. He shut the door and smiled at Rob.

"Harry..." Their father continued "You at least returned unscathed."

"There is another factor here." Uncle Robert threw in. "To add to our puzzle. Yesterday the Marquis of Kilbride threatened Rob."

Rob's father's eyes widened. "And you did not tell me."

"I did not tell you because you would react like this."

"Rob, he has beaten you half to death. You cannot take his threats lightly."

"I did not."

"Kilbride did what?" Now John knew too.

"His injuries were not from a curricle accident. He was found in the street beaten to an unrecognisable state, with broken bones, and taken to Robert's because he would not come here. It has taken him months to recover."

"You would not come to me for help, even then…" John looked offended.

"It does not matter." Rob had had enough of this.

"And the situation with Kilbride is solved, Rob did it alone. He is capable." Harry announced to the room. "He did not need your help, Papa, or yours, John, or yours, Uncle Robert. He was always the best shot at school."

It was not the time to brag.

"Shot!" The room erupted with the one word from three voices.

"You did what, exactly?" His father glared at Rob.

"He called him out." Harry stated in his brash I'll-show-you-all voice.

"Harry. The one thing I asked you for was silence," Rob charged.

"They will work it out anyway." Harry grinned at their father. "We called at Kilbride's home last night and Rob told him if he was so brilliant he ought to have the courage to fight fair. He challenged him."

"Are you mad, son? He almost killed you once—"

"Rob won," Harry protested.

"Robbie should never have been there." Their father growled.

"He won," Harry said again, as though the news eradicated all else.

"If you had not, Caroline would have been left without a husband, carrying your child. I say again, Robbie, you should not have been there."

448

"But I was," Rob answered, "and I won. He threatened me; he threatened us. He would not yield without a dose of his own medicine. I do not regret it. Caro needs to be free of him. He is the reason she is suffering, even now. What would you have done, Papa?"

"I would have taken her away from him."

"But then you may never be sure you are safe to come back," Rob's uncle walked about Rob and caught his father's eye. They shared a look and then his father sighed.

"What happened?"

"Rob knows what he is doing. Kilbride missed him, and then Rob aimed and shot him in the leg. It went straight into his bone."

"I broke his leg in the same place he broke mine."

"With one pistol shot," John stated, his eyebrows lifting as he leaned back against his desk. "You are good."

Rob smiled.

"I told you," Harry said.

How foolish that he'd discovered the one thing he could best his family in at this moment. Perhaps knowing he was the best at something, though, would give him more confidence in his politics.

"But do not expect me to pat you on the back for it. It was stupid to do it alone," John added.

"He was not alone," Harry stated.

"And what if I had lost two of my sons?" His father's hand lifted in a gesture of lack of control. But Rob did not wish to be controlled—and nor did Harry.

"It was my choice. Caroline is my wife, she is my responsibility and she will be waiting for me, and I can travel with her now and not fear Kilbride because I have taught him the lesson he needed to learn." Rob turned away then. He was no longer a child to be scolded and if he chose to manage his responsibilities alone, then it was his choice.

"And if he pays more thugs to come after you?"

"I will carry pistols in the carriage, and then I will go back to his house and shoot him in the head," Rob threw over his shoulder. He turned back and faced them all. "I can take care of myself. Not every man has an army of servants and connections about him, and they manage without it."

"He can take care of himself. I vouch for it," Harry stated. "He is the most independent of us all."

"Robbie, you are the most sensible of my children, you should not be the one who turns out to be the death of me," his father sighed.

Rob smiled and said no more, but left them.

Chapter 49

"Caro," Rob climbed into the carriage.

Drew and Mary had been waiting with Caro, but it was not them she wished to be with.

Rob pulled the door shut and waved at Drew and Mary as the horses pulled their new carriage into motion.

"Good luck!" Drew shouted.

"God bless you!" Mary called.

Rob was sitting in the seat opposite Caro, leaning forward, his elbows resting on his thighs, as she occupied the whole of the other seat, lying on her back.

"How are you? Sorry I took so long."

"I am bleeding again." The weight of the knowledge caught in her chest as a sharp, hard pain. She had seen it when she'd gone up to the retiring room, and then Drew had been outside and she had wanted to cry, but she had not.

Rob gripped her hand. "Do not worry. We will ride to the edge of the city, stop at an inn, and then I will send a lad from the stable to fetch the doctor. All will be well."

Yet he'd paled.

"Has she kicked since the wedding?"

"No." That was Caro's fear too. If she could feel the baby moving she would not feel so scared.

451

"Is there much blood?" Their carriage rocked and creaked over the cobbles.

"Only drops."

"Then let us not worry until we know there is a need to. It is you, me and our daughter here: mother, father and child. What will we call her when she is born?"

"Rob, I cannot—"

"She is living. You said you did not tell me about her because you wished to enjoy her life for as long as it lasted. Well, she is still alive, and if we do not know how long for, then let us give her a name now. What will we call her?"

Caro squeezed his hand. He always knew what to say. "Sarah. It was the name of a nursery maid we had when I was a child. She was the only one who was nice to me when I was young."

"What happened to her?"

"The Marquis saw her paying more attention to me than my elder sister, Elizabeth. Sarah was dismissed."

"Life has been cruel to you."

"No. Not now, and not then. I had Drew, and now I have you."

"Yes, you do have me, Mrs Marlow, and you must endure me at your side forever more, till death do us part… and that will likely be a very long time away as I am so young." His fingers played with the ring on her finger as he spoke, twisting it around and around.

"You are foolish."

"So my father has just been telling me. That was why I took so long." He smiled, but sadness hovered in his eyes. He was afraid for Sarah too. "But I will ask your forgiveness now, Caro, because you may become bored of me. I am not a man who will look for wildness or seek out constant things to stimulate life."

"You are not forgiven. I am not looking for a man like that. I would not like him. I will love the man I have married, who has high morals and will dedicate himself to changing this country's laws for the better, and I will be proud of him. But I will ask forgiveness of you now, because I am afraid I will be boring and

452

age too quickly, and you will grow tired of seeing my face and hearing me speak of mundane things."

His eyebrows lifted and his eyes widened. "You are not forgiven, Caro, I cannot forgive you that. You will always be loved. I shall always look forward to being greeted by your smile when I wake or return home, and to listen to you speak with me in the evening when we are sitting in our chairs, by the fire, an old, tottering couple, who have loved each other their whole lives."

"And now you have made me cry. You are not supposed to make me cry on our wedding day."

"No. I am sorry."

He leaned further forward, and she whispered over his lips before he kissed her, "You are forgiven."

Chapter 50

Caro reached across the carriage and touched Rob's knee. "I am still bleeding."

He sat up and gripped her hand. He was drifting into sleep. They were on the edge of the city.

He looked at her dress. She knew they were only tiny spots, but the blood scared her.

"Do not worry we will stop."

He turned to open the hatch and tell their driver to stop at the next inn.

They stopped at the Red Dragon, barely outside of London, and Rob sent a groom riding back into the city for the doctor. He arrived an hour later.

"You are married?" the doctor stated impudently as he glanced at Rob when he entered the room.

"We are married, but we ceased our journey because my wife suffered more bleeding and so we did not wish to go on without your reassurance."

"I told her to rest."

Caro was lying on the bed in a room in the inn. She felt very tired, but there had only been spots of blood. "I walked up the aisle, that was all."

"And also stood to receive our guests."

"I could hardly lie down to do that."

"And travelled in a rocking carriage…" The doctor stepped forward. "Will you lift your dress and I shall listen for the heartbeat and then we may see what ill has been done."

Caroline's heart raced, and her gaze met Rob's. He leant to help her raise her dress. There was a very definite outward curve. His fingers brushed over her skin for a moment. It was the first time he'd seen it.

This was not what he ought to be doing on his wedding night, unclothing her before the audience of a doctor.

Regret whispered in the air when Rob undid the ribbon securing her drawers and slid them below the curve of her stomach. She was afraid, and yet she felt guilty because this was not how a wedding celebration ought to be.

The doctor pressed her stomach gently. "Your little one has just kicked me, so I am fairly certain the babe is determined to remain within. But let me check for the heartbeat to ensure all is secure."

Caro reached out for Rob's hand. "I felt her."

Rob smiled as the doctor pressed the funnel end of the cold instrument to her stomach. He slid it around a little, and then said on a low breath, "Yes. I have it. The heartbeat is swift and sure."

"May I listen?" Rob moved about the bed as though, if the doctor said no, he would insist.

"Here." The doctor straightened up and held the horn as Rob leant down. Rob's free hand touched the first curve of her stomach.

When he straightened up, moisture glittered in his eyes. "I have heard her heart beating."

Caro wished that she could.

"The child is healthy, but there is still a high risk of infection, and for the child to be lost." He'd looked at Rob, but then he looked at Caro. She brushed her dress back over her stomach. "You must be careful and continue to rest, and I am afraid you must do so for the rest of your term."

"I shall ensure it," Rob stated. "But might I buy that thing off you, and then I may listen for the heart if we are afraid. We intend to continue our journey in short stages."

The doctor made an irritated sound, but he handed it over.

The man was so superior, she was glad she would not continue in his care.

"I shall walk downstairs with you," Rob said.

Rob was gone for ten minutes. Caro rolled to her side and curled up a little. Sarah was still within her, her little heart still beating, and her legs and arms thrusting out.

When Rob came back it was with bread, creamy butter, cheese and tankards of ale.

"How are my girls?"

"Happy and hungry. Fresh bread has never smelled so nice."

"Sit up a little." He set the tray he held down, and then came to put the pillows behind her back. Then he filled a plate for her and set it on her lap.

"Thank you."

"You are welcome. But Caro, when you showed your stomach… There is a large dark bruise at your hip. How—"

"It is where I fell. My hip struck the stairs when I lost my balance, when Albert came at me and George."

Rob sighed, his eyes telling her there was anger and grief in his heart. "I am glad of everything I have done today."

She held his hand. "I am glad we are married too, but I am sorry, this cannot be the wedding night you hoped for."

"No, but it is ours, and I am a patient man. Sarah and you are precious. You are what is important. I would not be selfish."

He took off his morning coat, then slipped off his shoes and filled a plate for himself before walking about the bed to sit beside her.

"I am sorry this is not the wedding night you would have wished for," he said, smiling.

She had thought her first wedding night heaven, then it had tumbled into hell. "I am happy just to be alone with you."

456

"And Sarah."

"And Sarah." She smiled.

After they'd eaten, Rob took her plate and called for a maid to come and clear away. Then Rob helped Caro undress and change into a nightdress, before undressing himself, down to only his underwear. Then he blew out the candles and slipped beneath the covers with her, in the dark.

His hand lay on her stomach for a moment, before he moved closer and kissed her. Warmth and desire flooded into her blood, though her desire would be redundant.

Her tongue danced about his, and her fingers combed into his hair. "You have a scar." It had been beneath his fringe.

"From when I fell from my carriage."

She kissed him again.

He broke the kiss after a while and rested his forehead against hers. "You ought to sleep. You were tired."

She nodded and when he rolled to his back, she rested her head on his shoulder.

Their wedding day resembled their entire journey north, it was slow and nerve-wracking and then at night it was quiet in whatever inn they found, and she lay with him, kissing him before she slept.

They reached their new home a week later than they had planned.

"I believe this is it," Rob stated, when they turned off the road.

"You have not seen the house…" Caro looked at him.

She was sitting up against pillows, and she could look through the far carriage window easily, but to see out of the one beside her she had to twist around. "Oh!" She turned a little more as a charming large red-brick house came into view. It had six sash windows along each floor, and there were two floors, and then attic rooms, and the portico was a half circle with two pillars supporting a decorated roof, where a cherub aimed a bow at them. "It is beautiful."

"It is," Rob confirmed, his hand reaching out to take hers.

This was their new home.

The carriage halted and people began appearing. A young man hurried to open the door as Beth came from the house. She had come up here to take on the role of housekeeper as soon as Caro had asked. She was smiling broadly, as though she loved her new post and their new home too. A tall, stiff middle-aged man walked beside her.

Another man, a groom, walked from about the side of the house.

"Sir, madam, welcome." Beth curtsied, as Caro lay like the Queen of Sheba on her pillows. "We have been keeping an eye out for your arrival," Beth stated as Rob climbed down. "This is Mr Birch, he is your butler, and Mr Brown, the head groom." They bowed to Rob.

"It is good to meet you," Rob said, before turning back to Caro. "I will carry you."

He had been carrying her in and out of inns for a week, and his leg had become stronger because of it. She wrapped her arms about his neck and hung on, and so they crossed the threshold into their home.

It was a sunny house, two of the huge windows opened into the large, square hall, where the servants stood in two lines, and Caro could see into a large room on either side of the hall. A dining room and a drawing room, and there were two more doors and two more rooms at the back.

"This is Jenny, Mary, Polly…" Beth introduced the two lines of servants, the women on the left and the men on the right. But Caro felt too silly being carried throughout the introductions, it distracted her mind, and she could not remember their names.

"Would you rather recline on a sofa downstairs or go up to our room," Rob asked when the introductions were done.

"May we go upstairs? I am tired."

"Yes, of course."

"All is ready. Polly will you show Mr and Mrs Marlow upstairs?" Beth said.

"Thank you, Beth." Caro gave her a smile.

"The house is beautiful. I am so happy, Rob," her fingers stroked the back of his hair.

He smiled. "I am happy too."

"Beth, please would you have some lemonade brought to the room and if you have any biscuits…" Caro called across his shoulder as he began walking upstairs.

"Freshly baked this morning, ma'am."

"Thank you."

"Oh, the room is lovely," Caro exclaimed when Polly led Rob into their bedchamber. Another two large windows shone light into it, and though it might not be a suite of rooms as she had known at Albert's and Drew's, it was a large room with two chairs and a chaise longue by the fire, and then a large four-poster bed in bright-orange toned, glossy wood.

"I had not expected the furniture to look this fine. I think your housekeeper has done a remarkable job of freeing everything from its covers and sprucing it up."

A knock struck the door. Another maid stood there with a tray bearing lemonade and biscuits. Jenny… Caro must learn their names.

"Where do you wish to sit?"

"In that chair before the window. Oh, look at the view! You can see some sort of ruins beyond the trees."

"It was an ancient abbey. The ruins are right on the border of my uncle's land."

"This is so perfect, Rob, I had not imagined it would be beautiful. We will be so happy here."

"Yes, we will."

He sat next to her and looked out through the window, as the maid poured their lemonade. Then she left them, closing the door. He was so strikingly handsome. Her husband would be her favourite view.

Yes, she would be happy.

459

Once he'd finished her lemonade and eaten three of the mouth-watering biscuits, she said quietly. "Tell the servants we will have a late supper and then let us lie down for a while." She was still hungry. She was craving. They had merely kissed ever since their wedding night and nothing more, because they'd been wary of the child, but she had not bled for almost a week.

He crossed the room and did not ring the bell but went downstairs.

Caro stood and looked from the window down onto flowerbeds full of shooting bulbs. It was spring, and her life felt like it had a new spring season too.

She walked to the edge of the bed and sat down, then released the first few buttons of her bodice.

Rob came back into the room and shut the door. "I have said we will eat at nine, but informally here. What are you doing? You should not be upright."

"I have only walked a few paces."

"It was only a few paces along the aisle."

"Will you help me undress, so I might be more comfortable?"

"Yes." He gave her a twisted smile.

"And will you lie down with me?"

"If you wish me to."

"I wish it." Her voice was breathless as his fingers released more of the buttons over her breasts, then slipped her bodice from her shoulders.

She lifted her bottom, and let him slide her dress down her body. Then she let her shoes fall off her feet before lying down.

He slipped off his shoes and removed his morning coat, then lay down beside her, one elbow bent as his palm supported his head.

He smiled at her as his hand ran over the rapidly increasing bulge of her stomach to caress Sarah. "Your figure is beautiful like this." He looked down as Caro felt a jolt. "She kicked."

"Her movements are becoming stronger."

Rob leant and kissed Caro. Then he rolled backwards onto the bed with a sigh, his palm resting behind his head as his other hand settled on his flat stomach.

She turned to her side and looked at him in profile. The determination, strength and independence he so prized were evident in his features, and yet when he looked at her, he was all gentleness and warmth. Her fingertips ran down his chest to his stomach, over his waistcoat and the front of his trousers, then back up. She ran them down and up again.

He smiled at her. The sunlight poured into the room, illuminating him, like some Greek god. Her fingertips played over the material of his trousers, touching him, as he stirred within.

She held his gaze. He said nothing. Nor did she.

Her fingers traced the path of his arousal as it grew, up and down, just gently running over the cloth which covered it. He must ache for this. He'd said he could wait, and yet it was only natural for a man to ache for a physical bond.

She ached too. The need was a pain in her palms and a dense desire between her legs.

Her fingers lifted and began freeing the buttons of his waistcoat.

His hand gripped hers, stopping her, "Caro… think of—"

"That is not what I intend. We need not have intercourse. Trust me and relax."

He shook his head, but let her hand go. She undid the buttons of his waistcoat then urged him to take it off.

When he lay back down she pulled his shirt free from his trousers and undid the buttons of his flap as they kissed.

His desire aimed like a spear; desperate to be known again. They had not touched each other like this since the end of September.

His hand gripped in her hair as his tongue pressed into her mouth with a growing hunger.

Of course he ached for this. She ran the heel of her palm down his length, pressing against the firm skin. She loved him.

He rolled over her a little so she lay on her back, and then one of his hands gripped her breast over the cloth of her chemise. It

461

was fuller, already preparing to feed their child and it hurt as he gripped it, but in a delicious way.

Her fingers caressed him, in an upward motion, then slid down. She repeated the movement continuously, while his tongue pressed in and withdrew from her mouth and his fingers kneaded her breast.

His breathing became faster, and the motion of her hand was not hers but his as his hips lifted, then pressed down into the mattress, so he ran himself through her fingers.

When he broke, a cry of triumph and gratitude escaped his throat as he spilled onto his shirt.

She smiled as he sighed out a, "thank you," into the air.

"You may return the favour…" she whispered in a husky voice.

"How?"

"With your mouth, I do not think it would harm with your mouth."

He gave her a devil's grin that was unlike Rob. "Your wish is my command, Mrs Marlow."

He rolled over, moved between her legs and stripped off her underwear. Then his hands gripped her thighs and pulled them wider.

He kissed her rounded stomach first, then kissed her inner thighs one at a time. Then his thumbs ran over her, one after the other, in a mesmerising rhythm, without trying to invade her. She would not wish him to take the risk and he did not.

She breathed hard, her arms reaching above her head and holding the pillow as his thumb began circling over her most sensitive spot, spreading moisture there. He kissed her lower lips, then his tongue tasted.

Her arms fell and she gripped his hair as his thumb continued to tease, and his tongue played the same game it had done in her mouth, simulating the action of sex, slipping a little within her and then slipping out.

Oh, she'd ached for this too, longed for it and she had not even known how much.

Her breaths released in short, little panting sounds, and her hips lifted to the rhythm of his tongue. She imagined the feel of him within her and longed for it, even though it could not happen, and yet even the thought made her break and shatter on his tongue. The release swept through her body and into her limbs as she cried out her relief just as he'd done.

He rose, wiped his mouth on his arm and came to lie beside her. "The next time we do this, I shall have to pleasure you first, because I wish for it again now."

She laughed, "You may have it again and use my mouth if you wish, if I move down the bed so I need not bend."

"Lord, Caro, how can a man refuse such an offer...?" Heat burned in his eyes.

"Kneel next to me, then."

A groan slipped from his lips as he rose. His trousers were still hanging open and a new erection pointed at her. She gripped him in her hand and let her tongue trace his tip. It was salty with the taste of his earlier release. "Lean over me, and then you might press into my mouth."

He gave her a look that said she was mad, desirable and beautiful.

One hand pressed into the mattress, holding his weight, while the other stroked through her hair as he pushed into her mouth, without trying to go too deep and choke her. She had never done it this way with Albert. It was new and just for Rob.

Each time Rob ran through her hand, sliding into her mouth, he sighed out a sound on his breath, as his fingers curled, combed and clasped in her hair, as though he felt guilt and wished to hold on to a non-sexual contact. Yet he could not have denied he was enjoying it because his body was engorged, hot and heavy in her hand, and pressing more and more firmly into her mouth.

When he reached his climax, she felt it shudder through every muscle of his body, and her free hand lifted to trace the back of his buttock to his thigh.

She swallowed as he rolled away.

"Caro," he said into her mouth. It was a statement of love, as he leant over her. He spoke with a depth she had never heard in Albert's voice, even when they had first married.

Yes, you do have me Mrs Marlow, and you must endure me at your side forever more, till death us do part… and that will likely be a very long time… That was what he'd said the day they had married, and the more time she spent alone with him the more she believed it was true.

Chapter 51

Rob was sitting with Caro in the drawing room. They were eating breakfast on their laps, so Caro could remain on the sofa, with her legs up.

He was enjoying it—the day—his marriage—and Caro's company. Yet he was eager to get out. That was why they had risen early. He was going to ride out and meet those who worked on the farms he now managed. His heart raced at the idea of responsibility and having something of meaning to do.

A noise breached the windows, an arrival, a lone horse-rider.

Rob stood as footsteps crunched on the gravel outside.

"I wish to speak with my nephew, Mr Marlow." The words rang from the hall.

"Lord Barrington."

"Uncle! In here!" Rob shouted.

Caro moved to rise, but Rob pressed a hand on her shoulder. "You need not stand."

"He sounded agitated."

"He will still not expect you to stand."

The door creaked as it swung back heavily and his uncle walked in with a purposeful stride. "I am sure you will not have seen the paper." He did not say, "welcome", or, "how was your journey?" but strode across the room, withdrawing a folded paper from within his riding coat. "So I have brought you a copy."

He held it out to Rob.

Rob took it.

"Would you like coffee?" Caro offered, trying to play hostess, even though she could not rise.

"Thank you, Caroline, but I shall pour it, you need not move." He poured as Rob opened the paper. "Look at the obituaries."

Rob sat down and scanned the open pages.

"You have done it now," his uncle stated, as he sat down facing them both. "But you are rid of him. Yet I do not know if you, with your high morals, can live with shooting a man and being the cause—"

"He is dead." Shock washed through Rob, draining all the blood from his head.

"He is indeed."

"Who is? Who did you shoot?" Caro sat more upright.

"She does not know?"

"She knows now," Caro answered looking at Rob, distress bright in her eyes, when she was not supposed to worry.

"I'm sorry."

"For what are you sorry?" she pleaded.

"He is gone." Rob still held the paper. He could not believe it.

"Kilbride, your former husband. Rob shot him in the leg, replicating the wound he'd caused Rob, in a duel Rob called on the morning of your wedding. Rob did not intend to kill him and yet Kilbride is dead."

"How?" Rob looked at his uncle, shock swelling through his veins. He'd killed a man.

"I have heard from your father that it was blood poisoning. The wound became infected."

"My God."

"Will you cope with this?" his uncle asked. "You are the last man on earth I would have thought might kill a man."

"I did not seek to."

"But you will feel the burden of it regardless. I know because I killed a man once. A man who deserved to die too, and that was in self-defence, but I have never forgotten it."

Rob looked at his uncle. "I do not regret what I did. I have morals, but I will not let a man threaten and hurt us. His fate is not my fault, it was fate that took him—"

"Then fate is just," Caro whispered. "But a duel, Rob… and what wound did he cause you?"

"It was nothing."

"Nothing… You have still not told your wife. One thing I learned early is you should be honest within a marriage. It looks as though I must leave you now I have set all your secrets in the air." Uncle Robert drank down the rest of his coffee, then stood. "Harry said the only person who knows it was you who shot him was a groom. Apparently the authorities are asking questions, but the groom has not yet told anyone how Kilbride was shot. Let us hope he holds his silence and you get away with this."

"The groom will not speak," Caro answered. "Albert was violent to his lower servants too. They hated him."

Rob stood. He did not want Caro concerned by this. "Thank you for the news. But I am not sure I wished to know it, and thank you also for sharing it with Caro when I was protecting her from this."

Amusement twisted his uncle's lips. "Well, if you have need of any more common-sense spoken to you, you will know where to come."

"Good day, then, to you and your common-sense."

Uncle Robert laughed. "Let me know if you need any advice on your farms."

"I am riding out to look at the farms in a while. I intended to ride over to you afterwards and discuss what I learn."

"Then I will be at home and await your visit." Uncle Robert looked at Caro and bowed his head, "Good day."

"Good day."

He turned away and walked from the room.

Rob sat. Pushed down by thought. He'd killed Kilbride, not physically, but... if he had not shot him...

"And now you must explain before I allow you to go anywhere. What did you do? What wound did Albert cause you?"

"I did not call him to a duel on my own account. It was for you and Sarah. He did not simply call at John's once, he was there for our ball too, and after he hurt you the day before the wedding he came to White's and threatened me. I know what he is capable of. I merely meant to teach him a lesson. An eye for an eye."

"What eye did he lance in you?"

Rob took a breath. He did not wish to tell her this.

"Rob..."

"Very well," he leant his elbows onto his knees and looked at her. "I did not have a fall from my curricle."

"But your leg, and your hand, I remember, was stiff too, and the scar at your temple."

He nodded.

"When?"

"The night of the Newcombs' ball. I left early and walked home alone in the dark. He paid some thugs to attack me. I was carried back to my uncle's, and my parents came there to care for me."

"They were out the morning Drew, Mary and I left town."

He smiled.

"How poorly were you?"

"They hit me over the head with an iron bar, broke my leg and my hand with it, deliberately I think, and then kicked me repeatedly. I think I was quite unrecognisable by the end. It was why I did not come to see you sooner. I would have come to reiterate my proposal had I..." He smiled and laughed suddenly as he remembered the conversations he'd shared with his father. "But perhaps not. It was my father who convinced me I ought to try and persuade you, not simply accept your refusal."

"I cannot believe you did not tell me. Why did you not?"

"Because you had just very squarely told me I was not good enough for you. Why would I have wished you to know and my family do not know? So do not speak of it before them, only Harry, Mama, Papa, Uncle Robert, Aunt Jane, and John. I do not wish people to know. I was embarrassed."

"That is stupid. I would have wished to be with you. I should have been with you. The next time I see Drew I shall tell him severely he should have kept his thoughts to himself."

"I have told him so myself."

She reached out. "Hold me for a moment, please?"

Rob rose and moved to perch on the edge of the sofa where she reclined. His arms slipped about her midriff as hers wrapped about his neck, and then she sobbed onto his shoulder. His palm ran across her back. "I am sorry, I know that you felt for him."

She pulled away, tears on her cheeks and glistening in her eyes, which shone gold in the sunlight. "Do not be silly, Rob, I am not crying for him, I am crying for you. I should have been with you. I should not have listened to Drew. I knew you loved me."

"It does not matter now."

"No. But you have still made me feel like crying."

With that she held him again and sobbed gently on his shoulder.

Chapter 52

Sensations of contentment rested in Rob's chest as he walked about the large farm with his steward. The stock here was good, the dairy herd, the pigs and sheep, and Rob had taken an active interest in breeding the cattle. He learned more about the arable crops every day, too, as they passed through the season.

He could hardly believe it was May. Everything was growing and the lambs were chunky little sheep bouncing about in the fields.

No, it was more than contentment in his chest, it was intense happiness. He rode out on a daily basis and worked on the farms alongside the people he employed, and then went home to Caro, to find her at some quiet activity, reading or sewing, and they would share an evening together entertaining themselves with conversation or music, or games.

Then there was night…

There had been no more blood, yet her new doctor had said that if the placenta had indeed broken partly away from the womb it would not have repaired and so Caro was ordered to continue resting, and so in bed they must be imaginative. He had learned to be imaginative.

He smiled to himself as he walked beside the farmer to see the litter of a dozen piglets which had arrived into the world last night. But then he turned as swift hoof beats struck the ground near him.

"Mr Marlow! Sir!"

Rob looked up, stepping back from the horses' fractious strides as the groom pulled the horse up. "Sir!" the groom said again as he jumped down, gripping the reins hard to hold the horse steady. "I've been sent to tell ye Mrs Marlow is birthin'."

Already? Sarah was not due for another month.

"Mrs Marlow bled, sir, and then the pains come."

Damn. "I will take this horse. You ride the animal I brought here once it's saddled."

The groom lifted his hat and bowed as Rob grasped the reins. His right leg had healed mostly and yet he still set his left foot in the stirrup to haul himself up, his right leg was not quite up to that.

"Thank you." His steward lifted a hand and bowed his head slightly, as Rob turned the horse and tapped his heels hard against the animal's flanks.

The chickens in the farmyard scattered as Rob cantered out. He'd come via road, but if he rode back through the fields and jumped the stone walls, it would be faster.

Once he was beyond the yard he kicked his heels and set the animal into a gallop, at a gallop he was probably only a quarter of an hour from home.

Was the doctor with her already?

Caro would only be thinking of the child, but blood. If there was blood there was risk to her.

He would not lose her. "Lord." He glanced up to the heavens, "Hear me, please, protect her and bring her through our daughter's journey into the world."

He set his mind on the wall approaching, kicked his heels and lifted the animal into a jump. It landed heavily, but Rob urged it on, his inner vision on Caro.

The horse's nostrils flared and its breathing was heavy when Rob rode into the stables and jumped down. "Where is my wife?"

"In the bedchamber, sir."

He turned and ran. At least his right leg was now fully able to

471

do that, even if he still favoured the left side a little.

"Caro!" he raced up the stairs, taking the steps two at a time.

"Rob!" Her urgent voice stretched along the hall as he hurried.

"I am here," he stated, as he entered and strode across the room. She was in bed, looking very pale, and she must still be bleeding because there was fresh scarlet blood on the sheets below her waist. "Lie back," he said as she reached out her hand and sat up.

"The doctor…" he looked at the housekeeper, who was with her.

"Has been sent for."

"Would you send a message to my aunt too, to Lady Barrington, and ask if she would come?"

The housekeeper nodded and turned away to send word.

"Rob." Caro's voice and her pale-hazel eyes expressed her fear. He could not express his.

He gritted his teeth for a moment, then swallowed back the pain and emotion in this throat. "Lift your hips a little. Let me set a pillow beneath you. It will make you more comfortable." And perhaps slow the blood. Yet if the child was coming, surely she would continue to bleed.

When he lifted the sheet to place the pillow, he saw just how much scarlet blood had soaked into the sheet. Bile rose in his throat. She might be afraid for Sarah; he was terrified for her.

Her fingers grasped at his shoulders, her nails clawing as he finished putting the pillow into place beneath her. "Ahhhh…" It was a long, loud, sharp cry of pain, and he saw her stomach move beneath the chemise she wore. It tightened like a vice.

As tears ran over her pale eyelashes, he stripped off his gloves and his morning coat, his hat had been left at the farm.

He held Caro's hand. "You are not to be afraid, you have to do the work, but do not let fear make it harder." *Leave me to be afraid.* He would pray. That would be his task.

He pressed a kiss on her temple and her gaze clung to him. "I am scared, Rob."

"I know, but you must not be. She is early, but it is not too early for her to survive, just a few hours of labour and she will be here and all will be well." *Please, Lord.*

But hours of bleeding…

His free hand settled on her hair and his thumb rubbed her temple to help her rest. When the housekeeper came closer again, he said in a low voice. "Fill a bath with ice."

"Sir…"

"Just do it," his response was snappy.

He'd heard at school that the poet Shelley had put his wife into a bath of ice when she'd miscarried and bled, and it had saved the woman's life.

His heart raced as more blood seemed to seep into the sheets with every moment. His fingers stroked Caro's hair and her hand gripped his as her gaze clung to him. "Breathe slowly," he whispered, as her contraction eased.

There was a knock at the door and a copper bath was carried into the room. Then there followed a stream of footmen arriving intermittently with newly crushed ice.

"What are they doing?"

"We need to stop you bleeding, Caro, and it is the only way I can think to do it."

She nodded, the grip of her fingers tightening about his hand.

"Ahhhh." She bit down on her lip to shut off her cry when the next contraction came. There were two footmen in the room.

Where was the bloody doctor? The ice bath maybe the best thing for Caro, but Rob had no idea how it might affect the child, and he wished them both alive.

"Sir, it is ready."

Rob threw the covers back. More blood had come with her contraction. "Put your arms about my neck."

When he put his hand beneath her legs, the blood on the cloth seeped from the cloth on to his arm and dripped onto the floor. *God, help us please!*

He was out of his depth and losing her. She could not bleed

this much if she had hours of labour to endure—and live.

His heart raced as he carried her to the bath. "This will be cold, and it will hurt, sweetheart, but it must be done."

Her head turned and her face buried into his shoulder as he knelt. It was freezing, burning cold, even though that was a stupid thing to think, that is what it felt like, a burn, on his arms, as he lowered her into the water. She gasped with a loud cry and began to shiver violently, but he could see the flow of blood had eased.

"Rob," she clutched his shoulders as another contraction came. "Is it this way?"

Rob heard the question reach from the hall. The doctor.

Rob looked up.

"Mr Marlow, Mrs Marlow. Good heavens!" The doctor set his bag down in a chair as the door shut behind him, then he stripped of his gloves.

"My wife is bleeding heavily and experiencing contractions. I did not know what to do. I have put her in ice only because I thought it would slow the bleeding and it has."

Rob moved out of the way as the doctor nodded and came to kneel by Caro, with a horn in his hand to listen to the baby's heart. "There is still a good strong beat. There is no harm done to the child, and we shall keep you in the cold, I am afraid, for a while, Mrs Marlow. I think your husband has been very sensible and is entirely right."

Caro nodded, her eyes looking up at Rob.

"Where is Mrs Marlow?" Another voice carried in from the hall.

His aunt. The door opened again. Her gaze caught on the blood-stained sheets before it turned to him. "Rob."

"Aunt Jane."

She crossed the room and touched his arm in a kindly way. "You ought not to be in here. Caroline will wish to maintain her dignity as the birth progresses. Robert has come with me, so you may go outside and sit with him, and I will take care of Caroline."

Rob turned and knelt and kissed Caro's forehead. He was in

a dreamlike state now that the responsibility was lifted from his shoulders.

He stroked Caro's hair back from her forehead and held her hand. "I will leave you and Sarah in the good hands of Dr Silver, and you must not be afraid, because he will guide you through. I will see you again when Sarah is in your arms."

She nodded, sickly pale and looking exhausted, even though this had only just begun.

When he rose, Jane's fingers closed about his arm again and she guided him to the door. "I have done this numerous times, Rob, you must not worry."

"I am not a fool," he whispered back, "I have known two dozen births in our family and the woman has never bled from the outset. She is at risk, and so is our daughter. Please have me come back if all is not well. Do not leave it until the last moment."

Jane nodded. She had known this was not good, too, but been trying to pacify him.

He turned away.

His uncle waited in the drawing room. He'd already helped himself to a glass of Rob's brandy, and he held a second full glass out in Rob's direction. "It will be a long day."

"Especially long. I don't know if you heard, she is bleeding."

"Rob, I know. You have it all over you."

He looked down and then internally collapsed. Externally he dropped to perch on the edge of a footstool, his hands gripping his head.

"You will wish your parents here, I am sure, but they are too far away to be of any use."

Truly, he did wish them here. He'd never been in so much need of someone to share the load of his burdens.

He looked up at his uncle, "If I were to lose her…"

"Do not think of it. We will believe and pray it will not happen."

Rob nodded, accepting the glass that was held out. He'd shunned the army of support his family always offered and yet now, if they might do anything he would ride a million miles and drag his father and every one of his uncles here.

The next few hours were long, and at least once every half hour, or perhaps more, Rob climbed the stairs to walk along the hall and knock on the door of his bedchamber, and ask after Caro.

Each time Jane's answer was, "She is working hard." Which told him nothing of Caro's health or safety, while from within he could hear her screaming.

"I do not wish for another child," Rob stated as he sat down next to his uncle for about the tenth time. "I cannot risk this happening the next time. The doctor in London said the cause may be the number of times she has carried, or perhaps from previous injuries Kilbride has caused. If she falls again, she may bleed again. I will not risk it."

His uncle's hand settled on his shoulder.

Rob stood and began to pace the room. He would write to Harry and ask about the condom he'd mentioned. They should be cautious from now on.

If she lives…

No. He could not think of any other outcome. She would live, and Sarah would live.

He walked across the room to the windows, then turned and walked back to the decanters, then turned and walked the same path again.

"You are making me anxious," his uncle said.

"You ought to be anxious," Rob growled.

"Except that working yourself up will change nothing. Come and sit down and tell me what you have been up to with the farms. I have heard good things. Are you turning a profit?"

"A slight profit, but I hope the autumn will bring much more."

"Sit and speak to me."

Rob did, but all the while guilt stabbed into his stomach. He should be with Caro, thinking of her, praying for her.

Perhaps he ought to go to the church, but that would feel too much as though he did not believe she would live. He had to believe.

It was two hours later when the housekeeper rushed into the room, her hair beneath her mob cap damp with sweat, and although she must have washed her forearms Rob could still see the marks of blood. "You may come."

Rob's heart stopped.

"The child is here… and Caro, Mrs Marlow…" Rob was on his feet, though he'd not known he stood and was already walking.

"Weak, Mr Marlow."

But alive. He'd never felt so hollow inside.

He ran up the stairs and along the hall to their room. The sheets had been changed, and Caro was in bed, and the bleeding must have stopped at least because there was no scarlet stain between her legs.

The emptiness inside him filled up with love. Caro wore a clean nightdress too, and it hung open as the small child sucked from her breast.

Caro looked up, her skin was grey beneath her eyes. She looked like his phantom again, so pale. "Rob," she said weakly. "She is here. You were right. It is a daughter. Sarah."

Aunt Jane clasped his arm before he could move. "The doctor wishes to speak with you."

He crossed the room in a trance, and then pressed a kiss on Caro's crown, before pressing another on his child's. Sarah was tiny, smaller than any child he'd known in his family. A vulnerable, fragile little thing, like Caro. "I will return in a moment. I need to settle things with the doctor."

She nodded.

The doctor lifted a hand so Rob might walk from the room before him and then Rob led the man downstairs, but not into the drawing room where his uncle waited—into the dining room, where they might speak privately. This was not about payment.

"How is she?" Rob asked in a low voice.

"She has lost a lot of blood. She should drink pigs' blood for a month, and eat liver daily. I would also seek a wet nurse. It will slow her recovery if she is feeding the child herself. I am able to recommend a woman who has a child a year old and would be willing. But there is another risk. Sometimes mothers who experience bleeding may die if the internal wound becomes infected. You should call me if there is any sign that she is developing a fever.

Rob nodded, although he knew there would be little the man could do. The wound was within her. There was no cleaning it. He thought of Kilbride, of Caro's judgement that fate had been just. Fate would not be just if it took Caro.

Rob returned to sit with her, and she and the child rested against his chest and slept. He let the tears run quietly. He had a wife and a child, and they were already in danger.

When it came to morning, Caro fed the child and drank the blood he gave to her in a glass, with a face that told him he was mad and it tasted horrible, but she ate her fried liver too. Then he told her the doctor had found a woman from the village who would feed Sarah, to help Caro become well.

Caro expressed her hatred of the idea, but accepted it, and he did not tell her why every half an hour he lay his palm over her forehead as he leant and kissed her crown.

After luncheon, when both Caro and Sarah slept, Rob went down to the drawing room and opened the secretaire. He picked up a quill as the tears flowed, and took a sheet of paper from the drawer.

Papa, I need you here. Caro has had the child, we have a daughter, Sarah, as we hoped, and yet she is early and very small, and Caro bled profusely during the birth. She is very weak and pale.

Rob had held so much of himself back from his family over the years, out of the belief that the others might fight for attention, but he would not because he was stronger and did not need it. He'd always convinced himself he ought not need help. Caro had taught him how to accept help in the same moments that

478

he'd helped her.

I am afraid.

The doctor has said Caro might still not survive.

I feel helpless and lost. I am doing all the doctor has said and yet I am terrified it will not be enough. Will you come? Please. I am not sure you will be able to do any more than I and yet you and Mama always seem to have an answer.

And even if they did not have an answer...

I would like you here. I need your help.

He signed the letter, *Rob,* and within an hour it was folded and sealed and in the hands of a groom, who was to take it to catch the mail coach.

When he returned to the bedchamber Caro was sleeping, but Sarah was lying in her crib silently studying the world with eyes that were a very dark grey. He hoped desperately they would become the colour of gold.

Epilogue

"George! Hold out your hands and cup them. Like this." Mary called out to her son. George looked at her with a face that said, *do not tell me, I know how to catch.*

Caro smiled at her nephew's frustration. The men, Kate, Mary and her sisters Helen and Jenny were playing a ball game with all the children who were able to walk. They threw a small ball at someone and if they dropped it they were out, and if they caught it they had to race around the outside of the ring and whoever returned to their place first was the winner and the other person was out.

Poor George had dropped the ball twice, only to be allowed to stay in the game as those times suddenly became practices. But his uncle Harry was very carefully aiming for George's cupped palms.

He hit them, and George's hands closed about the ball.

"Run!" everybody yelled.

Caro laughed as Harry set off at a charge, and George's short little legs raced, his feet pounding across the ground.

Sarah woke and gripped the sleeve of Caro's dress. Caro held her more upright so she could watch the game. She loved to watch everything—she was an inquisitive little girl. Caro wondered if she would have George's energy.

Harry raced up to him, but instead of running on he picked

480

George up by the waist and ran with him.

"Uncle BaBa!" George cried in complaint. "Put me down, Uncle BaBa!"

Harry didn't obey, he ran on and set George in his spot. George squealed.

"We are playing together now, George."

Harry had been nicknamed the black sheep of Rob's family and yet, at heart, he was as good as his older brother.

"'ook." Iris called and began crawling off the blanket. Look was Iris's newly discovered word, and crawling her newly mastered activity. Caro looked to one of the nursemaids to pick Iris up and bring her back.

Caro was still supposed to take things gently, and she'd been told strictly not to lift. Yet she was very tired of playing the invalid. The game looked so much fun.

Rob threw the ball to Mary. She caught it, hitched up her skirt and petticoats then raced off about the circle as he did too. She won, but Caro had a feeling he'd let her win.

He gripped his side as if he had stitch, then lifted his hand in defeat.

"They played endless games such as this as children." Rob's mother stated. She was sitting beside Caro.

Caro smiled at her. She could imagine it.

Mary threw the ball at Drew. He caught it and began running before she had even had a chance to react, "Papa! Mama!" George shouted, unsure who to cheer. His father won and Mary dropped out of the game. Drew winked at Mary as Rob dropped down on the blanket beside Caro, breathing heavily.

"Good day, Mr Marlow…" she whispered in a teasing voice, "You can fool them all but you cannot fool me… pretending you had a stitch so it did not look too bad losing to Mary… Have you lost all your morals now?"

He looked at her and smiled. "I did not lie to explain my losing to Mary, I used the ruse to run slowly so I could drop out and sit

481

with you and Sarah."

He leant forward and lifted Sarah from her arms. "Hello, my precious angel. Have you been looking after your mama?"

"She has done a very thorough job of it too. It seems as though she sees everything," his father stated behind them. Caro looked back and smiled.

Rob's parents had come the week after Sarah had been born. They had stayed at Rob's uncle's, but they had spent most days with Caro and Rob. His father had helped Rob learn how to manage the farms, and his mother had helped Caro with Sarah when Caro had still been bed-ridden in the beginning. This was the last few days they were staying. They were going back to their own home once the family party had come to its conclusion.

Sarah whimpered a little. She was not hungry; she had only recently been fed. She simply wished to be active. "Here, may I hold her?" Rob's father held out his hands. "We are only here for a few more days, I must get my fill of hugs."

Rob laughed, but handed her up, and then his father walked away with her, bouncing her a little as he walked, holding her so she might see the game still, as she looked over his arm. Rob's mother rose and followed.

Rob's hand took Caro's, and they sat together watching the game. His fingers wove between hers.

"May we do this every summer, do you think? Invite everyone here."

"It would be nice."

Mary and Drew and even John and Kate had come up for their parents' last week here. They were staying with Caro and Rob, and Rob kept teasing his ducal brother that he was slumming it in their lowly mansion. John did not seem to mind, and the evenings they'd spent together as a six had been very pleasant, and Rob had spent hours sharing his political views with John and Drew to win their support.

Yet when his parents came over, as they'd done today, with Rob's brothers and sisters, then it became a wonderful family event, but not as overwhelming as the large affairs with the extended family, which she'd watched from her glass gaol cell at Pembroke Place

Rob lifted her hand and kissed the back of it. "I love you."

"I love you also."

He looked at her, "Harry has brought us up a gift." The words were spoken in a low, husky voice.

"Has he…"

A gift from Harry might be anything.

"I will show you later."

~

Rob looked at Harry's gift as Caro slipped beneath the covers. He was not sure about this. It did not look particularly comfortable, and yet if it protected Caro then it was worth any discomfort to him.

He slipped beneath the covers beside her, naked. Then held up the limp tube of membrane to show Caro. "This is our gift from my brother."

Caro looked at it, a frown forming a crease between her eyebrows. "What is it?"

"It is a thing that will protect you from falling with child again."

Her eyes said it all. They were dark amber in the candlelight, and they said that she did not wish to avoid children.

"Caro, I did not speak to you of it through your term because I did not wish to make you afraid any more than you already were, but I was told by the doctor in London that throughout your pregnancy you were at risk of bleeding to death, or picking up an infection and dying from that outcome—"

"Rob." Her eyes said that she was about to protest. He covered her lips with his fingers.

"Listen. The doctor has told me that unless I had put you in that ice bath you would have died that day, and there has still been

483

a risk in the three months since because there may still have been infection, or a haemorrhage. But now you are safe and I will not risk losing you." The dryness in his throat, even at the thought, made his voice crack a little.

"The doctor in London told me that what occurred maybe due to your history, the number of times you have carried or perhaps Kilbride's brutality. I would not risk it happening again. We have Sarah. Sarah will be enough."

A tear crept from one corner of Caro's eye and ran onto her cheek.

He wiped it away with his thumb. "I was more scared the day you gave birth than I was the day I faced Kilbride as he aimed a pistol at my head, and I had been terrified for you for months. I cannot endure that again."

"And you took it all upon yourself." Caro's cool palm embraced his cheek, then slid up and ran over his hair. "I wish you were not quite as independent as you are. You need not have carried that alone."

"I would not have burdened you with it. It would have scared you when you were only thinking of Sarah and that was right, but that is why my parents came after the birth, because I was too tired to continue worrying by myself."

"I would love to have a large family, like your parents and your aunts and uncles, but I know it will not be so for me—"

"Us, Caro, this is our family."

"It will not be so for us." Her hand touched his cheek again and her thumb brushed his lower lip. "But I never expected to carry even one child full-term and yet I have Sarah. If you wish to take precautions then I will be content with Sarah. I will protect myself for you, and for Sarah. I wish us to grow old together and see her grow up more than I would fight for another child who may never come."

"Thank you. I feared you would disagree." Rob leant and pressed a kiss on her lips. Then said over them, "The doctor has said to me we may safely have intercourse again…"

"And so Harry's present."

"And so Harry's present," Robert repeated with a low laugh over her lips. He need not fear losing her now, and he would not think of it again.

His hand slid to her hip and began drawing up her nightgown. "May we remove this barrier?"

She sat up and laughed.

She was allowed to move more now too. He was looking forward to walking together. Last summer they'd walked together playing with George. In future summers it would be Sarah between them holding their hands.

He pulled the cloth over Caro's head and tossed it to the floor.

"We have had months of foreplay, will you forgive me now if I am too eager?" His fingers squeezed her breast gently.

"You are forgiven."

He laughed as he leant to kiss her and ran his fingers over her flat stomach to the place between her legs.

Heat gathered in his blood as he groaned into her mouth, and his fingers slipped inside her, where they had not been since the autumn. He reacquainted himself with the warm, silky flesh as his erection pressed against her hip.

He rolled back and reached for Harry's gift.

"Let me help."

It took them a few moments to sheath him, her cool fingers brushing his sensitised skin, and he would not admit the agony that pulsed within his groin. He'd longed for this, for so many months.

She rolled to her back and opened her legs for him.

The heat gripped about his heart throbbing there as hard as it did in his groin as he pressed into her. "Oh." The sound that came from his throat had been wrenched from his soul. The sheath covering him stole some of the finer sensations, but there was still warmth, and a feeling of being consumed.

He held her gaze as he moved and her fingers clasped his

shoulders, but the look in her eyes spoke only of love.

~

She had no doubts of the longevity of Rob's love, not anymore. She had learned the depth of his loyalty as well as his love in the months they'd been married, and he had feared losing her for months and never spoken.

She wished to cry for him again, as she'd done when she'd found out about his foolish duel, and yet how could she cry for such an elemental man. A man who had been patient with her, and kind, for all the months they had been unable to be intimate in this way.

Rob was special, he was a treasure she'd discovered when she'd looked out through the walls of her glass gaol.

"Oh." The sigh breathed out of her lungs, but it was from her heart. She'd craved him constantly since about three weeks after Sarah had been born, and yet he'd continued to refrain, to protect her.

She lifted her hips and thrilled at the feeling of his swift, firm strokes.

His movement became sharp, hard jolts into her, striking at her pelvis in a rough hunger, as his gaze clung to hers and his fingers clawed into the mattress beside her shoulders.

Her thoughts dissolved into sensations as he withdrew, looking down at where they joined, and then pulsed slightly, playing with her.

Her hips lifted, trying to catch at every feeling, and then when he invaded her with another hard thrust she pushed back up against him so they thrust at one another.

His gaze came back to hers.

It was a fast, thrilling, country dance of movement.

He rolled to his back, pulling her over him, and then the steps were the other way about as he thrust up and she sank down to meet his strokes, her hands on his shoulders as his clasped her breasts. She rocked against him, heat and pleasure skipping through the dance with them, and the little death danced beside her, almost there but not.

She tumbled, as though she'd missed a step, and fell, then inside her there was a flurry of petticoats, as the little death fell on top of her.

Rob's fingers gripped her hips as his heels pushed into the mattress.

His legs were bent up and she sat astride him, her toes curled into the mattress as he lifted her and pulsed up into her.

His face contorted with hunger, then he broke too, pulsing, his seed spilling into their gift from his brother.

He groaned with pleasure as she fell forward and lay against his naked chest, her cheek brushing against his shoulder. She could hear his heavy breathing echoing in his chest. Her fingers settled over the dusting of hair across his pectoral muscle.

"I love you" he declared as his fingers ran through her hair.

"I love you also. Thank you for giving me Sarah." She rose up and looked into his dark blue-grey eyes.

His palms cupped her face, as they'd always done when he was speaking to her of anything important. "You have blessed me, with Sarah, and with yourself. You have given me a life I did not know I sought. I am the happiest man."

"While I am the most honoured of women. I am truly the blessed one, Rob, and I will help you achieve everything you wish from life. I will not hold you back." It was a promise. She'd been a shadow of herself, and now she was whole—healed and wonderfully happy. She wished him to be whole and fulfil his dreams. "Must you wash that thing out if we wish to do it again?"

"Yes." He smiled.

"I wish to be intimate again," she breathed the words against his neck.

~

487

Pride raced in Rob's blood, making his heart beat at an outrageous pace, as the men in the rows of seats about him applauded his first speech. He'd won his seat a month ago, and he was already making his mark. He'd worked hard in the months before the election to become known, both in Yorkshire and its surrounding area, where he might earn the support of those who would vote. Here in London, amongst the Whigs, he'd been speaking of his hopes for future laws that would make men more equal and see women treated fairly.

Yet not all men were treated equally in the House of Commons. Birth and money made a difference here as much as it did anywhere, and yet the men in this room also judged a man who earned respect well, and Rob was fast gathering respect, and relying on that trade. Of course, his birth and his illustrious relations made a difference too, but Rob no longer shied away from that. He earned his own income, he was able to hold his head high when he spoke up for the working classes of the country, yet he would willingly use the power of his family when it came to making alliances that would push his bills through. All help from his family had been gratefully received since the moment Sarah had been born.

When Rob walked from the giant hall with its stacked, leather-lined seating, he was then in an equally grand and overwhelming hall, the ceiling was as high as a cathedral, and the walls as ornate.

"Rob." It was his father who'd come down from the viewing chamber first to greet him. His hand grasped Rob's shoulder as he turned him to face the crowd of other men who'd come to hear his first speech. Rob had been practising it for a week.

Rob's hand was shaken a dozen times as he carefully tried to extricate himself from the group of his friends, family, and even some of his supporters. He'd achieved his second step in his pathway in politics, and yet his mind was not in here with the men who patted his back in congratulations.

John said something and the group looked to him. Rob clasped his father's coat sleeve. "I must go. I will meet you back at John's." His father nodded and smiled.

Rob walked swiftly away from the group before anyone else might stop him, elation flowing in his blood. He'd done it. When he walked from the Houses of Parliament out into the street he did not walk but ran about the corner.

A carriage waited there.

He pulled the door open. "Caro!"

"Rob!"

He climbed up without the step. "How did it go? I wish I could have come in and heard you. That is another thing you must make equal in this country."

He smiled at that, although she'd heard his speech a hundred times, as he'd practised it in their rooms. "It went well. Very well. You will have to ask Papa to relate every element of the scene to you, though, I was so nervous I cannot recall a thing."

She laughed, then leant across the seat, offering her lips. He kissed them quickly. Then he bent and kissed Sarah's head. She was sitting on her mother's lap. Caro had insisted they both came and were close, so that he might know they were near and supporting him, even if they could not come in.

He had thought of them here the whole time he'd talked.

"You did not stumble or stutter…"

"Not once."

"I knew you would not. I knew you would be perfect."

"People applauded me."

"Well, of course they would, because your views are wise and righteous and they would look fools if they did not applaud them." Caro looked at Sarah. "We are very proud of Papa, aren't we?"

"Pa, Pa." Sarah echoed. Rob lifted her from Caro's lap, and held her up so her feet rested on his thighs.

Sarah was who he wished to change the world for now. Let her have equal choices in her lifetime.

He looked at Caro. She smiled at him, a broad smile that said

489

her heart was bursting in her chest with happiness, pride and love. He'd promised himself that he would see her smile and laugh for him two years before, but when he had made that promise to himself, he had not known what he'd truly wished for. He had wished for this. For this wonderful woman to love him as she did.

"I love you," he said as he smiled back at her.

She did not answer, but leaned forward to kiss him again.

Author Note

The inspiration for Caro's and Rob's story is a bit different from the other books in the Marlow Intrigues Series. Their story does not have one specific trigger from a real historical tale, but it developed from lots of threads of truth in the stories I research and share on my blog janelark.wordpress.com. Caro's story begins in The Dangerous Love of a Rogue, a book that was very much inspired by Caroline Lamb's and Lord Byron's life stories, but also included elements of inspiration taken from the records of the courtesan Harriett Wilson who shared lots of the things which went on behind closed doors in the Regency period. The inspirations for Rob's and Caro's story were far more of a patch work, but many ideas for scenes did come from both Caroline Lamb's and Harriett's tales. I think that is why these stories are darker, because they are inspired by the elements of real stories from women who suffered at the hands of men, and of course the young men who at times suffered at the hands of women.

The main reason behind this story coming to life, though, was that when we left Caro at the end of The Dangerous Love of a Rogue I couldn't leave her story there, she needed a hero, and like Ellen in The Illicit Love of a Courtesan, because Caro was a very damaged person, she needed a kind hero full of goodness, so who better than Edward's eldest son...

I'll look forward to sharing the next story in the Marlow Intrigues Series with you, The Reckless Love of an Heir. Simply like my Amazon page to make sure you'll know when it's available, even if you buy from other outlets www.amazon.co.uk/Jane-Lark/e/B00CF5WXKI.

Thank you to all the readers who have taken the time to leave reviews, or get in touch and tell me how much they are enjoying the series, I do really appreciate all your comments.

Best wishes, Jane.

Like Jane on Facebook www.facebook.com/Janelarkauthor

Follow Jane on Twitter twitter.com/JaneLark

See Jane's visual inspirations on Pinterest uk.pinterest.com/janelark/